Out of the Frying Pan...

"Y OU WOULDN'T WANT TO live forever?"

"I guess there might be perks, but no."

King smiled enigmatically and set down the small statue. "They believed that the soul, even after death, remained in the body. Remained there awaiting judgment, until granted entrance to the underworld by Osiris." He waved his hand at the table. "All of this, elaborate ointments and rituals, would secure the soul even in the face of human mortality."

"That's interesting," Elizabeth said and eased her way toward the door. "Really quite a collection, and thank you for sharing it with me, but it's late."

"Time is irrelevant," he said, "if you want it to be."

She definitely didn't like the sound of that. "I don't understand what you mean."

"Don't you?" he asked and walked slowly toward her. "Surely, you've sensed it."

She backed up against the door and tried the handle, but it was locked. "I'd like to go now."

"I haven't shown you everything."

"I've seen enough. Please, unlock the door."

He stopped in the middle of the room. "Don't be frightened."

He closed his eyes and Elizabeth couldn't stifle her gasp...

For more information, please contact writtenbymonique@gmail.com.

Cover Photo: Ioana Davies
Cover layout and interior formatting by TERy*visions* www.teryvisions.com

ISBN 10: 1466243430
ISBN 13: 978-1466243439

First Paperback Edition

Printed in the United States of America.

MONIQUE MARTIN

Out of Time

ACKNOWLEDGEMENTS

THIS BOOK WOULD NOT have been possible without the help and support of many people. I would like to take this opportunity to thank Robin, John, Trista, Shannon, Rachel, Mary, DJ, Michael, Yvonne and my entire family.

CHAPTER ONE

THE NIGHTMARES HAD COME again.

Simon Cross pushed himself off the bed and away from the cold, sweat-soaked sheets. His heart racing, his breath quick and rough, he forced his eyes to adjust to the dark room as the last vestiges of sleep faded.

He glared down at his bed, as if it were to blame, as if the sheets and pillows had knowingly harbored the nightmare. He felt a surge of panic and escaped from the darkened bedroom.

The moon was nearly full and cast its silvery light through the open curtains giving the living room an unearthly glow. Vague shadows stretched out like the taunting specters of his nightmare. Ignoring everything but his destination, he strode to the liquor cabinet. His hands trembled as he poured a stiff Scotch and downed it in one swig. Without pause, he poured another. His hands gripped the crystal glass as he tried in vain to keep it from clattering on the silver tray.

Disgusted with his weakness, he slammed the bottle down and clamped his eyes shut. His hands still trembled.

"Bloody hell."

The last time he'd had a nightmare like this was over thirty years ago. Yet, the memory rang with sharp clarity in his mind. His grandfather. The violence. The blood. And above all, the helplessness.

Simon let out a short burst of breath. He tried to convince himself this had merely been another dream. Another dream about her.

Ignoring the stacks of open boxes littering the floor, he tightened his jaw, grabbed the glass of Scotch and prowled across the room. He'd dreamt of her before. He was, after all, only human. She was attractive, intelligent and everything he wanted, but could never have. It was only natural she'd be in his thoughts. But there was nothing natural about this dream. This nightmare. This wasn't a fool's late night fantasy, brought on by loneliness and assuaged by a cold shower. This was something unspeakable.

Unconsciously, he clenched and unclenched his free hand. No concrete images remained, just an unwavering sense of horror, of an inevitable evil.

Exactly as it had been before.

He took another drink and concentrated on the warm burning sensation as the liquor seeped down into his chest. There was no avoiding the harbinger of his dream. With the certainty only a condemned man can feel, he knew one absolute truth.

Elizabeth West was going to die.

Elizabeth had heard it all before. But no matter how many times she listened to Professor Cross' lectures, she marveled at the way he held the class in the palm of his hand. As always, there wasn't an empty seat in the classroom. Introduction to Occult Studies was a favorite at the University of California Santa Barbara. Most students were there for the excitement of it, the dark abiding thrill of all things supernatural, like attending a semester-long horror movie. A few, like herself, were there for something more.

When she'd taken his class as an undergraduate, floating along in the sea of the undeclared, she had no idea that four years later she'd be his graduate teaching assistant working toward her Masters in Occult Studies. A meandering path through her Humanities requirements had left her still wanting for something. While all the courses were interesting, none of them sparked her interest. Until she happened upon Professor Cross' class.

In retrospect, she wasn't sure if it was the man or the subject that had first drawn her in, and in the end it didn't matter. It had taken persistence and a thick skin to convince him she was serious about becoming his graduate teaching assistant. At first, she didn't understand why he'd tried to dissuade her. After attending one Board of Chancellors' meeting in his stead, she had a pretty good idea. Occult Studies was nothing more than a curiosity in their eyes. The poor foster child of interdepartmental parents, Occult Studies was hardly recognized as a serious area of academia. Technically it fell under the auspices of Folklore and Mythology, but for Professor Cross it was a life's work and something very real. His passion inspired her, in more ways than one.

Elizabeth watched him pace slowly behind the lectern, hypnotizing the class with his fluid movements, setting them up for the kill. His keen eyes scanned the classroom, pulling each student under his spell. When his eyes fell upon her, he paused, almost losing his place. He frowned and continued. No one else noticed the minor lapse, but claxons went off in Elizabeth's mind.

There was something off about him today. His normally squared shoulders were hunched. His sandy brown hair was slightly unkempt as though he'd dragged his fingers through it too many times. She'd noticed that morning he seemed out of sorts, and chalked it up to overwork. But there really wasn't a time when Professor Cross wasn't overworked. Something was definitely wrong. The untrained eye would see only typical Cross—brilliant, terse and otherwise occupied. Elizabeth knew him far too well to believe the simplicity of his façade. Working in close quarters had given her insights into the man that most people never knew. What others saw as detachment, she saw as stoic vulnerability.

On the rare occasion he'd let his guard down, she'd seen the depths of the man inside. She knew nothing could ever come of it. Aside from the twenty year age difference, he listened to Stravinsky, she listened to Sting. He was from South of London, she was from North of Lubbock. He grew up with a silver spoon, she grew up with a spork. It was hopeless. She was used to dreaming about things she could never have. There was no reason to think this was anything different.

Simon walked across the stage, powerfully graceful and deceptively smooth. Elizabeth shifted in her seat and needlessly adjusted her skirt.

Why did he have to be so damn attractive? He was handsome. The overwhelming female enrollment in his class was testimony to that. Tall, a few inches over six feet, slender, but not lanky. Eyes of a deep green, tinged with the sadness of having seen too much of the world. And his voice—a hypnotic, deep baritone with a cut glass English accent. But those weren't the things she'd fallen in love with. It was something else, something gentle beneath the hard edge, something needful beneath the control.

"And unlike the overly sentimentalized versions of vampires we see in today's media," Professor Cross said, his voice dripping with sarcasm. "Calmet's writings spoke to the truth of the beast. An unyielding malevolence." He paused and leaned on the podium. "Purge Tom Cruise from your malleable little minds."

The class snickered, and he waited impatiently for them to settle. "The vampire would suck the blood of the living, so as to make the victim's body fall away visibly to skin and bones. An insatiable hunger that kills without remorse," he said and surveyed the classroom.

Elizabeth knew that look, a forlorn hope of seeing some spark of interest, or God forbid, hear some intelligent discourse on the subject. Instead, a blonde girl sitting in the back row made a sound of disgust.

Professor Cross frowned. "Must you do that every class, Miss Danzler?"

She had the good sense to look chagrined. "Sorry, Professor."

Before he could retort that perhaps she should consider a field of study other than the occult, as Elizabeth knew he would, a handsome, athletic student sitting next to her bared his biceps and chimed in, "Don't worry, baby. These are lethal in all dimensions."

Professor Cross assumed his well-practiced air of indifference. "Failing that, Mr. Andrews, you could always bludgeon the demon to death with your monumental ego."

A wave of stifled laughter traveled across the room. As much as the students enjoyed the dark fascination of Cross' Occult Studies course, they also loved his unrelenting sarcasm. Sometimes, he went too far of course, and Elizabeth was left to smooth down the ruffled feathers.

"Sadly, it appears the only thing thicker than your muscles is your skull."

This was one of those times.

The class ended and the students began to pack up. "Don't forget chapters seventeen and eighteen of Grey's Lycanthropy of Eastern Europe for next week."

Elizabeth left her seat and started toward the back of the classroom. Time for a little damage control.

Professor Cross gathered his notes from the podium and turned to look for his assistant. Miss West had already left her customary front row seat and was climbing the stairs toward the back of the amphitheater.

Simon closed his briefcase with more force than necessary and tried to look away. He frowned at the familiar way Elizabeth touched the young man's forearm. Not that he was jealous. That would be patently absurd. Simon simply didn't suffer fools gladly, even by proxy. His mood soured as Elizabeth said something undoubtedly utterly charming and won a laugh from the hulking imbecile. Simon gritted his teeth and waited impatiently for the scene to come to an end. Elizabeth smiled one last time and headed back down the stairs. He glared at her in greeting and gestured brusquely that they should leave.

His mood still sour, Simon opened the classroom door and held it for her. Elizabeth smiled her thanks and walked out into the corridor. He followed her out, moving quickly down the crowded hall, keeping his strides long, forcing her to almost jog to keep up. After a few moments of tense silence, he stopped abruptly and turned to glare down at her.

"I don't need a nursemaid, Miss West."

Elizabeth cocked her head to the side and frowned. "That's debatable, but I wasn't—"

Simon arched an eyebrow in disbelief, challenging her to deny it.

"All right, I was."

Simon snorted.

"But you've got to admit you were in rare form, even for you."

"Your point?"

"That a little browbeating goes a long way. Lance is a good guy. He was just showing off."

"For your benefit, I suppose?" Simon said and instantly wished he could take the words back.

Elizabeth laughed. "Hardly. I'm not exactly his type," she said with a rueful, lopsided smile.

He felt an odd urge to comfort her, to tell her Andrews was a simpleton, but the words died in his throat. How did she do that? One moment she was forthright and confident, challenging him; and the next shy and achingly vulnerable.

"Besides," she added. "It'd be unethical to date a student."

11

That was something he'd told himself daily. He cleared his throat uncomfortably. "Yes, quite right. Well, we have work to do. Shall we?" he said and gestured down the hall.

"No rest for the wicked," she said with a grin and started down the corridor.

Simon watched her disappear into the mass of students and took a deep breath. The scent of her perfume lingered in the air. "None indeed."

Elizabeth set down her pen and massaged her cramping fingers. She could swear she did more work correcting the papers than the students did writing them. And the tiny desk lamp that passed for light in the room was making her eyes cross.

It had taken Professor Cross a year to acquiesce to her request for an actual desk in his office. At first, he'd done everything he could to keep her out of what she liked to call his inner sanctum. He kept the room dark. Suitable, he'd said, for their work. The room was tiny, another testament to the lack of enthusiasm on the part of the Board. He'd been a professor there for nearly ten years and had labored in obscurity. Although, he seemed just as pleased that they left him alone.

Grant money was scarce, if not non-existent, and so he used his own money to further their research. For all the good it did. It seemed the latest get rich quick scheme in the former Soviet Union was the illegal export of so-called occult artifacts—a lock of genuine Baba Yaga hair or, her personal favorite, werewolf droppings. Capitalism at its best. For all the money spent, not one thing had been authentic. But Professor Cross was undeterred, and so their research trudged on.

Elizabeth rubbed her eyes and stole a glimpse of him in the reflection of the glass covering the Bosch print on the wall, the only decoration in an otherwise impersonal office. He really did look tired. More than that, he looked worried. Bent over his desk, one hand wrapped around his head casting a shadow over his face.

"You look like hell," she said.

Simon's eyes snapped up to meet hers. "Thank you," he said tartly.

"I just meant... Are you all right?"

Elizabeth steeled herself for his curt reply, but something stopped him. He looked at her and the hard light in his green eyes softened. "I'm fine," he said. "Thank you."

Then, as quickly as it had disappeared, his natural aloofness re-established itself. He indicated the large stack of graded papers on his desk. "I think that's enough for one night."

Elizabeth shook her head. "I'm okay."

"You can finish the rest tomorrow and drop them off at my house."

A yawn squelched any protest she was going to make. "All right. I could use some good sleep for a change. I've been having this dream. Very David Lynch. Totally and completely unnerving."

Simon dropped his pen and quickly retrieved it. "I see."

Elizabeth shrugged and packed her bag. "I'm gonna sleep like the dead tonight."

She turned back to say goodnight and found him staring at her again with the oddest expression on his face. "Are you sure you're okay?"

He seemed to come back to himself. "Yes, of course. Goodnight, Miss West."

"Good night, Professor," she said and left the office, her footfalls echoing down the empty hallway.

Simon gripped his pen so tightly his knuckles were white with the strain. The mention of her dream brought back the memory of his nightmare from the last few nights. He'd wanted desperately to ask her about her dream, to tell her about his, but felt too foolish. What could he say? *I dreamt about you last night. Don't know any details, but you died a horrible death. Have a good night. Pillock.*

He forced himself to put down his pen and pushed away the fresh wave of anxiety that threatened to pull him under. He'd managed for most of the day to forget, to feel safe in having her by his side. He couldn't say anything, but he couldn't let her walk away either. Before he knew it, he was on his feet and hurrying out into the hall. She was nearly at the corner when he caught her. "May I walk you to your car?"

Elizabeth started and then blinked at him in surprise. "I'm right outside," she said pointing to the doorway around the bend. "It's not really far enough for a walking to."

He hadn't expected her to refuse and felt like a schoolboy who'd been turned down for a date. "Yes, well then. Good night, Miss West," he said and turned back toward his office before he could make a bigger fool of himself. He walked into his office and closed the door. The main door to the building closed with a thud, and he put his hand to his forehead. Gibbering dolt. Tongue-tied over a woman half his age.

Moments later, he heard voices outside and looked out his office window. Elizabeth waved goodbye to someone then walked alone into the parking lot.

He watched her through the slats of the louvered blinds. He was used to being on the inside looking out. It was how he lived. The loneliness had become a welcome companion, reinforcing old memories and keeping him safe from new ones.

He scanned the darkness for unseen dangers, but the night was quiet and still. Elizabeth made her way to her decrepit VW Bug and unlocked it. She opened the door, but didn't get in. She paused and lifted her head as if she'd heard something. Simon felt his heart lurch. He strained to see the threat, ready to go to her. After a painfully long moment, she shook her head and got into the car.

Simon let out a breath he didn't know he'd been holding and watched her pull out of the lot. He stood at the window long after the red of her tail lights had been swallowed by the night. What was it about that woman that left him feeling so undone? He was a solitary man, by choice and by circumstance. He'd grown used to living according to his own whim and no one else's. Then Elizabeth West had come into his life. She was curious, honest, unafraid and completely maddening. He had managed perfectly well without her and yet, he couldn't quite remember how.

CHAPTER TWO

THE FALL EVENING AIR was crisp, as crisp as it got in Southern California. A cool breeze swept over the finely manicured lawn in front of Professor Cross' house. Elizabeth tugged her T-shirt down more securely over her navel and thought about grabbing a sweater from the backseat. She shifted the stack of papers in her arms and peered through the dirty car window. There was a sweater in there somewhere, buried under the piles of books. Wasn't worth the effort, she decided. After all, this was a hit and run. Drop the papers off and then back to the library. Again. Her tiny matchbox apartment was not conducive to studying. Neighbors who thought they were on a daytime talk show and pipes that liked to sing off-key were just a few of the joys of her time at home.

She turned back to the house and tried to tame her unruly hair, but the wind had other ideas. Maybe frazzled and windblown could be a new look for her? Not that he'd even notice. Another strong gust blew past her. Fallen leaves scraped against the pavement, the only sound in an otherwise strangely silent night. It wasn't that late, but the street was empty, as if everyone knew something she didn't, some coming apocalypse she'd missed the memo for. Maybe it was the full moon or the coming eclipse? She looked up into the bright moonlight, but the man in the moon wasn't sharing his secrets either. She stood a moment longer on the sidewalk and then looked at the imposing façade of the Tudor style mansion—strong and intimidating, reeking of old money. The windows were dark and the porch light wasn't on, and she wondered if he'd forgotten she was coming by.

A large, gnarled oak tree blocked out most of the light from the moon and kept the front door shrouded in darkness. She stumbled on the path and almost lost her hold on the papers. Leave it to Professor Cross to have cobblestones. Probably imported them from England for the sole purpose of tripping young Americans.

She rang the bell and waited. After a few moments, the porch light came on and Simon opened the door. He wore casual slacks and a loose-fitting, forest green sweater. Normally, the color would have set off his eyes; now it only served to draw attention to how bloodshot they were.

"Miss West. What are you doing here?"

She held out the stack of graded papers. "You said I should drop these off."

"What?"

"The essays from last night," she prompted with a frown. Simon Cross was many things, but forgetful wasn't one of them.

He ran a hand through his hair and nodded absently. "Right. Papers. Come in."

They passed through the dark foyer and into the warm living room. A fire blazed in the hearth, and a single floor lamp cast a pool of soft light onto a large, leather wingback chair. As she entered the room, she felt she was stepping inside the man. Outside, the exterior was cold and imposing, but the inside was inviting and comforting.

She'd been to his home before and took each opportunity to find some new artifact or personal item. To put one more piece of the Simon Cross puzzle in its place. She set the papers down on the edge of a long, fruitwood trestle table and tried again to force her hair into some semblance of human appearance. "Essays weren't too bad. I think a few of the students might actually be learning something."

Simon hovered uneasily in the center of the room. "One can only hope."

Elizabeth glanced around the room, guiltily sneaking a peek at the intimate details of his life. A grand piano sat in the corner. Although there was sheet music out, she couldn't quite conjure the image of Simon ever playing it. Then, she noticed two large, open shipping boxes next to the sofa and gave in to her absurd urge to make small talk. "Packages. I love getting packages. Get anything good?"

Good manners succumbed to curiosity, and she walked over to the crates. An old photograph rested on top of the crumpled paper inside the box. She leaned over to get a better look. In the photo was a young, lanky boy who stood with his hands planted firmly on his hips. Pure Simon Cross. Although, the cheerful smile was an expression she'd never seen him wear. A dapper, older man with a shock of white hair and an outrageously bushy mustache had his arm draped over Simon's shoulder. They looked like two great white hunters, their quarry just out of frame.

She'd been so caught up in the photograph she hadn't noticed Simon at her side until she smelled the musk of his aftershave. He reached down and picked up the photograph. "My grandfather."

"Sebastian Cross? The anthropologist?"

Simon fixed her with a piercing gaze, the flickering light from the fire reflected in his eyes. "And how did you know that?"

"Your university bio." Elizabeth had been curious about Sebastian Cross ever since she'd read the small blurb in the faculty biographies. "He was—"

"Insane?"

"I was going to say eccentric. His papers were... Unique."

Simon laughed. A cold bitter sound. "You read his papers?"

"Some of them. They were very interesting."

"If by interesting you mean they were derided in academic circles, you'd be correct." He crossed over to the fireplace and carefully set the photo on the mantle.

In the two years of seeing him battle the impolitic politics of university life, she'd never seen him this defensive or wounded. "I didn't mean that, Professor Cross."

Simon gripped the edge of the mantle and stared into the blazing fire. The muscles of his back, tense and formidable, stood out in relief against the taut fabric of his sweater. A loud, crackling pop accentuated the silence.

"I know it's none of my business," she continued, throwing caution to the wind. "But—"

"You're right." Simon turned to face her, any sign of his turmoil replaced with an implacable hardness. "It's none of your business."

Stung by his rebuke and feeling foolish for having tried, Elizabeth said, "I guess I should be going then."

Simon clenched his jaw, a deep frown furrowing his brow.

Elizabeth waited for another tense moment, courting the hope that he might ask her to stay. Finally, she gathered her wits and the shreds of her dignity. "Goodnight, Professor."

She was nearly at the foyer when she heard his voice, demanding and pleading at the same time. "Wait."

She stopped and slowly turned to face him.

"I'm—I'm sorry, Miss West."

Simon glanced back at the photo of his grandfather, as if he could find the answer to some unspoken question in the faded Kodachrome. She'd never seen him like this—so at a loss. It was strangely appealing and more than a little unnerving.

"There's something I'd like to show you," he said. "That is, if you don't have another engagement."

Elizabeth shook her head and smiled. He was actually asking her to stay, and she knew him well enough to know it cost him dearly to ask. Trying not to appear too giddy at the prospect and failing miserably, she said, "I'm all yours."

He nodded, the ghost of a grateful smile in his eyes. "Please," he said, gesturing to the sofa.

Simon waited until she'd taken her seat before he sat opposite her in the overstuffed wingback. He looked down at his hands, and the silence stretched out between them. He cleared his throat. "I'm sorry. Can I offer you something to drink? A glass of wine?"

She wondered if the earth had shifted on its axis. Two apologies from Simon Cross in under a minute. "Thank you."

He excused himself and went into the kitchen. Elizabeth couldn't imagine what had come over him. One minute he was distrustful and caustic, the next he was a gracious, even nervous, host.

She glanced around the room and hoped to find some clues to explain his aberrant behavior of the last few days. Small statues, one of them a very well endowed fertility god, were strewn around at the base of the boxes. Vases and more picture frames poked out of the crates. She noticed an ornate box on the coffee table in front of her. It was made of deep, rich mahogany and about the size of a shoe box. An intricate gold and porcelain inlay of a globe adorned on the lid. As she leaned in to get a better look, Simon came back into the room.

"I'm afraid I only have Cabernet," he said and handed her the glass.

Taking a sip of wine she leaned back into the soft cushions. "That's beautiful," she said, indicating the box on the table.

Simon glanced down at the small chest. "It was my grandfather's. All of this was his."

She knew from what little she'd read about Sebastian Cross that he'd died nearly thirty years ago. Why were the belongings just now being passed on?

As if sensing her question, Simon lifted his eyes to hers. "My aunt died last week and the family sent these along."

"Were you close? To your aunt, I mean."

"Hardly," Simon said. "She had a unique talent for making you feel very, very small. My family wasn't exactly what you'd call..." He frowned searching for the right word. "Functional."

"Functional is relative. Sorry, bad pun."

Simon took a sip of wine and set his glass down. "I wasn't very close to my family, except for my grandfather. I spent my summers away from boarding school with him in Sussex."

"He's the reason you teach occult."

Simon seemed startled by her insight, not that it was any great leap of logic. He leaned back in his chair and studied her for a moment. His expression eased from surprise to reluctant admiration. "He specialized in anthropology of the supernatural. And, not surprisingly, was ignored and ridiculed for what most saw as a specious field of study at best."

Elizabeth nursed her drink as Simon recounted his summers with his grandfather. She didn't dare interrupt with any questions, afraid he'd stop sharing. The most personal thing he'd ever said before was that, in his opinion, Thousand Island dressing was an abomination. She sat quietly, with rapt attention as the unfathomable Professor Cross, revealed fathom after fathom.

The old man had told him stories of his adventures with everything from the anthropomorphs of ancient Greece to the zombies of eighteenth century France.

"And, like any young boy would be," Simon continued. "I was enthralled. His 'brunch with the death eaters of Peru' was a personal favorite."

Simon looked almost ashamed. He seemed to retreat inside himself, pulled under by the riptide of a painful memory. Slowly, he ran a long finger against the smooth edge of the mahogany box. "I was never allowed to touch this when I was a boy."

Elizabeth's curiosity, as it was wont to do, got the better of her. "But you're not a boy anymore."

"No," Simon said, his voice stronger and his eyes clearer. He took a small key from the table and opened the box.

There were dozens of small items resting on a red velvet covering. Jewelry, charms, and coins. Simon picked up a small pouch by its leather strap.

"A gris-gris," Elizabeth said, barely able to contain her excitement.

"Typical of turn of the century voodoo practitioners, if I'm not mistaken," Simon said, handing the charm to her.

Elizabeth turned the bag over in her hand. For something supposedly a hundred years old, it was barely worn. She tentatively brought the pouch to her nose, sniffed and pulled back in surprise. "I can still smell the spices. There's no way they should still be this fragrant after so many years. It must be a replica."

Simon picked up another item from the box, a small silver coin no larger than a dime. He held it to the light. "This is odd."

Elizabeth pulled her attention away from the gris-gris. "What is?"

Simon gave her the coin. "What's wrong with this?"

"Well, it's Greek. A griffin on one side and the head of a bull on the other. It looks authentic enough, but—" Her eyes rounded as the realization sunk in. "No signs of wear at all. It looks newly minted."

Simon reached for the next anomalous item. His eyes locked upon a beautiful, gold pocket watch. "I remember this. He always carried the watch with him, but I never once saw him open it."

Simon's hand trembled as he took the watch out of the box. "I remember some men coming by the house asking about it not long after his death. I never did find out who they were."

He looked across at Elizabeth, his eyes clouded with worry and a tinge of fear, but he quickly averted his gaze and looked back down at the watch.

Elizabeth set down the coin and moved to stand next to Simon. The watch case was etched with an intricate replica of the Mercator globe. He turned the timepiece over and summoned the courage to open it. He flexed his fingers and carefully undid the small clasp.

The interior face was ringed by two thin bands, each marked with N, S, E and W. The face itself was a complex configuration of dials. Some dials were numbered with the standard one through twelve, while others were in increments of ten to one hundred. Near the stem was a cutout inset where the phases of the moon were displayed. The illustrated moon was full and there was a small black disk slowly moving across its face.

Simon's finger brushed against the crown. The stem clicked and extended. Elizabeth wasn't sure, but she thought the hand on one of the smaller dials had changed position. Very carefully, Simon pushed the stem back into place.

"It's beautiful," Elizabeth said, peering over his shoulder.

Simon nodded, but he was clearly lost in the watch.

Wanting to leave him to his private memories, Elizabeth peered into the box. "May I?"

Simon glanced up from the watch. "Certainly."

Elizabeth picked up a small, Egyptian scarab ring. The scarab itself seemed genuine enough, although there was a crack down the beetle's back, but the band and the setting were far too modern, probably from this century. She was about to comment on the irregularity when she noticed something odd about the gold watch in Simon's hand.

She frowned and looked at it more closely, then closed the small chest and studied the lid. The design on the watch was the same as on the lid.

"They have the same inlay," she said and moved back to look over Simon's shoulder. "What kind of watch is that? And how does it know we're having a lunar eclipse tonight?"

"Eclipse?"

"Yeah, I'm guessing that's what that little black disc thingy signifies."

As if on cue, the room darkened. The moonlight filtering in from the window was slowly obscured by the earth's shadow. Moving in perfect sync, both the disc on the dial and the darkness blotted out the moon.

Without warning, a crackle of energy erupted from the watch. Small blue streaks snaked out, shimmering over Simon's hand. Like azure lightning, the bolts moved up his arm and covered his entire body.

Startled, Elizabeth reached out to him, and as soon as she touched his arm, the blue light slithered onto her hand and enveloped her, paralyzed her.

The world around her began to vibrate, faster and faster. Like the wings of a hummingbird the motion was so quick the edges of reality began to blur. It was as if the universe were trying to shake itself apart.

And then, it did.

Chapter Three

THE SUN SLICED THE alley in two.

Simon groaned and rolled onto his side, his hand falling into a puddle of warm water. The strange sensation brought him back to the edge of consciousness. The blaring of car horns in the distance grew more insistent and drew him out of the haze.

The acrid smell of gasoline and burning coal filtered between the old brick buildings. He took a deep breath and gagged on the stale, dank air. Bright sunlight stabbed into his eyes, and he brought a hand up to shield his face from the glare. Squinting against the light, his head throbbing mercilessly, he forced himself to sit up.

The world around him finally came into focus. Battered trash bins and discarded wooden crates lay like victims of a firing squad against a brick wall. What the hell was he doing here? Or was this another vivid dream strangling him with realism?

The last thing he could remember was sitting in his living room. He'd been going through his grandfather's things. Days haunted with sleepless nights blurred his memories. Decomposing fragments slowly came back to him. He'd settled in for a night of warm whiskey and cold memories, but someone else was there.

Elizabeth! The aching pain of his dreams, the loss and desperation rifled through his senses in rapid fire succession. He pushed himself to his feet and stood on shaky legs. His mind refused to clear, except for one thought—he needed to find Elizabeth. Frantically, he scanned the alley, dreading what he might find. She was only a few feet away, lying face down in the shadows. His heart raced faster in his chest as he stumbled to her side.

She wasn't moving. This had to be a dream. Please let this be a dream.

"Miss West," he said insistently.

Nothing.

He steeled himself for the worst. Perhaps this was a nightmare after all. His hands trembled as he gripped her shoulder and cradled her head in his hand. Carefully, he rolled her on to her back. Her face was pale, as if all the blood had been leeched away. Her body was limp in his hands. An unerring sense of déjà vu overwhelmed him.

"Elizabeth."

She moaned and rolled her head to the side.

"Thank God," he whispered and without thinking, stroked her cheek. Emotions whirlpooled inside him. With shuddering breath, he wrestled for control and finally won.

Her eyes opened and struggled to focus.

"Are you all right?" he asked, clenching his fist to keep from caressing her. She brought a shaky hand to her forehead and groaned. "Professor?"

He scanned her for injuries. Her pupils were reacting to the light. That was a good sign. And she seemed to be coming around. "Are you hurt?"

"I'm okay, I think. Except for one hell of a headache," she said as he helped her to sit up.

"It'll pass soon," he said, knowing it was a lie. He felt worse than before. His own head pounded. He wasn't one to offer false comforts and did his best to ignore the fact that he'd done just that.

She glanced at their bizarre surroundings and shook her head, trying to clear it. "What the heck was in that wine?"

"Can you stand?"

She nodded and took the hand he offered. He watched her carefully. She swayed a bit and he reached out to steady her. "Are you sure you're all right?"

She wobbled and gripped his forearm.

Tightening his hold, he put an arm around her back to support her. "Miss West?"

"Fine. Sorry, I was..." she said as she looked up into his face. Her pale skin flushed pink. "I'm all right."

Slowly, more reluctantly than he wanted to admit, he moved his arm from her back. He wasn't quite ready to let go completely, so he held her arm tightly in his grasp.

"Take your time."

She smiled and nodded. "I'm okay," she said and then seemed to notice where they were for the first time. "I think. Where are we?"

"I'm not sure," he said as he glanced around the alley.

"This is definitely not your living room."

Simon laughed softly. "It's good to see your powers of observation are still intact."

She gave him a wry smile, but it faded. "This isn't even Southern California. At least no part I've ever seen."

She was right. The architecture, what he could see of it, was completely wrong. Not to mention the smell of coal thick in the air. A shrill, odd-sounding car horn blared around the alley's corner. And like a lemming to the ocean, Elizabeth started toward the mouth of the alley.

"Where do you think you're going?" Simon asked.

"Just having a look around. We're not going to figure out where we are standing in this alley."

He didn't know what bothered him more. That she was so willing to wander off into God knows what, or that she was right.

"Hang about," he said and hurried to catch up.

He grabbed her arm again, and she rolled her eyes. Petulant he could deal with. Out of his sight, he couldn't.

Staying close to the building's edge, she peered around the corner. After a long steady silence she croaked out a tremulous, "Oh, boy."

He looked around the edge of the building.

"Tell me that isn't a..." Elizabeth said. "I must be hallucinating. Tell me you don't see what I see."

"A Model T?"

And not just one. A mass of tall, long, rectangular shaped cars trundled past. Simon took an unsteady step backwards. Where in God's name were they?

"I was really hoping for hallucinating."

The cacophony was nearly deafening. High-pitched horns wailed up and down the endless street. A horse whinnied and reared, its hooves scraping the pavement. A sea of people, all talking at once, surged on the sidewalk in front of them. Men in suits and fedoras, women in vintage dresses walked by. A large horse-drawn cart clattered over the pavement.

"They must be making a movie," Elizabeth said hopefully.

Simon had a terrible sinking feeling. He tugged on her arm and she looked up at him with wide, frightened eyes.

"Miss West," he said, urging her to follow his lead and pulled her back into the alley. "What's the last thing you remember?"

She rubbed her forehead. "Being in your living room looking at your grandfather's things and then the watch went all higgledy-piggledy."

Adrenaline coursed through his veins. Of course, the watch. In his single-minded concern for Elizabeth, he'd completely forgotten about it. He moved back down the alley and scoured the pavement until he found the timepiece only a few feet from where he'd regained consciousness. Gripping the case tightly, he carefully opened it. His eyes darted over the complex dials. This couldn't be.

Elizabeth came to his side. "Be careful with that thing."

"I'm not an imbecile, Miss West," he bit out.

"No offense, but I'm not looking for a repeat performance."

Neither was he. He knew the answer to all his questions lay in the watch. The strange dials that had been a mystery before, now began to coalesce into a semblance of reason. If one could call it that. Simon's head was spinning and not just from the damnable headache that wouldn't go away. It was insane. Absolutely insane to even consider, and yet....

Was it possible that all the stories his grandfather had told him weren't stories at all? The destruction of Pompeii, a night at Valley Forge, the War of the Roses. Dear God. He'd actually been there.

Elizabeth leaned in to get a better look at the watch, her body brushing against his. "What the heck's going on, Professor?"

How could he expect her to believe what he could hardly comprehend himself?

Her hand gripped his arm, and she forced him to look at her. Her blue eyes, usually filled with confidence, danced nervously across his face. "Where are we?"

He tried to quell his growing sense of panic and keep his voice calm and detached. "It's not so much where we are, but when. Judging from the cars and style of dress, we appear to be in the late twenties."

"Twenties? As in Nineteen Twenties? You can't be serious."

"Perhaps early thirties, I'll need to check." Research—the haven for a logical mind. Simon always sought refuge in detail, in the search for answers. His entire career had been built on the foundation that anything could be proven, no matter how incredible it sounded, if the right research was performed.

"Check what?" Elizabeth asked. "I think you'd better tell me what the hell's going on."

Simon held out the watch and stared down at the complicated dials. "If I'm reading this properly, I'd say it's 1929. July Seventeenth, to be exact."

Elizabeth let go of his arm and stepped back. The color drained from her face, and her voice trembled. "That's impossible."

A fresh wave of guilt washed over Simon. He couldn't afford to give in to it. "It seems that my grandfather was more than merely eccentric."

Elizabeth stared at him, her expression blank. "Are you saying that thing's some sort of time machine?"

"Apparently."

"That's impossible."

"Apparently not."

She put her fists on her hips and looked at him accusingly. "You're awfully calm about this."

He was anything but calm. Still, he knew they had to keep a clear head if they were going to find a way out of this mess. "Would you prefer I panic?"

"A little, yeah. I mean—Hello! Time travel. Not an everyday thing," she said, a frown coming to her face. "Unless, you've done this before."

"Don't be absurd."

"Yeah, wouldn't want to be absurd standing in an alley in Nineteen Twenty-Nine."

Simon took a deep calming breath. "I assure you, if I had any idea what this watch was capable of..."

"I know. I'm sorry," Elizabeth said, wringing her hands. "It's like some bizarre episode of Star Trek. Where's Spock when you need him?"

"I don't see what Dr. Spock had to do with—"

"Mister Spock. Oh, never mind." She took a deep breath. "Okay. The watch got us here, right? So, it can take us back."

"Logical."

She giggled, but quickly subdued it under the heat of his glare. "Sorry. Must be time travel jitters. So, undo it. Put it in reverse or whatever."

"I don't think we should stumble ahead blindly."

"Worked getting us here."

Simon blanched at the remark. Whatever had happened to them was his fault. He could bear that, if there were a way to undo it.

"I didn't mean that the way it came out."

"No, you're quite right, Miss West," Simon said. The weight of their situation truly was dawning on him. If he'd been alone he could have faced it without pause. But now, for the first time in his life, he was responsible for someone else. "The situation is entirely my fault."

Elizabeth tentatively put a hand on his arm. "Who knew your grand-dad was a time traveler? And I can't believe I actually said that."

Simon felt the unaccustomed need to comfort welling inside him again. Compassion had never been a strong suit of his. If anything, the opposite was true. "You do know that I would never knowingly endanger you."

"I know that. I... You think I'm in... I mean, we're in danger?"

"We're in an unknown situation. I'd prefer to err on the side of caution."

"Agreed. Let's err there."

Simon couldn't shake the feeling that something terrible was going to happen. It was more than the lingering memories of his dream. More than the situation they'd been thrust into. He'd never given much credence to hunches, but he had a sense he'd started something in motion bringing them here. Something he wouldn't be able to control. Something inevitable.

"Not that it isn't unique, being here, wherever it is," Elizabeth said. "But maybe we should try to get back home?"

"Agreed."

"We'll just re-create everything," she continued. "You were holding the watch. Did you do anything to it? Push any buttons?"

"The stem did extend, but..."

"Okay. Just do exactly what you did before."

"I'm not sure that's wise. I'd much rather be sure of what I'm doing before I make another mistake."

"It's worth—"

A thick metal door swung open with a loud clang. Elizabeth jumped at the sound and grabbed Simon's arm. A large, burly, unshaven man stepped into the alley. His white undershirt was stained a sickly yellow with sweat. "What you doin' here?"

Simon put his hand over Elizabeth's and pulled her slightly behind him. He turned to glare at the man. "We were simply—"

"Do it someplace else," the man growled with a thick Brooklyn accent, as he threw his bucket of empty bottles into a nearby trash bin. "Go on, get out of here!"

Simon ignored the man and started to turn back to Elizabeth.

"You want I should call the cops?" the man said with a sneer, as he looked Elizabeth up and down. She was wearing a tight, blue T-shirt and jeans, but his eyes traveled her figure as if she were naked. Her clothes were far too form-fitting for the period to be anything other than something a tramp would wear. "Take your quiff and get a room."

Simon's body tensed. He slowly pulled out of her grasp and took a long direct stride toward the man. "I beg your pardon?"

The big man only smiled. "You heard me."

Simon started forward again, but Elizabeth pulled on his arm.

"We can't afford to see the police," she whispered. "Let's just go."

Simon's eyes flared, and he turned back to the big man. Long dormant emotions boiled to the fore. His instinct to defend Elizabeth crashed into his common sense. He'd known more than his fair share of bullies, and most could be cowed with a biting remark. But this was something different. He'd never felt such an overwhelming desire to punch someone in the mouth.

"Professor," Elizabeth urged and tugged on his arm.

Simon gave the man a long, steely glare before he turned back to Elizabeth. Without another word, he took her by the arm and led her out of the alley.

"Good idea, Professor," the man snarled.

They were half way down the block before Simon released her. He shoved his hands into his pockets. "I'm sorry."

Elizabeth grinned. "You'd better stop apologizing. Might be habit-forming."

Simon couldn't help but smile back. Why couldn't he have smiled like that back home? Had to be here, she thought, and looked around at the busy street. Wherever here is. Elizabeth self-consciously wrapped her arms across her chest and looked down the street.

The cars were huge, and there were so many of them. Big black sedans, with cloth-canopied tops and headlamps sticking out like bug eyes meandered along the street creating some semblance of lanes. The foot traffic surged around them, and Elizabeth suddenly felt terribly underdressed. Some men wore knickers and bow ties, or Oxford bag pants that ballooned as they walked past. Every one of them wore a hat. Fedoras and bowlers. And the women too. They all had on hats. Tight-fitting cloches or veiled peekaboos. And dresses.

A couple glared at her, whispering disapproval as they noticed her pants. Not one woman wore slacks, only dresses and skirts. Some wore their hose turned-down in a risqué fashion statement, but clearly wearing blue jeans was not something a lady did.

Hundreds of cars and thousands of people teemed around them in a dizzying rush. More and more passersby gave them odd, disapproving looks.

A young boy with a ragged, woolen cap strode past them. "Paper! Get your paper here!"

Simon startled her as he called out. "Boy!"

The young man came over to them and held out a paper. Simon reached into his pockets then realized he didn't have any change. And even if he did, she realized, they couldn't start spreading twenty-first century money into the past.

"Sorry, I don't," Simon showed the boy his empty palm.

The newsboy sighed, but then seemed to notice Elizabeth for the first time. He waggled his eyebrows suggestively. "Ain't you the stuff?"

Simon stepped closer to Elizabeth and narrowed his eyes. Elizabeth rolled her eyes and took the opportunity to get a glance at the paper.

"Just lookin'," the kid said quickly and started back down the street.

Elizabeth leaned in and whispered in Simon's ear. "You were right. July 17, 1929. And the Yankees lost again."

Simon raised his eyebrow in question.

"Read the headline."

"That's my girl," he said, but then cleared his throat and looked away.

Her stomach fluttered at the compliment, not to mention how adorable he was when he was flustered. "And we know that you can read the watch."

"True," he said, pulling her closer as the crowd surged across the intersection. He led her to an empty doorway away from the mass of people. "But, I'm afraid, reading and manipulating are far different things."

"You'll figure it out."

Simon didn't seem so sure. Elizabeth's eyes darted down the busy street. They'd actually time traveled back to 1920's New York. It was absurd, but she felt a growing sense of excitement. Even if they were only there for a day. What an adventure!

She looked back at Simon. His eyes were dark with concern and uncertainty. He looked down at the watch and put it in his pocket. "This may take some time," he said.

The doubt in his voice sent a shiver up her spine. He'd never been anything but certain, and to see him off-balance was incredibly disconcerting. But why should it all be on his shoulders? She wanted to allay his fears, but recognizing he had them would be an insult. Better to lighten the mood. If anyone was ever in need of a little cheering up, it was Simon. "If my boss doesn't mind that I'm late," she said. "Then I'm game."

His lips quirked into a smile. "You will be docked pay, of course."

Elizabeth laughed, but it didn't last long. They couldn't exactly stand around on the street while he figured out the watch. There was no telling how long that might take and the sun was already dipping behind the buildings.

"Speaking of pay," she said. "We should find someplace to stay the night. Just in case."

"Yes. I'd prefer not to stay on the streets. I doubt New York has changed that much in the last seventy years."

"Right. Wow. Seventy years. I'm still having a little trouble believing that."

"It is... difficult."

Elizabeth sighed. "Well, looks like the hand we were dealt anyway. So, we need a place to stay, but that's going to cost money."

"And clothes. I'm afraid we're garnering a bit too much attention as we are."

"I guess we'll do it the old fashioned way," Elizabeth said. "Pawn something."

"We can do that?"

Elizabeth swallowed the laugh that threatened to bubble up. He seemed genuinely alarmed at the idea. "It's not the best bang for your buck, but when you're in a pinch. And I think this definitely qualifies as a pinch."

"All right, but I'm afraid I don't know..." he said and then shrugged helplessly.

Elizabeth smiled. This she knew how to do. It was a good feeling to be able to help. "I do. We need jewelry, things like that are the easiest to pawn. What do you have?"

Simon took stock of his personal items. She'd never seen him wear jewelry of any kind, except for his wristwatch. He pulled back the sleeve of his sweater and took off the watch. "Will this do? It's not a very modern design."

Elizabeth took the watch and frowned. "Broken," she said. The crystal was smashed. "Must have happened when we crash landed."

Simon put the watch back on his wrist. "Your necklace?" he asked.

Elizabeth self-consciously tugged at the chain. "Not worth anything. My ring's a fake too," she added with an embarrassed smile.

She'd never had any real jewelry, certainly, nothing worth pawning. She looked down at her ring. Fat lot of good it would do them. They needed something real, something gold.

"The ring!" she blurted and then without further explanation took off back down the street.

When he caught up, she was on her hands and knees crawling around on the pavement in the alley.

"What in God's name are you doing woman?"

"Ah-ha!" she cried and jumped to her feet. She held out her hand to him in triumph. In her palm rested the small scarab ring. "I thought I remembered holding it when the watch did its thing."

Simon's face paled, and his hand trembled as he took the ring. Elizabeth watched the play of emotions across his face.

"It's a good thing, right?" she asked. His face was ashen. "Bad penny?"

Simon looked up at her and clenched the ring in his hand. "Very much so."

She waited, but he offered nothing else in the way of explanation. "We can find another way."

"No," Simon said and put the ring away in his pocket. "It should bring a good price."

He stood up a little straighter and nodded toward the street. What was it about the ring that frightened him so much? The tension in his body was palpable.

"It's getting late," he said. Everything about his demeanor had changed. All the emotions he'd let seep out were tucked neatly away. Even his voice was different. Crisp and business-like. "We should find a place to stay the night."

"Right."

Simon stepped back and gestured down the alley. His face was again an impassive mask. The prospect of adventure didn't seem quite as appealing as it had a few minutes ago. At least she wasn't alone. Much. She let out a deep breath and started out of the alley. Together they rounded the corner and stepped into the past and perhaps into their future.

Chapter Four

CALVIN COOLIDGE SAID THE business of America was business. And nowhere was it more evident than the streets of Manhattan in 1929. From the red-hot vendors and shoe-shine stands to the upscale Stork Club and New York Stock Exchange—money was in constant flow and so were the people.

Elizabeth could feel the energy of a city at the height of its power and purpose. People walked with a fast pace suited to the jazz rhythms of the nightclubs. Traffic surged along the streets in tempo with the city's heartbeat. Raucous, dizzying and intoxicating—New York was a party spiraling toward the inevitable calling of the cops.

The people were well-dressed by modern standards. The only ones casually attired were workmen in their coveralls. She felt as if she'd shown up for a wedding in a potato sack. Or worse. There was sharp disapproval in the eyes of people they passed and something she didn't want to define in a few of the men. She tugged self-consciously at the hem of her T-shirt.

"I wish everyone would stop staring," she whispered to Simon.

Simon arched a brow and said off-handedly, "I'm sure your T-shirt has nothing to do with it."

"What? It's brand new, mostly. What's wrong with it?"

"Nothing a little more of it wouldn't cure," he said and looked down at her uncomfortably. "It is rather on the small side, isn't it?"

Elizabeth stopped walking and tugged at her shirt again. Getting fashion tips from a man who thought a Windsor instead of a four-in-hand knot was accessorizing was really too much. "This is a perfectly good shirt."

"In another time, perhaps," Simon said, lowering his voice. "But here it's a little revealing."

She looked down at her shirt. It was small, but everything was covered. All the important stuff anyway. She looked up in time to see Simon avert his eyes.

He cleared his throat and struggled to find his words. The skin of his neck reddened. Was he actually blushing? He cleared his throat again. "Your...chest is...displayed."

Elizabeth looked at the clothes the other women on the street were wearing and finally understood. A part of her hadn't quite accepted that she wasn't just the observer here, but also the observed. She was really here. A wolf whistle from a passing truck put the exclamation point on it. She was a bright, perceptive person, but had a huge blind spot when it came to men. She never noticed them noticing her, and the realization always made her uncomfortable. Very self-conscious now, she hunched her shoulders and crossed her arms over her chest.

Simon sighed heavily and pulled his sweater over his head, leaving him wearing only a crisp white oxford shirt. He held the sweater out to her, but his eyes wouldn't meet hers. "Put this on."

It was ridiculously large for her. The sleeves fell well past her hands and the hem rested barely above her knees. But it was a good fit in other ways, better ways. It smelled like Simon—clean with a hint of aftershave. The weight of the soft fabric was comforting, like the pressure of a hand on the small of her back. She let herself snuggle into it and then noticed Simon looking at her with a strange, far off look in his eyes. Whatever he'd been thinking, he pushed it away quickly and found a fascinating spot of gum on the sidewalk.

Elizabeth pushed the long sleeves up to her elbows. "We should be..."

Simon put his hands in his pockets and nodded. Slowly they fell into step together again and joined the busy flow of pedestrians.

They started in mid-town and after a few inquiries headed south toward the lower class sections where pawn shops would most likely be found. Before too long, the neighborhood changed. The streets were a little dirtier, and the people a little harder. The Lower East Side was a haven for immigrants and the working class, all of them trying to find their piece of the American dream.

"There we go," Elizabeth said and pointed to a sign "Arbogast J. Smith, Pawnbroker".

As they stepped inside, she was struck by how every pawnshop was like the next—a sad mixture of lost hope and second-hand dreams. The owner stood behind the glass-cased counter and looked up sharply when the bell at the top of the door announced their arrival.

He was a tall, thin man with dark eyes that seemed unnaturally large behind the thick lenses of his glasses. Elizabeth shuddered. He looked like the proverbial spider, and she felt like the unwitting fly.

"Why don't you see what you can get for the ring and I'll try to find some clothes," Elizabeth said. She tried to shake the feeling she was being sized up for something unpleasant and browsed the shop's wares.

His large bug eyes followed her as she looked at the merchandise—clothes, jewelry and the inevitable saxophone. Why was it every pawn shop seemed to have a tarnished sax hanging in one corner? A bit of someone's soul dangling by a thin cord. A piece of someone's heart taken in trade. She'd left a few chapters of her life behind in glass cases.

She noticed Simon hadn't started haggling and nodded her head toward the counter to prod him along. She thought about doing it herself. Simon was clearly out of his element. But could a woman in the 1920's get the same price as a man? Hell, they couldn't even in the next century. Some things were slow to change. She reminded herself to try to check her impulses. A headstrong woman in this time would be as welcome as a skunk at a lawn party, and they couldn't afford to stick out at all. She spied a rack of second-hand dresses in the back and went to find something suitable.

Simon watched her disappear into the back of the store and then turned his attention to the owner.

The man wasted no time appraising Simon, and a thin smile stretched his pinched mouth. "Name's Smitty. What do you have for me today?"

Simon didn't have much experience in bargaining, but he knew a shark when he saw one. He took the ring out of his pocket but didn't hand it over just yet. "A family heirloom. It's quite valuable."

Smitty's lips quivered in anticipation. "Of course." He held out his bony hand.

Simon hesitated, looking at the man's black, smudged fingers. He had little choice though, and set the ring on the counter. He loathed the idea of pawning it. Even though the ring brought with it painful memories, they were the last he had of his grandfather. The watch and the ring had come to symbolize those final moments—frightening and confusing, but all he had left.

Elizabeth poked her head around the corner and held out a pale, floral print dress. "Is there somewhere I can try this on?"

"There's a partition screen in the back," Smitty said, as he stopped examining the ring and leaned over the counter to stare at Elizabeth.

She came around the corner and put the dress on the counter. As she started to pull the sweater over her head, Simon gave in to the ridiculous urge to block Smitty's view. Not that she was undressing, but there was something sensual about the way she moved, the way her hair fell across her shoulders.

She smiled and handed Simon his sweater. "Thanks for the loan."

He watched Elizabeth walk to the back of the store and then turned to Smitty, whose leer slid effortlessly into an oily smile.

"Mr. Smith," Simon bit out. "If you don't mind..."

Smitty's lips tightened, his mouth looking like a gash cut into the middle of his face. Simon clenched his jaw. He couldn't afford to say the things he wanted to. Not now, when they needed money so badly. The sooner they finished their business here the better. "The ring," he said tightly.

"Of course," Smitty said and examined the small scarab. He turned it over in his hands and looked at the setting closely. "You're not from around here, are you?"

"We're new in town," Simon said. Now he was going to be forced to make small talk with this creature.

"Where ya staying?"

Simon hesitated. "We haven't settled in quite yet."

Smitty looked up from examining the scarab. "You on the lam?"

"Of course not," Simon said and racked his brain for viable story. "We just got off the train and... I really don't see how it's any of your affair."

"You're a little jumpy aren't ya? No luggage, odd clothing. If this ring's hot it'll affect the price."

"Now, see here—"

"You wouldn't be the first."

Simon's patience was wearing thin. "We are not on the run."

"No?" He glanced down at Simon's hand and saw he wasn't wearing a wedding ring. "Out for a little fun then?"

"What exactly are you implying?"

Smitty shrugged. "You wouldn't be the first man to have a little milk without buying the cow."

Simon reached the end of his rope. No matter how badly they needed money he wasn't going to tolerate such insolence. "Mr. Smith," Simon ground out. "If I were you—"

"We're newlyweds," Elizabeth said as she came to Simon's side. She hooked her arm through his and turned to Smitty with her sweetest smile. "He's still getting used to the idea."

"Yes," Simon stammered. Smitty seemed to step back a little. Apparently, Simon's claim on her was enough to bring the man up short. It was a ridiculous charade, but if it gave Elizabeth a modicum of safety he'd gladly keep up pretenses. "It all happened rather unexpectedly."

"Very," Elizabeth said with a grin, her eyes bright with mischief.

Smitty narrowed his eyes. "You don't have rings."

"There wasn't time to see to everything properly," Simon said. "We were hoping you could help us with that. Unless, of course, you'd rather continue to insult my wife," he finished, laying his hand possessively over hers.

Smitty didn't seem to believe them, but if it meant more business he clearly didn't care what their story was. "I think I might have something."

"I thought you might," Simon said. He looked down at Elizabeth sternly, but his pique melted. The dress she was wearing was simple, but she looked wonderful. The pale blue-green pattern made her hair seem that much more striking. A series of ridiculously tiny buttons ran up the front, stopping at the base of the v-neck. Her pale skin led to the enticing arch of her collarbone. The scalloped hem fell to her knees, giving him a glimpse of her shapely legs. Elizabeth seldom wore dresses, and he wondered why when she was so enchanting in them.

Elizabeth ducked her head shyly. "Do you like?"

"Very much," Simon said softly.

Elizabeth blushed and stepped back. She couldn't quite meet his eyes. "I'm gonna need shoes too. I'll just go see what's back there," she said and disappeared again into the back of the store.

Simon watched her walk away. She should definitely wear dresses more often. Or perhaps it was best she didn't. He had enough trouble keeping his feelings under wraps as it was. The softening of his heart whenever she was near was untenable enough. Now, with seemingly every man they encountered leering at her, it was almost impossible to hide how he felt.

"I'll give you thirty for the ring," Smitty said.

"Thirty? It's worth ten times that."

"Got a crack in the stone. Thirty."

"Thirty-five."

Smitty's cold face split into a grim smile. "I say it's worth thirty."

"Unconscionable," Simon muttered.

"Take it or leave it. No skin off my nose."

Simon knew there had to be other pawn shops and glanced out the door. The light had already started to dim. They couldn't afford to search all night for another shop. It was a crime to sell the ring for so little, but they needed money. Now. "Fine," he said.

"The ticket's good for sixty days, then it goes in the general merchandise," Smitty said and wrote out the receipt. "Pleasure doing business with you."

"I assure you," Simon muttered. "The pleasure was entirely yours."

Once they'd made their purchases—one dress, one suit, one broadcloth shirt, one pair of ladies shoes, a pair of imitation gold rings and a small suitcase—they had less than twenty dollars left.

The street was dimly lit, but still filled to the edges with people hurrying this way and that. No wonder they called it the city that never sleeps. As far as Simon could tell it never even took a breath.

They walked aimlessly in an uncomfortable silence until Elizabeth suggested they ask someone for directions to some boarding houses. Simon didn't think they needed help, but when they passed the same little diner twice, he finally relented. With vague directions to head down Market Street, they set off again. The uncomfortable silence joined them.

"I'm sorry about springing the whole just married thing on you back there," Elizabeth said suddenly.

Simon looked at her, waiting for more of an explanation.

"It sort of came out, but it's probably a good cover. We can't exactly rent a room together if we aren't. I mean we could, but I've had enough of being called a prostitute for one day," she said with wan smile. "I guess we could get two rooms. Be most of our money, but if you'd rather—"

"No," Simon said. One room was the best idea and not just monetarily. He had no intention of letting her out of his sight while they were here. And if the few reactions she'd gotten from men so far were any indication, she was going to need some looking after. "One room will do, Miss West."

"Professor," she said. "I think maybe you shouldn't call me Miss West anymore. At least not in public. It's okay to call me Elizabeth. I know it's awkward, but..."

"We don't have any choice, do we?" he said too sharply. He rolled his shoulders to release some of the tension. It wasn't her fault he couldn't get a grip on himself. He was used to having a place for everything and everything in its place. This sudden turn into the unknown left him off-balance and he didn't like the feeling one bit. Not to mention being here with her. He'd managed quite well to control himself around her before. But then, he'd been able to hold academia between them. He could step back and regain himself, rebuild the wall she unwittingly felled. But now, they were forced together and he wasn't sure what to do. For the first time, he wasn't sure of anything. And they'd only been there three hours.

He turned his head away from her and kept his eyes on the opposite side of the street. Dilapidated tenements and brownstones nearly black at the base with soot told them they were in the right area. This area they could afford at least. Simon watched the people gathered on the stoops warily and gripped the handle of their suitcase that much tighter. Thankfully, it wasn't long before he saw signs for rooms to rent.

They settled on the Manchester Arms. It was an average sized residence hotel—three stories, no elevator, but the lobby was clean and the price was right. Seven dollars for the week, paid up front. Simon took the key from the desk clerk, and they started up the stairs.

"He was nice. I was beginning to wonder if everyone here was just nasty," Elizabeth said. "Gives me faith in humanity again."

"You're easily persuaded," he said, squinting to read the door numbers in the poorly lit hallway.

"You're such a cynic. I thought he was nice."

"A bit too nice, I think."

"Come on, newlyweds always get special treatment," she said. "Ah. Here we are. Room Thirty-four."

Simon set the suitcase down and unlocked the door. He pushed it open and gestured for Elizabeth to go first.

"Aren't you going to carry the bride over the threshold?" she teased.

She was impudent and absolutely charming. "Miss—"

"Elizabeth. You know, you haven't said it once."

Simon took a deep breath. "Elizabeth."

She blushed a little and grinned. "That wasn't so bad, was it?"

What could he say? Yes, it was. That saying it meant he'd crossed some invisible line he'd drawn for himself? That the mere thought of her name made his stomach drop with desire? That the way it fell across his lips felt like a prayer he wasn't worthy of?

"No," he said. "It wasn't."

"Good," she said with a smile and took a step into the apartment. The room was dark, and she felt along the wall for a light switch. She found it quickly and turned it on.

Simon picked up the case and followed behind. She stopped a few feet inside the door. He was about to ask what was wrong, when he saw it for himself.

The bed. There was one bed. One tiny, little double bed, for them both to share.

CHAPTER FIVE

ELIZABETH COULD FEEL SIMON'S presence behind her. When she'd pulled up short, he'd practically run into her and now they were standing so close, they were almost touching. Touching. The bed. Those two thoughts definitely needed to be separated. She tore herself away from staring at the small bed and walked over to the window.

The room was musty and could use some fresh air. And so could she. "Is it me or is it hot in here?" she asked, and then yanked open the drapes.

Simon cleared his throat and set the suitcase down. "Yes, it is rather warm."

She tried to jimmy the window open, but it wouldn't budge. "It's stuck."

"Let me," Simon said from close behind her. Too close behind her.

She turned around, and they were almost touching again. She smiled nervously and side-stepped out of his way. "I'll unpack," she said, desperate for something to do.

For all her bravado about making this an adventure, she hadn't considered this part of it. Alone in a bedroom with Simon Cross.

She was generally comfortable around men. Working with them, playing with them, but never simply being with them. She'd grown up surrounded by men. Her mother had left her and her father when she was too young to remember. It had been just the two of them, so she tagged along wherever he went. And he went a lot of places. Not the typical American childhood, growing up in backrooms and pool halls in towns all across Texas, but she wouldn't have traded it for anything. She'd learned an awful lot about people. How to read someone's face when they'd drawn an inside straight. How a man's hands told his life story. Or how the truth was easier to keep track of than a lie. But, even in all that, she hadn't learned much about being a woman.

She'd had relationships, but somehow there was always something eluding her, like there was a secret handshake she didn't know. Each time a man asked her out she was surprised, flattered and a little frightened. Inevitably, her insecurities brought things to a premature end. Not that she'd been heartbroken over any of them. They were good men, most of them, but none of them had managed to force her heart to overrule her head.

"Bloody piece of..." Simon grumbled and took off his jacket, tossing it over the back of a chair.

She opened the suitcase and put their old clothes away in the small dresser and armoire that served as a closet. It was a silly thing to do really. She didn't expect to be staying. But, she'd lived in hotels most of her life and the first thing she always did was unpack. It made the room hers instead of yet another place to stay.

Simon rolled up his sleeves and hit the wooden window frame with his fist. After a few more good bangs, the window finally opened. A breeze blew into the room, but the night air wasn't much cooler than the hotbox of their apartment.

He turned around triumphantly, and she offered him a smile.

"Here we are," she said.

Simon stared back, and the awkwardness hovered between them. They'd spent hour after hour in closer quarters than this, but then again, the office didn't have a bed in the middle of it.

"Yes, well," he said and sat down in one of the two chairs that accompanied the small, round table near the window. He took out his grandfather's watch and carefully opened it.

Elizabeth knew Simon worked best uninterrupted and tried to find something to occupy herself. She looked around the small apartment anxious to find anything of interest. The walls were an indistinct beige and the rug a darker shade of indistinct beige, stained and tattered at the edges. She could see the ghost of earlier wallpaper, some sort of dizzying stripe hidden beneath the hastily applied paint. The room itself was no more than ten by twelve. The ceiling light, a thin brass tube jutting straight down to a chipped smoked glass shade, hung down too low.

She made her way to the bathroom and nearly bumped into the sink when she opened the door. The fixtures were dull and rusted. The faucet arched high over the basin like a drooping branch, its constant drip leaving a dark yellow stain on the porcelain. The paint was bubbled and peeling.

There wasn't a showerhead, but she supposed she should be thankful they had a bathroom at all. It sure beat long walks down the hall in the middle of the night to a community bath. The bathtub was old, and she noticed a series of deep scratches gouged into the tub. What the heck could have made those? Maybe some bathtub gin, she thought with an odd thrill. Or a gangster shoot out, bullets ricocheting from a mob hit. Or not.

She looked at her reflection in the streaked mirror. Same old Elizabeth West. Hair out of place and eyes too big for her face. She shook her head. Didn't matter if she sprouted wings. Simon wouldn't notice the difference.

She went back into the bedroom and Simon was still hunched over the watch, completely oblivious to her. Some things never change. And on that depressing note, she busied herself with looking around the room again.

The furniture was plain, but practical. The bedside lampshade was crooked. She tried to straighten it, but like everything else in the apartment it did what it wanted and apparently it wanted to be crooked. She'd stayed in worse places, but those had been with her father. Being with Simon was an entirely different story.

A splash of red caught her eye. The only decoration in the room was a god-awful painting of a barn over the bed. The bed. She'd managed to ignore it for all of two minutes. Time for a little more ignoring.

"So," she said too brightly. "You got it figured out yet?" She thought she saw Simon smirk. She walked over to the table and looked over his shoulder.

"Incredible workmanship," Simon said. "These dials control the time—century, decade, year, month, day. Down to the very minute. Fascinating."

Elizabeth pointed to the thin bands that ringed the face. She leaned in closer and rested her hand on his shoulder to steady herself, and willfully ignored the feeling of his muscles beneath her fingers. "And those must be directional coordinates. Longitude and latitude."

He cleared his throat. "Exactly."

"Then shouldn't you be able to set it for the time and place we left? And voilà. Home again, home again, jiggety-jig."

"Or it could have a built-in homing device. Automatically returning the person to the point at which they left."

"What makes you think that?" she said and took a chair.

"I can't seem to change the dials anymore. They appear to be locked in place."

"Well, then let's hope it's got an auto-return feature."

Time travel was fun and all, but deep down she'd always believed Simon could control the watch without any trouble. The small room got a little bit smaller.

He tried varying the extension of the stem, but the dials remained fixed. "I wish I knew how it was activated in the first place."

"We could just recreate exactly what we did before."

Simon looked up from the watch and gazed at her intently. She needed to understand the seriousness of the situation. "It could be dangerous."

"Nothing ventured..." she said.

A smile tugged at his lips. Her confidence and bravery shouldn't have been surprising. She'd met each obstacle they'd encountered so far with enthusiasm and a very appealing sense of adventure. She really was quite bewitching. Abruptly, his smile faded. He had to stop doing that. Every time he looked at her his thoughts drifted to foolish schoolboy notions. Now was not the time. "Right, exactly as we were then."

Elizabeth stood and moved next to his chair, putting her hand back on his shoulder. "You were sitting, and I was looking over your shoulder. What did you do next?"

Simon pretended not to notice she was touching him, that the simple gesture made his heart beat a little faster. "That's the problem. I didn't do anything. The watch simply...started."

"You must have done something. Did you close the case?"

"No, I remember watching the moon phases as it—"

"The eclipse!" Elizabeth said excitedly. "Remember, we had a lunar eclipse and that little black disc slid over the full moon." The excitement ebbed from her voice. "You don't think we need an eclipse to make this thing work, do you?"

The moon displayed now was barely half full, and there was no sign of the small disc. He wasn't surprised she'd come to the same conclusions he had. It was one of the things that had drawn him to her when she first started working for him.

"It's not uncommon for astrological phenomena to play a critical role in the supernatural." The words were spoken by rote. He'd probably said the same thing in his class dozens of times, but he'd never considered what that really meant.

"So we have to wait for an eclipse?"

"Possibly."

His mind was racing now. Memories of conversations with his grandfather sped across his thoughts. Grandfather had always been obsessed with the phases of the moon. Simon had never paid it much heed. Sebastian Cross had been obsessed with many things.

Elizabeth started to pace. "I wonder how long we have to wait."

"A few days. A few months. A year."

"A year?"

"We'll have to research that tomorrow. There is another possibility. The watch could have broken when we landed, and we will never be able to return."

"You must be fun at parties," Elizabeth mumbled. She shook her head and pushed out a deep breath. "For now, I'm going to believe it's set on auto-return."

"Believing it doesn't make it so," he said matter-of-factly and went back to studying the watch.

"Sometimes believing something is all you have," Elizabeth snapped. "I'm going to get ready for bed."

"Miss... Elizabeth," Simon said, alarmed at her abrupt change in tone. "I didn't mean..."

Ignoring the worst was only an invitation to bringing it to bear. He couldn't let himself simply believe in things. He had to prove them first. It was the only way to avoid disappointment. It was a philosophy he'd lived by and it had never failed him. Until now. Part of him wanted to share her faith, but it meant offering far too much of himself.

Elizabeth shook her head. "It's okay. I didn't mean to bite your head off." She ran her hand through her hair and heaved a heavy sigh. "You're right. We have to be prepared for that possibility."

She looked suddenly very tired. Dark smudges hung below her eyes. Clearly, the day had taken a greater toll on her than he'd thought. Despite wanting to keep analyzing the watch, he closed it. "All of that can wait until tomorrow though."

"Right. Tomorrow," she said resignedly. "So, what side do you want?"

"Side?"

"Of the bed."

"Oh, I..." Simon said. "I'll sleep in the chair."

"For who knows how long? Don't be silly."

"I think..." he stammered and tugged at the collar of is shirt. "I think it's best."

"We're both adults," she said and then smiled wickedly. "I won't compromise your virtue."

Simon was so pleased to see her spirit back, he forgot himself and returned her smile. "Is that a promise?"

"I believe it is," she said.

They held each other's gaze for a long moment, but the playful exchange melted into something more. Before the tension became too much, Simon looked away.

"I'm going to get washed up," Elizabeth said and ducked into the bathroom.

Simon heard the door click shut and slumped down into his chair. She had to be part siren. What a wonderful idea. A little sexual repartee before sharing a bed with a woman you can't have. Bloody brilliant.

He spent the next few minutes reminding himself of why he'd put the barriers between them in the first place. Loving someone was a risk he couldn't afford. He'd spent too many years trying to close wounds that wouldn't heal to open a fresh one now. No, his life was fine the way it was. Distance meant control. And now, more than ever, he needed both. Feeling more himself, he turned calmly when she called out from behind the partially opened door that she was getting in to bed.

So much for calm. He wasn't sure what he'd been expecting, but it certainly wasn't this. She stepped tentatively into the room, tugging her tiny T-shirt down over her navel. Simon turned quickly away, but it was too late. The image of her wearing only the small shirt and panties was burned into his memory. Not to mention the fact he could see her reflection quite clearly in the window.

She slid under the covers and pulled them up to her chin. "S'okay. You can turn around now."

Simon stood awkwardly on the far side of the room. This was impossible. He looked nervously around the room and noticed the light switch near the door. "Do you mind if I shut the light now?"

"Sure."

Simon turned off the light, but instead of feeling relieved, he felt strangely more on edge. The darkness only heightened the sense of intimacy. The rustle of the covers as Elizabeth moved in the bed brought images to his mind the darkness couldn't hide. He walked back over to the table and began to undress.

His fingers fumbled at the buttons of his shirt. He hadn't been this nervous undressing since Eton. But he'd been a boy then, losing his virginity in the blink of an eye with a girl he couldn't even remember. Now he was a man. A man who had to spend the night lying chastely next to a woman he desired more than any he'd ever met.

He really had to curtail that train of thought before he embarrassed them both. Latin. Consummate—Conjugate verbs. Abstenero, absteneras, abstenerat...

Finally, when he'd finished undressing, he slipped under the covers and tried not to feel the heat of her body next to his.

A soft moan escaped her lips in the darkness. He lifted himself up on his elbow. "Are you all right?"

"Fine," she said and swallowed. "It's all just a little overwhelming."

"We'll be fine," he said in a voice far too husky to be reassuring.

"You don't snore, do you?"

He could see the vague outline of her face as she moved onto her side. The soft curves of her smile shone through the darkness.

"I don't think so," he said. "But I'm sure you'll tell me."

She laughed and let her head rest on the pillow. "Goodnight, Simon."

"Goodnight, Elizabeth."

She rolled away from him, and he let out a deep breath, closing his eyes.

Sleep was a long time in coming. As the night dragged on, he found himself watching her. It was soothing and comforting in ways he didn't dare explore. He listened to her slow breaths and watched over her until sleep finally claimed him. It was a ritual he would repeat every night they were together.

CHAPTER SIX

ELIZABETH ROLLED ONTO HER back and lingered in that foggy place right on the edge of sleep. She wanted to slip back into the haze, but something felt wrong, and slowly she started to wake. She stretched her legs and pushed the covers down to her waist. She blinked a few times, but her eyes didn't seem to focus properly. She squinched them shut and then tried again. It wasn't her eyesight, she realized; it was the room. This wasn't her apartment.

Then, the bed moved.

She gasped and carefully looked to her left. A man's back. Simon. New York. Time travel. For a moment she'd thought it had all been a dream. Moving through time to a strange place. Stuff like that didn't happen. Except in dreams. In some bizarre Nyquil hallucination with images coated in thick green syrup.

But it was real, she reminded herself, feeling the thin sheet in her hands and the lumpy mattress at her back. Very real. She was back in time. With Simon.

As if on cue, he moaned in his sleep and rolled toward her. She held her breath, afraid to move. She didn't want to watch him—it felt too peeping-tomish—but she couldn't help it. He looked younger, happier. His mouth was caught in a gentle smile; whatever he was dreaming about he seemed to be enjoying it. She realized with a pang of sadness that she'd never seen him so relaxed and content. He was always a little on edge, as if prepared for some unseen foe. A part of him always seemed to be struggling, always on guard. It must be an exhausting way to live. With all they had to face now, Simon was sure to carry an even heavier burden than usual. It would be just like him to fall into a brooding mode and push her away.

There had to be something she could do about that. Lying there in the early morning, she made a pact with herself. She would do whatever she could to ease his load. She'd put on her bravest face and swallow her insecurities. He had enough to worry about without adding her into the mix.

Greedily taking what fate offered, she watched him for a few more minutes. He mumbled something incoherent and rolled his head to the side. His breathing was slow and steady. She could see the muscles of his chest under his thin cotton T-shirt. How did he stay in such good shape? The idea of Simon going to the gym was laughable, but he clearly did something to have that physique. She tried not to let her imagination run wild with just how he worked out.

Memories of last night wheedled their way into her mind. Watching him through the darkness as he undressed. She'd tried not to watch him unbutton his shirt. She'd tried extra hard not to sneak a peek as he stepped out of his trousers. Tried like a trooper not to notice how broad his shoulders were. How strong the muscles of his legs looked silhouetted by the soft moonlight from the window. She'd tried not to feel the heat of his body next to hers as he slid under the covers. She'd tried not to let the moan escape her lips, but it did.

Bad Elizabeth. She pulled her eyes and thoughts away from his chest to safer territory. His face held a few worry lines, no surprise there. But his lips, curved in that smile, were irresistible. Sculpted and sensual. What would it be like to kiss him? To feel them against hers. To feel the rough stubble on his cheek scrape along her skin.

Oh, this was a dangerous train of thought. Derail. Derail.

Simon moaned again, more softly than before and rolled onto his side facing her. His arm fell across her hip. Her stomach dropped, and she froze.

His eyes opened, and he smiled sleepily.

She hoped her voice didn't squeak. "Morning."

Simon grinned, but then his expression changed with dawning realization. "Elizabeth," he said. "Miss West?"

"Right on both counts."

He blinked back at her. "What the devil is..." he said and then noticed his hand resting on her hip. He yanked it back and cleared his throat, moving to his side of the bed. Hastily, he sat up and tried to look as if nothing had happened. "Sorry."

"It's okay," she said with a blush.

Simon cleared his throat again, putting his hands in his lap. She had to hide her smile. He was absolutely adorable when he was befuddled, but she decided to take pity on him. "I'm going to use the bathroom, unless you want to go first?" "No," Simon said. "You go ahead. I'll...You go ahead."

Stifling a giggle, she escaped into the bathroom. When she caught sight of herself in the mirror, her laughter stopped.

An appalling case of bed head and raccoon eyes stared back. She combed her fingers through her hair, but it stayed poking up like a bouffant gone terribly wrong.

My kingdom for a hairbrush.

She tested her breath. Strong enough to kill a wildebeest. How humiliating. She'd actually sat there grinning like an idiot at him. Looking like this.

She searched the tiny bath. No toothpaste, no hairbrush, no nothing. What a way to make a debut in the twenties, looking like a day passer from an asylum. She did the best she could with the absolute nothing she had. A quick bird bath and finger brushing later, she felt marginally human and slipped on the dress they'd bought yesterday.

First stop, a pharmacy, she thought. Her stomach rumbled in protest. Breakfast first, pharmacy second. She took one last look in the mirror and sighed.

You can do this, she told herself. A city was a city. It's not like they were in the middle ages. How different could it be?

"I'm tellin' ya that ump was blind. Fletch oughta get him some cheaters. The Babe was robbed. That was a two bagger!" a man growled loudly and thumped his hand on the counter.

"Don't see what you're gripin' about. Yanks won, didn't they?" his companion said.

"It's the principle of the thing. Ain't right."

Simon glared at them, but their argument continued. It seemed everyone in the diner felt the compulsion to converse loudly enough to wake the dead. He turned back to Elizabeth, who'd been listening to the conversation with glee.

"Can you imagine getting to see Babe Ruth play?" she said. "If we have time, we are so going to a game."

"This isn't a vacation, Miss West," he said, picking up his menu.

"It isn't a prison sentence either. Think of the opportunity we have. We get to see what it was really like. Not some revisionist history from a book, but the real deal. And I've always wanted to go to Yankee Stadium," she added with a grin.

"Miss West—"

"I'm kidding. Mostly. And it's Elizabeth, remember?" she said, wiggling her ring finger.

He hadn't forgotten, but after the incident in bed he felt more compelled than ever to keep his distance. It wasn't bad enough that he'd dreamt of her and that the dream had coalesced, in a frighteningly smooth way, into reality. But if he was going to wake up every morning with a raging morning erection, this was going to be impossible.

"First thing we should do is visit the local library," he said. "We need to know the exact time of the next eclipse."

"Wouldn't want to be caught with our pants down."

Simon cleared his throat. "No," he said and quickly went back to his menu. The prices were absurdly inexpensive. Steak and eggs for a quarter. Coffee and a donut for a dime. Blue plate special only fifteen cents. Remarkable really, or would have been if he had more than twenty dollars to his name.

He heard someone snapping gum and looked up to see their waitress impatiently tapping her stubby pencil on a pad. "What'll it be?"

"You don't have Wheatina."

Snap. Pop. Snap. "Nope."

He stared down at the menu looking for something that didn't sound positively dreadful.

"We'll have two specials," Elizabeth said. "And two coffees, unless you want tea?"

Simon was about to say something about being able to order for himself, but the idea of some tea in his future blocked out everything else. "Do you have Chinese Gun Powder?"

"This look like an armory to you, buddy?"

Elizabeth handed her menu to the waitress. "Two coffees will be fine."

Simon pursed his lips and gave up, handing his menu to the waitress. He watched her walk away and looked around the diner. Steam billowed from behind the cook's counter. A corpulent man with a sour face and a grease-stained T-shirt tossed ridiculously large slabs of meat on the grill behind the long curved counter. There wasn't even an empty stool, so Simon was pleased they'd managed to get a booth. At least here, they had a modicum of privacy.

"We won't be having tea at the Ritz any time soon,"

Elizabeth said. "Better get used to it."

Simon wiped the tabletop in front of him with his napkin and set it aside. "That much is clear."

"So, how'd you sleep?"

"Well enough, thank you," he said uncomfortably. But she smiled back innocently, and he felt his tensions ease a little. "Did I snore?"

Elizabeth grinned. "Nope."

"You did," he said.

"I do not snore."

"Like a locomotive," he teased, thoroughly enjoying her look of embarrassment.

"That's not a very nice thing to say."

"The truth is often ugly," he said, trying not to smile.

She blushed. Beautifully. "Did I really snore?"

"It was more of a gurgling sound really."

"Oh, really? Well, better a gurgler than a bed-hog."

"I beg your pardon."

"You practically pushed me off the side."

"I did? I'm sorry. I..." Who knows what he'd done in his sleep. If it was anything like what he dreamt of...

"I was joking. Mostly. You did bogart the middle a little, but it is a small bed and well, by size rights you should have two thirds anyway. It's only fair."

Simon was about to argue the point when the waitress arrived with the coffee.

Elizabeth took a sip and let out a contented sigh. "Oh, I needed that. So, after the library, what's next on the hit parade?"

Simon tried the coffee. It was too strong and too bitter, but he forced it down. "That depends on how long we have to stay here. I had considered trying to contact my grandfather."

She seemed surprised at that.

"He was living in London at this time, I believe. Although, aside from the difficulty of tracking him down, I'm not sure we should. There's no guarantee he knows anything about the watch at this point in time. We have no idea when it came into his possession, and if I were to tell him something about the future, the consequences could be disastrous."

He took another sip of coffee. It didn't taste any better than the first. And his beard was beginning to itch. "We have to do everything we can to ensure the integrity of the timeline."

"I've been thinking about that. Your grandfather seemed to get pretty involved in the times he visited. Brunch with the death eaters and all."

"No doubt he embellished his adventures for my benefit." Although at this point, the line between fact and fiction seemed blurred beyond recognition.

"Could be. But then again, maybe not," she said, her brow furrowing in thought. "The Heisenberg Principle says that we change what we study by the very act of studying it. Maybe he was telling the truth."

"Perhaps." Regardless, he thought, the less they were involved in the unknown here the easier it would be to keep an eye on her. There were far too many factors as it was, in a city and a time he was unfamiliar with. Adding in more could only spell disaster. She was far too open and accepting, but she wasn't a fool. She had a good head on her shoulders, and he decided to appeal to her logic. "But, you must admit, reason dictates, the less we interfere here the better."

Elizabeth nodded grudgingly. "Well, we're going to have to do a little interfering. If the eclipse is more than a day or two away, and judging from our luck, my money's on months, we're going to have to find a way to earn money. Even at these prices twenty dollars won't last much more than a week. We're going to have to get jobs."

She was right, of course. How did she manage such calm, even enthusiasm in the face of this gaping maw of uncertainty? Didn't the prospect of spending months, perhaps a lifetime here unsettle her in the least? Simon sighed and forced his mind back to the issue at hand. Money had to be a priority. It was a rather daunting prospect. He had never wanted for money in his life and he sincerely doubted there was a great call here for professors of the occult. "I don't think it's quite that simple."

"Two specials," the waitress said, putting down plates laden with eggs, hash browns, bacon and toast. "Anything else?"

"Know where we might find some jobs?" Elizabeth asked. "We're new in town and really don't have any idea where to start."

The waitress raked her eyes over Simon and arched a thinly plucked eyebrow, before turning back to Elizabeth. "There's a chalk board over on Fourth and Broadway. Lists all sorts of jobs, but I don't think they're exactly your type."

Elizabeth grinned. "You never know. Thanks."

The waitress snapped her gum and ripped their bill off her pad. "Good luck, honey."

Elizabeth smiled triumphantly. "That wasn't so hard. Library, job boards. Looks like it's going to be a busy day," she said and dug into her food with relish. "Better eat yours before it gets cold."

Simon poked a fork into his runny eggs. Busy indeed.

Elizabeth had never ridden a subway before. The cars bumped along, jigging from side to side, as they clattered through the dark tunnels. She felt like a native, bouncing in her seat like the rest of the passengers. If they only knew.

The train's brakes squealed as it ground to a halt at the 42nd Street station. She and Simon fell in with the press of people hurrying out the doors and up the steps. She could see the library looming down the block.

It was enormous and oddly comforting. Inside, it looked like every other public library in a big city. Same vaulting architecture and marble floors. It felt like a little bit of home.

They found a book on eclipses easily and settled into one of the long tables in the main reference hall. Elizabeth watched Simon skim through the pages until he hit the one they'd been searching for. His face was unreadable as he closed the book.

"Well?" Elizabeth prompted. "You going to tell me or what?"

"It could have been worse."

It was an annoying habit of his, withholding information just for the privilege of watching someone squirm in anticipation. "And?"

"The next lunar eclipse will occur September 3rd of this year."

"Six weeks?"

"So it would seem," he said.

September third. That was a month and a half before the stock market crash. She hated to admit it, but Simon was right—they should limit their involvement in the culture. She'd read enough science fiction to know that, but it was so tempting. To be able to avert one of the darkest periods in American history. Not that she really could. What was she going to do? Walk the streets wearing a sandwich board that said, "Sell your stocks! Black Tuesday approaches!" They'd lock her up and throw away the key. Still, it was an enticing idea. But there were definitely more pressing matters to think about. Six weeks was a long time. And even then, there was no guarantee the watch would work. They might be trapped there forever.

"Are you all right, Miss West?"

"Just thinking."

"Indeed," he said with a sigh. "Since we seem to be stuck here for an extended period, I suppose we should look into employment."

The way he said employment nearly made her laugh, as if he were being asked to live in a basket of snakes. Her own fears about what may or may not come fell away. Why was it facing adversity was easier when someone else needed you? "It's not that bad."

"You almost sound as though you're pleased with this turn of events."

"Like you said, it could have been worse. Now that we know, it's not so bad really. It's kind of an adventure."

He frowned, but it didn't quite reach his eyes. "Your definition of adventure is deeply skewed."

After they'd finished at the library, they started back to lower Manhattan. Fifth Avenue was a far cry from their neighborhood, at least the little she'd seen. Huge buildings stretched toward the sky, except for one huge hole in the ground. A large, elaborate sign stood at the rim—"Future Site of the Empire State Building - Starrett Bros. & Eken". The Empire State Building, something that seemed so old in her mind, hadn't even been built yet.

Everything about the city seemed about to happen. As if every person, every thing were on the verge of something better. She always thought New York would feel oppressive, impersonal, but it was just the opposite. Energizing and inspiring, where the only limit was your own imagination.

Reality, however, came back with a swift vengeance when they reached the job boards on Broadway. Most of the offerings had already been erased, leaving only dishwashing for fifty cents a day. So much for getting a job easily.

But, as she always told herself back home, if you can't make money, spend money. Simon had balked at first, until she pointed out that he could simply never shave again. Off they went to F. W. Woolworth Co. 5 and 10 Cent Store.

The Woolworth's back home had been nothing like this. Complete with a soda fountain, which Simon wouldn't let her try, the store had everything a person could want. Clothes, canned goods, jewelry, personal items.

For someone who'd never lived on a fixed budget, Simon was absolutely miserly. She managed to finagle a few items anyway. Toiletries were a must. The sales woman suggested a new product—Charmin bath tissue. What in God's name did they use before? The soap smelled more like lye than lilacs, but at least it was something. They bought all the necessities: toothpaste, hairbrushes and a safety razor looked anything but. They purchased towels and undergarments (Simon had delicately disappeared for that one), and one pair of pajamas. Simon hadn't thought her suggestion that he be tops and she be bottoms was all that funny. But with less than ten dollars left, they couldn't afford a second pair.

It was early afternoon when they dropped off their packages at the apartment and hit the pavement again. For such a big city, there were precious few jobs to be had. It certainly didn't help not having the faintest idea where to look.

They wandered aimlessly for a few hours before Simon suggested they work on a grid. Walking the business districts block by block, east to west.

By late afternoon, they'd traveled from Columbia Street on the East to Bowery on the West. Still no jobs, not even a nibble.

As the day wore on, Simon grew more and more quiet. She knew he held himself responsible for them being there. She also knew that no amount of talking would make him feel otherwise. Screwing on her best smile, she suggested they get an early dinner.

They walked a few more blocks when the unmistakable smell of garlic cooking in olive oil caught her attention. She sniffed the air like a bloodhound on the scent and led them further down Delancy. Even before she saw the street sign, she knew where she was—Mulberry Street, the heart of Little Italy.

"Just like in 'The Godfather,'" she said in awe.

Simon was unimpressed. "Quaint."

"Oh, come on, look at it," she said, tugging on his sleeve and pulling him into the fray.

The street was small, barely wide enough for two cars, and bursting with life. Sidewalk cafes crowded with men playing cards and dominoes. Groceries with large wooden boxes displayed fresh fruits and vegetables on the sidewalk. Push carts selling every food imaginable clogged the streets. A few cars trying to weave through the mass crawled along more slowly than the people on foot. Green and white awnings jutted from the brick facades. Lace curtains covered the lower half of etched glass windows. And the smells. Garlic and oregano. Basil and simmering olive oil.

Three men in black pants with crisp white shirts leaned against a light pole smoking cigarettes. "*Ah, bambina. Molto bella. Venga averci una bevanda con.*"

Elizabeth giggled. "Hello."

Simon grunted and moved between the men and her, taking her arm and hurrying her past.

"Isn't this great?" she asked.

Simon let go of her arm. "Charming."

He could be a spoilsport all he wanted to. She'd wanted to come to Mulberry Street since she was a little girl. A friend of her father's, Tony Funnico, used to tell her stories about growing up there. Fun Tony, that's what the other men called him, was always ready with a story. She'd spent many nights sitting with him, after he'd lost all he had to lose. As she looked at the young boys running down the street in their caps and knickers, she wondered if he might be one of them.

They had a quick dinner, eaten standing on the sidewalk, of sausages and onions wrapped in flat bread. She really wanted a canoli for desert. Fun Tony said Mulberry Street had the best in the world. However, with their money so tight, a canoli was a luxury item they couldn't afford. Later, when they had money, she'd come back and eat one of every kind.

After dinner, on their way home, they zigged when they should have zagged and found themselves off the beaten path. The street was deserted and eerily quiet. Elizabeth hummed a Cole Porter tune she'd heard playing in a music store. It was a nervous habit she'd picked up from her father. She glanced over at Simon and could tell from the way his back was ramrod straight and his eyes were narrowed that he was tense.

"We'll find work soon," she said. "I can feel it my bones."

"Your bones are very optimistic."

"Better happy bones than sulky bones."

"I prefer to think of them as realistic."

"All right, if it—" she started, and then stopped walking. She grabbed Simon's arm. "Do you hear that?"

The soft scrape of shoes being dragged along uneven pavement, a cry of pain muffled by pride, a sharp crack of something hard against something broken—the unmistakable sounds of a struggle. She'd heard them from behind closed doors before and knew the images that filled the keyhole. The sounds filtered down the street, seeming to come from an alley barely twenty feet ahead.

Elizabeth started toward the sound. She heard more thumps and sobs of pain as she neared the darkened alley. She rounded the corner and stopped dead in her tracks.

CHAPTER SEVEN

ELIZABETH'S BREATH CAUGHT IN her throat. A man was on his knees holding a shaking, bloodied hand out before him. He was flanked by two large men. One casually toyed with a small blackjack, while the other leaned against the high fender of a large, expensive car. There must have been someone inside the car, because the leaning man stepped forward and lit a match, extending it inside the back seat window. Elizabeth saw a black, gloved hand steady the flame. The suffering man continued to moan, and Elizabeth was about to call out when she was yanked back around the corner.

Simon's eyes blazed down at her in the moonlight. She tried to struggle out of his grip, but he only held her more tightly. He pulled her away until they were pressed up against the brick of the corner building.

"Let go," she said.

"Quiet," Simon hissed. Once he seemed sure she wasn't going to do anything rash, he peered around the corner. After only a few seconds, he pulled his head back.

"He needs our help," Elizabeth whispered.

Simon gripped her arm again and pulled her back the way they'd come.

"What are you doing?" she said as she tried to slip out of his iron grip.

"Getting the hell out of here." Once they were more than a block away, Simon let go of her arm and stared down at her angrily. "What in God's name do you think you were doing?"

"That man was being beaten," she said. "We should have done something."

"Of all the idiotic—They had guns. What do you propose we should have done? Getting yourself killed wouldn't have been much help now, would it?"

Elizabeth quietly seethed. "I still think we could have done something."

Simon took her arm again and his eyes bore into her. "You must promise me you will never do that again."

"I didn't do anything," she said bitterly. She hated being a helpless bystander. One thing she'd learned in her life was that you took help when it was offered and gave it when it was needed.

"Miss West...Elizabeth, please?"

She was about to argue when she saw the look in his eyes. He was frightened. Not for himself, but for her. "I'm sorry. I...I just wanted to help."

"And we will. We'll find a policeman and report it. It's the best we can do."

Elizabeth didn't say it wouldn't be enough, Simon knew that as well as she did. They made their way back toward Mulberry Street, and told the first policeman they found what they'd seen.

If his ruddy complexion and red hair weren't enough, his accent pegged him as one of the many Irish immigrants who found their niche in the NYPD. She'd always thought it was a bad movie cliché, and yet, here he was.

Officer O'Malley diligently scrawled the details in his small notebook, but his face paled when Elizabeth told him about the car.

"A black and tan, ya say?"

"Yeah, maybe a limousine. There were three rows of windows and a man sitting in the back. He was wearing black gloves. That's all I could see."

The policeman's face was a blank slate as he nodded and tucked his notebook back into his breast pocket. He absently brushed his cuff over his badge to polish it.

"Aren't you going to do something?" she asked. He didn't seem in a hurry to do a damned thing.

"Don't worry, Miss. You folks go on home now."

"But—"

Simon intervened. "Thank you officer. Good night," he said and led her down the street.

"What was that all about?"

"Isn't it obvious? The policeman recognized the description of the man in the car and judging from his reaction, it's someone even the police won't become involved with. We should follow his lead and stay out of it."

"But that's crazy."

"The twenty-first century doesn't have a monopoly on corruption," he said. "Remember where we are. When we are. Prohibition, gangsters. This isn't a romantic period; it's a dangerous one."

She started to argue, but stopped. He was right. It was frustrating as hell, but he was right. Suddenly, she felt very tired.

"It's been a long day," he said, his expression softening. "Let's go back to the flat."

She nodded and they started back to the apartment.

Their room was stifling even at nearly midnight. Clouds hung over the city keeping the air thick and still. Without a breeze, their little apartment housed the heat like an unwanted relative who comes to visit and simply won't leave.

Simon took his place in the chair by the window while Elizabeth brushed her teeth and had a bath. He was happy for the respite. Not that she was bad company. Far from it, she was managing their predicament better than he was. He'd never considered having to provide for someone, and it seemed his first foray was a titanic failure. Where she'd met the day with unflagging enthusiasm, insisting the answer lay just around the next corner, he'd been dour and judgmental.

The people were coarse and uneducated. The streets were crowded and dirty. The only thing that lay around the next corner was another problem. He shifted in his chair and tried to relax. He hadn't slept well the night before, but at least the nightmares hadn't come. Perhaps the danger to Elizabeth existed in the future and not here in the past. As tempting as that notion was, he refused to accept it. Their little night adventure was proof enough of that. He felt certain she was threatened. Not knowing how or when was the rub.

They agreed to try their best to put the incident out of their minds. Their best wasn't good enough, not for Simon. What took place in the alley was a reminder of what he'd feared since they first set foot here. He'd been a fool to let his guard down, even for a moment. And her reaction. Good Lord. She'd practically run headfirst into the mess. Where angels fear to tread indeed.

Even though the day had been exhausting, he found he couldn't quite sit still. He stood and looked out the window at the dark street below. The lamps glowed, but left only faded pools of light on the pavement. The fire escape was less than comforting. It was spindly thin and looked ready to give way under the slightest weight.

"Oh, that felt good," Elizabeth said as she emerged from the bath.

She was wearing the pajama top. The shirt was long enough to fall mid-thigh. With the sleeves rolled up, she looked like she was wearing one of his oxford shirts. An image lifted from his dreams. Thick, damp tendrils of hair clung to her cheeks and curled about her shoulders. Her skin, pink from the heat of the bath, still glistened with droplets of water.

The situation was difficult enough without her walking around the apartment looking like sex personified. She clearly had no idea of the effect she had on him. Her unassuming sensuality only drove him that much closer to madness.

"A nice warm soak. Can't recommend it enough," she said.

Or a cold one, he thought grimly.

"Good idea," Simon said and hurried into the bath. He closed the door and let out a long breath. The room smelled of the shampoo she'd used. He knew that scent would drift over to him in the night and carry him off to dream of things that shouldn't be. He twisted the taps and concentrated on the rush of cold water. At least that would solve his body's reaction; if there were only something for his heart.

He really had to stop thinking like this. He wasn't the sort of man to ogle a woman. He'd never been one to daydream. Now, his mind was in a constant state of drift; thoughts of Elizabeth always under the surface.

Bath finished, he pulled on the pajama bottoms and a T-shirt, took a deep breath, and stepped back into the bedroom. It was empty. "Elizabeth?"

His heart began to race as he searched the room. "Elizabeth!"

"Out here," she said and poked her head in through the window.

Simon closed his eyes for a brief moment and collected himself. "What in God's name are you doing out there?"

"It's much cooler. Come on out, there's room."

"Come back inside," he said.

"You don't know what you're missing."

"It's not safe. Elizabeth..."

"Don't tell me you're afraid of heights."

"That's not the point."

"I am actually," she said, leaning one elbow on the windowsill. "Afraid of heights. Not really in the 'oh, I'm gonna fall' kind of way. More in the 'oh, I sort of want to jump' kind of way. Nutty, huh?"

"Yes, now come inside."

"All right, don't get your knickers in a twist," she said, putting a leg inside. Simon held her forearm and tried not to look at the smooth skin of her thigh as she clambered back into the room. "I'm in. Happy?"

"Thank you," he said. They stood awkwardly for a moment. Simon realized he was still holding onto her and quickly let go. Needing something, anything to purge himself of the image of her very shapely leg, he gave the fire escape a cursory inspection. "Rusted, shoddy construction. I should speak to the management about it."

He stayed looking out the window for a long moment, before summoning the courage to turn and face her again. The pause did him little good. She looked as charming as ever.

"Perhaps we should go to sleep," he suggested. "It has been a trying day."

"Not really tired anymore. Bath gave me a second wind."

"Did it?" he said, hoping he didn't sound as anxious as he felt. He looked around the room, desperate for a distraction.

"How about a game of cards?" she asked.

"Since you insisted on wasting our money on them," he said with a wry smile. "I suppose we should put them to use." He gestured toward the table.

She walked over to the bureau and picked up the pack. "A deck of cards is one of life's necessities."

He wasn't sure about that, but at least they were a safe diversion.

She sat down opposite him and opened the deck. "So, blackjack or strip poker?"

Simon nearly choked as libidinous images flashed through his mind. With the little she had on, it would only take a hand or two. He massaged his temple, trying to rub the thoughts away.

Elizabeth laughed. "I'm only joking. You do know how to play cards, don't you?"

"Of course. I went to boarding school."

"Of course," she said with a smile. Settling the cards in her hand, she shuffled them once, then again with a bit more flair. A waterfall shuffle and a skilled fan were followed by a few more difficult flourishes. He arched a questioning brow, surprised and impressed.

She shrugged and performed another impressive flourish. "Daddy taught me well."

She cut the cards one-handed, but the top stack slipped. Her forehead wrinkled in a thoroughly endearing scowl. "Damn hands," she muttered. She held them out, palms up and frowned at them. "Too small."

Simon had always secretly admired her hands. They were small, even for a woman her size, but he thought they suited her well. They were delicate, almost fragile, but there was strength there too. In his weaker moments, he'd wondered what it would be like to hold them.

"Daddy said I could have been one hell of a gambler if it weren't for them," she said with a wistful smile. "But there's one thing a card player never has. A small hand."

"Your father was a gambler?" Simon asked. She'd never offered much about her family.

"Yup. Just not a very good one."

"I'm sorry."

She smiled, but there was sadness behind her eyes.

"Don't be," she said. "He was good at the important things." She set the deck down on the table. "How about a little gin rummy?"

Simon wanted to know more, but it was clear she'd put an end to the subject. "Gin it is."

A comfortable ease in companionship and gentle sparring made the hours slip by without notice, until, in the end, Elizabeth and fatigue finally won out.

They removed their rings and set them on the nightstands. Smitty had warned them that the fake gold would turn their fingers green if they didn't. The tension from earlier in the night returned, as they slid under the covers, each too aware of the other.

Once Elizabeth was asleep, Simon rolled onto his side and saw the moonlight reflect off the fake gold of his wedding band. It was eerily familiar somehow. A ring caught in the moonlight. He closed his eyes and tried to place the memory, but each time he almost grasped it, it slipped away. The uneasy feeling lingered and carried him to a night of fitful sleep and taunting dreams.

The next day was spent much as the first, in a vain search for employment. Block after block they walked, hoping to see a help wanted sign in a window. They asked for leads at various stores, but very little was forthcoming. One job was going to be hard enough to find, but two was looking downright impossible. The late afternoon sun started to fall behind the taller buildings and sent long shadows stretching down the street.

A man at the haberdashery had suggested they try closer to the Bowery, so they decided to take a short cut over to Canal Street and try their luck there. A group of children huddled in the middle of the street arguing. Barely visible among them was a small priest. His face was shiny with sweat, and he mopped his brow as he tried to settle the boys down.

"Now, Jimmy," he said with a delightful Irish lilt. "If your toe's not touchin' the base there's not much chance you're safe, now is there?"

A pimple-faced boy scuffed his shoes on the pavement and pointed toward a dirty shirt on the ground. "But he yanked the bag away!"

"Who's the umpire here?"

"You are," the boys chorused in what was obviously a trained response.

"That's right, I am. And what I say goes. And I say you should get back to playin' ball before this old priest melts in the sun."

The boys reluctantly agreed and went back to their positions in the street.

"And you were out by a mile, Jimmy," the priest added with a wink.

Elizabeth and Simon stood on the sidewalk with the priest as the stickball game resumed. It was nice to watch something so normal, so human regardless of the time. She caught the priest's eye and he bowed his head in greeting. He looked like he'd fallen off a charm bracelet. No more than five foot two and with hair that swooped back from his forehead in gray waves, he was Barry Fitzgerald incarnate.

"They're a lively bunch, but they keep me young. Name's Father Cavanaugh," he said extending his hand for a shake. "I don't think I've seen you two around before. New in town?"

Elizabeth grinned. "Does it show?"

His bright, pale blue eyes crinkled at the edges. "A little."

"My name's Elizabeth and this is Simon, my husband," she added quickly.

"Father," Simon said and took the priest's hand.

"I don't suppose you know of any jobs available in the neighborhood?" Elizabeth asked.

The father tugged on his ear in thought. "Not off the bat, no. But I'll be sure to ask around. I'm over at St. Patrick's," he said. "If you need a little hand."

"Thank you, Father. That's very kind of you."

"You're very welcome," he said, before his attention was pulled back to the game. "Now, Vincent, none of that! We play a clean game or we don't play at all." He walked out into the street and was once again lost in the crowd of children.

"We still have time for a few more blocks before it gets dark," Simon said.

"Right. Once more unto the breach."

Elizabeth wiped a bead of perspiration from her forehead and sighed. "I don't know about you, but I could use a drink."

"A little early for that, isn't it?"

"I meant a soda," she said.

He looked almost chagrined, but covered it with a frown. "Why don't you rest for a moment in the shade. I'll get us something."

Elizabeth smiled gratefully and walked over into the shade. She watched Simon disappear down the block into a small grocers. Leaning against the brick wall, she closed her eyes. At this rate, they were going to run out of money long before they ran out of time.

"What am I supposed to do now?" she heard a deep, gruff voice say.

Elizabeth glanced over and saw a large, brawny man talking to a pretty little red-head. The woman smiled up at the older man. "I'm sorry, Charlie. We didn't plan it, but..." her voice trailed off as she placed a hand over her stomach.

Charlie smiled wistfully. He looked like a bear, barrel-chested with a belly to match. "He take good care of ya?"

"The best. I know I'm leavin' ya in the lurch, but Tommy's kinda old-fashioned. Specially now I'm in a family way and all."

Charlie shook his head. "Don't know what I'll do without ya, Viv. Where am I gonna find another girl like you?"

Viv grinned and laughed. "We're everywhere." She looked around the street. "See there's one right there," she said pointing at Elizabeth.

Elizabeth quickly looked away and pretended she hadn't been blatantly eavesdropping.

Charlie laughed. It was a rich, wonderful sound. "You're a pip."

"I hate to do it to ya, Charlie, but I gotta go. Thanks for everything," she said sadly and went up on tiptoes to kiss his cheek.

Charlie cleared his throat and blushed. "Go on. Go home."

"I'll see ya around, Charlie," she said, turned and walked down the street.

Charlie watched her for a moment and shook his head. He turned to go back inside when he took another look at Elizabeth. He gave her the once-over and smiled. "Don't suppose you're lookin' for a job, are ya? I got girls havin' babies and..." He shook his head and waved his big, meaty hand in defeat. He turned and reached for the door.

"Wait," Elizabeth said. "I am."

"Are what, honey?"

"Looking for a job."

He smiled and looked her over again. He walked toward her and sized her up quickly. "You're pretty enough. Ever wait tables?"

She hesitated and decided to lie. "Sure."

Charlie saw right through her. "I ain't got time for nobody green."

"I'm a quick learner," she said. This was their first job offer, and she wasn't going to let it slip by. "If you give me a chance, you won't be sorry."

Charlie cocked his head to the side. "Turn around."

Elizabeth knew she should have felt uneasy, but there was something gentle in his eyes. Some people just feel right, and Charlie was one of them. His face was big and round, with jowls like a hound dog that shook when he laughed. He seemed the sort of man you could lean on, good broad shoulders to cry on and big, brawny arms to hold you up. His shirt was wrinkled and she could see crude patch jobs at the cuffs. A bachelor if ever there was one. She trusted him instinctively and turned around as he asked.

"What's a doll like you doin' hanging around here?"

"I'm waiting for my... husband."

"Married, huh?" Charlie said with a shake of his head. "Well, best of luck to ya."

He moved to walk away, but Elizabeth grabbed his arm. "Wait."

"Husbands. Don't go over so good. I got enough problems," he said and gently lifted her hand from his arm.

"It is just waiting tables, isn't it?" she asked.

"I run a clean joint," he said obviously affronted. "No funny stuff in my place." He looked her up and down again. "I don't know."

"I really need a job. We're new here, and well, we're kind of running out of money. And don't worry about my husband. He's very forward thinking."

"I don't know."

"Please?" She put on her best pout. Charlie frowned, but she could see she'd gotten to him.

"I always did have a soft spot for dames in trouble. All right," he groused. "We'll give ya a try."

Elizabeth was so excited she stepped forward and pulled him into a hug. "Thank you!"

"And your husband. You sure he won't mind?" Charlie asked.

"Positive."

Charlie looked over her shoulder and his expression darkened. "Cause he looks like he minds."

Elizabeth didn't understand until she stepped back and followed his gaze. Simon stood behind her and looked like a brewing storm.

Chapter Eight

SIMON GLARED AT CHARLIE with a look that had made the first year students tremble. "Who are you?"

"Simon, darling," Elizabeth said sweetly, as she took his arm. The muscles under her fingers were corded. When Simon wanted to, he positively oozed danger. "I've got a job."

Simon narrowed his eyes at Charlie. "Doing what exactly?"

Charlie shrugged and looked at Elizabeth. "I told ya, doll. Husbands."

"No, no. He's just excited. Aren't you, Simon?"

Simon set his jaw, his piercing gaze never wavering from Charlie. "You still haven't answered my question."

"Waitress. At Charlie's place. Isn't that good news?"

"You own a restaurant?" Simon asked, skepticism dripping from every syllable.

Charlie crossed his arms over his big chest proudly. "A club. We serve a lot of tea, if ya get my meaning?"

Simon's lip curled in distaste. "A bar."

It was Charlie's turn to be suspicious. "You ain't a G-man are ya?"

Elizabeth laughed. The idea of Simon as Elliot Ness, pulling down the brim of his hat and shouldering his gat was... not so funny really, and pretty darn sexy. Regardless, Simon clearly failed to see the humor in the situation. His arm tensed under her hand.

"Don't worry. Nothing like that," she said.

Charlie eyed Simon apprehensively, then softened. "A limey Fed. That'd be a first."

Simon bristled at the word *limey* and seemed ready to make a scene. Things were going from bad to worse in a hurry. Elizabeth hoped she could keep Simon from ruining their one chance at some money. She needed to move quickly. "When can I start?"

Simon glared down at her. "I think we need to discuss this first."

Charlie looked from one to the other, the wheels turning in his head. He let out a deep breath. "Tell ya what. You come by tonight at six, and the job's yours. I don't see ya, I find somebody else. Jake?"

"I'll be there," she said.

"Help if I knew your name, doll."

"Elizabeth. Elizabeth We—Cross," she said and held out her hand.

Charlie chuckled and shook her hand. "You got moxie, kid. I like that."

Simon mumbled something under his breath and Charlie released her. "Hope ya got enough," he said, casting a quick glance at Simon. "Well, I gotta see a man about a dog."

He pointed to a heavy metal door. "Knock twice and tell em Charlie said you was okay."

"Thank you," Elizabeth said. He gave her a quick grin and headed off down the street. She hated to see him go. He was the first person who'd actually given them a chance, and Simon had to go and be a big pill.

She let go of Simon's arm and stepped back. "What was that all about?"

"I'd prefer to have this discussion in private."

"Fine," she said and started toward their apartment. If Simon said anything in return, she didn't hear it. By the time they'd reached their room, they'd both worked themselves into a lather.

"So talk," Elizabeth said, slamming the door behind them.

Simon stalked over to the window. "I don't approve."

"Well, it's a good thing I'm not asking for it then, isn't it?" Who did he think he was? And what the hell was wrong with him? They'd spent two days looking for jobs and when one fell in their laps he decided to have issues?

"Elizabeth—"

"I can't believe you have a problem with this."

He folded his arms smugly over his chest. "Need I remind you that working in a speakeasy is illegal?"

"Prohibition was idiotic." She knew he had Puritanical tendencies, but this was too rich. "Let's make booze illegal so the underworld can thrive. What a good idea."

Simon took off his coat and tossed it onto a chair. "The law is still the law."

"And I suppose you've never broken the law."

"I understand that having a gambler for a father might have skewed your—"

"No." Her hands balled into fists. "You keep my father out of this."

"Miss West," Simon said, clearly trying to control his temper. "We are not so desperate that we need to resort to something of this sort."

"Maybe having two dollars to your name isn't real to you. But it's real to me. And if taking a job waiting tables means we can pay the rent then I'm grateful for it."

She narrowed her eyes and continued, "If I didn't know any better I'd say some Paleolithic gene kicked in and you were angry that a woman got a job before you did."

Simon clenched his jaw and turned to look out the window. "Don't be absurd. You don't know anything about this Charlie person. You've known him for ten minutes, for God's sake. Who knows what sort of man he is."

She knew exactly what sort of man he was. With some people, you could just tell. And with others, she thought, as she stared at Simon's back and felt like she was looking at a stranger, you never knew them. Suddenly, the argument seemed more pointless than ever. "So, don't trust anyone? Not even you?"

Simon turned around, but didn't offer any argument. His face was hard and unreadable. Any closeness they'd achieved in the last few days evaporated.

"Maybe you can live that way," she said. "Keep everyone at arms length, but I can't do it. I can't afford to do it."

"You can't afford not to," he said fiercely, covering the distance between them with two quick strides. "Our position is difficult enough. You have no idea what that man's motives are, what sort of situations you might find yourself in."

"Yeah, like getting a paycheck," she said and then shook her head. "Since we got here, I've been leered at, called a whore and generally treated like crap. Charlie's the first person who's given me a break and I'm gonna take it."

"It's a mistake."

"It's mine to make."

He glared at her, but she wasn't about to be cowed by him now.

"I'm going out," he said.

"Fine."

"Fine." He slammed the door and stormed down the hall.

Elizabeth slumped down onto the bed. "That went well."

The street was crowded with people. For most, the workday was ending. Vendors packed up their wares and trundled their carts off for the night. Shopkeepers pulled metal grates closed with a resounding clang. The entire city was in transition. The long work week was giving way to a hard fought weekend.

The world had certainly changed in the wake of the First World War. At least, Simon had vague memories of his grandfather telling him as much. The twenties began with a pause. Never had there been such loss, such senseless destruction. It left the world stunned and somber. But as with all great times of darkness, once the veil lifted, the sun shone brighter than before. Nothing makes life sweeter than a reminder of its tenuous nature.

Cars were now a luxury most Americans could afford. The city and the country, once worlds apart, grew closer. Buildings sprouted out of the landscape. Higher and higher they reached, echoing the newfound desires of the people. Bigger was better, and nowhere was it truer than in New York City. Movie palaces, grand ballrooms, and high-rises stood testament to the new age. The jazz age.

Jazz embodied the time. From its primal, blues riffs to the complex melodies of Gershwin, it all cried out to the soul of the New Yorker. You've worked hard, now it's time to play hard. And play they did.

Not since the rise of the Roman Empire was a society so hell bent on excess. Women painted their faces and bobbed their hair. As buildings went higher, so did women's hemlines. Men built spectacles of human achievement: the Chrysler building, Holland Tunnel and the beginning of the Empire State building. So quintessentially American.

Lubricating the party was a never-ending supply of booze: bathtub gin, Havana rum and whiskey with a kick. Women who would never have been seen drinking in public now frequented the dark speakeasies that dotted the landscape. There were more than five thousand to choose from in Manhattan alone. Everything from the upscale Conga Room to the hole in the wall, like Charlie's Blues in the Night.

"A speakeasy, of all places," Simon mumbled to himself. He made his way down the sidewalk shouldering against the tide of humanity. Why was it he always seemed to be going against the traffic?

What in God's name could she be thinking? Hadn't she gleaned anything from that scene in the alley?

"Damn woman."

She was clearly without a grain of sense in her head.

The wailing of car horns and early evening chatter were no more than an annoying buzz in his ear. His thoughts were filled completely with Elizabeth West and her damnable talent for making him feel completely undone. His temper had always been quick to light, but he'd been its master. Bloody hell.

Why was she so damn obstinate? He was merely looking out for her welfare, which she seemed more than content to completely ignore. Rushing off down that alley last night had been idiotic. She must have been dropped on her head as a child.

And then to accuse him of trying to keep her from working because of some male pride on his part. The idea was laughable. Absurd. It was mere happenstance she'd found employment first. It wasn't a reflection of his lack of skill. It didn't mean that he was incapable of providing for her.

"Bugger."

He wasn't entirely without skills. Surely he could secure some employment and they could afford to find her more suitable work. His search would have to wait until tomorrow, he thought as he noticed the sun had all but disappeared from the horizon.

He'd never given a moment's thought to caring for someone else. And now, suddenly it seemed to be the only constant in his world. He'd happily lived his life barely registering the other people in it. How did this damn woman find her way inside him? And for her to see him so clearly, so easily. She must be some emotional idiot savant.

He'd wanted other women, had been with other women, but not one of them had gotten under his skin the way she had. Even her friendship, if he could call it that, ran deeper than the trysts at Oxford or the stunted relationships he'd bungled in the years after. Intimacy was simply not part of his makeup. It required skills he'd never cultivated and he felt no inclination to do so. Until now. But it was too late for that. He was comfortable with the life he'd built.

He spent years refining the layers that buffered him from the outside world. His work had always been enough. The search for answers. Facts could be categorized, put in their proper place. Text books were conveniently black and white, but now the world was a swirling mass of murky grays. Feelings he couldn't grasp, much less control, were getting the better of him day by day.

And now, the one thing he'd been able to cling to, the one thing that centered him, was gone. If there were no way to get home, he thought and felt for the watch in his pocket, he'd be trapped here without his work. He supposed he could start a research project here, check some texts that were lost to the future. But it would do little good. She'd become an inexorable part of that too, he realized. There wasn't a facet of his life she hadn't slipped inside of, even his past—the one thing that separates each of us from the other. His grandfather's death, his nightmares were now all inescapably linked with her.

A fresh wave of guilt and dread washed over him. If ever there was proof that he should have kept her away from him, this was it. If he'd never given in to her curiosity, never allowed her into his life, she'd be safe right now. Instead, she was trapped here with him, and about to walk headfirst into God knows what.

It was impossible. She was impossible. The way her eyes sparked with fire when she argued with him. The way her cheeks flushed. The way her pulse pounded out her fury. He wanted to strangle her with one hand and caress her with the other.

Why did the simple act of watching her sleep make him feel more content than he could remember? Why did he care so much what she was thinking? What she was feeling?

Why did he want her so very much?

He stopped walking, and the crowd surged past him. He stood like a rock in a stream of humanity. Their current pushed against him, silently urging him to join the human race. Shapeless faces passed him by, dimly lit by the night stars and glow of the streetlamps. Each a life, each on their way to something, to someone.

He let out a long breath, stepped into the current and started home.

Father Cavanaugh wiped the sweat from his forehead and hastily shoved the handkerchief under his robes. Those boys would be the death of him. Extra innings for goodness sake!

He pulled open the heavy wooden doors to the church and took a deep, calming breath. Old St. Patrick's wasn't what it once was, since the diocese had been moved to the larger cathedral uptown, but he wouldn't have traded his parish for the world. The air inside the church was cool, even in the midst of summer. The smell of candle wax and incense filtered from the side altar. Breathing in the soothing mixture, he smoothed down his robes and brushed a bit of dirt away.

It was time.

He walked over to the confessional booth and pulled back the plush, velvet curtain. This wasn't the regularly scheduled confessional session. It wasn't even, in the strictest sense, a confession. Sins were spoken of, not in coarse whispers of repentance, but in cold detachment. A dangling soul suspended between good and evil. A man nourished by the dark side and seemingly abandoned by the light.

Father Cavanaugh settled himself on the small bench and pulled the curtain closed. He lit the small candle that served as light in the booth, the wick struggling to come to life.

"You're late," came a voice through the thin mesh window.

The vague smell of stale cigarette smoke infused in the man's clothing drifted through the partition.

"Yes, I'm sorry," the father said, trying not to be unnerved by the subtle venom that laced every word the man spoke. "As always, your confession is sacred, kept in the strictest confidence, with only God as—"

"Please save your prattling for someone upon whom it won't be lost," the man said. "You should know me well enough by now that I wouldn't talk to you if I didn't trust your...discretion."

Father Cavanaugh laced his hands in his lap, deciding to plunge head-first into the matter at hand. "Would you like to talk about what happened last night?"

"My business matters are irrelevant to our conversations."

"It's not a line so easily drawn, my son. A sin committed—"

"He got what he deserved," the man said in a smooth voice. "Make a deal with the devil and you pay the price. Right Father?"

Father Cavanaugh could hear the sneer in the man's voice. "Is that how you see yourself? As the devil?"

A long silence followed, and Father Cavanaugh wondered if he'd overstepped. It was a delicate dance, his relationship with this man, and one he couldn't afford to ruin.

"You tell me," came the hushed response.

"The devil wouldn't be here with me now," the father said. "In God's house."

Another protracted silence followed, and the flame on the candle danced. "I'm not here to find God."

"But to find your soul. Is there really such a difference? Every soul seeks redemption. In that, you're no different than anyone else."

"Oh, but I am, Father. Or have you forgotten?"

"No," the priest said. He could never forget. "But you must be patient. God will show you the path, but you must have the strength to take it."

"You make it sound so simple."

"No, it's never that. But you must have faith, my son. God will show a sign, you need only have the wisdom to recognize it."

"A sign," he said, testing to see how the word felt across his lips. "I hope you're right."

The father heard the whisk of the curtain being pulled back, and the man was gone. The small candle that lit the tiny room flickered in the residual breeze and was nearly snuffed out. Such a fragile thing, so easily extinguished. But even a small flame can light the darkness.

He closed his eyes and prayed.

CHAPTER NINE

"TWO YACK YACKS AND a Panther," Elizabeth said, as she leaned against the far end of the bar and waited for her order to be filled. Only three hours into her shift, and her feet were already killing her. She glanced at her reflection in the long mirror hanging behind the bar. Between photographs of Clara Bow and Mary Pickford, her own coal-rimmed eyes looked back. She barely recognized herself. Her hair was in a loose ponytail, lips painted in a bright, red cupid's bow. Her eyes shone a brighter shade of blue as the thick, black Egyptian-style liner stood out against her pale, powdered skin. The effect was a popular style of the day—an odd mix of Lolita and wicked city woman.

The green-spangled bandeau headband and its crimson feather made her feel like a reject from some bizarre Hiawatha Christmas pageant. But she could live with all that. It was the rest of her outfit that made her feel uncomfortable. Her uniform amounted to no more than a one-piece bathing-suit covered with green sequins and few strategically placed feathers. Every nuance of her figure was on display for all to see. That was the point really—to appeal to men's vices, all of them. Charlie, bless him, had seen how nervous she was and reassured her. He had a strict "look but don't touch" policy. If anyone got out of line, Lester was there to give them the bum's rush.

Lester, the bouncer, was easily over six foot four and nearly as wide. His square, bald head sat directly on his shoulders, making him look like a Rock 'em Sock 'em Robot. His muscles threatened to burst out from under the strained material of his tuxedo. The upscale outfit was an odd counterpoint to the rest of the club. Not that it was the low end of the spectrum, where décor was a page ripped from a magazine and the only clean glass was one you brought yourself. Charlie's club was the top rung of society's bottom ladder. It was just nice enough to lure the uptown crowd looking to go slumming, but not too expensive to scare away the working Joe who wanted to find a good way to burn his hard-earned money. Tendrils of cigarette smoke wound their way up into the thick haze covering the room like a cloud. Stools lined the long, wooden bar and small, two-top and four-top tables filled nearly every inch of the modest floor space. A small, upright piano was pushed against the far wall, but no one was playing it. The crowd didn't seem to notice the lack of music. They were having a good time and didn't mind showing it.

The club was dark. Two weak, overhead lights cast a yellow glow that barely made it to the plank floor. Dark stained, wood paneling and deep red brick made the place feel even smaller than it was.

Elizabeth was more than a little overwhelmed at first. The doors opened at eight o'clock, and people had been streaming in ever since. They barked out orders for Panther and Scat and a hundred drinks she'd never heard of. She'd laughed when Charlie loaded her first tray with tea cups. He explained all drinks were doled out in tea services, a rather thinly veiled attempt at confusing police raids. It made the room look like a mad tea party, or something out of a Fellini film.

Charlie patiently taught her what each drink was and, thankfully, she was a quick study. A Yack Yack was a glass of bourbon flavored with iodine and burnt sugar. A Panther was whiskey with a touch of fusel oil. When the bartender asked you to pick your poison, he wasn't kidding. But the danger didn't seem to bother anyone. They were already living dangerously, breaking the law by being there, so what was another risk? After all, that's where the fun was.

Charlie set down the drinks she'd ordered and gave her an encouraging smile.

Dixie, the club's other waitress, slid in beside her. "You doin' okay, honey?"

She felt as tired as Dixie looked. Dix couldn't be over thirty, but looked ten years older. She wore too much make-up, trying to hide the lines, but it only made her look used up. Peroxide blonde hair one shade too pale for platinum curled in tight waves around her face. She was the type of woman life liked to kick around. Always getting the fuzzy end of the lollipop, she'd said with a hint of southern twang. She'd come to New York from Georgia when she was seventeen. Lookin' for somethin' better, she'd said. When Elizabeth asked if she'd found it, Dix had just smiled and cast a quick, rueful glance at Charlie. Not that they were an item or anything. Can't compete with a ghost.

"I'm all right," Elizabeth said with a smile. "Hanging in there."

"Servin' swill with a smile. You'll do okay, kid."

Elizabeth nodded and, armed with her tray and a new round of drinks, went back to work. As tiring as it was, she hadn't realized how much she missed having something to do. It helped her keep her mind off Simon. The big jerk.

She served the drinks and put the money in a small clasp box she kept on her tray. "Y'all need anything else?"

"We'll let ya know, honey," the man said with a smirk.

Elizabeth smiled and turned to take another order. So far the patrons hadn't been too patronizing. A few propositions and one loud proposal were about it. She wasn't used to being stared at, but it was oddly intoxicating. She'd spent most of her life trying to downplay her sexuality, but there was no where to hide in this outfit. Much to her surprise, a part of her found she liked it—the attention, the subtle power, the confidence.

"What in God's name are you wearing?" said an all too familiar voice.

She turned to head back to the bar and felt herself flush. Men had been watching her all night and one off-handed comment from Simon made her feel self-conscious again. Quickly, she shoved that feeling aside and lifted her chin in what she hoped was cool detachment. "Simon."

He continued to look at her with his patented disapproving face.

"What are you doing here?" she asked with forced disinterest.

"Another round, doll!" a man from a nearby table shouted.

"Comin' right up," she said and then turned back to Simon. "If you don't mind, I've got work to do."

He followed her to the bar. "It took me two hours to find this damnable place. The least you can do is talk to me."

Charlie had clearly heard the damnable place remark and frowned. Elizabeth gave him an apologetic smile, before turning back to Simon. "Get lost, did you?"

"I couldn't remember the address. I was a bit out of sorts when we were here last."

"So you came here to what? Remind me you don't approve?"

"I came to apologize," he said through gritted teeth.

She set down her tray and crossed her arms under her chest. "Okay."

His eyes darted down to her cleavage, and she quickly uncrossed her arms.

"Hey, baby. You new around here?" a man on a stool asked with a sloppy wink. Apparently Simon wasn't the only one to notice her breasts nearly spilling out.

"I beg your pardon?" Simon said coldly. "I'm trying to talk to my wife."

The man snorted and mumbled something under his breath.

Charlie leaned on the bar. "Problem, Lizzy?"

"Yes," Simon said.

"No," Elizabeth said quickly. "No problem, Charlie. Is it okay if I take a break? Just for a few?"

Charlie looked at Simon and frowned, before giving Elizabeth a quick nod.

She smiled at Charlie and brusquely led Simon over to a relatively quiet corner of the room where the dirty dishes were stacked.

"Well?" she said, nearly crossing her arms again, before thinking better of it. She did feel more at home in her own skin, but not quite that comfortable.

"I'm sorry."

"That's it?"

He glanced irritably back over to the bar. Charlie was watching them out of the corner of his eye. "While I don't like the situation, this place isn't what I'd choose. I... I respect your decision."

"Thank you."

He nodded curtly and shoved his hands into his pockets. "I reacted badly this afternoon. The stress of our situation. I apologize for taking it out on you. It won't happen again."

She could tell how hard this was for him. Admitting he was wrong came at a high price for Simon. Although, he did deserve it. He'd acted like a prize mule this afternoon and she really had no idea why. She wanted to make him squirm, but she felt oddly touched by the nervous way he pushed his hands into his pockets and looked away, almost shyly. "It's all right," she said. "I was kind of in your face."

"Yes, you were a bit—"

She put her hand on his arm to interrupt him. "You better stop while you're ahead."

Simon smiled gently. "Right." He looked down at her small hand resting on his arm.

She was about to pull away, when she looked over Simon's shoulder. "Charlie's watching us," she whispered. They were so awkward around each other, so aware of the other physically, it was hard not to notice. Charlie did. If they were going to fly under people's radar, they had to look and act the part of a couple. She tentatively ran her hand down Simon's arm. "We need to play our parts remember?"

"Parts?"

Elizabeth nodded slowly, gaining confidence from the tremor in Simon's voice. "We're married, remember? Newlyweds. Charlie may not look it, but he's damn savvy when it comes to people. Just play along."

She licked her lips and moved a little closer. She realized under this pretense she could play out things she would never allow herself otherwise. This was a chance to touch him, to feel him. She laid a hand on his chest and could feel his heart beat faster at her touch, see his eyes grow darker. She moved closer, all her reasons forgotten. She let her eyes slide down from his eyes to his lips. They were so sensual. She could almost feel the warmth of his breath on her cheek. She wanted to kiss him. Knew she could, and leaned that much closer.

Simon's hands, strong and warm, wrapped around her upper arms. For a moment she thought he might push her away, but his head inclined a fraction, his eyes dipping down to her mouth. The rest of the room blurred around the edges and left only him. Inescapably, she was pulled closer and closer, her lips nearly on his.

"Doll! How's about some service?" a man at a nearby table called out.

Startled, they both jumped back. As quickly as it had been woven, the spell was broken. All her courage drained away, Elizabeth stepped back and looked down. "I...I should get back to work."

She wanted that moment back, but the brief intimacy had dissolved, replaced with their usual guarded tension.

"Of course," Simon said awkwardly. "I'll be going." But he didn't move.

"Right."

"Right."

He looked like he was about to say more, but merely nodded and turned for the door. She watched him walk away and let out a quick breath. As almost kisses went, that was a doozy.

Simon left the club as more patrons were coming in. A thick, burly man shouldered past him and surveyed the room. With a quick nod to Charlie, he went back and pulled open the door, motioning the all clear. Slowly, conversation waned. When the newcomer stepped inside, it stopped entirely.

Whoever he was, he certainly knew how to fill a room. He was tall, but it was the ineffable way he commanded attention that made him seem larger than life. He walked down the few steps that led to the floor, surveying the room the way a lord surveys his subjects. He not only accepted their rapt attention, he demanded it. The initial silence gave way to anxious murmurs. He caught Charlie's eye, and with a nod, summoned him.

Elizabeth watched the interplay from across the room. Dix set down a stack of dirty cups and whispered in her ear, "Just play it cool, kid."

"Who is that?"

"You really aren't from around here are ya? That's King Kashian," Dix said as though that explained everything.

King's bodyguard approached a small table near the bar and said something to the young couple seated there. Their faces paled, and they quickly took their cups and fled.

King moved like a big cat, all sinew and grace, a careless prowl. He and Charlie sat at the vacated table. Where King was the definition of calm, Charlie was jittery and nervous. He bobbed his head in answer to some unheard question.

Elizabeth had never seen Charlie anything but affable and at ease. She'd only known him a day, but still... "What's up with Charlie?"

"I dunno, but King never comes here himself unless it's something bad. The payment was on time. Gave it to Vic myself when he came in last week."

"Payment?" Elizabeth asked. "You mean protection money? King's a gangster?"

"Jeez," Dix said anxiously and looked around to see if anyone heard her. "Just take some orders and don't look him in the eye, okay?" She hurried back to work as far from King as possible.

Elizabeth stood rooted to her spot. A real live gangster. It was kind of exciting. He wasn't what she'd expected. He was young, maybe thirty and very handsome with naturally olive-colored skin and hair as black as pitch. A well-tailored suit covered his athletic physique. He was attractive in a danger-ous, might makes right, sort of way. There was something cold about him, though. She could feel it even across the room. Maybe it was the way his black gloved fingers moved so sinuously, like snakes. Definitely, cold blooded.

His expression was an odd paradox of disinterest and keen awareness. As if on cue, he looked away from Charlie and caught her staring. His eyes were piercing even from a distance. He seemed to be seeing right through her. She wanted to disappear into the crowd, but couldn't look away. His lips curled into a thin smile.

King said something to Charlie who shifted nervously in his seat and shook his head. King turned his gaze on Charlie and a moment later Charlie stood and called out, "Lizzy, come here for a sec."

Now she'd done it. She took a deep breath and approached the table.

Charlie looked like he was about to have kittens. "King," he said, and shot Elizabeth a quick apologetic glance. "This is Mrs. Cross."

Elizabeth would have giggled if Charlie hadn't looked so pale. Mrs. Cross.

King nodded slightly and leaned back in his chair. His eyes, the color of dark, bitter chocolate, traveled the length of her body. He reached into his coat pocket and took out a silver cigarette case.

Elizabeth fought the urge to run, but stood her ground. His gaze inched up her body in a salacious caress. It was all she could do not to shiver. There was something terribly unnerving about the man. The way he moved, so fluidly. The way his eyes bore into her in a casual assault.

He tapped the end of his cigarette on the table and then lifted it to his mouth. His bodyguard appeared at his side and flipped open a silver lighter, extending the flame. King leaned forward and steadied the light.

She felt her stomach drop with sickening realization. It was all too familiar and suddenly the pieces fell into place. The night in the alley. The man wearing gloves.

King was the man in the car.

Chapter Ten

Exhaling a billowing cloud of smoke, King leaned back in his chair. Elizabeth wracked her brain for something to say. Nice to meet you. Have anyone offed lately? Finally, she blurted out nervously, "Those things'll kill ya."

King's lips curled in a Cheshire smile as if enjoying a private joke. "I wouldn't worry about that."

The smile was even more unnerving, and she self-consciously pulled on her fingers. "Can I get you something to drink?"

Charlie, who'd been standing to the side, shifted nervously. But Elizabeth couldn't tear her eyes away from King. Instinct told her never to turn her back on this man. The surge of something unmistakably feral that flickered across his eyes told her she was right.

"Perhaps another time," he said.

His voice was mesmerizing—smooth with a touch of melancholy, like a French horn. How very Peter and the Wolf, she thought. She wanted to walk away, to get as far away from this man as possible, but his eyes held her captive. There was a flame behind them, searing and dangerous. The flash inside them dimmed, but still smoldered beneath the surface. It was more than that though. There was something unnatural about them. She couldn't quite place it. Like looking into a reflection of a flame, a mirror image of something once removed, something that existed in the periphery, lying in wait.

She knew he wanted her to submit, to show her deference somehow. He was the predator, and she was the prey. As idiotic as it probably was, as dangerous as she knew it to be, she wouldn't give him the satisfaction. Men, modern or not, who expected blind deference weren't going to find it in her. She stood her ground with as much calm as she could muster. Turnabout being fair play, she stared back at him, meeting his challenge with one of her own.

A ghost of a smile crossed his face—surprised and pleased. He took another drag from his cigarette and flicked the ash onto the floor. "You're an intriguing one, aren't you?"

"Not very," she said. "I'm really more intrigue adjacent."

"Somehow I doubt that," he said, amused, and then turned to Charlie. "I like this one."

Charlie cleared his throat and frowned. "She's a hard worker. Maybe you should get back to it, Lizzy?" He looked to King for permission. "Lotsa thirsty people."

King nodded and narrowed his eyes once more at Elizabeth. "Yes, of course. Charles and I have some business to attend to. We'll talk again soon, I'm sure."

There was an implicit promise in the way he spoke. Or was it a threat? She nodded once in his direction and carried her tray over to Dix.

"You okay, kid?"

"Yeah. Fine," Elizabeth said and cast a glance back over to the table. "I think his bark's worse than his bite."

Dix started and dropped her tray. "Damn it," she muttered.

Elizabeth knelt down to help her pick up the broken cups and noticed that Dix's hands were trembling. "Are you all right?"

"Yeah, sure," Dix said, who was clearly anything but. She grasped Elizabeth's wrist and looked at her with uncharacteristic seriousness. "Just stay away from him. He's... just stay away, okay?"

For someone who'd been around the block and back again, Dix was awfully jumpy about King. "Don't worry," Elizabeth said. "I'm not looking for any trouble. Believe me."

Dix nodded nervously and moved to dump the broken dishes in the trash. Elizabeth stood and took up her tray again. A pair of men at a nearby table called her over, and she went to take their orders. Grateful to be back at work, she tried to let the tension from her meeting with King fade away. But no matter where she went in the small room, she could feel King's eyes on her.

A few minutes later, King's henchman whispered something in his ear. The gangster stood and said something to Charlie, who nodded vigorously. Finally, King left. The strangling energy that came with him began to lift, and the bar came to life again.

Charlie hurried back behind the bar, mumbling to himself. "Damn Sully. Goin' and gettin'... now what am I supposed to do?"

"Anything I can do?" Elizabeth asked.

"Not unless you play piano."

"Sorry. All thumbs," she said. Once again, her curiosity got the better of her. "What happened to Sully?"

Charlie's ruddy face crumpled as he sighed. "King said he had an accident. Broke his fingers last night. All of 'em."

Elizabeth's stomach dropped as she realized what he meant. She remembered the man's cries from the alley, the way he held his trembling hands.

"I think I saw King and Sully the other night," she said, thinking out loud.

Charlie's frown deepened. "No, ya didn't."

"Yeah, in an alley. I was—"Charlie reached out with his big, meaty hand and clasped her wrist. "You didn't see nothin', ya hear me?" he whispered urgently. "You didn't see nothin'."

"Okay, Charlie." The knuckles of his hand were gnarled and swollen. Silently, they spoke louder of pain than any words could, and she shivered.

He must have noticed because his face softened and he patted her hand gently. "You stick to your own business. For my sake, all right?"

"Sure, Charlie."

He sighed again and picked up his dishrag. "Where the hell am I gonna find another piano player? Sully wasn't much, but he was cheap. They don't fall outta trees ya know." He rubbed down the bar and a small smile lit his face. "Course, you did, didn't ya, Lizzy? Fell right outta the sky."

"Something like that."

"Maybe old Charlie Blue's luck is finally changin'."

Elizabeth grinned. "You old softie, you."

"Don't let it get around," he said with a wink and went back to work.

By the time Charlie gave last call, it was almost three in the morning. He ushered out the last straggler, and she and Dix set about closing up for the night. It was a little past three-thirty by the time Elizabeth finished her chores, changed and said her goodnights.

She stepped out of the smoky club and took a deep breath of the fresh night air. She was about to start down the street when she noticed Simon. He was leaning against a lamppost, his shirt sleeves rolled up, jacket hanging loosely over one forearm. Waiting, and looking damn sexy doing it.

"What are you doing here?" she asked.

Simon pushed himself upright and took a step toward her. "Waiting for you."

In the dim light, she couldn't quite make out his expression, but his voice sent shivers up her spine. The good kind. She'd been anxious to tell him about King, but all thoughts of the gangster fled as Simon approached. Memories of how she'd felt when he came to apologize resurfaced: the racing of her pulse, the temptation to kiss him. The balmy night air seemed to grow that much warmer against her cheeks.

"You're flushed," Simon said, as he drew nearer. "Are you all right?"

"Fine. I just...You waited for me?"

Simon shifted his jacket unnecessarily from one arm to the next. "I don't like the idea of you out alone at this time of night."

He'd had far too long to think about things, to think about her. He'd tried to concentrate on creative ways to research time travel. The library, not surprisingly, was of little help. In his desperation, he'd even gone so far as considering tracking down H.G. Wells, who according to a recently published article was living somewhere in France. Perhaps his science fiction was as much thinly veiled truth as his grandfather's work had been. But keeping the timeline intact forbade even that preposterous wild goose chase. Hours of work later, and with nothing to show for it, his mind drifted back to Elizabeth and the way she'd looked in the club, the way she'd looked at him. The way she was looking at him right now.

He cleared his throat and attempted to clear his mind. "A respectable woman in this time would not be walking by herself. I'm only being practical."

"Right."

The blush on her cheeks faded, and her eyes seemed dark and troubled. "You sure you're all right?" he asked.

"Just a long night."

"Understandable," he said. He gestured down the street with one hand, the other hovering behind her back, resisting the urge to touch her, if even only for a moment. "Shall we?"

The streets were deserted. It was the only time New York was still. A pause between the end and the beginning. The sounds of their footfalls echoed against the brick walls.

"The rest of your shift went well?" Simon asked. When he wasn't uselessly lost in the stacks, he found himself wondering what she was doing and trying to forget how she looked doing it. He was loath to admit it, but even in such a short separation, he missed her. It wasn't a comforting thought. Surely, it was unnatural to think about someone so much. But no matter how hard he tried, his thoughts always came back to her.

"Work was okay," she said. "Charlie gave me an advance so we're okay, in the money department at least."

"Thoughtful of him," he said, unable to keep the slight sneer from his voice.

"I thought so. I seem to remember asking another boss for an advance once. He wasn't quite so generous."

Simon barked out a quick laugh. "If I remember correctly you needed the money to buy a pair of Italian shoes."

"They were on sale for a limited time," she said. "Charlie's a good man. He worries almost as much as you do."

"I don't—" Simon started in protest. "What does Charlie have to worry about?"

"Gangsters, piano players: it's a regular Scorsese film fest."

"A what?"

"Scorsese. Do you even go to the movies?"

Simon ignored her jibe and took hold of her elbow. "Gangsters. You're sure?"

"Well, one anyway." Elizabeth went on to tell him about her encounter with King, her realization about the attack in the alley and Charlie's warning. Simon asked her detailed questions about each conversation. When she finished, he fell into a thoughtful silence.

Barely three days into their journey and already she'd caught the eye of the most dangerous man in town. If his reservations about her taking this job hadn't been justified before, they surely were now. Tomorrow, he'd find employment, no matter what it was. Perhaps, he'd found the lead he needed tonight.

"All and all," she said, "an interesting night. And can I just say my dogs are barking. If I'm going to make it through tomorrow night, I have got to get some better shoes. I wonder if I can find something Italian."

"Tomorrow? Surely, you're not thinking of going back there?"

"Surely, I am."

"Elizabeth—"

"Simon," she said and stopped walking. "We've already had this conversation, and I'm too tired for a repeat performance. I know you don't like me having this job, but I have it. We need it. And besides, Charlie already paid me for the week. And I ain't no welsher," she added with a grin.

Simon frowned, intent on not being swayed by her smile. "You are the most stubborn, pig-headed, obdurate woman I have ever met."

"Just some of my many charms. Actually that's one charm."

Simon shook his head. There was no use arguing with her tonight. She yawned, and he noticed for the first time how tired she looked. Her eyes were beginning to glass over, and her slim shoulders curled forward weighted with fatigue. She'd taken on all of the responsibility, and he'd done nothing but berate her for it.

"I realize I haven't been exactly supportive of your decisions the last few days, but I do...I wanted to...thank you."

Elizabeth smiled and touched his arm tentatively before pulling away. "You're very welcome." She stifled another yawn. "We better get me to bed before I turn into a pumpkin."

"To bed," he agreed and then realized how that might have sounded. "Right. Well then." He gestured nervously down the street, and they walked home in companionable silence.

Exhausted, Elizabeth took a quick bath and then fell asleep almost before her head hit the pillow. Simon watched the gentle rise and fall of her chest. The corners of her mouth were turned up in a quiet smile. She looked so peaceful, so beautiful. Only in the dim predawn light would he allow himself such thoughts. Well, that wasn't quite true really.

He remembered the way she looked at the club. Every curve of her figure leading his eyes to the next. He'd drunk them in greedily. He couldn't help himself. Unassumingly seductive, she had no idea what she did to him. How his body reacted to her nearness. How when she'd moved so close, he could have closed his eyes and still felt her presence. Still felt the desire. He almost wished he had kissed her. Maybe if he could taste her once, he could get her out of his system. Be free from the endless thoughts of what might be. It was folly, of course. He knew there wouldn't be just one kiss. Not that it mattered. She deserved a better man than he could ever be. He was carved from an old stone. Rough hewn edges and a cold, hard center.

Elizabeth's gentle snoring interrupted his thoughts. She rolled onto her side, moving closer to him. Her arm snaked out from under the covers and fell onto his chest. His breath caught at the intimate touch, but that wasn't the worst of it. She wiggled closer still, and snuggled her head into the crick of his shoulder, her warm breath fluttering against his neck.

Even a stone can feel heat.

He could smell the clean fragrance of her soap and feel the silk of her hair as it brushed against his neck. She felt so wonderful against him, the gentle pressure of her along his side. It was far too tempting to slip his arm around her, to give himself over to the feeling of her in his arms. But it was a pleasure that wasn't his to take. If his performance at the club were any indication, he desperately needed to keep her at a distance. He couldn't afford to let his guard down. His brain was muddled enough as it was. His heart couldn't take one more blow. And he knew it would happen. He could never forget that. Time was his enemy, slowly inching toward the inevitable, the culmination of his nightmares. A week? A month? A year? The end would come.

Elizabeth shifted again in her sleep. He rolled away from her onto his side and closed his eyes.

Tennyson was wrong. Sometimes, it would be better never to have loved at all.

CHAPTER ELEVEN

BARELY A RIPPLE DISTURBED the surface of the water. The sun shone brightly and soft puffs of clouds drifted lazily across a cerulean sky. Simon sat alone in a small rowboat. Only thirty feet away, Elizabeth drifted in her own. She smiled gently and waved to him. He loved the ease of the day, the mild rolling motion of his boat as it bobbed slowly in the water. Elizabeth leaned back and raised her face to the warm sun. She looked like an art deco goddess, her lithe figure in a pose of supplication to the sky above. He wanted to be with her, by her side, and started to row his boat closer. His boat cut easily through the water. The small wake it created pushed gentle swells toward the distant shore.

A billowing cloud slipped in front of the sun and cast a dark shadow over the water. Simon felt the beginnings of a cold wind sweep across the bow of his boat. It sent chills across his skin. His desire to be with her blossomed into a need. He dug his oars into the water and watched as they sliced into the murky depths.

The wind grew colder, stronger. He looked for Elizabeth, but she was further away, not nearer. Her boat had turned away from his, as if pulled on an invisible string toward the horizon. He should have been getting closer, but with each moment that passed, she was further and further away.

The icy wind bit into his cheeks. He gripped the oars more tightly and deepened his stroke, plunging them into the water. The harder he struggled, the rougher the water became. Another cloud, larger than the last, darkened the sky. Whitecaps broke over the growing swells like angry mouths searching for something to sink into.

Simon fought against the roiling sea and called out to Elizabeth. But the wind was fierce and threw the sound back at him. Her tiny boat rocked back and forth, drifting further and further away. She gripped the gunwales as a large wave nearly capsized her. Simon called out again as he struggled to reach her. She must have heard him this time, because she turned and cried out, but any sound was lost in the wind.

Rowing desperately, Simon's muscles burned. The cold wind sliced into his face, and his fingers ached with the effort. But none of it mattered; he had to reach her. She called out again and held up her hand, urging him to stop. But it was too late. He looked down into the water and saw the small wave he'd created growing larger and larger until it became a huge wave, heading straight for her boat.

The cresting water was too powerful and crashed into her, flipping the boat over. Simon called out again and strained to see her. His boat was finally making progress. He rowed with all his heart and when he saw a glimpse of color his heart soared. But as he drew closer, the color grew brighter. A scarlet red, blossoming like a stain.

Blood.

Her body bobbed to the surface. A wave rolled her onto her back. Her bloody, lifeless face stared back at him.

"No!" he cried and lunged forward. The covers fell off his body, as he sat up with a start.

"Wha? What? Simon?" Elizabeth said breathlessly.

He panted furiously and twisted around to see Elizabeth awake and alive by his side. He gripped her tightly by the shoulders.

"What's wrong?" she asked, trying to blink herself awake.

He searched her face, desperate to reassure himself she was all right. The horrible gash and lifeless eyes he envisioned in his dream overlaid her worried face. For a moment, the two images existed together in grotesque harmony. He clamped his eyes shut and when he opened them again, the nightmare was gone.

"Nothing," he said. "Just a nightmare." He released his iron grip on her and tried to calm his thundering heart.

"Mmmm," she said, rubbing her eyes. "What happened?"

Simon looked down at his shaking hands and wound them into the sheet. "I don't remember," he lied. In fact, he remembered every horrifying detail. That unnerved him more than anything else. All his other nightmares had been vague at best, disturbing images that faded quickly. This dream was still vivid in his mind. Too vivid. "I'm sorry I woke you. Go back to sleep."

"You're okay?"

"Fine. Go back to sleep."

Elizabeth yawned and lay back down. "Just think good thoughts. You're in a field of wildflowers," she mumbled into her pillow. "Lots of..."

He glanced over at her, still amazed at her ability to fall asleep so effortlessly. He watched her burrow under the covers and curl up on her side of the bed.

Letting out a long breath, he lay back. The damn nightmares were getting worse. At first, he'd tried to write them off as nothing more than subconscious manifestations of his inner turmoil. But the frequency and power of them foretold something much more sinister. He'd studied the occult far too long to overlook the significance. Portents and harbingers of death were part of his stock and trade. But objective, intellectual discovery and personal experience were far different things. And it wasn't as if this were the first time either. His grandfather had died days after his first night terror. He'd been too young and traumatized to see the correlation. And now, he felt like that frightened boy he had been thirty years ago. He simply couldn't bear that sort of loss again. Elizabeth was alive, but the nightmares still came. Try as he might to rationalize and deny, there was a truth in the dreams he couldn't escape.

He fought against sleep and the horrors it brought. Eventually, he lost the struggle and fell once again into the world of nightmares.

The late afternoon sun warmed Simon's back as he faced the heavy door. He held up his hand to knock, paused, and then rapped his knuckles against the metal. It had been a long enough day already. Elizabeth took bloody forever to find her perfect shoes for work. Thankfully, she seemed too tired to tag along when he mentioned he might have a lead on a job. She offered to go with him, but he would have none of it, and insisted she rest. The last thing he needed was her standing over his shoulder. If this incredibly asinine idea fell apart at the seams, at least without her there, she'd never be the wiser. He'd left her at the apartment and headed out on his errand. Before he could finish his thought, the small rectangular peep hole door slid open and Charlie's bright eyes peered out.

"Oh, you," he said, the light dimming noticeably. "Lizzy's not here."

"I came to see you."

Charlie paused for a moment, then undid the locks and opened the door. "Come on in."

Simon stepped inside. The club was empty and quiet, a stage waiting for the curtain to rise.

"Something wrong with Lizzy?" Charlie asked.

"No, she's fine. I... I came... I understand you're in need of a new piano player."

Charlie laughed in surprise. "I am. You know somebody?"

"I'd like to apply," Simon said, trying to sound as though he weren't mortified at the very thought.

"You? Lizzy said you were a professor or something back in England."

"I am. I was, but I also play. The two are not mutually exclusive, you know."

Charlie laughed again. "Well, ya sound like a professor. I'll give ya that. Let's see what ya got, Maestro." He gestured to the small upright in the corner.

Simon nodded and walked over to the piano. He sat down on the small bench and rubbed his sweaty palms on his thighs. He didn't play very often, but perhaps all those lessons his mother had forced him to endure as a child might actually serve a purpose. He wasn't familiar enough with the music of the day to play any by memory and paled when he didn't see any sheet music.

"Do you have any songs, any sheet music?"

"Ya read music?"

"Of course I do."

Charlie rolled his eyes. "You're touchy enough to be a player. In the bench."

Simon stood and lifted the seat. He chose a Cole Porter standard, "Let's Misbehave", and said a silent prayer as he started. Luckily, the few times he'd sat down to aborted attempts at seeking solace in playing had been enough, and his fingers limbered as he played. In spite of his earlier misgivings, Simon found himself enjoying the music. There was something so alive in it. The allegro defied even the most morose mood. As his fingers danced over the keys, he felt himself growing lighter by the moment, getting lost in the playful, knowing wink of the melody. In the twenties, the glass was always half-full and touched with a splash of Vermouth.

"Not bad, Professor," Charlie said when he finished.

"Thank you. And the job?"

Charlie leaned onto the piano and watched Simon carefully. "You're good enough. But..."

"But?"

"Why do you want it?"

Simon closed the music and kept his eyes away from Charlie. He'd never been in this position before and it was decidedly uncomfortable. "We need the money."

"And?"

Simon frowned. He thought about an elaborate explanation, but Elizabeth had been right about Charlie. He was a shrewd judge of character. "We do need the money, but more than that. Elizabeth needs... looking after."

"You're right on that score," Charlie admitted. "But she's got a job to do and—"

"I won't interfere," Simon promised.

Charlie looked skeptical. "You sure you can do it?"

"Wasn't my playing adequate?"

"Not that. You can play all right. I mean, can ya look me in the eye and say you won't do nothin' when a man catches an eyeful of your wife or offers to take her to the boat races? I run a clean joint, mind ya. But this ain't exactly church on Sunday either."

Simon knew he had to make the promise, even if he wasn't sure he could keep it. "She'll do her job, and I'll do mine."

Charlie sighed heavily and shook his head. "All right. I get the feeling I'm gonna regret this, but ya got the job."

"Thank you," Simon said, relieved. "Now, about my salary..."

"I think I regret it already."

Elizabeth waited impatiently for Lester to open the door to Charlie's. It was after six, and Simon hadn't come home. Lester slid the peep hole open, and she saw his eyes crinkle in a smile. "Hiya, Lizzy," he said, as he opened the door for her.

"Thanks, Lester," she mumbled and made a beeline for Charlie, who was standing behind the bar.

"You're late," he said, as he counted inventory for the night.

"I'm sorry. I know, but Simon didn't come home, and I don't know where he is."

Charlie's big face split into a grin and he looked over her shoulder. "Turn around, doll."

"What?" She followed his gaze and turned around. Simon stood on the other side of the room. He leaned casually against the piano, enjoying his moment of triumph.

He was wearing a black tuxedo and a smug grin. Elizabeth blinked a few times. She hadn't expected to see him here, and certainly not looking absolutely devastating. The tux was simple and classic. The long straight lines made his shoulders look broader. His legs were long and set apart in a casually confident stance. The vee of his crisp, white shirt drew her eyes up to his face. She'd always thought him a handsome man, but a handsome man in a tuxedo was something else entirely. Elegance and power combined.

She realized she was staring, that her jaw was probably scraping the floor. She pushed away the fluttering feeling in her belly and walked towards him. "What are you doing here?"

Simon nodded toward the piano. "Working."

"You mean, you... You can do that?"

Simon laughed and brushed a piece of invisible lint from his lapel. "I can do a great many things."

She remembered the piano in his living room. "I had no idea you had a love of music."

"A man should have more than one love, don't you think?"

97

Elizabeth smiled. Life affords few opportunities and this one was too good to pass up. "Well, that depends," she said, and stepped closer. "On the man."

His Adam's apple bobbed nervously in his throat. "Indeed."

"You could have told me."

Simon's expression remained amused and in control. "And miss this? Hardly."

"The mysterious secret life of Simon Cross?"

"Hey, Lizzy!" Charlie called out from across the bar, interrupting them. "You better get changed."

"Will do," she said, and then turned back to Simon. She smiled slyly and eyed him up and down. "Well, I do love a good mystery."

Simon swallowed hard and seemed at a loss as to how to respond to that salvo. She enjoyed his discomfiture for a long moment before giving him a saucy wink and heading toward the back room. Point, Elizabeth.

This was how Saturday night was meant to be. The club was packed to the rafters with people ready to revel. Simon's piano playing was just the touch the club needed. Keeping the selections lively, he realized that, much to his chagrin, he actually enjoyed himself.

He kept a not so surreptitious eye on Elizabeth. A few men were overly solicitous, but she handled them smoothly. Her ability to appease people without losing ground was a skill she'd had years to hone as his assistant. Even if she didn't know it, she was masterful. He found himself simply watching her. The easy way she engaged people was alluring. He was sure more than one man ordered well past his limit just to talk to her again.

The bar wasn't quite what he'd expected. His imagination coupled with his brief glimpse last night had given him the impression of a tawdry bacchanal. Crowded, loud and dirty. But the people were amiable, even generous. Charlie ran the place well. He stayed on top of countless drink orders and kept things running smoothly. Not to mention Simon had seen him have a few harsh words with one of the men who'd given Elizabeth a hard time. All in all the evening went well. And, thankfully, King Kashian was nowhere to be seen. Although, judging from what Elizabeth had told him about her encounter with the man, they would certainly be seeing him again. His hand went unconsciously to his pocket and he felt the outline of the watch. It was their only chance of getting home and suddenly he needed the reassurance that it was there.

The bulk of the night passed in a blur. Just when it seemed they'd barely begun, their shift was over and Charlie gave last call. Only Simon's aching wrists and Elizabeth's sore back let them know how hard they'd really worked. They changed into their street clothes and were ready to head home when Charlie offered them a nightcap.

"None of that rotgut," he said. "The good stuff. Glenlivet do ya?"

Simon arched an eyebrow. The other bottles were of indeterminate origin, homemade labels sloppily pasted on. Brand name drinks were a rarity during prohibition.

Charlie understood the unasked question and set the bottle down. "Fella I know brought a few bottles back from the war. Smooth as a baby's bottom."

A drink sounded wonderful, but it was outrageously late. "Some other time perhaps."

"Just one?" Elizabeth said and cast a quick glance at Charlie. "Besides, it's tradition. Your first night working in the club. Gotta have a drink."

"Right," Charlie said too quickly. "Uhm, it's tradition."

"Tradition?" Simon said, easily seeing through her ruse.

"Well, traditions have to start somewhere," she said and settled herself on a stool. "Just one drink and then we'll go."

His inability to deny her would surely be the death of him. "All right," he said taking the stool next to hers. "But just one."

Charlie set up the cups. "Dix, you want a snort?"

She set down her dishtowel and came to join them. "Don't mind if I do."

Charlie raised his cup. "Here's mud in yer eye."

They toasted and drank. The scotch was warm and soothing and reminded Simon of home. He wasn't a social drinker, preferring his own company to most other's. He'd never given much thought to the notion that he drank alone. The idea of sitting at a bar making idle chitchat was vaguely nauseating, and yet, here he sat. And it wasn't so bad after all. Elizabeth made conversation, while Simon merely listened, content as usual, to simply watch.

She was animated and engaging as she regaled them with stories of her father and their misadventures at the race track. Dixie and Charlie chimed in with stories of their own, but Simon's attention was swallowed whole by Elizabeth. The way the soft light brought out the golden highlights in her hair. The gentle timbre of her voice as she laughed. Her small fingers delicately tracing the rim of her empty cup.

"What about you, Professor?" Charlie asked, breaking him away from his reverie.

"I'm sorry?"

"He asked where you learned to play?" Elizabeth said.

"Play? Oh, piano. My mother insisted," he said, hoping that would satisfy them. He should have known better.

"Insisted?" Elizabeth asked. "Doesn't sound like much fun."

"It wasn't," he said, but something pricked at his memory, something warm and long-forgotten.

Elizabeth must have noticed a change in his expression. She was too astute by half. "Except," she prompted gently.

"There was one Christmas," Simon started, not sure why he felt compelled to tell the story. The words simply came of their own volition. "I was eight or nine, I can't remember. I'd been taking lessons for only a few months, and my father decided I should give a recital. My mother took the task of molding me for the occasion."

He could still see their living room. Victorian furnishings, Chippendale chairs he was forbidden to sit in except on special occasions. The grand piano looming in the corner.

He looked down into his empty tea cup, almost as though the scene were playing out at its bottom. "I was petrified," he said and cast a quick glance at Elizabeth. Her smile was perfect. Not patronizing nor overly sweet, just perfect.

He looked away and continued, sliding down the slope of memory. "The entire family, great aunts, uncles had come home from India, every possible relation there to witness my inauspicious debut."

He pushed the empty cup away and shook his head. "Greensleeves," he continued with a soft laugh. "Of all the songs. I think my mother was more nervous than I was. I can see her face. She used to wear her hair up in a loose sort of bun," he said, his voice temporarily trailing off at the sharpness of a memory nearly forgotten. "When my father announced the time had come, I felt like I'd suddenly sprouted ten thumbs. But there was no turning back. I started playing. Terribly. I wanted to run away, and then... I'd nearly forgotten this. Mother started to sing. She just smiled at me and stepped forward. She was doing it to cover for me, to drown out the shambles I was making of the song. Slowly, others joined in. Even my father."

He'd completely blocked out that memory, more than willing to put darker ones in its place. Odd that he'd remember it now.

"That's so sweet," Dix said, pulling him abruptly back to the present.

Simon cleared his throat uncomfortably. What had possessed him to tell that story? He didn't know, until he felt Elizabeth's hand slip on top of his. She squeezed it reassuringly and smiled. And for once, he didn't pull away.

Chapter Twelve

$\int$UNDAY, ELIZABETH THOUGHT LAZILY as she started to wake. Her eyelids were heavy with sleep, and she forced them half-way open. The late morning sun filtered through the thin curtains as they fluttered in a warm breeze. Even with the city outside bustling with weekend foot traffic, the room was quiet and peaceful. Reluctantly, she began to push herself upright, but the bed beneath her hand didn't feel right. Too firm, too warm, too Simon.

Instantly awake now, she dared to open her eyes. Well, this is embarrassing, she thought. Sometime during the night, she'd practically crawled on top of him. One arm lay across his chest, one leg draped over his thigh. And a nice thigh it was. She felt the long, taut muscles beneath her. She could almost picture the sculpted strength of them. The way they might tighten and relax if he were... She quickly glanced up to see if he'd heard her thinking and sighed softly. He was still asleep.

She started to pull her hand away from his chest, but the broad planes of muscle felt solid and comforting under her fingers. She felt his heart beating. quickly. Too quickly for sleep.

She looked at his face again and noticed things she'd missed before. His jaw wasn't slack, but slightly clenched. His lips weren't as full as usual, and lay in a flat line. The corners of his eyes crinkled with the effort to keep them tightly shut. The big faker. The big, adorable faker. She nearly laughed out loud. It wouldn't do to embarrass him and, after all, she was the one who'd climbed on top of him. Not that he'd resisted apparently. His arm curled under her shoulder, the long fingers of his hand barely brushing against her.

Maybe she could pretend with him, for just a few more minutes? She laid her head back down on his shoulder and closed her eyes, letting herself drift into a fantasy. This was how Sundays always were. Waking up early in his arms—safe and content. Maybe they had breakfast in bed? Or made love?

As her mind floated along in the pleasant current of her daydream, his hand slid down her arm and tightened ever so slightly. Was he caught in the same current? With a contented smile, she sighed and fell back asleep.

When she woke up again, Simon was out of bed and fully dressed. "What time is it?" she asked with a yawn.

"Nearly one in the afternoon," he said and turned the page of the paper with a snap. "Did you sleep well?"

Elizabeth felt the blush steal over her face. "Very."

Maybe it was her imagination, but she thought she could see him smile behind the paper. She grabbed her dress and slipped into the bathroom. A few minutes later, she emerged washed, dressed and ready to meet the day. After last night, who knew what it might bring.

"So," she said and took the chair opposite Simon by the window. "What should we do today? We've got all day. Or what's left of it anyway."

"I'm not sure," he said, putting down the paper and picking up the watch from the table. "It seems our time is our own. For six weeks at least."

"At least?" She didn't like the way he said that.

"My research has generated absolutely nothing in the way of leads. We have little choice but to trust the watch will do what we think it will," he said as he slipped it inside his jacket pocket. "If not, we're on our own, I'm afraid."

Their little adventure suddenly took on an epic scope, and she felt a yawning abyss of uncertainty opening at her feet. A few days, weeks even, she could handle. That was manageable. The idea that they might never return was unnerving, to say the least.

"It'll work," she said.

If Simon saw through her bluff, he didn't show it. "And since we are here," she continued. "We might as well make the best of it. Starting today."

"Well," Simon said, picking up the paper. "We could go to a movie, I suppose."

Elizabeth raised her eyebrows in surprise.

The corners of his mouth twitched and he added, "Yes, I do go to the movies on occasion."

She grinned and tried to picture him with a bucket of popcorn and a thirty ounce soda. Somehow, the image wouldn't gel. "That would be fun, I guess," she said with calculated indifference.

He set down the paper and eyed her suspiciously. "But?"

She leaned forward and hunched her shoulders with barely contained excitement. "We're in 1929. Think of all the things we could see. A movie would be interesting, but what about... I don't know, the Ziegfeld Follies, or is Houdini alive? Wouldn't that be amazing? What about the Hippodrome? Wait a minute, that's not here anymore more, is it? I can't remember. But there are tons of things. Like..."

"Yes?"

"Coney Island!" She loved amusement parks, and a chance to see Coney Island as it was meant to be was thrilling. "Wouldn't it be fascinating to see it in its heyday. You know, before it got all kitschy and gross."

"I'm not sure I'm—"

"This is living history. How many people get a chance to see that?"

"Be that as it may—"

"Haven't you always wanted to go to Coney Island?"

"I think I can safely answer that with a resounding no."

"Oh, come on," she said. "It's too good to pass up. And it'll be fun. Roller coasters, strange freaky side show things."

"As appealing as that sounds, which by the way, is not at all, I don't—"

"Okay. You don't have to go," she said quickly.

"Thank you." He watched her for a moment, then picked up the paper again. "I understand there are free concerts in Central Park."

"I'm sure you'll have a good time, but I'm going to Coney Island."

"Elizabeth," he ground out.

"Simon," she mimicked. "Really, you don't have to go," she said, as she coyly played with the collar of her dress. "I think it would be fun and educational. A double whammy. But, if you want to mope, I mean, stay around here, you're perfectly welcome to."

Simon put the paper down and sighed. "I'm not really the amusement park type."

"You didn't strike me as the piano player in a speakeasy type either, but..." she said with what she hoped was a dangerously engaging smile.

"Lord help me."

The early afternoon train was packed with people heading out to the island. Back to front, side to side, two to a seat, people crowded into the subways and the elevated train to Brooklyn. The crowd jostled with every bump and turn as the train moved steadily toward the Nickel Empire, where five cents bought everything from a red-hot to a turn at the Tilt-A-Whirl.

Simon gripped the overhead handhold, and Elizabeth gripped Simon. Unable to reach a pole or a hand grip, she'd tried standing on her own for the first few minutes. The shimmying of the car nearly knocked her off her feet and would have if Simon hadn't caught her. She smiled bashfully and wound her fingers into the fabric of his jacket. He kept an arm loosely around her waist.

She looked up at him with a questioning glance.

He looked away shyly and then lifted his chin in poor imitation of indignation. "Purely for safety reasons."

Elizabeth slipped her hand onto his shoulder. "Safety first, I always say."

The car was stifling, or would have been if either had been paying the least bit of attention to anything but the other. The tiny windows let in only the barest warm breeze, and the mass of bodies filled the car with an unrelenting heat.

Elizabeth felt a single drip of sweat inch down her back with torturous slowness. It started to tickle, and she arched her back to help it along. In the close quarters, her tiny movement forced her hips up against Simon. She thought she heard him groan, but the bustle of conversation and the thrumming of the train made it impossible to tell.

"Sorry."

He shook his head. "What?" he asked loudly.

She started to push herself up on her tiptoes to move closer to his ear, when the car abruptly lurched. She threw her arms around him to steady herself and felt his hand press firmly against her back. She was only inches from his face now. The sharp rise and fall of his chest pressed against hers. His lips were so tantalizingly close. Full and masculine, seemingly waiting to be kissed. She looked up into his eyes. They were dark and intense. They lingered with hers before dipping down to her mouth, then back again. An unspoken question hovered between them. Her heart was about to answer when the car jerked violently and started its swift deceleration.

Once again, their moment was gone and reality crashed back in. People shouldered for the door, each having to be the first one out. Simon glared at a large sweaty man and his wife who shoved their way past them.

Elizabeth reluctantly eased her arms down from Simon's shoulders. That was the second time she'd been in his arms, not that she was counting. Okay, she was counting. And each time to have someone ruin it when they were so close. Not that there was anything to ruin. Was there?

The crowd pushed up against her and when the doors opened she was swept away with them. She lost sight of Simon the moment her feet hit the platform. She struggled back to him, but it was no use. Caught in the tide, she edged her way to a large stanchion. Wriggling her shoulders and giving a few people a good elbow in the ribs, she managed to grab hold of the pillar. She stepped up onto the lip and scanned the crowd for Simon.

He was being swept along as she had been, but was fighting it all the way. "Simon! Over here! Simon!"

His head jerked around, and he saw her. His expression both frustrated and relieved. He forced his way through the crowd, which was finally thinning.

"What the devil?" he ground out.

"Pretty enthusiastic bunch, aren't they?"

"Ill-mannered, rude—"

"They're not that bad. And anyway," she said with a gleam in her eye. "We're here."

His face was flat. "Hooray."

"Oh, come on sourpuss. This is gonna be fun. You're gonna love it. Trust me," she said and held out her hand.

He looked at her hand suspiciously. Finally, he took it and sighed. "All right, I'll come, but I'm not going to enjoy it."

But he did enjoy it. Walking among the throng, holding Elizabeth's hand, he felt like he belonged. He wasn't apart from life now, but a part of it. He glanced down at her hand resting in his. It really was so small, his fingers seemed to engulf it completely. And he liked the feeling. The constant, subtle reminder that he wasn't alone.

Surf Avenue swarmed with tens of thousands of people. Cars tried vainly to weave their way between the pedestrians. Simon pulled Elizabeth onto the crowded sidewalk, and she gawked at the scene.

Barkers sang out their outrageous promises of the fantastic to lure the unsuspecting to their attractions. The roaring sound of the roller coasters rumbled like thunder, and the smell of garlic and cooking meat drifted through the crowd, tempting each passerby.

"This is amazing!" Elizabeth cried.

"It is quite a spectacle," he admitted.

"Ooo, the Cyclone!" she squealed and pulled Simon down the street.

They passed by Nathan's Famous Redhot stand, where people stood ten deep waiting for the best dog in town. They walked past the bilious entrance to Luna Park, which was one of the three existing self-contained amusements parks. Coney Island was a controlled sort of chaos. Luna Park, Steeplechase Park and the Bowery were separate entities. Mixed in between them were independent rides. Coasters and spinning cup machines, rides of every variety, all owned and operated apart from the big parks. The world famous Cyclone was the most majestic of them all.

The ride was a behemoth, a figure eight design with a ridiculously steep drop. The cars screeched overhead, flying past the street below at over seventy miles an hour.

Elizabeth looked up into the bright sunlight shining off the wood and steel giant. "This is gonna be great."

"You aren't seriously considering going on that deathtrap?"

"You bet yer bippy I am," she said and hurried over to get in line.

Simon watched her with veiled amusement and no small amount of alarm. Safety wasn't exactly of paramount concern during this decade. Did they even have seatbelts? He did his best to swallow his worry and found a shady spot to wait. He watched her chat with a pair of young children behind her in line. She was smiling, laughing, and absolutely lovely.

The line was atrociously long and snaked in and out of his sight. At each bend he could see her, and she waved to him, bouncing on the balls of her feet in anticipation. Content with the warmth of the sun and the vicarious pleasure of her excitement, he waited patiently. Before too long, he was rewarded with a breathless, wind-blown Elizabeth.

"I am definitely doing that again."

Simon shook his head in defeat. "Go ahead."

"Later," she said with a wave of her hand. "We haven't even been in the park yet. Come on, time's a'wastin'." She started back up Surf Avenue without him.

They paid the quarter admission price and stepped inside Luna Park. A large, artificial beach and long, rectangular pool rested just inside the gate. He could smell the salty air rolling in from the Atlantic ocean, barely a block away. Bright, white towers topped with intricate spires and lattice work reached for the sky in the distance. Elizabeth turned around in a circle, taking it all in. People swarmed around her, excitedly buzzing about the afternoon's pleasures. Eclectic architecture ringed the outer perimeter, a series of snapshots of faraway lands, transporting each visitor to places they'd only dreamt of.

"It's amazing," Elizabeth said.

After the constant browns and grays of the city, the pristine white buildings and red shingled roofs were another world. She wasn't the only one gawking at the splendor of the park. There was an electricity in the air. People who had never traveled more than a few miles from their homes were suddenly thrust into a replica of an ancient Egyptian tomb or a jungle oasis filled with headhunting natives, anything the imagination could conjure.

The frantic strains of a ragtime band seemed to catch Elizabeth's attention, but before she reached the bandstand, another spectacle pulled her away. There in the middle of the park sat a huge lagoon. She ran to the railing and leaned over to look down into the murky, deep, green water.

Simon, who'd been trailing behind, finally caught up with her. She moved around the park with exhausting, childlike enthusiasm, reminding him how young she really was. As she leaned against the rail, a gentle breeze blew the hem of her skirt, and he caught a glimpse of her legs and the black garters that hugged her thighs. He felt his pulse race and forced himself to look away. Perhaps, not quite so young after all.

"I've said it before, and I'll say it again. Wow. Look at that," she said, pointing to the far end of the lagoon. A boat, large enough to hold six people, slid down a wide flume more than one hundred feet long before it plunged into the lake. A crowd standing on platforms around the Shoot-the-Chutes applauded as each boat took its turn on the giant slide and splashed down into the lagoon.

The hairs on the back of Simon's neck prickled with anxiety. The water, the boats, it was all too eerily reminiscent of his nightmare. It was an unreasonable fear, he knew, but as he watched Elizabeth lean farther over the railing, a cold panic washed over him. He gripped her arm tightly and pulled her away from the edge.

She looked at him in surprise and he let go. "I... This looks interesting," he said too casually and gestured to another attraction a safe distance from the water.

If she noticed the strain in his voice, she chose to ignore it and happily continued her giddy exploration of the park. He grumbled good-naturedly as she dragged him from one end of the park to the other. He pointed out the egregious historical and cultural inaccuracies of each exhibit they visited: the ridiculous errors of confusing the Fourth and Eighteenth Dynasties of Ancient Egypt, the headhunters of Borneo sporting Central African headdresses. It certainly wasn't the way he'd choose to spend an afternoon. But she met each new discovery with such unremitting wonder, he found himself actually having a good time. She stared wide-eyed from one attraction to the next, and he was content simply to watch her.

After a rather nauseating spin on the Tilt-A-Whirl, Elizabeth was ready for something a bit more sedate and forced Simon to choose their next destination.

He balked. She cajoled. He relented.

He suggested the cyclorama, not mentioning that the short line was the main appeal. Cylcoramas were shown in cylindrical rooms with the crowd seated in the middle. A large, movable painted canvas was stretched around the circle with sound and lighting effects used to heighten the drama. The Battle of the Marne was a spectacular recreation of one of WWI's epic battles. Despite the antiquated effects, Elizabeth jumped in her seat when a miniature car crashed from a small platform. Thunderous explosions echoed from behind the walls and a thick smoke swirled overhead. It was frighteningly effective, perhaps too much so. The costly battle was still fresh in the minds of the world. When the lights went on, the small crowd was quiet and reflective. The somber Zeitgeist cast a pall on the day. Simon had the absurd feeling that things had somehow taken a turn for the worse. When they left Luna Park and headed back down toward the Bowery, he knew he was right.

CHAPTER THIRTEEN

THE ALL-MONKEY ORCHESTRA AT the Hippodrome was too good for Elizabeth to pass up. Or so she thought. After the depressing show at the cyclorama, she hoped something fun and silly would lift her mood.

The performance consisted of fifty trained monkeys dressed in band uniforms playing miniature instruments. It was certainly silly, but not the fun she'd been hoping for. Maybe it was the color of her mood as she took her seat on the long wooden benches. Maybe she was trying too hard to regain the excitement of earlier in the day. But as the animals wriggled and jumped on the stage, she felt her mood growing darker. She tried to remind herself this was a different time, with different sets of morals. The notion of animal protection was still in its infancy. It wasn't as though the creatures were being overtly abused, but the sight of them subjugated in such a ridiculous farce set her mind into a tailspin of judgments. The SPCA was hardly a blip on the radar, no one was going to look after them, and with shows throughout the day, there was no way they were treated properly. At best, they were no more than props. At worst, she didn't want to think about.

Simon took her hand and gave it a gentle squeeze. When the show ended, he led her silently out of the amphitheater.

Had she been looking, but not really seeing? Now that the idea had been planted, everything she saw was cast in a disturbing light. Bonita's Fighting Lions looked thin and haggard in their tiny cages. Before, the park patrons seemed merely excited. Now, they looked frenetic, jigging madly from one spot to another. Even the carousel horses seemed twisted and disturbed. But it was Wagner's World Circus Side Show that was the straw that broke the camel's back.

Elizabeth shuddered when the barker paraded the freaks out for display. The Tattooed Man, the Spider Boy and the Wolfman. Simon muttered something about the obvious lack of any true lupine qualities. Elizabeth barely registered his remarks as Wagner brought out Pipo and Zipo, two microcephalics, or Pinheads as they were more commonly known. The crowd gasped in shock as the pair walked across the makeshift stage. Children hid behind their mothers, only to be encouraged to gawk at the poor couple.

It was more than Elizabeth could bear, and she hurriedly slipped through the crowd. She had to get away from it all, and didn't stop walking until she reached the edge of the Boardwalk. Black waves lumbered ashore in the distance, a dull roar in the background of the night. She leaned against the wooden railing and breathed in the salty, ocean air. Simon came up behind her, but she didn't turn around.

"God, this place is awful. I'm sorry I made you come," she said. The sand close to the walkway glistened like pyrite.

He leaned back against the railing. "It's a different time."

Elizabeth mimicked his pose, turning back to face the park. The sun had set and thousands of fairy lights sparkled in the night. "It's just a Potemkin village, isn't it? A beautiful façade hiding a dark reality."

"Aren't most things?"

He sounded so resigned to it. Was this the world he lived in all the time? Never seeing the magic, only the man behind the curtain.

"I guess so," she said and pushed away from the railing and started back slowly toward the Bowery.

They walked the short distance up 12th Street, passing the huge two-hundred foot Wonder Wheel. People giggled and screamed from their tiny, swaying cars on the Ferris wheel. Elizabeth barely noticed. The side show carnies and their nickel games of chance lined the sidewalk: age old scams waiting for the next sucker. Hucksters and conmen were all too familiar to her. A little three card Monty, a shill game; the fix was always in. Her daddy always believed that one good hand, one good roll of the dice was only around the corner. And it might have been, if the cards weren't marked and the dice weren't weighted. Even up until the end, he never lost sight of the brass ring, always just beyond his reach. Now it all felt like an illusion. A dream stripped away to the cold, bleached bones of reality.

"We have a winner!" The stall owner handed a man a kewpie doll. The woman with him threw her arms around his neck and squealed in delight. The happy couple walked away arm in arm.

Simon grew increasingly distressed by Elizabeth's silence. More than once, he'd wished she would curb her enthusiasm, but now he found he missed it. Her smile that had warmed him during the day had faded with the afternoon light. He wanted to reassure her, but false comforts weren't his nature. He knew it was absurd, but he felt compelled to see her smile again. He noticed the byplay of the couple and had an idea.

"This way," he said and led her toward one of the ring toss stalls.

"Nickel for three tries," said the carny. "Win something for the pretty lady?"

"What would you like?" Simon said confidently. How hard could it be? Elizabeth laughed, but it was still lifeless. "It's okay."

Simon surveyed the prizes. The kewpie dolls were grotesque. He looked over at Elizabeth and saw her eyes lingering on a small stuffed animal on the top shelf. "What do I have to do for the tiger? That one in the back?"

The carny's lips curled in pleasure. "Just gotta get one ring on the blue bottle and it's yours."

Simon took off his coat and handed it to Elizabeth. She smiled, a bit of the spark he so loved lighting her eyes. Shouldn't be difficult really—one ring out of three.

Ten minutes and three dollars later, he still hadn't hit a sodding thing. He slammed another quarter down on the wooden ledge.

"Really, it's okay," she said, biting her lip in an obvious effort to keep from laughing.

"No, it's not," he said.

He tossed the ring, and it clattered off to the side. The second rimmed off the blue-necked bottle. Finally, the third hit its mark. It looped around the bottle and settled in place.

Simon grunted in triumph. "About bloody time."

Elizabeth laughed and gave him a round of applause. He suddenly felt embarrassed. He wasn't one for overt, or covert for that matter, shows of testosterone. But the way she looked at him, almost adoringly, it was enough to turn lead into gold.

The carny used his long pole to retrieve the stuffed tiger and handed it to Simon. Elizabeth positively beamed when he turned back to her. Whatever the cost, it had been well worth it.

Feeling the carny's eyes on them, Simon led Elizabeth to a secluded spot near a darkened stall for more privacy. He looked down at the tiger. It was ridiculous really, poorly made and covered with a layer of dust. The stitches were loose and haphazard, ready to split apart at the slightest provocation.

He turned it over in his hands, feeling suddenly foolish. Such a paltry thing for all the money he'd spent. Money they didn't have to spare. He took a deep breath. "I think he belongs to you," he said softly and handed her the tiger.

Elizabeth brushed the soft fur and played with one of the ears. "I love him," she whispered. She steadied herself on his shoulder and leaned up to kiss him. Just the barest caress on the corner of his mouth, but the feeling was electric. She pulled away just far enough for him to see her face—surprised, questioning, and desiring. A breathless moment hovered between them.

A voice inside Simon's head screamed at him to step away, to stop this before it went too far. She moved closer again, her lips brushing against his. And the voice fell silent. Everything Simon knew, every good reason, every second thought, disappeared in that instant. The only thing that mattered was the feeling.

Her lips, tentative and soft, pressed against his. His hands moved without thought and pulled her body closer. Fueled by desires too long buried, he kissed her with all that he was, all that he dreamt of being. She opened herself to him, and he took all she offered. The gentle kiss blossomed with passion, as he tasted her, drank her in, devoured her. He felt her breasts crush against his chest as he pulled her closer still. His hands splayed across the arch of her back and the delicate curve of her neck. The silk of her hair wound its way around his fingers as she wound her way around his heart.

She eased her mouth from his, and he could feel the soft warmth of her breath against his cheek. He groaned with pleasure and opened his eyes.

"Simon," she whispered breathlessly.

He pulled back and looked into her face, flushed with the heat of the moment, lips swollen and slightly parted. Her eyes glistened in the moonlight, pulling him in. He was falling, spiraling, completely out of control. Out of control. Slowly, a swelling terror rose in his chest. The panicked feeling from his dream, the loss and desolation, surged inside him. Dear God, what had he done?

It was a moment he would revisit for years to come—the moment he pushed her away.

He still held her, not to him, but away from him. His fingers dug into her arms, as his grip tightened. He couldn't do this. He'd been a fool to think he could lose himself in her. He could never outrun who he was, who he wasn't. Love was a luxury for other men. He shook his head slightly and winced as pain and confusion colored her expression.

"That was a mistake," he said.

Her face blanched, and she gripped the small, stuffed tiger tightly. "I... I don't understand," she stuttered.

He couldn't explain it. How could he confess that he could never be the man she wanted, the man she deserved? Wanting her in return couldn't change that. No matter how much he wanted her. He'd selfishly taken what she'd offered without thought to the consequence. He could love her. He did love her, he thought with a deepening sickness in his heart, but he couldn't bear to be loved by her. To have something so beautiful and know it couldn't last. To know each day spent with her was one fewer day left to them. The swell of panic from his nightmares overwhelmed him again. He could not bear to let her in, only to have to let her go again. His heart couldn't take the risk.

"But on the train," she said. "And this morning, I know..."

The pain in her voice cut into his resolve, but he couldn't waver. He knew he was a coward. That realization only reaffirmed he was right in pulling away. He wasn't capable of being what she needed. He was selfish and afraid. The sooner they both faced it, the better. She deserved a whole man, not broken pieces.

"Mistakes," he said more firmly.

She looked as if she'd been struck. Every fiber of his being screamed for him to comfort her. He reined them in. Better a clean cut. He would watch over her, loving her safely from afar. If he kept his distance, maybe one day he could forget her. Or perhaps, if he stayed away from her, the terrible fate he'd dreamt of would never come to pass.

"We should be getting back," he said. He set his jaw and let his eyes fall to the ground.

Elizabeth glared at him for a long moment. He could feel her eyes boring into him, but he didn't have the courage to meet them. Didn't have the strength to weather the questions and the anger he knew they held. Then, without another word, she turned and walked away.

The train home was crowded, but there were still seats to be had. Elizabeth took one next to a window. Simon had kept his distance as he followed her back to the station, and now stood alone in the back of the car as it shimmied down the track.

He watched Elizabeth lean her head against the cool glass of the window. The dark scenery passed by in a blur. He'd done the right thing, he told himself. The only thing he could. He'd always walked along the periphery of emotion, never willing to submit. It was a lonely way to live, but it was the only way he knew. He was too old to change now, too afraid, if he dared admit it. His demons were too familiar, too insidious, killing him by inches instead of miles. A way of life that wasn't living. A heart as little used as his couldn't bear the strain. He'd have lost her eventually. He was sure of that. Better to stay that way from the start than be cleft in two.

When the train reached the station, Elizabeth rose and walked out without so much as a backward glance. He deserved it. Far worse really. He waited for the other passengers to leave before making his way up the aisle. Passing the seat where Elizabeth had been sitting, he saw the small, stuffed tiger abandoned on the empty train. He nearly reached out to take it, but it was useless now. He'd made his choice. He left the train car and followed her home.

He knew this journey into the past would be fraught with dangers. He just hadn't realized that losing his heart would be one of them.

CHAPTER FOURTEEN

ELIZABETH COULDN'T BEAR TO look at him, not without yelling, or worse, crying. She wasn't going to give him the satisfaction of either.

The walk home was silent. She wanted to run; she wanted to run and hide and disappear. Her father's voice was the only thing that kept her from losing it completely. Never let 'em know you're scared. Eddie West's kid didn't run away. No matter what.

The door to the apartment closed behind her. She shivered and wrapped her arms around her chest. It was so damn cold. Eighty-five degrees and absolutely freezing. She walked into the room and stood in the middle of the beige carpet with her back to him. For a fleeting moment, she wished he'd come to her. Say he didn't mean it, that it was all a mistake.

A mistake. How those words cut. She heard him pad over to the table by the window. He wasn't going to take it back. He meant it. She was a mistake.

She lowered her hands to her sides and tightened them into fists to keep them from trembling and walked into the bathroom. She simply couldn't be in the same room with him. Slamming the door behind her, she looked into the mirror.

How was she going to face him again? The look in his eyes when he'd said it, shocked and appalled, almost angry. She'd put her soul into that moment, into that kiss. She offered him her heart, and he'd looked at her like she was a fly in his soup.

Why was it the things you want to forget the most are the things that stay with you forever? She closed her eyes, fighting back the tears that threatened to spill out. There were precious few times she missed her mother. Daddy was all she'd ever needed, most of the time. But what she wouldn't give to have her mom, right here, right now.

Elizabeth grabbed a handful of toilet paper and wiped her runny nose, sniffling back the tears that clogged her throat. There was no one here for her to talk to. No one was going to rub her back in those reassuring circles. No one to tell her it was going to be all right. And besides, it wasn't going to be all right.

What an idiot. How could she have done it? What the hell was she thinking? He'd spent a few dollars on a cheap stuffed toy, and she threw herself into his arms.

She pushed away from the sink and slumped down onto the toilet. She was a complete fool. He'd been nice to her. Nothing more. Just nice, which, okay, for Simon was tantamount to a proposal. Or so she'd thought. A few looks, and she'd melted like butter. Was she that desperate for the illusion that he cared? Seeing things when nothing was there. A few longing looks that were probably all in her head anyway. Simon was right. Believing something doesn't make it true. It just makes you look like an ass.

Elizabeth ran a shaky hand over her eyes. God, if she could only take it back. Rewind, call a do-over. She replayed the scene in her head again and again. The way he looked at her right after she thanked him for the tiger. He wanted her, he felt something. Or was that revisionist history? Did she see desire because it was there, or because she wanted it to be? And the kiss. God. The kiss. She could remember every nuance, every place his hands had touched her. That was even more pitiful. It didn't mean anything to him. He was caught up in the moment, she was there. Nothing more.

Could she be more pathetic? She'd actually discovered a whole new level of humiliation. Maybe they'd name it after her, like Lou Gehrig's disease. West's Shame: not fatal, but you wished it were.

But the way he'd held her. She could still feel his body pressed against hers, strong and protective. She could still taste him on her lips. He hadn't fought her. He didn't push her away. Not at first. He'd responded. She might not be a femme fatale, but she knew enough to know when a man was excited. There are some things you can't hide. And it was more than that. This wasn't just another kiss. She'd kissed enough horny underclassmen to know the difference. Lust was hands up your shirt and tongues down your throat. Simon caressed her, held her. It had been more than the twenty year difference in experience. It was passion, tempered. But tempered with what?

He could have stopped it before it started, if it was such a big mistake. But he didn't. He kissed her back. He wanted to kiss her. He felt something. She was sure of it. So what the hell was he doing pushing her away? What was he running from? Was the mighty Simon Cross afraid?

She let out a long sigh and moved back to the sink. She turned the taps and let the water rush over her hands. The cold against her face made her gasp, but she wasn't going to be red-faced and puffy-eyed if she could help it. Rivulets of water ran down her chin, and she rubbed them into her neck. She looked at herself in the mirror again, when a knock on the door interrupted her thoughts.

"Eliz—Miss West?" Simon's voice came from the other side of the door. "Are you... Is everything all right in there?"

She stared into her reflection and felt a new heat rising in her. Anger. It was a damn sight better than the abject humiliation of a few minutes ago. If he wanted to be a repressed schmuck, he could do it on his own damn time. You don't make someone feel something and then pull the rug out from under them. You just don't do it.

Her T-shirt was hanging on the thin clothesline over the tub. Thank God she'd done laundry earlier and didn't have to go back into the room to get her clothes. She wasn't about to wear the top of their matching set of pajamas. Shrugging off her dress, she pulled the tiny shirt over her head. The hem fell slightly above her panties and she started to tug it down, but the hell with it. What did it matter now anyway? She grabbed a towel and dried her face. Taking one more steeling breath, she opened the door.

Simon took a step back and shifted nervously.

She glared at him for a moment until he had the good sense to look away. She walked over to the bed and pulled the coverlet down on her side. It was probably foolish to even ask why, but she couldn't help herself. And maybe in the asking she could find a little bit of control.

"There's only one thing I want to know," she said, as she turned to face him. "What are you so afraid of?"

Simon frowned and shook his head. "I... I'm sorry."

"You're sorry?" She waited for more, but he just looked at her with those shuttered eyes. That was all he had to say? She tensed her jaw and fought the urge to shake him. He could barely look at her. He should at least have the decency to look her in the eye. A screaming match would have been better than the defeat, the complete lack of anything. Was he that shut down? Maybe it all wasn't a façade. Maybe he really was a cold-hearted bastard.

They stood in an awkward silence for a painfully long moment before she shook her head with undisguised pity.

"Fine. You be sorry. You can do whatever the hell you want. I'm going to bed."

Simon turned the corner onto Mulberry street, already planning his next move. If she wasn't there, he'd try Saint Patrick's then go back uptown and retrace their steps from earlier in the week.

Damn that woman.

The last thing he'd wanted was the one thing he'd gotten. She'd been gone that morning when he woke up. No note, nothing, except an empty bed. It was just like her. To rush off to God knows where.

He rolled his neck, trying to work out the kinks. A night in the little wooden chair had done little to help his mood. Now, his body was twisted in the same knots as his heart.

He went from store to store, pushing his way through the crowd. She had to be here. This was the sort of place she'd seek. Get that canoli she'd talked incessantly about. Pastry shop after pastry shop and still no Elizabeth.

Could he have made a bigger cockup of the situation? He'd behaved like a fool. He should never have let things get as far as they had. Never should have given in for one moment of perfection. One blissful moment when everything else faded away, except the feeling of her in his arms.

Damn her. She should have, at the very least, had the decency to tell him where she was going. She could be anywhere in the city. Anything could be happening to her.

With a force of will, he pushed that thought aside and continued through the crowd. He'd find her sooner or later. Not that he had the slightest notion of what to say when he did. His stuttering apology last night only drove her further away. What could he say? How could he keep her only at arm's length when the feeling of her by his side was all he thought about?

He shoved his hands into his pockets and felt the cool, embossed metal of his grandfather's watch. His fingers ran over the surface. Odd, how in only a few days it had become a talisman. An anchor to reality. But it was nearly meaningless without her. He gave a short painful laugh. What wasn't?

As he neared the end of the block, he mentally mapped out his next move. Take the subway uptown and work his way back. Surely she wouldn't leave the city. No. He had the watch. She'd come back to him, if for no other reason. Cold comfort.

He was about to reverse his course when he felt someone watching him. He turned around quickly, scanning the crowd, hoping to see a glimpse of her. The hairs on the back of his neck prickled.

No Elizabeth. Who'd been watching him? He was sure he'd felt the weight of someone's eyes on him. In the shadows of a doorway stood an old woman, arms wrapped under a black shawl, dark eyes boring into him.

Then he noticed the hand-painted sign that adorned the window next to her—Rosella: Spiritualist and Medium. Undoubtedly, one of the many charlatans that had found a way to profit from people's suffering. A legacy of the first World War.

After the war, after any time of great sorrow, people looked for answers. So much loss led to questions about life, death and what lay between. Some turned toward religion, and people like Aimee Semple McPherson came into power. Some turned away from everything, and others turned toward the slightly less ordinary.

Spiritualism had been reborn. Finally out of the back rooms and dark alleys, the movement was big business. From the average housewife to the cream of society, nearly everyone embraced the prospect of speaking to a lost loved one.

Simon eyed the old woman with undisguised disdain. His years in the occult had led him to more than his share of impostors. He'd even, for a brief time, considered following in Houdini's footsteps and spending his life debunking those who'd gain from other's pain. But he'd had his own battles to fight and had forgotten about it, until now.

"You have lost something?" the woman said, in a thick Italian accent.

It hardly took a clairvoyant to see that. "I know your type," Simon said. "Don't waste your time on me."

Rosella narrowed her eyes. "Ah, but your time is not your own, is it?"

Simon felt a cold shiver, but ignored it. Vague remarks were the hallmark of her kind. The subject's imagination was key in any deception, and he wasn't about to be drawn in by her games. "I don't see—"

"You do see, what will be," she said and then spat on the sidewalk. "La malvagità disegna vicino. Near to the one you love."

Despite his misgivings, he found himself struck by her warning and took a step closer. "What evil?"

She reached out a wrinkled hand to stop him, her withered fingers feeling something unseen between them. "I am mistaken," she said quickly and wrapped her shawl more tightly around her narrow shoulders.

"What do you see?" Simon said more fiercely. Did she sense the same danger he did? "Tell me what you see."

"Nothing," she said, keeping her eyes to the ground. "I see nothing."

Her frightened denial unnerved him even more. "You said you saw evil. Coming nearer—"

"Go," she said, turning and opening the door behind her.

Before Simon could get in another word, she slammed the door in his face. The locks clicked into place and the shade was hastily drawn.

He raised a hand to knock on the door, but stopped in mid-motion. It was absurd. This little charade was undoubtedly all part of her scheme. Tantalize the customer with an indistinct warning and leave them begging for more. He wasn't that much of a fool.

Turning on his heel, he walked down the crowded street berating himself for having wasted the time. He rounded the corner and headed toward

Old Saint Patrick's. He tried to put the incident out of his mind, but the old woman's warning lingered like a circling hawk in the sky.

He spent the rest of the afternoon searching for her. Charlie hadn't seen her, and the small tremors of anxiety he always carried with him grew until he was frantic with worry. He'd make one last check of the apartment, then he'd go to the police. Timelines be damned.

He keyed into their small apartment and stopped dead in his tracks. Elizabeth was sitting at the small table, very much alive.

He breathed a sigh of relief and closed the door behind him. "Where the hell have you been?"

Elizabeth kept her gaze out the window and gave a bitter laugh.

His relief was pushed aside by a wave of anger. "The least you could have done is left a note. I looked all over the damn city for you."

She turned slowly in her chair. "Now, you found me."

Her calm was maddening. "What were you thinking?" he said and strode toward the table.

She stood and met his anger with her own. "I don't think you want to know."

Simon clenched his jaw. She was right about that. He didn't want to know.

"But since you asked so nicely," she said icily. "I think it's best if we don't share an apartment anymore. I wouldn't want any more mistakes, would you?"

He winced and tried to think of something rational to say, which was distinctly lacking in this conversation. "Elizabeth—"

She walked away from him and busied herself with preparing her outfit for the club. "I should have enough money by the end of the week."

She couldn't be serious. He couldn't let her move out. There simply had to be a way to convince her not to. God knows, it was hard enough to protect her as it was, but if she weren't with him... If she weren't with him. He choked on the thought. He felt his hands begin to shake, and he tamped down the feeling. He couldn't afford another bout of emotion. He'd let himself slip last night and created nothing but another nightmare. He had to be in control of himself. He had lived the last thirty years in well-measured restraint. He wouldn't fail now.

"Don't be absurd," he said and winced as soon as the words left his mouth.

She arched an eyebrow in challenge. "Oh, I'm sorry. Was I being absurd?"

"That's not," he stuttered and shoved his hands into his pockets. "That's not what I meant."

"It doesn't matter anymore. You made yourself quite clear last night. I'll have my own place by the weekend."

He fought against the urge to take her in his arms. Tell her it was all a mistake. That he'd made the mistake in pushing her away. But his feet wouldn't move. He had done the only thing he could yesterday, but he couldn't let her leave.

"Like it or not," he said, as evenly as he could. "We're in this situation together."

"No. We're not." She picked up her costume and lifted her chin. "We need to keep up appearances. But since that's all they are, where I spend my nights is none of your business."

Elizabeth ignored him all the next night at the club, never once even glancing in his direction. Simon managed to play the music, but he wasn't sure how. Her anger was well deserved, but that was hardly a comfort.

He finished his set and sat on the piano bench watching her lean against the bar, waiting for her order to be filled. She tucked a few stray strands of hair behind her ears and gave Charlie a fleeting smile.

The night dragged on painfully slowly. The bar was doing a brisk business for a Monday night, but every couple, every happy reveler was nothing more than painful reminder of something he'd never have. He watched her as she greeted each table with a smile. He hadn't realized how much he'd come to rely on her smile. How much that simple thing meant to him. Now they were all for someone else. He was starting to feel truly maudlin when the buzz of the crowd softened to a whisper. Every eye in the club was on the man in the doorway.

"King!" Charlie said with forced enthusiasm. "Your table is waitin' for ya."

The dark haired man nodded his head once and took a seat along the far wall. Simon nearly forgot his place in the song as he leaned to his right to get a better view. So this was King Kashian? He used so much oil in his hair, there was enough left over for his smile.

Dix went to his table, but he waved her off. His dark eyes traveled across the room until they found their prize. Elizabeth. Dix signaled for her to come over. King's gaze raked over her body, and Simon hit a sour note. He covered quickly, then strained to see them through the crowd.

The man's look was positively indecent. King waved a gloved hand and gestured for Elizabeth to join him. She shook her head. Good girl. King leaned forward and narrowed his eyes. Elizabeth put her tray down on the table and took a seat.

They spoke for a few minutes until King turned and nodded toward Simon. Elizabeth followed his gaze and said something in response. King laughed, and they both turned away.

What the bloody hell was she doing?

CHAPTER FIFTEEN

SIMON GROUND HIS TEETH with growing aggravation. He wished he could see Elizabeth's face, but all he could see was King's smug expression. They were too far away for lip reading, but it was clear enough that the gangster was enjoying her company. A bit too much.

Simon played a few more standards, trying not to race the tempo, but his heart wasn't in the music. After a few more minutes, King pushed his chair back and stood. He gave Elizabeth a courtly bow and a not so courtly leer, before heading for the door. She took up her tray and walked to the bar. Simon finished the last bars of "S'Wonderful", ignored the smattering of applause and walked over to her.

She was waiting for an order to be filled when Simon gripped her by the arm and forced her to turn toward him. "What was that all about?"

Her eyes were cold, and she wrested her arm from his grip. She turned away and grabbed her tray. "Thanks, Charlie," she said, and moved back into the crowd without giving Simon another glance.

He grunted in aggravation and ran a hand through his hair. What did she think she was playing at? They knew King was dangerous. Why didn't she just go and play in traffic, for God's sake?

"You all right, Professor?" Charlie asked as he served up a particularly vile smelling concoction.

Simon gave a terse laugh. "Fine."

"Sorry about King. Fancies himself a real cake eater."

"I'm sorry?"

"Ya know, good with the ladies."

"Really?" Simon said, unimpressed. "And I suppose fraternizing with the clientele is part of Elizabeth's job."

Charlie frowned. "It ain't like that. When King wants to talk, ya talk." He put down his dishrag and leaned against the bar. "I don't know what you did, Professor. But if I were you, I'd fix it."

"I don't know what you mean," Simon said, bristling.

Charlie shrugged. "I'm just sayin' flowers might not be a bad idea."

"I don't remember asking you for advice on our relationship. I'm fairly certain it's none of your business."

Charlie's kind eyes grew hard. "Anything affects the club is my business."

Simon cocked his head to the side in challenge. "If you have a point, I suggest you get to it."

Charlie sighed. "Look, I like ya. Well, I like Lizzy; you're a pain in the ass. But Lizzy likes ya, so you can't be all bad."

"Thank you," Simon said dryly.

"Alls I'm sayin' is: men, we mess up. Don't always know why, but I know one thing. You got a good thing in Lizzy. Do what you gotta do. Cause trust me, there's always somethin' or somebody there waitin' to take it away from ya."

Simon nodded and turned to watch Elizabeth. If Charlie only knew how true that was.

Back at the apartment, Elizabeth kept her distance and her silence. They hadn't said more than two words since their brief contact in the bar. Simon continued to sleep in the chair. Nightmares plagued him. Awake or asleep, it didn't seem to matter. No matter how hard he tried, doubts crept in. He told himself time and again that he'd done the right thing. That he was sparing her, but the truth inched its way to the surface. He wasn't protecting her at all. It wasn't a matter of sparing her the infliction of his inevitable failure, it was something much simpler. Something far less noble.

She was right. He was afraid. Petrified actually. The idea of loving someone, of being loved in return frightened him beyond words.

His family had never been a source of comfort. The idea of the Crosses as a loving family was laughable. It seemed they shared one heart among them, and it had withered and died with his grandfather. The pain of that loss was so shocking, so final, so gruesome. Being a witness to death had taken the life out of Simon, as if a part of him died with his grandfather. The utter and complete desolation he felt was his alone to bear. The one person he'd loved, who'd loved him in return had died a horrible death. And even now, thirty years later, the scars were still fresh and the guilt still suffocating. The family, of course, had pretended it was an accident, a doddering old man falling down the stairs. They concocted ridiculous stories to save their precious reputation. It wouldn't do to have a member of the family die under mysterious circumstances. Mundane death was so much more palatable.

Sebastian was a slight on the family name in life, and nothing changed that in death. He was swept away from sight, another skeleton to hide in the family closet. Simon did his best to crawl in after him, to hide in the darkness. Even his life's work was best suited to the shadows. The few times he'd let someone in had ended badly. More often than not, he'd ended the relationships before they could begin. Then Elizabeth had come into his life. All the walls he'd built were slowly being worn away. Until now, when the cracks became fissures, and the walls started to crumble. He could feel the past repeating itself. Was he strong enough to face it all again? Or could he change his destiny?

The things that had once defined him, detachment and control, lay in rubble at his feet. She'd given him the chance to live again, and he'd thrown it in her face. Judging from the way she'd treated him since, she wasn't about to forgive him. Not that he deserved her forgiveness. Or would even know what to do with it if it were given. Not much to worry about there either; she would be gone in the morning, just as she had been every morning since Coney Island. Yet, somehow, hope flickered in his chest, refusing to be snuffed out completely.

Knowing Charlie's was the only place he'd see her, Simon went in early. The bar was eerily quiet. Empty tables, empty chairs: the perfect place for an empty man. Charlie was putting a new picture of Lillian Gish on the wall behind the bar. He straightened the corners and stood back to admire his work.

"Pretty little thing, ain't she?"

"Hmm? Oh, I suppose," Simon said, as he took a seat on one of the wooden stools. He'd never felt so at sixes and sevens; a bleak future ahead, and nothing but mistakes behind him.

Charlie shook his head and pulled out the bottle of Glenlivet from behind the counter. "You got it bad," he said and set-up two cups. "Lizzy still givin' ya the cold shoulder?"

Simon's frown was answer enough, and Charlie nodded in commiseration. "Want a snort? Cure what ails ya?"

Simon desperately wanted a drink, but feared he wouldn't be able to stop with just one. "I don't think that's wise."

Charlie opened the bottle and poured the drinks. "Naw, probably not." He slid one cup across the wooden counter to Simon. "Sometimes wise ain't all it's cracked up to be."

Simon laughed and took the cup, but he didn't drink. Charlie raised his cup in toast. "Here's mud in yer eye."

Simon breathed in the scent, letting it fill his lungs with pungent warmth before taking a sip. "quite good."

Charlie nodded and stared down into his empty cup. His usually jovial face was lined with worry. "You try the flowers?"

"I think we're well beyond that," Simon said, surprised at his willingness to talk to the man, but he felt too tired to fight it anymore.

"I know you don't want me stickin' my nose in, but bein' alone ain't good for no man."

Charlie's wide shoulders seemed bowed under some unseen pressure. He looked at Simon with unaccustomed passion, a ghost of pain floating in his eyes. Simon knew the look. He'd seen it often enough in the mirror. "Who was she?"

Charlie's meaty face wrinkled in a mixture of chagrin and sorrow. "Mary. She was beautiful, my Mary." He poured another drink and looked down into the cup, his eyes dreamy and distant. "Seems like yesterday."

Charlie closed his eyes for a moment and smiled ruefully. "A real looker. And a sweeter girl you never will find. Met her in the park. Saw her walking with her sister, real pinched-face sort of broad. Just made Mary look even prettier. Not that she needed the help."

He stopped for a moment, poured another and took a deep drink of the Scotch. "Minute I laid eyes on her, I knew she was the girl for me. Crazy, huh?"

Simon shook his head, remembering the first day he'd seen Elizabeth. She was a student in his class then and had the gall to interrupt his lecture. She raised her hand and challenged his theory on the motivational hunger of lycanthropics. He was annoyed at the disruption and impressed with her audacity. But it wasn't her question that lingered in his mind later that day. It was the sound of her voice, the tilt of her head, the fire in her eyes.

"Anyway," Charlie continued, breaking Simon from his reminiscence. "I walked right over to her and introduced myself. Tipped my hat and said, name's Charlie Blue and I think I love you."

Simon grinned in spite of himself.

Charlie laughed and reddened at the memory of his boldness. "I know, but ya say some pretty stupid stuff when you're in love. She laughed at me, but I was a cocky son of a gun and didn't give up. She said it was improper for her to talk to a man she hadn't been introduced to. See? Her sister piped up that no matter what, it wouldn't be proper for her to be talking with the likes of me, but Mary, she had this look in her eyes. They were brown, but there were these little red flecks in 'em. Sorta like cinnamon. Then she, I'll never forget, she asked me if I knew anyone in the park. Told her I knew the cop over on the southeast corner. Course, I didn't tell her how I knew him," he added with a wink.

"Luck was on my side that day. She knew the fella too. God bless him, old Pete the cop, never let on and gave us the proper how do ya do's. Her sister was ready to pop a button, but sweet Mary," he said, his eyes glazing over at the memory. "Well, from that moment on, I couldn't think of nothin' else, but her. It was like a fever, ya know? A wonderful fever."

Charlie started to take another drink, but his cup was empty, and he set it aside. "I courted her best I could. She was from a good family. You know, the kind that lives so high up they can't see nothin' without lookin' down their noses. Me, I was a regular Joe, but Mary, she made me feel special. Like me, Charlie Blue, was somebody."

Simon knew the feeling, the way Elizabeth had looked when he gave her the stuffed tiger—like he was the only man in the world.

Charlie looked at the bottle for a moment, then pushed it aside with the back of his hand. "One day, we hadn't seen each other for a week. We're supposed to meet, and she don't show. That's not her, so I get worried. I go round to her house, and her mother tells me she won't be seeing me no more. Seems she's found another fella. Somebody who could give her the things I couldn't, I guess." His voice couldn't hide the bitterness, even after all the years.

"I didn't believe it at first. Not my Mary. So, I went back the next day and told 'em I wasn't leavin' till she told me face to face."

Charlie shook his head, and his eyes misted over. "I was such a God damn fool. She came down and stood behind the screen door. Looked me in the eye and told me it was over."

Simon remembered all too well the expression on Elizabeth's face when she told him she was moving out. An ending before a beginning.

Charlie's brawny hands clenched around the empty cup. "I was so angry, I couldn't see straight. Didn't see straight. Didn't see what was right in front of me. She was thin. Too thin. And so pale. But I didn't see it. All I saw was red." He laughed bitterly. "Last time I saw her, and I didn't even really see her."

Simon fought down the panic that welled inside his chest.

Charlie sighed heavily and played with the frayed ends of his bar rag. "Got a letter from her sister 'bout two months later. Mary had the influenza and...died. Didn't want me to know. Didn't want me to watch it happen."

The desperation Simon had felt during his nightmare prickled at his skin. Watching Elizabeth die.

Charlie nodded slowly, once again resigned to his fate. "I woulda taken those two months over the nothin' I got any day. I shoulda kept on tryin'. Never be another Mary. Not for me."

"I'm sorry."

"Eleven years ago. Coulda been yesterday." He looked up from the tattered edges of the rag and made sure he caught Simon's eye. "You're a lucky man, Professor. You've got your Mary. Don't let her go."

Simon nodded thoughtfully and drank the last of his Scotch. Elizabeth wasn't his to lose. Or was she? The real question was, did he have the courage to find out?

Elizabeth gave Simon a wide berth all night. A few times he made tacit overtures; a gaze that lingered a moment too long, the beginnings of an unsure smile, and he even stuttered something about her hair. If she didn't know better, she might let herself believe he was feeling contrite. But this was Simon Cross after all. The same man who'd just two nights before rejected and humiliated her. The same man who had nothing more to say than that he was sorry.

She'd fooled herself into believing he was something he wasn't and paid the price. Working at Charlie's used to be fun, but now it was all she could do to keep a smile plastered on her face for the customers. It wasn't bad enough that she had to work with him all night, but the walk home was unbearable. Once they were in the room, she could crawl into bed, hide in the darkness. But the silence and awkwardness of walking home on the deserted streets was strangely too intimate.

Tonight she was lucky, it was bank night. Growing up around pool halls and race tracks, Elizabeth knew what that really meant. Banks, the kind Charlie and some of her father's friends used, were no more than glorified bookies. A safe house to store your cash. The locations changed to keep the bad guys and the feds guessing. It was a risky way to handle money, but when you made your living under the table, it came with the territory.

If she could make the run with Lester the bouncer, then he could walk her on to the apartment, and she could avoid the death march with Simon. It was a good plan. Of course, convincing Charlie wasn't so easy. He rejected the idea at first. He wasn't too crazy about letting her go to the safe house. Guns, money, and a pretty girl—nothing good ever came out of that mix. She promised to stay out of the way, but he wouldn't budge. When she pushed out her lower lip in her patented pout, his resolve began to weaken. She knew it was dirty pool, using her feminine wiles, but what good were wiles unless you used them now and again? Finally, Charlie agreed, the old softie, but only if she did everything Lester told her.

For his part, Simon accepted her announcement with resignation. She'd expected a lecture, or, at the very least a disapproving glare. He simply nodded and asked her to be careful. With one last significant look at Lester, he left to walk home alone. For a brief second, Elizabeth wanted to go after him, but thankfully the moment of madness passed.

Once the money was bundled, she and Lester started out. The strain of the last few days was finally beginning to hit her, and she was more than grateful that Lester was a man of few words. They walked quietly along the empty streets. The sound of their footsteps and the occasional clatter of a milk horse cart were the only noises to disturb the night and her thoughts. Had it been her imagination or was Simon less Simony tonight? He seemed distracted and softer around the edges somehow.

She shook her head and walked a little faster. No. She was not going to fall for it again. She'd take the little, shreddy remnants of her heart and move on. She was moving on. Definitely, moving on.

If he wanted to apologize, really apologize, he'd had ample opportunity. Well, maybe not ample. She'd been gone each morning before he woke up, ignored him at the club, and didn't talk to him at home. But if he really wanted to, he'd have found a way. So, clearly, he didn't want to. He liked it the way it was. Her suffering and burning in the hell of abject despair was obviously the way he wanted things.

And that was fine by her. Not the suffering, she could definitely do without that part, but she didn't need him. She was a rock. She was an island. And channeling Simon and Garfunkel was never a good sign.

She sighed so heavily, Lester actually spoke. "You okay, Lizzy?"

"Yeah. Just thinking."

"Ah," he said and nodded sagely. "Gotcha."

"We almost there?"

"Yeah, it's just—" Lester stopped walking and grabbed Elizabeth's arm. He cocked his big, bald head to the side.

"What is it?" she asked anxiously. His sausage-sized fingers dug into her arm.

"We're bein'—"

The figures came out of the darkness too fast for either of them to react. A pair of iron hands clamped onto her arms, pulled her out of Lester's grip and tossed her into the shadows of the alley.

Chapter Sixteen

THE BRIGHT MOON CAST its silvery light through the thin curtains. Simon sat in his chair, his personal prison, and waited. The minutes dragged on and still Elizabeth wasn't home. The streets below were empty and still. The only sound piercing the night was the clatter of an old-fashioned milk cart, the horse's hooves beat out an unnatural cadence in the city night.

Simon pulled back the curtain and looked down into the darkness, willing her slender silhouette to walk down the sidewalk. Not a soul was there. Slumping back into his chair, he absently felt for the gold watch in his pocket. The feel of the etched case under his fingers wasn't as calming as it had been a few short days ago.

He took a deep breath and tried to content himself with waiting. As the minutes grew into an hour, an uneasy sense of foreboding welled deep inside him. He should have protested her accompanying Lester on Charlie's errand, but he knew it would have fallen on deaf ears, or worse yet, driven her further away.

He'd been an absolute fool. He'd pushed her away and then idiotically wondered where she went. He should have gone after her tonight. The niggling voice in the back of his mind whispered his darkest fears. Was tonight the night his nightmares became reality?

The room was empty without her. He was empty without her. He should have laid his heart out for her, but he'd run away. Simon pushed the chair back and stood. Time to bloody well stop running.

He retraced the path he'd taken home—up Market Street and down Madison. He vaguely thought of calling Charlie at the bar, when he realized pay phones weren't commonplace in the twenties. He rounded a corner when he heard a voice filtering up the street. He stopped for a moment and listened. There it was again. He crossed Madison and the sounds grew more distinct—a low guttural moan and a higher voice talking in hurried, anxious tones. His long legs quickened their stride and came to a sudden stop at the mouth of an alley.

Lester lay on his back, and the small huddled form of Elizabeth bent over him.

"Dear God," Simon choked out.

Elizabeth swung her head around at the sound. Her eyes were wide with fear and a trickle of blood on her forehead stood out in stark contrast to her pale skin.

"Simon," she gasped in relief. "How did you..." Her voice trailed off, and her expression changed. Her eyes hardened. "What are you doing here?" she asked and turned back to Lester, who moaned and tried to lift his head. "It's all right, Les."

Simon managed to get his legs to move again. It was all he could do not to take her into his arms. He knelt down next to her and tried to slow his thundering heart. "You're hurt. What happened?"

Ignoring him, she gently touched the side of Lester's face, below the growing knot on his forehead. "How do you feel?"

"Like I went twenty with Sullivan," he croaked.

He reached for his breast pocket and his thick brow furrowed when he found it empty. "Damn. You okay, Lizzy?"

"Of course, she's not," Simon barked. "Look at her."

She glared at Simon before smiling back down at Lester. "I'm okay."

"What happened?" Simon asked, as she raised a shaky hand to her ashen face. She wasn't all right, and he damn well wished she'd stop pretending she was. He helped Lester push himself into a sitting position, but his eyes never left Elizabeth.

"Old-fashioned mugging," she said in a tremulous voice that belied the flippancy of her words.

Simon's heart took another step into his throat as images of Elizabeth being thrown against the hard, brick wall flashed through his mind. "Mugged?"

"Naw, they musta followed us," Lester said.

"Followed you?" Simon asked.

"Musta known about the deposit," Lester said as he tentatively felt the mouse growing on his forehead. "Charlie's gonna skin me alive."

Elizabeth put a comforting hand on his arm. "Money can be replaced."

Lester laughed and then winced in regret. "Not this money, but I was talkin' bout you. Charlie made me promise six days to Sunday I'd look out for ya."

Simon bit back the derisive comment that rolled on his tongue. He was in no position to cast stones; his glass house had shattered days ago.

Lester leaned against the wall and managed to stand up. "You sure you're okay?"

"I'm fine," she said and ignored Simon's offer of help as she got to her feet.

Lester shook his head and sighed. "Guess I better go face the music." He looked at Simon and his dull eyes glinted in the lamplight. "You take care of her?"

Simon didn't trust his voice and simply nodded.

Elizabeth took a shaky step toward the street. "We'll walk you back."

Simon was at her side in a moment and held her elbow for support. Whether she liked it or not, he was going to help her.

"Hell no," Lester said. "It's gonna be bad enough without him seein' ya like that. I really am sorry, Lizzy. They came outta nowhere."

"It's okay."

"It ain't, but thanks," he said sheepishly. Lester shook his head once to clear it and started down the street mumbling to himself.

"We should follow him," she said, taking an unsteady step forward.

Simon gripped her arm more tightly and shook his head. "He'll be all right."

"He was out for too long," she said. "I should—"

"Would you stop! Just stop for one moment and let me take care of you!"

She stared at him for a long moment in obvious shock. He saw a flicker of vulnerability cross her eyes, but she pushed it away. He'd seen it though, and it gave him hope. "Please," he said softly. "Let me take you home."

"Home," she said, and a near hysterical burst of laughter bubbled out of her throat. She glanced nervously around the darkened alley, and he felt her arm began to tremble. The trauma of the night finally caught up with her.

"Elizabeth," Simon said.

She looked up at him, eyes bordering on tears.

He slipped an arm around her back, and she nodded numbly.

Once they were safely back in the apartment, Simon maneuvered her to the bed and piled pillows behind her. "I'll get a cloth," he said and disappeared into the bathroom.

His hands shook as he turned on the cold tap. He glanced into the bedroom to reassure himself she was still there. She was, but it didn't calm his pounding heart. He wet a washcloth and hurried back into the bedroom.

Elizabeth's head was tilted back against the headboard, her eyes closed. His heart clenched again. He'd come so close to losing her. He dragged a chair to the bedside, the sodden rag dripping in his hand as he leaned forward. "Do you need to go to hospital?"

Elizabeth opened her eyes and shook head slowly. "Not that bad," she said and reached up to touch her forehead.

"Let me," he said, holding out the cloth. "Are you going to tell me what happened?"

"Mugged," she said stonily. It was her turn to put up a wall. Was this what it felt like to be on the other side? Is this how she felt every time he shut her out?

"They grabbed me," she continued, closing her eyes briefly. "And I hit my head. I think I saw them. I'm not sure. It's all a little fuzzy."

"It's all right," he said, then held up the washcloth. "May I?"

She nodded and watched him warily, but he made sure to be gentle as he probed the wound. The cut was nestled below her hairline. It wasn't very big, and the blood was already starting to congeal. He carefully wiped away the few dark, crimson lines that streaked her face. She hissed in a quick breath when he touched a particularly sore spot.

He pulled his hands away quickly. "Sorry."

"Doesn't matter," she said.

Simon rested his elbows on his knees and looked down at the soiled carpet at his feet. It did matter. If he could only find a way to tell her just how much. "I am sorry."

"You already said that." Her voice was bitter and harsh. The tone, even more than the words, struck a cord in him. Wounded and lashing out. And it was all his doing.

"I don't mean..." he said and sighed in frustration. He simply couldn't remain seated. He stood and walked to the far side of the room, tossing the bloody cloth onto the table. "I'm a fool."

Elizabeth folded her arms over her chest. "Go on."

"You have every reason in the world to hate me," he said hoarsely. When she didn't deny it, he felt his resolve weaken. There were so many things he wanted to say, needed to say, but he couldn't find the words. He touched the back of his chair by the window and nearly fled into the safe confines of lonely misery it provided. The little, wooden chair had come to symbolize his retreat from life. Twice, he'd sought refuge there, hiding from his emotions, but it was a lost cause.

Closing his eyes, the images from his nightmare flashed before him. He remembered the desolation he'd felt at the end of each dream, the unspeakable torment of watching her die. He'd never been more frightened in his life. Until tonight.

"I understand if you choose not to forgive me," he said slowly, unable to look at her. "I behaved abominably. It was a mistake."

"You said that too."

Simon turned to look at her, letting her rebuke find its mark. He nodded in acceptance and started to pace. Words drifted just beyond his reach, and he moved more quickly in a futile attempt to capture them.

"I've never been good at expressing my feelings and, bloody hell, why should it be different now?" he said with exasperation. "No matter what I do, I can't get a moment's rest from thinking about you. You're always there. Did you know that?" he said, accusing her. He put his fists on his hips and sighed. "Of course you didn't. How would you? I could barely admit it to myself. Deny and rationalize. I'm a master at that, you know. Finding ways to mine misery out of pleasure."

She moved to sit on the edge of the bed, her hand fleetingly going to her forehead. "What is it you want, Simon? You want me to feel sorry for you? Doesn't sound like you need my help for that."

"That isn't what I want."

"Then you better start saying what you want because I don't have any idea. You're scared. Who isn't? You think I'm not? You think I wasn't terrified tonight when..." Her voice trailed off and she clasped her hands in her lap. "If all this is about asking my forgiveness, we can cut to the chase. Consider yourself forgiven, and we can forget this ever happened."

"I can't forget. And I don't want to."

"So far this week is pretty high on my things to forget list. It's not exactly filled with picture postcard memories."

"I take full responsibility for—"

"Would you stop that," she said, jumping to her feet and fighting for balance. "Not everything is about you. It's so convenient to take too much on your shoulders, isn't it? So when you collapse under the weight no one can blame you."

He whirled around to face her. "Do you think I wanted this? Do you think I wanted to hurt you?"

"The results speak for themselves."

"No they don't. The last thing in the world I wanted to do was hurt you. When you kissed me, I...I panicked. I'm not proud of it and I'm not trying to make excuses. You said that I'm a selfish man. Perhaps I am. For wanting things I can't have," he said and let out a deep breath, "for wanting you."

He stood there, raw and vulnerable for the longest moment of his life, before he turned away.

"Don't say that if you don't mean it," she said, her voice trembling.

"I've never meant anything more in my life," he said. "I don't expect you to understand. God knows, I don't. I've spent the better part of my life avoiding any sort of personal entanglement. But you, you're...unavoidable. I tried. You have no idea the hours I spent trying not to think about you. Trying not to imagine what it would be like to hold you in my arms."

He forced himself to look into her eyes. "You absolutely terrify me. Whenever I'm with you it's as though someone has reached inside my chest, until the pain is almost more than I can bear. And when I'm not with you, I'd give anything to feel that way again."

He heaved a deep sigh and continued. "Tonight when I saw you in the alley... I...No, it was before that. I know it doesn't matter. I know you can't possibly return my feelings after the way I've treated you," he said and felt his courage failing. He turned away, unable to bear the rejection he knew he'd see in her face. "But I...I couldn't go another day as I was."

The silence was oppressive. Slowly, he eased back around to face her. Her small hands were clenched tightly at her sides, eyes pleading. She was trying so hard to be strong, defying him to hurt her again.

"And who are you now?" she asked.

"A man hopelessly in love with you."

She closed the space between them, and his heart raced with each step. She stopped a few feet away and then slowly, beautifully, a smile came to her face. "Nice to meet you."

If he could only stop time, he would lock this moment away for eternity. Tentatively, he lifted his hand to her cheek, barely a caress, and gently pushed a stray lock of hair away from her face. He searched her eyes for any sign of resistance, but she leaned into his touch. Emboldened, he loosely cupped her face with the palm of his hand. He moved slowly, giving her every chance to pull away.

His lips met hers in a tender kiss. Her hands came to rest on his chest and for a fleeting moment he feared she'd push him away, but her fingers curled into the fabric of his shirt and pulled him closer.

Simon brought his other hand to her face, trying to convey his love and desire in every touch, to show her how precious she was to him. Finally, he could let himself out and let Elizabeth in. A world he'd only imagined, one he'd feared to even dream of, was born before his eyes. The impossible and unreachable had fallen into his hands. His heart still ached, but it was a sweet, beautiful pain.

Somewhere in his life he'd lost his way and now he'd found it again in her kiss. A piece of a puzzle he didn't know was missing slid into place. Supple lips pressed against his, caution forgotten in the sublime feel of her mouth upon his. Tentative at first, the kiss flourished with passion. He felt her nimble fingers brush against his throat and then move down his chest to unbutton his shirt. He wanted this so badly, wanted her more than he thought possible, but the last shreds of coherent thought clung to his brain. He had to be sure she wanted him. This had to be her decision. He pulled back breathlessly and looked at her. As much as it frightened him, she was the one in control.

Elizabeth's smile faltered. Afraid she might think he was pushing her away again, he gently ran his hands along her arms and took her hands in his. "Are you sure?" he asked.

Her smile blossomed again; the love he'd been denying himself shone back. How had he possibly survived without it? Now that it was his, it was as much a part of him as breathing, and he would never let it go.

She caressed his cheek, and then kissed him, more demanding than before. Her hands slid from his face and moved back to the buttons of his shirt. She worked her way down to his belt and rucked the fabric up from his waistband, then tugged on his undershirt. Reluctantly, he moved away from her kiss and pulled the shirt over his head and tossed it aside.

Elizabeth's eyes, dark with passion, swept over his body and he watched as she took him in. She hadn't turned away, she didn't leave him as he so deserved. Instead, she laid her palm flat against his skin, feeling the beating of his heart.

A maelstrom of emotion swept over him. He felt himself falling again, and knew this time there was no turning away. She loved him. As unthinkable as it was, one look in her eyes told him a world of truths.

Her hand slowly slid down his chest and stopped at his sharp intake of breath. With an intoxicating half-smile, she pulled away and began to undo the buttons of her dress.

His hands caught hers, and she looked into his eyes. Silently, he asked permission, and she let her arms fall to her sides, offering herself.

Without taking his eyes from hers, he unbuttoned her dress, his long fingers trembling. The thin, cotton dress fell open. The lace of her bra peaked out from behind the edges of the fabric and begged for his touch. He reined in the impulse, wanting to take this as slowly as possible, to savor each moment as it was given.

He brushed the tips of his fingers along her collarbone, easing her dress from her shoulders. Leaning forward, he lifted her hair away from her neck and kissed the sensitive skin at the nape.

She rolled her head to the side, allowing him to work his way along her neck and down again to her shoulder. With each kiss his need for her grew.

His hands slid down her sides and came to rest on her waist, gently pulling her body to his, until his hardness pulsed against her belly.

She sighed and he moved away slightly, shifting from one shoulder to the other. He nudged the dress further off her body. It slipped completely off and pooled at her feet.

She ducked her head in embarrassment. Was it possible she didn't know how attractive she was? Touching her cheek, he urged her to lift her eyes. If she doubted before, she never would again. As long as he had breath in his body, she would know how beautiful she was. "And even the angels were jealous."

Her skin blushed a bright red that rose from her cheeks and traveled deliciously down her chest. His eyes followed the path in a loving touch.

Emboldened, she stepped forward and ran her hands down over his quivering stomach muscles, finally working at the clasp of his belt. Simon grasped her waist, his hands nearly large enough to encircle her, and trailed his fingers up her sides, stopping just shy of the swell of her breasts. His thumbs slipped over the lace and he felt her nipples tighten in response. Each time she inhaled, her breasts brushed harder against his fingers. A deep, groan rumbled in his chest, and she stopped pulling on his belt.

Flicking the front clasp of her bra, he eased the straps off her shoulders, and her breasts were laid bare for his touch. It was too much to resist, and he cupped her in his hands. The hard tips of her nipples rubbed against his palms as he tenderly caressed the supple flesh.

Elizabeth closed her eyes and tilted back her head. Dear God, she was beautiful. After a moment, she opened her eyes, the shyness long gone, and took hold of one of his hands. Slowly, she urged him back toward the bed, slipping off her shoes as she walked.

Simon stood by the bed and watched as she lay down, reaching out for him to join her. He knew in that moment, he'd follow her anywhere, and without question to the heaven she offered now. He stretched his body out next to hers, lost in the smoky haze of her eyes, of her lips, swollen and moist. He leaned down to take them in a kiss, his hips pressing against her side, as he felt her hands run along his back, urging him closer still.

Trailing kisses down her neck, he stopped to suckle the heated skin above her pulse point. Licking and tasting every inch, he slowly made his way down her neck until he reached her breasts, soft and round, topped with dark pink. He kissed the valley between them. One hand moved to brush the underside of one, as his mouth descended on the other. How could something be so soft, so absolutely perfect? She fit into the palm of his hand as if God had designed it be so. The taste of her grew more exquisite with each kiss.

Her hips rose and rubbed against the thigh he had nestled between hers. He looked up into her eyes and found he wanted nothing more than to pleasure her. It surprised and shamed him. He'd never truly thought of his partner's wants before. He'd seen to their needs only to expedite his own. It was a painful truth to realize what a selfish lover he'd been. With Elizabeth, everything, things he hadn't even begun to realize, changed. He could be content to please her, could spend a lifetime doing it and it wouldn't be enough.

Simon eased himself down the bed and moved between her thighs. He kissed the juncture of her hip and smoothed his hand across the soft swell of her belly. Smelling the musky scent of her arousal forced him to push his own hips down into the mattress.

Slipping a finger under the elastic of her waistband, he looked up the bed for permission. Her soft moan answered him, and she raised her hips. His fingers caressed her legs as he slowly pulled her panties down and set them aside. He wanted so much to bury himself inside her, to find his own release, but more than that, he wanted to please her.

With one last look at her flushed face, he settled his elbows on either side of her thighs and ran his hands over her stomach. Her muscles quivered at his touch, and he felt a thrill knowing she wanted this as much as he did. He dipped his head down and tasted her for the first time. Her sharp intake of breath urged him on and he lapped gently at the moist warmth between her legs, licking and suckling until he felt her legs tense. He quickened his pace, drinking deeper. Her breath came faster, growing more ragged with each passing second. He gentled his movements and then watched in rapture as she pushed her head back into the pillow, her mouth open in a silent cry of pleasure.

He kissed the soft skin of her inner thigh as she came back down. Once he was sure she was ready, he slipped a finger inside her, then another.

"Again," he whispered, a gentle urging bringing them both that much closer to the edge.

She cried out and he nearly lost himself as her body spasmed. With another gentle kiss, he eased himself back up her body. His erection tight in the confines of his clothes, rubbed against her body.

She opened her eyes, still blurry from her release. How many times he'd dreamt of that look, of being the man that brought her over the brink. She lifted a weak hand and ran her fingers through the hair at the back of his neck. He took her mouth in a passionate kiss, pressing himself more tightly against her heated body.

Elizabeth's hands fluttered down his back and slipped inside the waistband of his pants. She tugged at his hips, and he shifted away slightly. Her hands moved between them and molded over him. His arousal jumped, and he stifled a groan.

Simon shook his head. "I'm afraid it will all be over too quickly if you do that," he rasped, and rolled to the side, quickly shedding the rest of his clothes.

He smoothed his body against hers, the first unfettered touch. He closed his eyes and fought for control. Just the feeling of her was enough to push him over the edge. But he needed her so much more than that. It wasn't her body giving him pleasure. It was fire to a cold a heart, life to an empty soul.

He moved his body over hers, until he was resting just above her. Any fears he had were allayed in her kiss. She pulled him to her and with one smooth motion he slipped inside her.

The feeling was such unimaginable bliss, he had to stop. He savored the feel of her surrounding him, body and soul. Burying his forehead in the crook of her neck, he tried to slow his breathing. God, she was perfection. A fleeting sense of sadness swept over him. He knew he'd never feel this whole, this complete again.

Her hands ran down his back, and he lifted his head. Her eyes were soulful and so achingly beautiful. The words came out as naturally as their bodies fit together.

"I love you," he whispered and then took her mouth in a tender kiss.

She shifted her hips, and he pulled out slightly before thrusting back slowly. Each movement drew them both closer to the brink. He wanted it to last, for this moment to last forever, but each time he pulled away, her body drew him back deeper, until he was drowning inside her soul. He felt her begin to pulse around him and with one final thrust he lost himself.

After a long moment, the world slowly coalesced and he nuzzled her cheek.

"Elizabeth," he whispered.

"I love you, Simon," she said, still breathless from their lovemaking.

He kissed her tenderly, humbled by her words. He was sure he wasn't worthy, but he'd spend the rest of his life trying to be.

Gently, he eased off to the side and pulled her into his arms. She rested her hand above his heart. Such a small hand held everything he was.

The bright hues of dawn's first light filtered through the window. He held her as she drifted off to sleep and prayed when he woke, that it all wasn't a dream.

CHAPTER SEVENTEEN

.

ELIZABETH AWOKE TO THE feel of warm skin, hard muscle and a distinctly male scent. Simon. He'd been so tender, so unsure. She could remember the moment the shutters of his eyes opened. How hard it must have been for him to lay bare everything he'd kept so carefully hidden. The way he'd looked at her, waiting for the rejection, and the surprise when she touched him.

She could feel his arm around her, strong and loving, and nuzzled her cheek into the crook of his shoulder. The lump on her forehead reminded her of last night's other activities, but any pain was lost in the feeling of being in his arms. The thin sheet was pooled around his waist, and her hand rested against the bare skin of his chest. A soft sprinkling of hair tickled her palm, and she slid her hand across the muscles to the dark coppery skin of his nipple.

Simon cleared his throat. "Good morning."

Elizabeth smiled at the formality in his voice. Even with a naked woman in his arms, he was still Professor Cross. She knew Simon was in there somewhere, he just needed a little coaxing. Her fingers drifted down his ribs to his abdomen. He sighed, almost sadly, and she pushed herself up onto one elbow. He was watching her carefully, bemused but apprehensive.

"Good morning yourself," she said and dropped a kiss onto his chest.

His hand touched her shoulder tentatively and his eyes fell away from hers. "How do you feel?"

Nervous as hell. "Wonderful."

He smiled, but still his eyes didn't meet hers. She gently eased his face back to hers and kissed him reassuringly. When she pulled away, his expression was still troubled. He pushed a lock of hair behind her ear, and his eyes fell on the bruise on her forehead. He sighed and closed his eyes for a moment. When he looked at her again, his brow creased and she could see it was difficult for him not to look away again. "About last night..."

Her body tensed and he quickly shook his head. "Not that."

"If you're worried about birth control, I've got that covered."

"Dear Lord. I hadn't even thought of that," he said, clearly appalled at his lack of foresight.

"We did have a lot on our minds."

He relaxed a little and nodded. "I just wanted to..." he said and then shook his head again. "Thank you."

Elizabeth laughed in relief. "If I remember correctly, I should be thanking you."

Simon chuckled and she could feel the rumbling in his chest beneath her. "I'm fairly certain I don't deserve you."

"Why don't you let me be the judge of that."

A trace of a smile lifted his lips. "And if your judgment's impaired?"

"I guess you'll just have to trust me."

He paused and nodded slightly. A nearly imperceptible movement acknowledged something so profound. His long fingers brushed the hair away from her face and trailed down her cheek.

She leaned into his touch and settled herself more comfortably. "And how do you feel?"

He smiled for a moment, but then something else won out and he looked up at the ceiling, letting out a long breath. "Like I'm on top of the bloody world."

She could hear the tremor in his voice. "And about to fall off?"

Simon's eyes flicked back to hers, seemingly surprised and a little embarrassed by her insight.

Elizabeth shook her head. "Not gonna happen."

"You seem terribly sure."

She arched an eyebrow and slipped her body onto his. "I like it on top."

Charlie hadn't stopped grinning all night. Only when Elizabeth mentioned the mugging had his expression faltered. He shrugged off her concern over the money with a wave of his hand. She was all right, and that was all that mattered. The club was doing a land office business, but Elizabeth had a feeling his ear-to-ear smile was something a bit more personal.

"You look like the cat that ate the canary," she said, as she waited for another order to be filled.

He shrugged innocently. "Just a happy man."

She saw his eyes dart over to Simon and his smile broaden even further. She fought the urge to giggle. Charlie, the two hundred pound cupid.

However it had happened, she was grateful. Was it only yesterday she stood in this very same spot and thought her world had come crashing down? She looked across the bar at Simon. He really did play beautifully. She couldn't see his hands, but could imagine the way they moved across the keys with sensual grace. She grinned to herself, remembering how they'd moved across her body that morning.

The warmth of the memory and the velvety melody of "Someone to Watch Over Me" lulled her into a pleasant haze. She didn't notice the hushed voices and the newborn tension in the room until King was standing at her side.

"Penny for your thoughts," he said in a voice smoother than silk. "Although, I'm sure they're worth much more."

She tried not to let her fluster show and busied herself with rearranging the nearly empty tray. "Mr. Kashian."

"King."

She nodded once. "What brings you here again?"

His dark eyes flashed with something almost preternatural, but he schooled himself quickly. "A little business," he said and then moved ever so slightly closer. "And perhaps a little pleasure."

She tried not to shiver. She was used to space invaders, people who infringed on your personal bubble, but King was something else entirely. It wasn't simply the fact he was a gangster, although she knew that should have been more than reason enough. It was that something in his eyes. Some mysteries are better left unsolved, a tiny voice told her. For once, she listened.

"I hope you have an enjoyable evening," she said with as much finality as she could muster.

King merely smiled, and she was saved from any more conversation when Charlie appeared with her drink order.

"Here ya go, Lizzy."

She took the tray, but couldn't help one last glance at King. Expecting his usual entitled, insouciant expression, she was surprised to find a tinge of sadness and even a glimmer of uncertainty.

She was about to leave when she noticed her order wasn't complete. Damn. "I need another Scat, Charlie."

"Right, sorry."

King shifted his shoulders and rested his gloved hands on the bar. "We have business matters to discuss, Charles."

The bottle of whiskey trembled in Charlie's hand. "Yeah?"

"Nothing to worry about really. The local police department will be paying you a visit tomorrow."

Charlie's face blanched. "A raid? You sure?"

King snorted derisively. "I assure you, my sources are never wrong."

"I didn't mean—"

King waved him off impatiently. "You'll close tomorrow."

Charlie had completely forgotten about the drink order. "Right."

King fastidiously tugged at his kid gloves. "The situation is an aberration. An error in someone's judgment," he added darkly. "It won't happen again."

The cold resolve in his voice reminded Elizabeth exactly why she should avoid this man. He turned to her and bowed slightly, extending his hand. Reluctantly, she gave him hers. When he leaned down and kissed the back of her hand, she nearly gasped. His lips were ice cold.

His eyes fell on her wedding ring as he released her hand. "Mrs. Cross," he said, the enigmatic exterior once again fully in place.

Without another word, he gave her his back and left. Elizabeth was still recovering from the shock when she felt Simon come up behind her. Funny how she could feel his presence now without looking.

"That was quite a display," he said.

She turned around and did her best to push away the skin crawlies she felt lingering from King's touch. "He was just being theatrical," she said.

"That's one word for it," Simon said, shooting daggers at the door.

She placed her hand on his chest, and he covered it with his own before looking down. His face was clouded and he seemed to struggle for words. "I... I don't like his touching you."

"It didn't mean anything."

"To you perhaps. But it did to him and most assuredly to me."

Elizabeth felt a rush at his words. Proprietary and jealous. It was silly, but the threat he exuded made her feel safe.

She smoothed his lapel and leaned closer. "Do you know how sexy you are when you're jealous?"

"Elizabeth..."

"I can't help it," she said with a breathy sigh and whispered in his ear, "if I want you."

She felt his body surge closer to hers, his hands gripping her hips, even as his hands shook. "We're in public," he managed in a rough voice.

But he didn't pull away, as she slipped her arms around his neck. "But we have all day off tomorrow. Raid," she said and blew a soft breath onto the flushed skin of his neck. "Any ideas?"

He pulled back to see her face, and she felt a thrill at the passion in his eyes. "A few."

Heat flooded her body and she brushed a tempting kiss against his lips before leaving his embrace. She picked up her tray and looked back at him over her shoulder. "Only a few?"

"Dozen."

Tomorrow could not come soon enough.

They spent the next morning and an indecent part of the afternoon in bed. Simon would have gladly stayed where he was, but Elizabeth's growling stomach reminded him they hadn't eaten in nearly twenty hours. Truth be told, he needed a little sustenance himself.

He went out alone and found a small deli down the block and bought roast beef sandwiches, two bottles of some strange lemon cola and an afternoon paper. He'd only been gone fifteen minutes and already he missed her. How quickly he'd grown accustomed to having her by his side. It seemed that everything before her was merely an echo. Life was suddenly vibrant, colors sharper, the world alive around him. Even the people on the street seemed different, or perhaps he was only really seeing them for the first time. The smudge of newsprint on the paper boy's cheek. The apple vendor's stern concentration as he meticulously scrawled a new sign for his cart. The grin on a small girl's face as she was pulled down the sidewalk in a little red wagon. They'd all been there before, he simply hadn't bothered to notice. Simon tucked the newspaper under his arm and started back to the apartment.

When he returned, Elizabeth was still in bed, although she had gotten up long enough to put on one of his shirts. She looked absolutely adorable, sitting on the rumpled sheets, swimming inside his shirt. It was so oddly familiar, he had to remind himself this wasn't the way it had always been. A wave of nervousness coursed through him, suddenly far too self-aware. He forced himself to ignore it.

"Aren't you ever getting up?" he asked, as he set down the paper bag.

She pouted theatrically. "Don't wanna."

"Lunch is served."

"In that case," she said and walked over to the table. But she ignored the food and slipped her arms around his neck and kissed him. "I thought you were hungry?"

"Oh, I am. Starved," she said and insinuated her body against his. "Sex makes me hungry. And I'm very hungry."

"Elizabeth..."

With a grin she eased out of his arms and plopped down into a chair. "What'd ya get?"

"Cold sandwiches and warm soda, I'm afraid."

Elizabeth peered inside the bag. "Sounds good to me."

"And a paper," Simon said as he took his seat. "There is a whole city to explore, you know?"

"Bored with me already?"

Simon reached across the table and rubbed his thumb across the back of her hand. "Hardly. But as much as I'm loath to admit it, I'm not seventeen anymore."

"Could have fooled me," she said, and took an outrageously large bite from her sandwich.

He watched her devour her lunch. For such a small thing, she ate like a horse. He carefully unwrapped his sandwich and picked up the newspaper. Studiously ignoring the gory headline emblazoned across the front page, he flipped to the middle section. "I wonder what's playing at the Roxy."

Elizabeth giggled. "You're certainly getting into the spirit of things."

"Just swimming with the tide."

Simon skimmed the pages, waiting for something to catch his interest. "There's a new Marx Brothers movie," he said and peered around the edge of the paper. Elizabeth's expression stopped him cold. Her face had gone white. "What's wrong?"

Never taking her eyes from the paper, she took it from his hands and laid it down on the table.

"This...this man," she stuttered and pointed to the picture below the "Butchered!" headline. In grainy black and white, a man hung upside down in a butcher's window. Her fingers trembled as she turned the paper around. "I think he was one of them. One of the muggers."

"Are you sure?"

"No. I...It was dark and it happened so fast." She squinted at the picture. "I can't tell. Maybe."

Elizabeth read the lead of the article. "Drucker's Butcher Shop had more than its usual fare hanging in the window this morning—side of beef, pig and Dutch O'Banion."

She nervously rubbed her forehead just below the small cut at her hairline.

Simon felt his stomach clench. "Elizabeth?"

She startled and her eyes darted back and forth. "I think one of them called the one that grabbed me Dutch. I think."

"Try to remember."

Her eyes flashed to his. "I am," she sniped.

Simon took a deep breath and nodded. Of course, she was trying. But if that man was one of those who attacked her, they'd managed to become embroiled in something far greater than a mugging. Unerringly, his hand felt in his pocket for the watch.

"I don't know," she said and looked at the photograph. "God, this is sick. Who would do something like that?"

Simon moved his chair next to hers. He squeezed her hand and gave her a smile he didn't feel. "What does the article say?"

"In what looks to be the third in a trio of gangland slayings, a message has been sent. The bodies of Fish Brody and 'Mustache' Pete Arnold were found near the East River earlier in the day. Both had been seen frequenting clubs in the Lower East Side with none other than Dutch O'Banion."

She leaned in closer to the paper. "I wish I could see his face more clearly. Or maybe it's better I can't."

The photograph was blurry, but the gruesome details were clear enough. The gaunt man had been strung upside-down in the window like another side of beef. His mouth hung open, his blank eyes fixed and unseeing. A severed pig's head rested beside him.

Simon didn't know what to say to comfort her. He'd imagined the things he'd do if he ever came across the man who'd attacked Elizabeth, but this, this was inhuman.

"Father Cavanaugh of St. Patrick's parish," Elizabeth read, "found the body after returning from a late night call. O'Banion's death is eerily reminiscent of the murder of the Weasley twins three months ago. Stabbed twice in the neck, bodies drained of blood..."

Simon's hand clenched over hers. "What?"

Elizabeth kept reading. "A pair of stiletto sharp cuts on the neck and the odd loss of volumes of blood. In each case, the blood at the scene was minimal, leading police to believe the murders occurred elsewhere. The small puddle of blood doesn't account for the shriveled, desiccated skin of the corpse."

"Dear God. The vampire would then suck the blood of the living, so as to make the victim's body fall away visibly to skin and bones," Simon recited, feeling the first rush of possibility.

"A vampire? You don't really think..."

Simon took the paper from her and scanned the rest of the article. "I don't know. The marks on the neck could be stab wounds, and the blood loss could be explained through conventional means."

Part of him felt the exhilaration of potential discovery. The photograph was too hazy and taken from too far away to get a good look at the wound. But if it were what he thought it might be....

Simon set down the paper and tried to clear his mind, but it whirled with the possibilities. Years of research, a lifetime of endeavor, and the evidence to justify it all could be within his grasp. "Imagine if this is tangible proof of the occult. What I've been, what we've been searching for."

"I'd feel a whole lot better if I weren't stuck in the middle of it," she said.

In his enthusiasm, he'd nearly forgotten the circumstances. "I'm sorry. I've just waited so long for something like this."

"I could have waited a little longer."

"Yes," Simon said. "But still, it is a possibility." As much as he hoped it was true, a part of him was disgusted by the prospect, to wish something so vulgar into existence was shameful. He glanced at Elizabeth and could feel her nervous energy coming off in waves.

She pulled her hand away from his. "And the tiny little fact that this man was murdered and strung up like an animal is what? Extraneous?"

The rebuke was well aimed and stung. "Of course not."

"You'll forgive me if I'm not overjoyed at the prospect of finding a vampire when I'm trapped in the middle of this whole depraved mess."

She was right. This wasn't an academic exercise, this was frighteningly real. He made a conscious effort to squelch his research instincts. Was he really such a man who could see death and find only what helped his cause? "It's probably nothing of the kind."

He needed to touch her again and reached for her hand. Thankfully, she didn't pull away.

"I know this means a lot to you, Simon. Under any other circumstances I'd be right there with you. But reading about vampires in books is one thing, this..."

"Is something else entirely," he said and squeezed her hand before rising to move around the room. As much as he tried to deny it, the possibility was there. A chance to find the proof he'd spent a lifetime searching for.

Elizabeth pulled her knees up to her chest and watched him pace for a few moments. "Why do you believe it? I mean, all of it."

He leaned against the far wall and paused for a moment before he answered. "Because the man I most admired believed it, and was ridiculed for it," he said simply. "If I can prove he was right, find some empirical evidence…"

"You'll clear his name?"

"Yes." It was a simple motive really, one he realized she couldn't possibly share. "What about you? Why the occult? Why not General Anthropology? History?"

She gave him an embarrassed smile. "It sounds silly."

He nodded in encouragement and walked over to the bed.

She took a breath and shrugged. "I guess part of me can't believe human beings are really capable of atrocities like this," she said and nodded toward the paper. "And I hoped, maybe, there was another explanation. That people weren't doing those awful things. That evil wasn't just an idea, but a real, tangible thing. And if it had form, if you could find it, you could stop it. That's me, saving the world from evil." She shrugged again. "Told you it was silly."

"Not at all. I think it's…" he said and smiled gently as he sat down, "wonderfully you."

"Naïve and all catty whompus?"

"No," he said and held out his hand for her to join him. She took it and sat on the bed. "You see the best in people. Don't ever be ashamed of that. Even though I might act differently on occasion, it's one of the things, the many things, I love about you. You saw the best in me when I didn't deserve it, and for that," he said, as he kissed her hand, "I'll be forever grateful."

"You know, for a stuffy Englishman, you're pretty damn eloquent."

"Am I?"

She ran her fingers along his neck, tickling a particularly sensitive spot behind his ear. "Makes me all puddley."

He leaned into her touch and felt her lips follow the same path as her fingers. "That's good?"

"Oh," she breathed softly. "Very good."

Her mouth was doing something marvelous to his neck, barely nibbling on the skin, when she suddenly pulled back.

"What's wrong?" he asked.

She stared at his neck, her eyes clouding with worry. "Do you really think it was a vampire that killed that man?"

He considered, briefly, lying to her. "It's possible."

"God, I hope you're wrong."

He wanted to say he hoped so too, but he didn't. He wanted it to be a vampire. As unthinkable as it was, he wanted it.

His thoughts must have shown on his face because Elizabeth pulled away. "You hope it is one."

"No," he said quickly, but couldn't manage the lie. "Yes. I know it's irrational, but I've spent too long searching to turn back now. If this is a lead, a real lead, I have to follow it."

Elizabeth was quiet, considering what he'd said. After a long moment, she nodded. "I guess I should put on some clothes then."

She read his confused expression and sighed again, this time in exasperation. "If you think you're going vampire hunting by yourself you really are nuts."

"You don't have to be involved in this. I'd really rather you weren't."

Her face was a mixture of resignation and sadness. "I already am."

CHAPTER EIGHTEEN

Elizabeth didn't feel like a vampire hunter. She sure didn't look like one. She'd always pictured them as grim men in long cloaks, stalking through the cemeteries of seventeenth century Europe. Her light floral pattern dress and ankle strap pumps were hardly de rigueur.

Simon, on the other hand, could have slipped back a few centuries and fit right in. Judging from his dour expression, he had grim down to a science.

He'd tried to talk her out of coming with him. He'd said, vampire or not, mucking about in a murder was dangerous business. But, she'd been his assistant back home and that wasn't going to change now. Besides, if she was somehow connected to this mess, the more she knew, the better off she was. Not to mention the fact that she was curious too. She hadn't sat through Professor Hayes' endless lectures on Slavic folklore for her health. As frightening a prospect as it was, if a vampire really was involved in the killings, she wanted to know as badly as Simon. It seemed highly unlikely they'd actually find anything, but the possibility was there. Hell, they'd traveled back in time. Anything could happen.

They went to the crime scene first. No yellow tape cordoned off the butcher shop. No large crowd was held at bay by the police. Even the severed pig's head still sat in its place. A closed sign in the window was the only hint that it wasn't business as usual.

Simon looked from storefront to storefront trying to divine some clue in the location itself. He was as meticulous now as he was back home. It was one thing she envied about him. He could patiently work through endless stacks of materials, painstakingly sorting through them for that one kernel of evidence.

People were a different matter. It was as though all his patience was spent on inanimate objects, leaving none for the rest of the world. Only the most brave or naïve students dared to darken his door during office hours. She wasn't sure which category she fit into. A little of both, perhaps.

In the end they complemented each other. Maybe the same would be true in a relationship. A thrill of both excitement and fear rushed through her. A relationship. She was in a relationship with Simon. At least, it felt like one. A day old and already she wondered how long it would last. She was being silly. Simon told her he loved her and he certainly wouldn't have said it if he hadn't meant it. But nagging doubts pricked at her. One night of bliss does not a relationship make. He was still the same man who'd pushed her away. The same man who'd spent thirty years keeping the world at arm's length. Could he really simply push the reset button? Was it even possible?

"There's nothing of use here," he said. "Are you ready to move on?"

Lost in thought, she stared at him blankly for a minute.

"Elizabeth," he said, and held out his hand.

"I'm ready," she said and took his hand. After all, miracles did happen.

The sun had finally set, but instead of providing relief from the stifling heat, it merely cloaked it in darkness. The sharp spires of old St. Patrick's rose in the distance like a fist full of daggers. Gothic architecture had never bothered her before, but now it seemed too jagged, too oppressive. The dark gray façade loomed over the small street, and a cold shiver ran down her back.

As they walked up the steps of the cathedral, Elizabeth saw a familiar face. "Dix!"

Happy to have any distraction from her increasingly uneasy thoughts, she walked over to the other woman. "What're you doing here?"

"Just sayin' hello to the father," Dix said, nodding her head in the direction of the large double doors where Father Cavanaugh stood talking to a young family. "Not that I'm religious or anything. Just droppin' in, ya know?"

Elizabeth recognized protesting too much when she saw it, but wasn't about to pry. "We were doing the same," Elizabeth said. "He offered some help a while back. We wanted to let him know we were doing okay."

Dix nodded, and her eyes darted to Simon and then back to Elizabeth. "Glad to hear it," she said with a smile.

Elizabeth could see the sadness tugging a bit too much at the corners of her mouth. Oh, Dix was happy for them, but her eyes had the look of a woman who wanted the happiness she saw and didn't think she'd ever find it. Unrequited love was an albatross Elizabeth knew too well.

They stood awkwardly for a moment, having run out of small talk and neither wanting to discuss why they were really there.

"Well," Simon said, breaking the stalemate. "We should say hello to the father before it gets too late."

"Yeah. I gotta be goin' too."

"See you tomorrow, Dix," Elizabeth said, as Simon led her away. She was about to say something to Simon about Dix when he called out to the priest.

Father Cavanaugh said his goodbyes to the young family and waved them over. "Ah, good to see you two again. Elizabeth was it?"

"Simon and Elizabeth Cross," Simon said.

A girl could get used to that.

"Of course," the father said with a broad grin. "What can I do for you?"

"I was hoping to ask you about yesterday. I understand," Simon continued, "you found the body in the butcher shop."

"Oh, yes. Terrible, terrible business."

"Did you get a good look at the body by any chance?"

Father Cavanaugh was surprised at the question, but he hid it quickly. Curiosity and a tinge of concern colored his face. "And why would you be wantin' to know about such things?"

Not accustomed to having to explain himself, Simon stumbled for a reason.

"He thinks he's Sherlock Holmes," Elizabeth added. "Trust me, it's better to humor him."

"Ah, likes to play detective, does he?" the Father said with a wink.

Elizabeth thought of all sorts of replies to that, but managed to merely smile.

Simon ignored the byplay. "Can you describe the body? The markings on the neck seemed rather unusual."

Elizabeth could have sworn a flash of fear passed over the priest's placid face.

"I'm afraid people are always findin' new ways to do each other harm," he said noncommittally.

"Yes," Simon persisted, "but the wounds, were they slits or small and round like a snake bite?"

There it was again, a brief glimmer of alarm. His eyes shifted from side to side, trying surreptitiously to make sure they weren't being overheard. "A bite? Surely you don't think a giant serpent is loose on the streets of New York City. Now that would be news," he said with a laugh. "No, it was as the paper said; a sad example of the darkness some men find themselves driven to these days."

"Yes," Simon said. "But the draining of the blood seems almost ritualistic."

"I'm afraid the newspaper man overstated that."

"But the photographs..."

"To sell papers. I'm afraid they paint a more gruesome picture for effect."

"Really?" Simon said.

If Father Cavanaugh noticed the skepticism in Simon's voice he chose to ignore it. "We live in different times. Newspapers aren't what they once were. Hearst and Pulitzer have seen to that," he said, then offered them an embarrassed smile. "That was bitter, wasn't it? Before the seminary I tried my hand at reporting. Fresh to America from Ireland and my first assignment was the Spanish-American war. Somewhat of a birth by fire."

"You were a reporter?" Elizabeth asked, trying to get her mind around a young Father Cavanaugh.

"Ancient history."

"That is fascinating," Simon said dryly, obviously recognizing a diversionary tactic when he saw one.

Father Cavanaugh smiled genially again and checked his pocket watch. "Well, I've talked your ear off, haven't I? I really should be going. I'm sorry I couldn't be more help, but it's probably best to leave the evils of our society to the professionals, eh?"

"Thank you, Father," Elizabeth said with a quick glance at Simon, hoping he wouldn't press the issue.

"Good night to you," the priest said with a nod, and hurriedly disappeared into the crowd.

"Well," Simon said, his eyes narrowing and following the priest as he disappeared behind the heavy wooden doors to the church. "That was... interesting."

"Yeah." Interesting was one way to put it. Terribly unnerving was another.

"He obviously knows more than he's saying," Simon said.

"Maybe he can't say more. Father-client privilege, or whatever it's called."

"It could point to someone in the parish being involved."

"But what are we going to do? Pretend we're census workers? Make sure you check the creature of the night box, should it apply."

"The library."

"I'm sorry?"

"Have you forgotten everything I taught you?" he said, and then got that gleam in his eyes. The wheels in his head were spinning in overdrive. "If this is the work of a vampire, it would need to feed. Which means more victims. Just the sort of thing a sensationalistic paper would print, don't you think?"

They poured over newspapers at the library until it closed. Three similar cases were reported in the last few years. That would have seemed like a decent lead if it weren't for the fact that there had been six murders with ice picks and four beheadings. Maybe the butcher shop murder was nothing more than a gangland signature killing.

Simon wanted to talk to the reporter, but Elizabeth calmly pointed out the downside. Imagine the headline: Future Couple Seeks Vampires in Gotham.

Their initial foray as vampire hunters had turned up bupkis. Elizabeth wasn't sure whether to be relieved or frustrated.

As the days passed, and the incident drifted further away, she fell into an easy routine. Simon took a bit longer to let go, but eventually he stopped asking questions. Stopped asking them out loud at any rate.

The limited avenues for research frustrated Simon. At least twice, he'd reached for a phone that wasn't there to call contacts who weren't born yet. Even if there were documents that might give him clues to the existence of vampires in the city, he couldn't afford to find them. Aside from not having the credentials in this time to gain access to them, he couldn't risk the inevitable questions that would follow. His logical mind told him to give up the ghost, but his instincts wouldn't be silenced. There was more to the murder than a gangland killing, but without any more paths to follow, he was at a loss. Being so close to what he'd been searching for would have sent him into a tailspin if it hadn't been for Elizabeth. He'd always thought that finding proof of the occult was the most important thing in his life. It had been the only thing in his life, until recently.

She gave him things he didn't know he needed. Now that he had them, he was sure he couldn't live without them, without her. The days spent in their small apartment were a revelation to him, discovering her likes and dislikes. Her passion for American football confused him almost as much as her nearly pathological hatred of the innocent lima bean. His confession of a fondness for mushy peas made her face squish up in the most adorable way. Each discovery, from the ridiculous to the sublime, left him wanting more. She could make him laugh with a freedom he'd nearly forgotten, and melt his heart with a few gently whispered words.

He could spend a lifetime trying to understand her and never tire of the challenge. Stories of her threadbare childhood left him wanting to give her the world. Not that she complained about it, to the contrary really, she had the gift to see what she had and not focus on the things she didn't. He could envision her as a small child sitting in some poxy hotel room making jewelry out of gum wrappers. She'd faced the cards life had dealt her with the equanimity only a gambler's child could. Even so, he could see the hollow spaces inside her, the missing pieces of her life he'd never been aware of before. But, as she said, Swiss cheese wouldn't be any fun without the holes.

He, on the other hand, had clung to the injustices and wore them like a protective cloak.

It was overly dramatic to say he'd been reborn, but the truth of it was, that's exactly how he felt. Like he'd stepped into the sunshine for the first time after a life spent underground.

He found himself speaking freely of things he hadn't thought of in years. Memories secreted away now spilled out. The summers spent at his grandfather's knee where he listened to fantastic tales of faraway places. He'd visited them in his imagination, escaping from the cold rigidity of boarding school and the arch pragmatism of his parents. He hadn't realized it at the time, but he would spend the rest of his life searching for those fantastic places, even if he didn't quite believe they were real.

He told her how after his grandfather died, the chasm had grown between his parents and him; and again, when he told them he wasn't going to be a barrister. One black sheep was one too many, and Simon didn't have the excuse of being a doddering, old fool. They never let him forget their disappointment. He'd always considered Grandfather Sebastian his only real family, and once he was gone, Simon turned inward. His years at Oxford were empty and lonely. It all sounded so clichéd. Poor little rich boy. But Elizabeth listened intently, without judgment. All these were things he'd never shared, and now, not only was it painless to do so, it was oddly comforting. He wasn't sure what was more surprising, the ease with which he revealed himself or how much it pleased him that she wanted him to.

Loving someone and being loved in return was a shock to his system. Like any muscle that hasn't been used, his heart didn't always run smoothly. In the quiet of their room, life was bliss, but add in a few outside factors and the mixture became volatile. Fleeting moments of insecurity passed quickly enough, but the next Saturday night at the club, something else came to the fore. Unprovoked jealousy spiked to the surface.

King Kashian was back.

Simon did his best not to watch the man watch Elizabeth, but it was a losing battle. He tried busying himself with some new sheet music Charlie had bought recently, when a little man sidled up to the piano.

He looked to be in his late fifties, but the years hadn't been kind to him. His legs were bowed and spindley; it looked as if it took a great effort just to cross the room. But it was his face that most struck Simon, etched with deep lines only grief can carve.

"You're British, right?" the man slurred.

"Yes," Simon said. Why was it Americans felt the need to ask him what was obviously apparent?

"Good," the man said with a lop-sided smile. He reached into the breast pocket of his wrinkled coat and took out several pieces of folded paper. "That's real good. Right and proper."

He leaned heavily on the piano and unfolded a few pages of sheet music, methodically smoothing the creases.

Charlie came up behind him, his usual genial demeanor tempered with a melancholy smile. He laid a hand on the small man's shoulder. "That time again already, Frank?"

Frank nodded and continued to lovingly smooth out the papers. "Woulda been thirty today."

Charlie gave his shoulder a comforting squeeze. "Frank's son was killed in the war," he explained. "Comes in every year on his birthday, and the player sings this song."

Simon felt distinctly uncomfortable. The last time he'd sung, well, to be honest, he couldn't remember. "I'm afraid I'm not much of a singer."

"You in the war?" Frank asked suddenly, his hand jerking with a phantom spasm.

Simon wracked his brain. This was 1929; he would have been in his late twenties during the war years. As an able bodied Englishman, he would surely have served. "Yes, I was."

Frank's eyes brightened with something more than the bourbon. "Maybe you knew my son? Where'd you see action?"

Simon knew he should have seen that question coming. He blurted out the first thing that came to mind. "The battle of the Marne."

The cyclorama at Coney Island had given him a superficial understanding of the battle at best, but it was, he thought sadly, the only specific battle of World War One he could remember. Shameful.

"Marne," Frank said softly. The name a curse and prayer at the same time. "First or second?"

"Second."

Frank's smile faltered as he rubbed the faded sheet music. "Jimmy was there." He looked at Simon, a glimmer of life, of hope, in his eyes. "Don't suppose you ever met? Thin as a reed, all arms and legs and hair like wheat?"

Simon shook his head and felt sick at his deception, but there was no turning back from it now. "I'm sorry."

Frank clapped Simon on the shoulder. "S'ok." He turned unsteadily to Charlie and said, "I'd like to buy this man a drink. Served with my son."

"Sure thing, Frank," Charlie said and held up two fingers to Dix. "But it's on the house."

Frank nodded solemnly. "I thank you." He looked down at the sheet music, his kindly eyes growing moist with unshed tears. "Mother doesn't come out anymore. But I do. Honor his memory and all. And I'm pleased to share a drink with you."

"Thank you," Simon said as he took the glass from Dix.

"But first we sing!" Frank said too loudly. He poked at the sheet music with a gnarled finger and slid it across the top of the piano to Simon.

Simon wanted to protest, but how in good conscience could he possibly disappoint this man? He looked at the music and realized he was actually familiar with it. "Keep the Home-Fires Burning" was a stirring ballad from early in the war. Vague memories of his grandmother's voice came back to him. She'd died when he was very small, and he'd all but forgotten her. As he read the words on the page, a latent feeling of loss welled inside him. Like the light of a dying star, the grief reached him years after the fact.

Simon cleared his throat and set the papers on the music stand. As he played the first few bars, a reverent silence fell over the room.

He sang the first lines, unsure and nervous, but his voice steadied by the second verse. The poetic recounting of a time when sacrifice was the norm, when men left their lives when called, brought a hush to the crowd. Until the chorus came, when an amazing thing happened. Each man, each woman, joined their voices in the song.

"Keep the home-fires burning, while your hearts are yearning, though your lads are far away, they dream of home."

What had been only a page in a history book was suddenly brought to life. Even ten years removed from the horrors of the war, the scars were still fresh.

The wave of emotion was palpable as they came to the last chorus. Thoughtful voices raised together, "There's a silver lining, through the dark clouds shining, turn the dark clouds inside-out, till the boys come home."

Simon played the final note, and the room was completely silent. Each man and woman raised their glass. Frank wiped a tear from his eye and raised his glass. "Thank you."

Charlie put an arm around the little man and took the sheet music from the piano. He led him to an empty chair and smiled his thanks to Simon.

The conversation in the bar slowly started to pick up again, but the feeling of loss still hovered in the room. Simon had never been one to seek comfort; if anything, he'd avoided it. Of course, he'd never trusted anyone enough not to use the moment of weakness against him. Now, his eyes unerringly searched out Elizabeth and found her at the bar placing an order. He caught her eye, and she seemed to know exactly what he was feeling. She smiled gently and he nodded toward the back. She told Dix she was going to take five. He passed by King Kashian, intent on ignoring him, opened the door to the storeroom and followed Elizabeth inside.

Wooden crates lined the walls, leaving a gap only for the door to the alley. Simon leaned back against a shabby old desk cluttered with papers and sighed. Without needing to ask, Elizabeth moved into his embrace. His arms wound around her and he held her to his chest. The feel of her was the palliative he needed.

He dropped a kiss on the top of her head. "Thank you."

"What for?"

He paused for a moment and then shook his head. "Everything."

She blushed and played with the lapels of his jacket. "That was beautiful, wasn't it?"

"Yes," he said, but she could hear the reservation in his voice.

"But?"

"Remind me to tell you about my grandmother some time."

"Sebastian's wife?"

Simon nodded and tucked a stray hair behind her ear.

"She must have been something. I doubt Sebastian would have loved just any woman."

Simon ran the back of his hand gently along her jaw line. "Must run in the family."

Elizabeth leaned into his touch and sighed dramatically. "Is it time to go home yet?"

"Another hour I'm afraid," Simon said, as he pulled her closer for a kiss.

Elizabeth loved the way he held her when they kissed. She felt treasured and desired. It was that way with everything about him, a gentle intensity that made her stomach drop. She would have laid odds that she'd never hear Simon Cross sing, much less sing with such emotion. The tentative vulnerability and need in him only made her want him all the more. They shared a few more longing kisses before it was time to get back to work.

The hour seemed to pass quickly enough, even though she had to weather the constant gaze of King Kashian. Thankfully, he didn't ask for another command appearance at his table and before she knew it, Charlie made last call. Slowly, the bar emptied. The poor, dear man who'd asked Simon to play for his son had long ago passed out at his table.

Charlie gently shook his shoulder to wake him. "Come on, Frank. Time to go home."

The man mumbled something incoherent and ran a hand roughly over his stubbled chin.

Charlie patted him on the shoulder and looked over to Simon. "Professor! Gimme a hand, will ya?"

Simon helped the older man to his feet, but he swayed precariously and leaned against the wall.

"Ah, a real snootful tonight. Do me a favor, Professor?" Charlie said. "Take old Frank home for me? I let Lester go early. Wife's ailin' and I can't leave the club."

Simon frowned. He did feel an odd responsibility for the old man's well-being. It was a strange sensation—concern for a stranger's welfare. Before, he wouldn't have given the man a second thought, but now, it was simply the right thing to do. However, he didn't want to leave Elizabeth alone with King, and his eyes quickly sought her out.

Charlie nodded his understanding. "I'll keep an eye on things. It's not too far down on Delancy. Four twenty, right Frank?"

The man grunted and licked his lips. "I can make it."

"S'alright. Professor here's gonna give ya a hand."

Simon looked anxiously at Elizabeth, who set down her tray of dirty dishes and walked over to them. "Something wrong?" she asked.

"No, I just have to," he glanced at Frank who was softly humming to himself, "make sure he gets home. I won't be long."

Elizabeth squeezed his forearm. "I'm not going anywhere."

Simon looked over her shoulder at King, who lounged idly in his chair. "I'll be back soon."

Charlie helped Simon guide Frank to the door, and Elizabeth resumed her chores. Once the dishes were stacked and the tables wiped down, she was ready to change. She had to pass by King, whose table was near the door to the stockroom. His eyes continued to follow her, but his expression was dispassionate, even a little bored.

She shut the door behind her and draped Dix's robe over her shoulders. She usually felt completely safe changing in the back, but with King in the bar, being totally naked felt, well, totally naked.

She turned her back to the door and began to undress. She'd barely managed to slip off her costume when she heard the creaking of a door opening. She wrapped the robe tightly around her body and spun around, ready to tell King a thing or two about privacy. But it wasn't King, and the door to the club remained shut. Then she heard the cough and wheeze and looked to other side of the room. A rail thin man stood in the doorway to the alley. His face was sallow, covered with a sheen of sweat. In his trembling hand was a black revolver, the thick muzzle pointed right at her.

"D-don't scream," the man sputtered. His fingers clenched spasmodically around the handle.

Elizabeth went cold with fear and held up her palms and, insanely, tried to keep the robe from falling open. Modesty even in the face of death. "Okay."

The man's cheek twitched and his blood-rimmed eyes blinked at uneven intervals. "The money. Heard there was money here."

It was like a scene out of a movie. A bad movie. She tried to make her voice as calm as possible. "Take it easy, okay?"

"The... The money!" he blurted out loudly with another severe twitch.

Elizabeth's mind raced. What the hell was she supposed to do? "All right. Just put down the gun."

He shook his head so hard she thought it might swivel off his shoulders. "They said there was money here."

His hand trembled so badly, he had to grip the gun with both hands now to steady it.

Elizabeth was about to say something when the door to the club slammed open. King filled the doorway.

The next few moments passed in slow motion. The man with the gun panicked. He looked at King and then back to Elizabeth. His shoulders hunched as he braced himself. With a wild look of panic in his eyes, he pulled the trigger.

CHAPTER NINETEEN

THE WORLD MOVED IN liquid time.

A bright, sparking flash of fire spewed from the muzzle of the gun like a roman candle caught on slow motion film. Elizabeth could have sworn she saw the dark streak of the bullet flying toward her. It was a mutated version of reality, both sluggish and swift, blurring her senses. Before the scream could escape her lips, she felt herself being shoved out of the way.

She had a vague sense of something rough and bleached rushing toward her. Too late she realized it was one of the wooden crates as she crashed shoulder first into the hard planked box and fell to the floor.

The thundering crack of the gun's report filled the small room. A dull thump was quickly followed by a deep grunt from King, and she heard him stagger backwards, his shoes scraping against the floor. Partially obscured by the boxes, King's broad back hunched slightly as he faced the robber.

"Sweet Jesus," the man whispered.

She could only see a hint of King's profile, the smooth contours of his face distorted by excruciating pain. She heard the gun slip from the robber's fingers and clatter to the floor. Peering around the edge of the whiskey crate, she saw the intruder's face. He was ghostly white now, his eyes bulged out of their sockets, bright with a primal fear, and locked onto King. A low guttural sound, deeper and more feral than any animal, rumbled from King. The robber gasped and ran out the back door. King stood motionless for a moment, then he rolled his shoulders and bowed his head.

Elizabeth pushed herself up on shaky legs. "Are you okay?"

King flinched at the sound of her voice, as though he'd forgotten she was there. He took a lurching step away from her and leaned heavily on the small desk.

She rose to her feet and hurried to his side. "Were you hit?"

He kept his face turned away from hers and merely shook his head. She started to reach out to him when the door to the club banged open.

"Nobody move!"

Elizabeth spun to see Charlie, shotgun at the ready. "What happened?"

"I think King was shot," she said, trying to keep her heart from hammering its way out of her chest.

Charlie took a step forward, but stopped short when King spoke, "I'm fine."

He kept his face turned away and judging from the way he was hunched over, he was anything but all right. "King—"

"Leave it," he barked.

She turned back to Charlie, but he merely shook his head. He scanned the room quickly until his eyes fell back on King and narrowed with suspicion and tempered fear. Charlie's ruddy face finally slackened as he lowered the huge, double-barreled shotgun. "You all right, Lizzy?"

She let out a quick breath and nodded. "There was a man. A burglar. He ran out there," she said and pointed toward the alley door.

Charlie looked gravely at King and then back to Elizabeth. "You sure you're okay?"

"Yeah."

Charlie puffed out his cheeks and ran a hand over his sweaty brow. "Good."

She managed a weak smile. "We're okay. King scared him off, I think."

Charlie seemed about to say something, but must have thought better of it. "Long as you're okay." He put the shotgun in the crook of his arm and headed back into the bar. "S'okay, Dix. You can get out from under the table now."

Elizabeth waited till she was sure Charlie was gone before turning back to King. She could have sworn he'd been shot. There was no way he could have gotten out of the path of the bullet in time.

Steeling herself against the bloody wound she imagined she'd find, she tentatively touched his shoulder. He flinched again, but didn't pull away. "King?"

Slowly, he straightened and tugged at the edge of his waistcoat as he turned around. His face was implacable, but the strange fire in his eyes burned even brighter.

"Disgusting," he muttered. "Drug addicts. Barely worth their own skin."

He ran his gloved hand over his vest again and Elizabeth saw a small, scorched hole about the size of a dime next to the bottom button. It didn't make any sense. If he had been shot, where was the blood? And he certainly wasn't acting as if he had a bullet in his stomach.

He must have known what she was looking for and quickly buttoned his coat, smoothing out the material. "Are you all right?" he asked placidly.

She wasn't about to be put off and leaned in closer to try to see the hole. "You're hurt."

He smiled, but it came off as more of a grimace. "You needn't worry about me."

"There's nothing wrong with worrying about another person's welfare."

"That depends entirely on the other person," he said, his trademark smirk back in place. "That filth from this evening deserves nothing more than contempt."

He appraised her for a moment, then strode to the alleyway door. "I'm sure my men will find him. Eventually."

He turned back to her, any trace of the incident was washed away from his expression, and he walked toward the bar.

Elizabeth reached out and touched his arm again. "Thank you."

He looked down at her hand and she thought he was going to tell her to let go. When he raised his eyes, his cold exterior was flushed with humanity, as if no one had ever genuinely thanked him for anything. It was only the barest of glimpses, but she saw another side to King in that moment. A mere second's exposure of his soul. A flicker of need that belied the stonework façade.

As quickly as it had appeared, the glimmer of something more receded into the darkness of his eyes. "Good night, Mrs. Cross."

Simon closed the door to their apartment and turned impatiently to Elizabeth. She'd told him about the attempted robbery, but she was clearly holding something back. What could be worse than almost being shot? His stomach lurched. He didn't dare follow that thought to its natural conclusion. "All right, we're home. Are you going to tell me what really happened or not?"

She sighed, as she turned on the light. "First things first. I'm okay."

His natural frown deepened. Any discussion that began with an assurance that she was all right was not going to be one he enjoyed. "Go on."

"Well, you could be a little happier about that part."

He was already impatient and her delaying tactics were only pushing him closer to the edge. "Elizabeth..."

"Maybe I'm imagining things."

"Would you please—"

"I know, it's just...I'm not even sure I saw what I saw. Does that make any sense?"

"At the moment you're not making any sense at all."

"Oh, I'm sorry. Almost getting killed sort of threw me."

He forced himself to try and relax. Bludgeoning her wasn't going to help, but how could she expect him to be calm? She'd been white as a sheet when he'd come back from taking Frank home. In typical form, she'd downplayed the incident, as if aggravated assault was nothing more than an annoyance. As absurd as it was, he could live with that. She'd been spared. Thank God, she had. It was the secret she'd kept, insisted on keeping till they were home. He sighed in frustration.

"I know," she said with sad resignation. "I'm just a little frazzled."

She wrapped her arms around her chest. He crossed the room and took her into his arms, kissing the crown of her head. Eventually, she pulled out of his embrace and sat on the edge of the bed. "I didn't want to say anything in front of Charlie and Dix. But...when the man fired the gun, I swear King was hit."

"Wouldn't it be rather obvious if he had?" he said, taking a seat next to her.

"You'd think so. He says he wasn't," she said, her eyes filling with insistent fire. "I'm sure he was."

"I don't understand."

"I'm not sure I do either. He pushed me out of the way, and then there was this sound. This whoomp, and no ricochet. If it had missed I would have heard it hit the crates or the wall. Something."

Simon gave in to the need to touch her again and took her hand, but even that couldn't assuage the growing sense of dread in his chest. Did they have bullet proof vests now? Most likely not. "It all happened so quickly, you could have missed it."

"Maybe. But he had this little hole in his waist coat. And the way he acted. He was in pain, I know he was. It didn't last long, maybe a minute, then he was normal again. Well, normal for King."

She squeezed Simon's hand and the fear she'd kept at bay glistened in her eyes. "Sometimes when he's looking at me, there's something in his eyes."

Simon tried to quell the surge of possessive jealousy that shot through his veins. Apparently, he did a poor job of it because Elizabeth shook her head. "Not like that," she continued. "Well, sometimes like that, but there's something not right, something shadowed."

The hairs on the back of his neck prickled, but he wasn't going to give in. Elizabeth needed assurances, not more to worry about. "He is a gangster."

"I know this sounds incredibly lame, but I've known gangsters before. Sure, they were just two-cent hoods, but they didn't see themselves that way. With King, it's different. There's something about him. It's not...natural." She paused in thought then shook her head. "Or maybe I have vampires on the brain."

Simon let go of her hand, and his fingers curled into fists. The niggling suspicion he'd been harboring was finally given voice. "You don't think King is..."

"No," she said too quickly. "Not really. I don't know. I guess I'm a little shaken, not stirred. Addled my brain. I'm not even sure what I saw. Maybe I didn't see anything."

"You've never been addled in your life," he said, pushing himself up off the bed. "Did you see any signs of transformation? Changes in his face?"

"I couldn't really see his face. He was turned away from me. I just don't know."

Simon did his best to slam the door on the voice that screamed "Harbinger!", but the door wouldn't close. Losing her was more than untenable, it was absolutely unthinkable. If this man were the creature they'd been searching for...

A thousand thoughts swirled in Simon's mind. If King was a vampire, how could he destroy him? Lead bullets wouldn't harm a vampire. Silver, perhaps, but only a few species. Nosferatu were never sighted out of Romania and not capable of taking on human guise. Uboir had been seen outside of Bulgaria, but weren't susceptible to silver poisoning. If only he could call his colleagues at Oxford.

"Simon?"

Her voice pulled him from his thoughts. She looked so small, it nearly broke his heart. In that moment, his needs seemed so unimportant next to hers. She needed comfort, not a lecture on the occult. He held his hand out to her and she stood and stepped into his arms. "I'm sorry. I'm sure there's a perfectly logical explanation."

Ockham's razor dictated that the simplest explanation was the best. Then again, he'd never been a believer in accepting the obvious. Except, of course, when it was standing in his arms.

He took a deep breath and wrapped his arms more tightly around her waist, pulling her securely into his embrace. He was not going to obsess about what was possible when a surety was standing right in front of him. "It's a miracle you weren't hurt."

"That's something, coming from a man who doesn't believe in miracles."

He slipped a finger under her chin and tilted her face up to his. "I didn't, and yet, here you are."

She blushed delightfully, and Simon brushed the pad of his thumb across her bottom lip. "Next thing you know, I'll be composing sonnets. And, as we both know, in that way madness lies."

She laughed and the sound lifted the edges of the shroud that had fallen over the room. He leaned in and kissed her, gently at first, but with a growing fervor.

However, the shadow had been cast, and even in her kiss, he couldn't quash the feeling that the thing he'd been searching for had found him.

An hour later, Elizabeth rolled onto her side, and her arm fell across the empty bed. She could still smell his scent, but where his strong, warm chest should have been was only the cool smoothness of sheets long-abandoned. The unexpected change forced her awake. Still groggy, she looked around the room and found him sitting in his chair by the window. Even in the dim light of predawn, she could see him watching her.

"Simon?"

He didn't respond, but she saw his shoulders rise and fall with the intake of a deep breath.

"What's wrong?" she asked.

He shook his head almost imperceptibly.

"Simon." She started to get out of bed, but he leaned back in his chair, lifting his elbows from his knees and curling his long fingers tightly around his thighs. She could feel him retreating, almost see the emotional shield he wielded in defense. With a deep breath of her own, she settled herself against the headboard. "Nightmares again?"

"Go back to sleep," he said, but the strain in his voice betrayed him.

"Did you try—"

"Visualizing your wildflowers wasn't quite up to the task," he said with a touch of sarcasm, reminding her of her advice to him from what seemed a lifetime ago. "Go back to sleep, Elizabeth."

There was something so despairing, so anguished in the way he said her name. She came instantly awake. "You want to talk about it?"

"No." quick, terse, definitive.

"Maybe talking about it'll help."

"I doubt that."

She couldn't let it rest. "You've been having them since we first got here, haven't you?"

He ran a hand through his hair. "Please..." She could feel the tension in his body even from across the room. "Some things are better left to the darkness," he whispered.

The silence pressed down between them until she couldn't stand the weight of it. "Are they about this? Being here? Me?"

His head snapped up and she knew she'd hit a nerve. The fierceness of his expression surprised her, frightened her. Before she could learn more, he tore his eyes away and clenched his long fingers tightly against the muscles of his leg, digging in against her, against the truth. His chest heaved with frustration as he pushed himself out of the chair and stared out the window. "Don't ask me about them."

The harshness of his voice triggered something inside her, and she felt the unstoppable need to make him talk about them. His tension was catching and her growing unease blossomed into anger. "If you think pretending nothing's wrong is best," she said coolly.

He turned back to face her, his eyes glinting in the cold moonlight. "You don't know what you're asking."

"Because you won't tell me." She knew her rising anger was unreasonable, but he was pushing her away again. With every passing second, he pulled further inside himself. If he wouldn't be drawn out, then she'd get behind him and shove. "Don't shut me out."

"I'm not. I just..."

"Just what? You open up only when it's convenient?"

"That's not fair."

"And neither is this."

"You don't understand."

"Then explain it to me."

He moved toward her, but stopped in the middle of the room. He started to say something, but clamped his jaw shut and shook his head. His hands, always so still and sure, hovered nervously in front of him. Finally, they dropped to his side, and his expression moved from frustration to loss. His eyes, which had been looking everywhere but at her, fell on her face. When he spoke, his voice was barely a whisper. "You die."

The hairs on her arms stood up. It wasn't just the words, although "You die" would have been enough. It was the way he said them. Like a confession.

"But it's only a dream," she said, trying to comfort him, or was it herself?

He moved back the chair and slumped into it. Relieved or defeated, she couldn't tell. She ran her hands over her arms trying to smooth out the gooseflesh.

When he began, his voice was a crumbling whisper. "Thirty years ago, when I was barely ten years old..." he began, his eyes flicked to hers, sensing her confusion. "Everything begins before we think it does."

She could feel him ebbing away like the tide, but after a brief pause, he continued, "I was spending the summer at my grandfather's home in Sussex. He told me stories of amazing, impossible things well into the night. Just the two of us," he added with a brief, wistful smile. "I'd had nightmares all that week, but they were vague. That night, he had an appointment, or so he told me. I went to bed, but I knew something was wrong." He closed his eyes and replayed the scene in his mind. "I finally managed to fall asleep and then the nightmare came. Formless, forbidding images, punctuated with one final horror. I remember waking suddenly, my heart bursting through my chest. One thing, and only one thing was clear to me. My grandfather was going to die."

He paused and she could see his Adam's apple bob as he swallowed and tried to control himself.

"This wasn't like any other dream, it was a vision, a moment in time that would play out, no matter what I did, it would come to pass. I knew that as surely as I knew anything."

She could picture young Simon, as he'd been in the photograph on his mantle, full of the fear and helplessness of being so young and afraid.

He sighed heavily and ran a shaking hand through his hair. "That's when I heard a sound coming from downstairs, like someone falling. I tried to convince myself it was one of the servants, but I knew it wasn't. I knew it was him. There was no reason, no logic in it. And I ran. Stumbled down the stairs and... there he was." His voice began to quiver and the words came out in a rush. "Just like in my dream. I saw him, lying on the floor."

Elizabeth shuddered at the image. What a terrible thing for a child to see. No wonder he had nightmares.

"I'd never seen death before," Simon continued, "but I knew it was there in the house that night. I think I knew it before I went to bed, but I didn't do anything. Didn't do a damn thing. I just stood there. His face was... blood gushed out of his mouth, spilling down his neck over a jagged gash. The front of his shirt was soaked in it. And the smell."

Elizabeth felt a chill. Was this what his nightmares about her were like?

"Everything about him was just as it had been in my mind. That final, horrible image of him lying there, dying. He looked at me with such urgency I wanted to bolt for the door. He was lying there in a pool of his own blood, reaching out to me, and I wanted to run."

Simon wiped a hand across his face, briefly pausing to massage his temples. "He tried to say something, but there was too much blood. His lips were moving, but I couldn't hear him. I don't remember doing it, but I must have knelt down next to him. He whispered to me, in a voice I couldn't forget in a thousand lifetimes. 'We're running out of time,' he said, and then his eyes cleared and he... he smiled at me. The tension faded away. 'You made a fine man,' he said. A fine man." Simon shook his head and groaned in self-derision.

She wanted so much to go to him, to wrap her arms around and him tell him he was a fine man, that everything would be all right. He wouldn't welcome it. He was hanging on by a thread. If he needed space, no matter how much she wanted to hold him, she'd give him that.

His breath caught and he shook his head, struggling for control. "And then he was gone. Just like that, this man, who meant everything to me..."

He flexed his hands and cleared his throat. "It wasn't until the servants came in that I even noticed his hands. The watch, our watch, was in one."

"And the scarab ring was in the other," Elizabeth said suddenly, remembering Simon's reaction when he'd seen the ring for the first time.

He didn't look at her, but nodded slowly. "And a scrap of black cloth," he added, and then pulled himself from the memory. He wiped his palms on his pant legs. "Of course, the family did their best to keep it quiet. Announced his death as a tragic accident, a senile, old man falling down the stairs. Falling down the stairs? It wasn't any accident and they couldn't have cared less," Simon said, his voice rising in anger.

No wonder he never spoke about his family. How could they have been so callous?

He pushed out a quick breath and continued, "They took the watch and the ring. Locked them away with everything else he owned. Everything he was, just swept away and covered with lies."

"So, you hadn't seen the watch until we opened the boxes in your house that night," Elizabeth said.

Simon leaned back in his chair. "The nightmares started the night I received the crates."

"That's natural. Seeing his things, triggering old memories."

"They weren't about my grandfather."

"Oh," she said softly. "You mean you dreamt about me before we got here. Before we even—"

"Yes. The night his things arrived. I'll admit I'd had dreams about you before that," he said with an almost shy smile that faded quickly. "But not…"

"With me dying."

He glared at her so fiercely, she thought he might try to grab the words out of the air and cram them back down her throat. She drew her knees up to her chest and watched him stride back to the window. He pressed his fist against the glass.

"It's happening all over again. Inch by inch, night by night, I'm drawn closer to it."

"Tell me about them," she said, knowing even the worst had to be better than the helplessness she felt.

His back tensed, and he gripped the window sill. "No."

She eased off the bed and laid a hand on his back. He jerked forward, but she wouldn't relent. "Simon."

He turned around, and she'd never forget the haunted look in his eyes as they bore into her, beseeching and desperate. "Don't make me relive them."

"I don't think you need my help for that. You're doing that right now aren't you? You close your eyes and they're there, aren't they?"

He let out a shuddering breath. "Yes."

"Then if I have a starring role in them, shouldn't I—"

"Don't make light of this," he bit out and stepped around her. He stalked back over to the chair and sat down heavily. "Not this."

"I'm sorry. I didn't mean to. But nightmares are normal. They—"

"This isn't some subconscious manifestation of my fears. They're real, Elizabeth. The things I see in them," he said in low rasping voice. "They will happen."

She'd never heard him so desolate. The agony in his voice, the defeat was sweltering. Her hands trembled, but she couldn't believe it, wouldn't believe it. She walked over and knelt before him, taking his hand in hers and waiting.

He sat perfectly still for a moment, warring with his fears before turning her trembling hand over. "So small," he marveled. His fingers traced slowly over her hand, gently caressing the skin. His touch soothed her, even as his words sent cold shivers up her spine. "A boat," he said softly, "sometimes fire, sometimes smoke. Each dream is different, but they all end the same way."

She squeezed his hand and forced him to look at her. "I'm not going anywhere."

"I don't think I could bear it, if..."

She gripped his hand more firmly. He pulled her hand to his lips and kissed her palm. His eyes shut tightly against the overwhelming emotions.

Elizabeth slipped into his lap. His arms tightened around her, and he let out a long breath before opening his eyes. He tried to smile, but faltered and it fell away. She kissed the corner of his mouth and felt his mouth open to hers. His kiss was quietly desperate. Without words, he eased his hand under her bare legs and carried her to the bed.

He made love to her with surprising slowness. The dark intensity in his eyes drilled into her, but he moved gently, trying to prolong each touch. Instead of ravishing her, he worshipped her.

Each moment was a study in contrasts. Desperate for release and fearing just that, burying himself inside her and enveloping her at the same time. The heat of his breath on her neck mingled with the cool sheen of perspiration that coated her skin. Long fingers dug into her shoulders, only to ease, and then grip again.

Elizabeth savored every touch, every motion. Her skin was burned by the roughness of his unshaven cheek, then soothed with supple kisses. His body, long and hard, moved over hers with gentle pressure. Strong hands stroked her with barely restrained passion. Every brush of his fingers, every facet in his eyes called out to her. It was amazing to be loved so much, to be needed with such consuming desire.

She could feel the riptide of his need, pulling her under. She went willingly into the depths with him. Each thrust was a deep breath, filling her.

But nothing lasts forever, and the moment he'd tried to stave off came like a wave crashing over them. His body tensed in a silent cry as he spent himself inside her.

The moment was gone and the oneness slipped away.

Dawn's bright light sliced through the window and heralded a new day. All the things they'd run from, the solace they'd found in each other's touch, were gone. She'd tried to rationalize his dreams about her, but he'd sounded so certain about them. He was so sure they'd come to pass. The one thing he seemed to believe in was the one thing she refused to. Simon was a man with issues. Big, fat issues. No wonder they came out in his dreams. So what if the dream about his grandfather had come true? That didn't mean these dreams were portents. Did it?

Eventually, exhaustion took hold of her body and she snuggled closer to Simon. She could feel him watching her. And she knew, when she awoke again, he would be watching her still. Watching and waiting.

CHAPTER TWENTY

THE NEXT NIGHT AT the bar, Simon's mood was black even before King appeared. Sleeplessness and worry had conspired to shorten his fuse. The smug, far too gratified smile that curled King's lips as he took his drink from Elizabeth made Simon's stomach churn. It wasn't enough that he hadn't been there to protect Elizabeth, but to have this creature be the one who came to her rescue gnawed at him. Being beholden to anyone was uncomfortable enough, but to owe her life to King was impossible.

Simon jabbed at the piano keys, indifferent to the romantic melody. The set seemed to drag on endlessly, as he waited for the moment he'd been dreading. The thought of thanking that bastard forced the bile to rise in his throat. But if there were a chance to draw attention away from her, he'd take it. If he could make it a duty owed to him and not to her, he'd swallow his pride gladly. It was undoubtedly a deal with the devil, but better him than Elizabeth. If there were even a vestige of honor in King, surely he'd accept the debt as Simon's alone.

Once he was sure Elizabeth was well occupied with other customers, Simon made his way to King's table. "I'd like to speak with you about last night," Simon said struggling to keep his voice even.

Pulling his attention away from Elizabeth, King arched an eyebrow in mildly amused interest and gestured for Simon to take the empty chair.

The arrogance of the man was infuriating, but Simon stilled the barbs that stood at the ready on his tongue. He ignored the offered chair and enjoyed the feeling of looking down on King. "I don't believe we've been properly introduced."

King lit a cigarette and leaned back in his chair. "No, we haven't."

"But it seems you know my wife."

King's lips curled in a self-satisfied grin. "Yes," he said, as his eyes unerringly sought her out in the crowded room.

"My wife," Simon said sharply and with unmistakable emphasis, "tells me I owe you a debt."

Simon clenched his jaw as King watched Elizabeth. Everything about the man was an affront. Even the most casual glance at her was prurient.

King looked back across at Simon. "It was my pleasure. Elizabeth is an exceptional woman."

Simon's voice dripped with venom as he said, "More than you'll ever know."

King gave a short laugh, and Simon kept himself from taking a small step forward. How he hated this man. He almost wished King were a vampire so he could drive a stake through his cold heart.

King smiled casually, unruffled by the hatred Simon knew was clear in his eyes. They understood each other all too well.

"I'm in your debt," Simon said, with a final incline of his head. At least for now, King's focus was on him and not Elizabeth.

Simon walked away from King and took his place back at the piano. A sense of satisfaction coursing through his veins. He'd never been proprietary before and was pleasantly surprised at the feeling.

King soon turned his attention back to Elizabeth, and Simon wondered if his coup hadn't been more of colossal blunder. The gangster invited her to sit with him. Even though he knew she couldn't really refuse the request, Simon felt a flare of jealousy and anxiety as she took the chair.

He tossed the sheet music aside and moved to interfere when he saw Elizabeth shake her head and give him a worried glance. Simon paused, then started toward the table when Charlie grabbed his arm.

"Don't go makin' a scene now, Professor," Charlie warned as he deftly slipped between Simon and King's table. "'Sides, I could use a hand in the back."

Simon let Charlie guide him past the table, but it took all of his control not to wipe the grin off King's face with his fist. In the back room, they moved a series of crates digging out some Panther whiskey. The physical labor did little to quell the anxiety Simon felt, but thankfully, King was gone when they returned. Simon instinctively sought out Elizabeth.

She was setting up cups on her tray when Simon noticed her hands were shaking. A teacup clattered out of her grip and the liquor spilled.

"I'm sorry," she said and took the rag Dix offered.

"No problem, kid," Dix said. "But ya better wipe it up before it eats through the bar."

Elizabeth laughed nervously and dabbed at the spill.

Simon came up behind her. "Are you all right?"

She jumped and nearly knocked another cup over.

"Elizabeth?"

"I'm fine," she said, but wouldn't meet his eyes. "Just clumsy."

She handed the rag back to Dix, gathered her tray and gave Simon a forced smile.

He touched her arm gently and she looked at him with an odd expression. Whatever it was that crossed her face faded, and she gave him a genuine smile. "I'm okay. Really."

He let her go and watched as she served a table. He knew she was lying; she was far from all right. As the evening wore on, Simon kept a close eye on her. Slowly, her body language eased, and she engaged the customers with her usual charm. The strange way she'd looked at him earlier kept tugging at his mind. He wasn't sure if it was only his dour nature or there really was something looming on the horizon. But as work ended that night, he had the feeling that their journey had taken a sharp left into the unknown.

Two hours later, Elizabeth sat on the bed and aimlessly picked at the coverlet. She knew she should have told him right away. The longer she waited, the harder it was to get the words out, and the worse his reaction was going to be. He'd known something was wrong straight off and tried to ease it out of her. When that failed, he poked and prodded, until her silence rubbed off on him, and he withdrew to the isolation of his chair by the window—his fortress of solitude.

What a hypocrite she was. Last night she'd badgered him into telling her his worst fears. Now, given an easier task, she was taking the chicken exit. She knew what he was going to say, the argument they would have. Just for a few more hours she wanted the closeness they'd found to stay. For all the good it had done her. He'd withdrawn his questions and himself. Anything would be better than the chilling silence. The cold, gray light of predawn glowed outside the window. Time to own up.

He sat stiffly in his chair, his back ramrod straight, glaring out the window.

Rock, meet Hard Place. Hard Place, this is Rock.

"King invited me to dinner."

Whatever he'd been expecting her to say, that wasn't it. He turned to her and looked almost relieved. "Did he?"

"I know I should have told you right away, but I was afraid of how you'd react."

"Is that all this is about?"

"Well, yeah." Where was the anger? The possessive, 'Bess, you is my woman now'?

He almost laughed and then rose from the chair. "Good lord, I thought it was something dire."

"It isn't?"

He grinned and sat next to her on the bed. "Comparatively? No."

"Really?" That wasn't quite the reaction she'd expected. He seemed almost nonplussed. She'd expected him to be plussed all over the place.

Seeming to think the issue was finished, he slipped off his shoes and tugged off his socks. "You're a beautiful woman. He's a man completely without a shred of decency. I'm actually surprised it took him this long. How did he take it when you refused?"

That explained the reaction, or lack thereof.

"I can't imagine he was too pleased," Simon said with a small smile. "I wish I could have seen it."

"I accepted." She hadn't meant to blurt it like that, but the words came out in a big, fat, ugly blob.

His hands stopped in mid-motion and his head snapped up. "You what?"

For all the time she'd had to come up with a plausible story, everything slipped out of her mind at the anger and betrayal in his eyes. "It's not what you think."

"Then you're not having dinner with him?"

"No, I am. It's—"

"What the hell can you be thinking?" he shouted and stood, towering menacingly over her.

Even though that was the reaction she'd expected, it frightened her. "If you'd let me explain."

He glared at her for a long moment, the muscles in his jaw working feverishly. "By all means," he said sharply. "Enlighten me."

She tried not to squirm under the intensity of his gaze and to sort out her thoughts. "He saved my life," she said, ignoring his derisive snort. "I owe him for that."

"And I'm sure dinner is all he wants."

"Simon—"

"Don't be naïve. Do you really think all he wants is the pleasure of your company? At worst, he's a vampire and you won't live the night. Or he's a gangster, hardly better. At best, he's a man whose interest in you goes far beyond dinner conversation, I can assure you. How can you possibly expect me to roll on my back while this creature, this man, goes after my wife!" His expression faltered and he turned away.

She moved to stand behind him, but he moved away before she could reach out to touch him. "Simon, please?"

The desperation in her voice must have penetrated his anger, because when he turned around his eyes softened for a moment, and the Simon she loved peeked through. He looked as if he were about to touch her but thought better of it.

She closed her eyes. She'd been hoping, stupidly hoping, she wouldn't have to tell him the whole of it, but there didn't seem any other way now. "Do you really think I'd do this if I had a choice?"

"What do you mean?" He took a step closer. "Did he threaten you?"

"No," she said, and let her shoulders sag under the weight they'd been carrying. "Not me."

"Me then?"

She nodded. "You and Charlie. Oh, he didn't say it flat out, but it was clear enough."

"I see."

"So, I go."

"Don't be absurd. You're not going to dinner with that man. My God. What if he really is a vampire? How can you even consider this?"

"Maybe you missed the whole threatening part, but that sort of made it a lock for me."

Simon walked over to the armoire, took out their suitcase and set it on the bed. "We'll leave immediately. If his threats are legitimate, and we have to assume they are, we can be miles away before he suspects."

"We can't leave."

He ignored her and took their clothes from the hangers and tossed them into the case. "Perhaps Philadelphia," he said to himself. "Or maybe a small town. We'll see what tickets are available at the train station for the money we have."

"I can't leave," she said in a mixture of defeat and resoluteness.

Simon crossed to the dresser and pulled open the drawers. "Of course you can. What choice is there?"

"Staying."

"Don't be ridiculous."

She bristled at his tone and moved into his path. "I'm not being ridiculous, and I'm not going anywhere."

"Elizabeth—"

"How could we? What about Charlie? How can you turn your back on him?"

Simon tossed the clothes he had in his hands onto the bed and sighed heavily. "With surprising ease. When it comes to a question of your safety or his."

"I'm not the one in danger."

He looked at her as if she were one of his more backward students.

"If he wanted to hurt me, why would he save my life? Or have you forgotten that?"

"No," he said through clenched teeth. "Not when you keep throwing it in my face."

She refused to take the bait and closed her eyes for a moment. "I am not going to run away and leave others holding the bag. You think this is what I want? You think this is easy for me? If I don't go to dinner with King, good people will be hurt and I can't live with that and I'd expect you to know me well enough to know that. I won't let that happen."

"And when the eclipse comes? And King finds you're gone? What happens to Charlie then? One way or the other, we're leaving town, Elizabeth. There's no reason to wait. The outcome is the same either way."

She hadn't thought of that. She'd been so caught up in the here and now, what happened after they went back to their time didn't even cross her mind. "All I know is, right now, I can keep Charlie and you safe by going. So, I go."

"It's insane."

Elizabeth let out a shuddering sigh. "I know."

He grunted and moved to the window. "How can you possibly be considering this after what I told you last night?"

"Because this isn't a dream. This is real. What King does to people is real. You think the men who mugged me were killed by some random murderer? It was King."

Simon whirled around. "You think I don't know that? You think I haven't considered that every waking moment? Even if he isn't a demon, he's a killer. Didn't you listen to anything I said last night? How can you expect me to let you go when you know what I dreamt." He crossed the room in three long strides and gripped her arms tightly. "You may think they're just dreams, but I know what they are. They're as real to me as you are right now."

His grip loosened and his hands slid up her arms, and then cupped her cheeks. "Losing you is real to me."

"And losing you is real to me."

He let go of her and shook his head. "You can't do this, Elizabeth."

"I have to."

"No, you don't. I won't have you going off with that man to protect me. It's madness."

"And if I don't go and something happens to you, what then?"

"We should run. Now, while we have a chance."

"I can't," she said. "But you can. You can leave. Maybe go upstate and when it's time for the eclipse we can meet somewhere. King couldn't find you and you'd be safe."

"Don't be absurd."

"It makes sense. King hasn't threatened me, he's threatened you. If you went somewhere—"

"No! Absolutely not. Impossible."

"Then I don't have much choice, do I?"

"You damn well know you do."

She clenched her fists. Why was he being so damn stubborn? "I'm not going over this again. You can deal with it or not. I hoped you might be supportive."

"Supportive? Of what? This idiocy?"

She looked at him stonily. "Of me." She turned and walked to the door. Her hand stilled on the doorknob. "I'll have King's car drop me off at the club."

"Elizabeth…"

She shook her head. "I think you've said enough," she said and closed the door behind her.

Bloody, fucking hell.

The harder he tried to hold her, the further he pushed her away. But this was madness. The idea of her going to dinner with that man to protect him. Could she possibly find a better way to emasculate him? Good God, was that what this was really about? His male pride. Was he that selfish? Yes, he was. He was a selfish bastard. A complete idiot who'd somehow cleverly managed to hurt the one person in the world he wanted to protect.

She'd come back not long after storming out. No words were exchanged. They shared the bed, but nothing else. They were two people separated by a chasm of inches. His sleep had been fitful at best, a few uneasy hours tossing and turning, before he gave up.

They spent the morning sharing a tense silence. The afternoon scratched along, until it was nearly time for the dinner. Everything that could be said, had been.

Elizabeth dressed quietly and left. He ground his teeth and stood stupidly in their small room. He knew he couldn't stop her, but damn well had to at least try. He grabbed his coat and bolted out of the apartment.

She was standing in front of the club waiting for King's car when he found her.

"Elizabeth, I..."

She crossed her arms over her chest. "You what?"

"I came to say I'm sorry, but I'm not. Honestly, I hate this. I detest the very idea."

"Thanks for rushing down and sharing that."

"You're not making this any easier."

"Making what easier? You've made it clear where you stand—this is stupid and I'm stupid for doing it."

"That's not what I meant."

Just when the words he'd struggled to find were almost in his reach, King's two-tone sedan pulled up to the curb, and the driver stepped out. A hundred protestations, a thousand pleadings choked his throat. All that came out was one simple word. "Please?"

The driver opened the door and waited.

Elizabeth smiled sadly and touched his cheek. "I'll be back," she said and then stepped into the car.

He watched numbly as the sedan pulled away, slipped into traffic and disappeared. He stood on the sidewalk long after it had gone, staring down the busy city street.

Chapter Twenty-One

TWILIGHT BLANKETED THE CITY. Dull, gray light swallowed the afternoon shadows. Depth and perspective muted into a flat, colorless world. Simon stood motionless, only dimly aware of the city bustling around him. Cars, no more than blurs of black, crowded the street. People, hurried and faceless, wove their way around him. And he stood.

He'd let her go. It all seemed an impossible dream, a scene from one of his nightmares. Perhaps it was. His heart thrummed against his ribs, every sinew in his body taut, and yet, he couldn't move. He vaguely wondered if he was suffering from apoplexy.

He was a fool. A simple, excruciating answer to a complex question. The constant barrage of his nightmares had somehow left him in submission to fate. An entropy of will in the face of the inevitable.

But what could he have done? Thrown her over his shoulder and carted her off to parts unknown? She would have hated him for it, but she would have been safe. Did he really need her love and acceptance more than her life itself?

He'd been so dazed by the revelation that she loved him, that he could be loved, that he'd accepted the transience of it all. After all, to love someone was to lose them. But now that he'd tasted what life could be like, there was no going back. The few weeks they'd shared weren't enough. A lifetime with Elizabeth wouldn't be enough.

It was a graceless epiphany, but one nonetheless. Invigorated with a purpose, Simon turned on his heels and marched to the door of Charlie's Blues in the Night. He pushed past Lester and called out to Charlie. Charlie leaned against the cash register talking to Dix when he noticed Simon. "Professor, what can I—"

"King," Simon interrupted. "Where can I find King Kashian?"

"Ah, you don't need to—"

"Where?"

Charlie cast a quick, nervous glance at Dix and then rubbed his nose. "I don't know, Professor."

Simon grunted impatiently. "Then I'll ask elsewhere."

"Wait!" Charlie said, as he came out from behind the bar. "Why do you want to find King?"

Simon hesitated, but then what was the point in lying now? They'd hear about it sooner or later. "Elizabeth's gone to dinner with him," he said. "And I plan on interrupting."

Charlie's eyes went round with alarm. "Lizzy? Why would she do that?"

As if he weren't worried enough, Charlie's near panicked voice sent Simon into overdrive. "Where does he live?"

"You can't just go bustin' in. King's not a man you wanna cross."

"Neither am I."

They stood at an impasse. The silence in the room stretched out between them until it was paper thin.

Charlie gave him a measured look. "There's somethin' you need to know, Professor."

Dix paled and gripped his arm. "Charlie."

"Get me a bottle of the good stuff," he said without looking away from Simon.

Didn't this buffoon realize every minute was precious?

"I don't want a drink."

Charlie shook his head. "Ain't for you. Come on," he said. "Give it over, Dix."

Her hands trembled as she held the bottle, her eyes beseeching. "We ain't supposed to say nothin', Charlie."

Charlie took the whiskey from her hand and then opened the door to the storeroom. "You might think I'm one stop from Bellevue, but...there's something you need to know."

Elizabeth had never been claustrophobic before, but she had the feeling the walls of the elevator were closing in on her as she neared King's penthouse. She took a few deep, calming breaths and swallowed the urge to make inane small talk with the elevator operator. Not that he would have responded. He hadn't met her eyes once since she'd gotten in. He looked straight ahead like a soldier, working the car's levers with quick, sure movements. He brought the car to a stop and the doors opened to reveal a lavish foyer.

Art deco moldings circled the high, arched ceiling of the rotunda. Stark, white, Greek marble statues stood sentinel to over-sized doubled doors. She hesitated and then stepped off the elevator. The doors shut quickly behind her.

She was debating whether to knock or run away when the double doors opened inward. For a second, she thought they'd opened by themselves. Then she saw one of King's men standing there, devoid of expression. He stepped back and gestured for her to enter. A ghostly butler would have been better.

There was no turning back now, Elizabeth realized as she steadied her jangled nerves and walked inside. She flexed her hands and tried to relax. The last thing she needed was to go into dinner already on edge.

Antiquities from every imaginable period lined the walls of the main hall. Cloisonné vases, intricately carved ivory statues mingled with marble busts and classic paintings. Thick tapestries covered most of the walls. There wasn't an empty space to be found. It wasn't exactly cluttered, but full. Too full. The overly ornate chandelier hung overhead like a crystalline storm cloud. Candlelight reflected in jumbled prismatic colors. She shuddered; it wasn't the cold room temperature, but the impersonal chill of things to be admired, but never touched. Oppressively rich and heavy fabrics covered the windows.

Lines from Coleridge's "Kubla Kahn" came to her mind: "In Xanadu did Kubla Kahn a stately pleasure dome decree: where Alph, the sacred river, ran through caverns measureless to man down to a sunless sea."

The henchman gestured for her to follow, and she trailed along behind him down the hall. She'd never seen such an ostentatious display of wealth. In spite of her nerves, she couldn't help but stare. An exquisite soft-paste porcelain vase painted with Roman soldiers and Cleopatra sat nestled on a glass case. Under the glass was row after row of jewelry. Jade, gold, every kind of stone imaginable rested in ornate settings.

To the left was a brown ink drawing of a woman holding the hands of small children. She stopped walking, drawn in by innocence of the piece, so atypical to what she knew of King.

"Beautiful, isn't she?"

She jumped back and crashed into King, who'd silently moved behind her. "S-sorry. I...quite a collection."

He smiled down at her before turning his attention back to the artwork. "I've always collected beautiful things."

She smoothed down her already smooth hair in an attempt to gather her composure. "One of the perks of being richer than God, I guess."

He laughed easily and looked at her. "Money has its benefits, but there are some things beyond price."

Small talk. Small talk was safe. She gestured to the drawing. "Rubens, huh?"

"Yes. I prefer his animals. They're majestic and powerful. The essence of life."

Her art history class knowledge was quickly running out. "So, you bought all these?" she asked lamely.

"A little money. A little creativity."

"You mean you stole them?" It was a stupid thing to say, but her foot was lodged firmly in place.

He didn't seem offended at all, in fact, he looked amused. "I paid people to steal them. It's entirely different. Would you like a tour?"

She didn't. She wanted to wolf down whatever passed for dinner and run like hell. And where had that bodyguard gone? They were alone now, and she swallowed nervously.

"There's something I'd like to show you," he added.

That sounded ominous. "You do know this is only dinner, right?"

"You wound me," he said with a mocking grin, placing a hand over his heart.

"I just want us to lay our cards on the table. I'm here because, well, because you coerced me. And because I do owe you for saving my life. But that's it," she said and lifted her chin defiantly. "Nothing more."

His eyes flashed briefly and a smile crept to his lips. "Of course."

With that vague assurance, he led her down the main hall. The tour was blessedly brief, and he completely ignored one wing of the penthouse. She figured it must have been his private chambers and felt a surge of relief that he hadn't asked her if she wanted to see his etchings. King was a cad, but so far at least, he was behaving like a gentleman.

The dining hall was formal. A long, mahogany table filled the floor space. Wingback chairs, enough for a dozen guests, rimmed the edge.

"You must entertain a lot," she said.

"Hardly," he said and held out her chair. She wished she'd been seated at the far end of the table, but the place settings were tucked together at the end furthest from the door. "Only on very special occasions."

That was the rub. "And what's so special about this occasion?"

He opened his linen napkin with the flair of a magician. "You."

She wriggled nervously in her chair and studied the silver salt and pepper shakers. He was actually being charming. Under different circumstances, if she weren't already in love, if he weren't a murdering gangster and possible vampire. But then if wishes were horses, she'd saddle one up and ride it the hell out of here.

He leaned back in his chair confidently. "Is it really so wrong that I want to get to know you better?"

"I guess not," she said. Keeping the conversation neutral was probably the best idea, but there was nothing neutral about King. Besides, he seemed to appreciate her honesty. "If you're looking to make friends, threatening them...not a good first step."

"Would you have come if I hadn't?"

She rubbed her sweaty palms on her dress and managed to meet his eyes. "No."

He inclined his head and reached for a crystal carafe. "Precisely. Wine?"

She eyed the wine suspiciously. Why did it have to be red wine? Dark, red, the color of blood. "No, thank you."

He set the carafe down with a thud. His face tightened, and his voice was low and harsh. "If I'd meant you any harm, I wouldn't have bothered saving your life. Don't make me regret that decision. I suggest you drink the wine."

Elizabeth pressed herself back in her chair. Aside from the obvious threat, there was a cruelty in his voice that scared her even more. God, how she wished Simon were there. And what a bad idea. Simon's temper would surely get them both killed, and the object of the game was staying alive.

She twisted the napkin in her lap, fumbling for a way to diffuse King's anger. If she was going to get out of here in one piece, she'd be wise to play the well-mannered guest. She forced herself to sit up straight and not fidget.

"I suppose one glass wouldn't do any harm."

As quickly as it had come, the storm cloud passed from his face and he smiled. "It's an excellent vintage, I assure you."

Great. Dinner with Dr. Jeckle and Mr. Hyde—an intimate portrait.

She managed a small sip and an even smaller smile. "Good."

"I'm pleased you approve."

King, once again the genial host, leaned back in his chair. As if on cue, two servants appeared with silver trays. "I'm sure you'll find the meal satisfactory. Far better then that diner you frequent, I assure you."

The fork slipped from her hand. "How did you know about that?"

"I'm not a man without means."

"You've been spying on me?"

"Spying has such a negative ring to it. I'm merely... keeping an eye on you. It's a dangerous city and the Manchester Arms isn't in the best neighborhood, but then I don't need to tell you that, do I?" he said and lifted one of the silver coverings from a tray. "I think you'll particularly enjoy the duck."

She felt sick. He knew where she lived, where she ate. Who knows how long he'd been having them followed. "I'm not feeling very hungry anymore."

King smirked and set the covering down. "Very well. I'm a patient man. We'll simply enjoy each other's company until your appetite returns."

There was no getting out of it. No getting out of any of it. Maybe the sooner she ate, the sooner she could leave. She picked up her fork and managed to get a mouthful down.

The dinner, what she ate of it, was excellent, or would have been if her stomach hadn't been on strike. The chef at the Ritz owed King a favor, for what she didn't ask, and had prepared an elegant meal. King rearranged the food on his plate, taking small bites. The strange thing was he never took off his gloves. She hadn't seen him without them. Odd enough in the middle of a heat wave, but at dinner, in his own home?

He must have noticed her staring, because he set down his fork and rubbed his gloved palms together. "An affectation," he said, with a mild grin. "My hands are always cold. But as they say, cold hands, warm heart. As it were."

She smiled and went back to her meal. Cold hands, ice cold heart was more like it. Or was it even more than that? She remembered the feeling of his ice cold lips the night he'd kissed her hand. Vampires lacked normal blood circulation and were rumored to be cold to the touch. And, she thought, looking at his untouched food, they didn't eat.

Maybe her imagination was running away with her. There were other explanations, but she couldn't shake the feeling that the man sitting across from her wasn't a man at all.

The conversation was sporadic and more often than not ended with a dangling question or an ambiguous answer. Once the final course had been served, King leaned back in his chair and regarded her with calm appraisal. "You are a charming guest. When you set your mind to it."

"Thank you, I think. And it was a lovely dinner, but I really should be getting back. Simon will be—"

"Ah, yes. Professor Cross," King said, lingering over the name with mild amusement. "I don't think he likes me very much."

He hates your guts didn't seem like a profitable thing to say, and so Elizabeth merely shrugged.

"But I see why he likes you. You're different, Elizabeth. Very different from the women I've met. A man could spend several lifetimes looking for a woman like you. There's a uniqueness, I can't put my finger on it, an unusual quality about you."

"I could say the same about you."

"Touché. So, tell me," he said casually. "How did you meet your husband?"

The way he caressed the last word made her tense. "Simon?"

"Unless you have more than one."

"No, just the one." She crammed a spoonful of crème brûlée into her mouth to buy time. She could make up a story, but there was no guarantee she'd remember it. Best to stick with the truth. "We met at college. I was a student there, and he was a professor."

King's smirk reached all the way to his eyebrows. "Dating the professor? I'm shocked."

"We didn't actually date until after I graduated."

"A college graduate working as a waitress. That's odd, isn't it?"

Elizabeth shrugged. "Good jobs are hard to find."

King grunted noncommittally and sipped his wine. "Where did you go to school?"

"Out of state." This was getting worse and worse. Time to go on the offensive. "But enough about me and my boring life. Tell me about you. How does somebody become a..."

"A gangster?" he said with that damn smirk. "Family business. Tell me more about yourself. I do find your...story fascinating."

Elizabeth grew nervous at the word "story". Best to stop this conversation now. "Didn't you say there was something you wanted to show me?" she asked.

King smiled. "Yes, there is."

Out of the frying pan into the fire, she thought. Smooth.

King set down his napkin and pushed back his chair. "Shall we?"

Knowing she had little choice, Elizabeth agreed and followed King out of the dining room and down the main hall. They veered into the wing King had avoided earlier. He stopped at a dark paneled door and took a small key from his pocket. He opened the door and waited for Elizabeth to enter first. The room was dark and there was a thick odor of strange spices. King stepped in behind her and turned on the overhead light.

She blinked to let her eyes adjust to the sudden light. It was like stepping into the Egyptian section of the British Museum, at least according to the brochures she'd seen. Artifacts ranging from small statues to a complete sarcophagus filled the room. Large, limestone blocks were piled in one corner. The paint had faded, but the images were still clear.

Despite her fears, her curiosity couldn't be contained and she walked further into the room. "This is amazing."

King closed the door. "Beautiful, aren't they?"

"Yeah," she said and moved to keep her distance as he crossed to the small table in the center of the room.

He picked up a small statue and held it reverently in his hand. "A shabti," he said and held the brightly painted figure for her to see. "They're said to come to life once their master is awakened in the afterlife. Do you know much about Egyptology?"

"A little." In her research with Simon, she'd studied some of the ancient beliefs about eternal life. They'd managed to acquire a few artifacts for his collection, but the market for them was ridiculously overpriced. Even their few visits to the local museums couldn't compare with the collection in this room.

"I'm something of an enthusiast," he said in gross understatement. "They believed that a person never truly dies. Eternal life. Quite an intriguing concept."

"I suppose."

"You wouldn't want to live forever?"

"I guess there might be perks, but no."

King smiled enigmatically and set down the small statue. "They believed that the soul, even after death, remained in the body. Remained there awaiting judgment, until granted entrance to the underworld by Osiris." He waved his hand at the table. "All of this, elaborate ointments and rituals, would secure the soul even in the face of human mortality."

"That's interesting," Elizabeth said and eased her way toward the door. "Really quite a collection, and thank you for sharing it with me, but it's late."

"Time is irrelevant," he said, "if you want it to be."

She definitely didn't like the sound of that. "I don't understand what you mean."

"Don't you?" he asked and walked slowly toward her. "Surely, you've sensed it."

She backed up against the door and tried the handle, but it was locked. "I'd like to go now."

"I haven't shown you everything."

"I've seen enough. Please, unlock the door."

He stopped in the middle of the room. "Don't be frightened."

He closed his eyes and Elizabeth couldn't stifle her gasp.

His face changed. Thick, corded veins bulged out on his forehead, slicing over his temples and popping out along his neck. Swollen and pulsing, the deformities stripped away any illusion of humanity. His mouth gaped open and his incisors grew before her eyes, grotesque fangs like a serpent's, curved and wicked. Finally, he opened his eyes and they glowed like amber lit from within. It wasn't the face of a man anymore.

It was the face of a vampire.

CHAPTER TWENTY-TWO

"**H**OLY CRAP!"

Elizabeth shrank back and tried to push herself through the door. King's yellow eyes glowed brighter. His nostrils flared as he tilted his head up and stole her scent from the air, a predator finding its prey. He took a step forward, and she flattened herself against the door as tightly as she could. Her blood pounded in her veins and she knew he could sense it too. Slowly, the rhythm of her beating heart was pulling him closer.

"King," she whispered, barely able to get the word past her dry throat.

He took another step, closing the distance between them. His bulk blocked out the light, and his face fell into shadows. Only the surreal glow from his eyes filled the void between them. He raised one hand, the gloved fingers stretching out and nearing her face.

She was going to die. She pressed her palms against the door, as she raised her chin, one final act of defiance. Then, King's hand halted its approach and hovered inches from her face, trembling.

"King," she said again, more strongly than before. If the man was in control of the demon, she had to reach him.

He closed his eyes and lowered his head. The demon visage faded. When he opened his eyes, he was a man again, but the cool restraint she'd seen before was gone. He pushed out a quick breath and took a step back. He looked nearly as shocked as she was by his lack of control, but he recovered quickly.

Elizabeth licked her dry lips and tried to speak, but her voice came out in a croak. "You're a vampire."

"Not just that," he said, fully in control again. Whatever battle had waged inside him was over. "If that's all I were, you'd be dead right now."

Her head was spinning. How could this be happening? It was one thing to read texts, to read two hundred year old accounts, but to be standing face to face with... She could barely bring herself to think it. Even having considered the possibility, facing the truth was shocking. Vampires were real. Real and staring at her.

"How?" she asked. That was too simple a question, but the best she could do.

King seemed pleased at the question. "Let's start at the beginning, shall we?" he said and then shook his head, ever the gracious host. "Would you like to sit? Your legs look about to give way. It is quite a shock."

He was right about that. Her knees hadn't stopped wobbling. "Standing's fine, thanks."

"As you wish," he said and then walked to the center table. He ran his finger over one of the small figures. "Eight years ago, when Carter discovered Tutankhamen's tomb, I knew I had to have a part of the treasure. From one King to another. It began merely as avarice, to have something so unique. To own it. But once the artifacts began arriving, it grew into something much more." He looked around the room proudly. "Much more."

"I'd recently inherited my father's business," he said without an ounce of sarcasm. "He was killed by rivals, and I assumed the mantle of command but had no desire to die an early death. They're quite common in my line of business. I'd read of the ancient Egyptian's beliefs in eternal life, and set out to discover their secrets. How to cheat death."

Elizabeth's knees had stopped wobbling, but she didn't dare move. King walked smoothly around the room as he told her his story. It was so shockingly antithetical to the demon she'd seen, the pleasant timbre of his voice, the graceful movements.

"My brother, it seems, had different ideas. He'd always been jealous of me. Jealous of the favor our father showed me," he said and shrugged indifferently. "His jealousy devoured him, until he tried to kill me. Technically he succeeded, but his plans, like everything else in his life, didn't quite work out. He aligned himself with a group of vampires."

"You mean there are lots of you?"

He smiled indulgently. "Not anymore. But I digress. My brother's first mistake was to trust them. They're stupid creatures, guided only by lust and hunger. They exist only to feed. No better than drug addicts." As if sensing her unspoken question, he continued. "I am, as I said, not just a vampire. The demon doesn't control me, I control it."

She knew that was only partially true. When he'd let the demon out, his control had faltered. For those brief, infinitely long moments, he'd been nothing more than a beast, wanting only the kill.

"But these creatures were like animals, no discipline, no thought. Pathetic," he said and gave a mirthless laugh. "This group, although rather inept, had managed to function as a small gang. Buoyed by meager successes, a series of artless murders and minor robberies, they'd garnered a bit of a reputation in the underworld. My brother offered them a chance for a bigger score, to climb the food chain, as it were."

Even in her fright, Elizabeth found herself listening with rapt attention. A gang of vampires loose on the streets of New York City. The underworld run by, well, the underworld.

"The ambush was ill-conceived and poorly executed," King continued. "My brother wanted to strike me down here, in this very room. His version of irony, I suppose. But I'd gotten wind of his plan and was prepared. Prepared in ways they couldn't imagine. Of course, they were supposed to kill me, but they betrayed my brother, to no one's surprise but his own. Why take the runt of the litter when you can have the best? They wanted to make me one of them, add to their cadre. Fools."

He stopped pacing and turned to face her. "The Egyptians were right. Death isn't the end, it's merely a bridge. That very day, I performed the ritual for preserving the soul. When they tried to turn me, I retained my soul. The typical victim is no more than a shell, a husk that provides the demon with access to this world. But my soul was bonded to my body, and it made me more powerful than they could imagine. A demon and a soul yoked together."

Elizabeth shuddered. That explained the dual personality she'd sensed. "And your brother?"

King's eyes sparked. "He was the last to die, and the most pleasurable to kill."

Her knees threatened to buckle. She was standing in a room with a mass murderer. A demon. How often did he kill? How did he choose his victims? Was she next? Why hadn't he killed her when he had the chance? She tried the door handle again, and to her surprise, felt it turn. It wasn't locked. In her panic, she must have turned it the wrong way.

"You were always free to leave," he said. His confidence slipped, and she saw the ghost of insecurity flit across his face.

Despite the voice in her head screaming for her to run, to run and never look back, there was a chorus of other voices asking questions, questions she and Simon had spent years trying to answer. Simon! How was she going to tell him? Oh, by the way, that proof you've spent your life looking for, well, I had dinner with it.

She looked at King and said the only thing she could. "I'm sorry."

His back straightened. "I didn't tell you this for pity."

"Why did you tell me?"

He regarded her calmly. "Because it's what I am."

"But why me?"

He walked over to her, and she somehow managed to stand her ground. He stroked her cheek with his gloved hand. "How does any man answer that question? You are an amazing woman."

She tried not to shrink back from his touch. "I don't understand."

He smiled enigmatically and stepped back. "I don't suppose you do. Yet."

Her head was throbbing and his cryptic answers weren't helping any. She ran a hand over her forehead and massaged her temple. She had the beginnings of one hell of a headache.

He pulled a watch chain from his pocket. "It's late, and you're obviously tired," he said, once again the well-mannered host. "We can continue this another time."

"You're letting me go?"

"I told you that you were always free to go."

There had to be a catch. There was always a catch. "And you won't hurt anyone. Simon or Charlie?"

"That's up to you. Every action has a consequence."

She could leave, but he'd know every move she made, and Simon would pay the price. "So, I'm not really free at all, am I?"

"We're all bound by the choices we make," he said and reached into his breast pocket. "I don't think you'd want to leave town without this." He held out his hand, and resting in his palm was Simon's scarab ring.

She felt her stomach drop. "Where did you get that?"

"I could ask you the same question," he said and held it up to the light. "Very unusual. One of a kind?"

"That doesn't belong to you."

"Oh, I think it does. But I am curious. How did you come by it?"

"A family heirloom, and I'd appreciate it if you'd give it back to me," she said and held out her hand.

"Perhaps," he said and slipped it back into his pocket. "In time. As I said, I'm a patient man."

And one who had, literally, all the time in the world. Her head throbbed even harder. "I'd like to go home now."

"Of course," he said and opened the door. "My man will take you."

She choked back the bitter taste the evening left in her throat and managed a tight, "Thank you."

King watched her disappear into the foyer before closing the door. He reached back into his pocket and took out the scarab ring and set it on the table. Slowly, he took off his right glove and there, on his finger was the exact same ring, with the exact same crack down the stone. He slid it from his hand and put it down on the table with its twin.

"A sign indeed."

Simon leaned on the far end of the bar and stared down at his clenched fists. It had taken all of Charlie's strength to keep him from forcing his way out into the night and blindly banging on doors until he found King. He knew it would have been useless, but anything had to be better than waiting. He'd spent the first two hours pacing in the back room, until the walls started to close in. Being in the bar was no better. Every time someone laughed he wanted to cram it back down their throat. Every minute that scratched by took another layer of skin. Every glass of whiskey that passed over the bar called his name. He ached for a drink, anything to blur the horrific images that cluttered his mind.

A vampire. His worst suspicions confirmed. Elizabeth was with the creature and there wasn't a damn thing he could do but wait. He clenched his fist until the knuckles strained white. Useless. Bloody fucking useless. He wanted to rage, to hit something until his hands were as raw as he felt inside.

A man shouldered up to the bar and tapped Simon on the shoulder. "Ain't ya gonna play or what?"

Simon blinked a few times and then turned to the man with a withering gaze.

Charlie interrupted before things got worse. "Ankle it. Go on. Get," he grunted and pulled the man forcibly by the lapels away from Simon. "Sorry 'bout that, Professor."

One more hour. He'd give her one more hour to return, then he'd take the city apart brick by brick till he found her. Charlie's assurances that if King wanted to hurt Elizabeth he'd have already done it weren't comforting. Going in half-cocked and getting himself killed wouldn't help her either. Damn it. There had to be something he could do.

If only he'd been more careful with the watch. If he'd only pushed her away when the light had enveloped him. If only. A thousand chances to keep her out of harm's way, each one missed. Each missed opportunity had brought her a step closer to him, and the death his very presence would inevitably bring. Or had it already? Was she...?

He pushed that thought aside ferociously. No, she wasn't. She couldn't be. It was his fate to watch. He knew that as surely as anything. When the time came, he'd bear witness to it. He took morose comfort in the thought. A drowning man will grasp even the blade of a sword.

Was he so pathetic as to let fate wrench away the only thing that meant anything to him without a fight? There had to be something he could do, some way to protect her. He'd spent years studying the bloody things. They had weaknesses. King had to have a weakness.

Vampires could be destroyed, he knew that much. They were strong, but not invincible. He needed weapons, tools, something, anything. And if King harmed one hair on Elizabeth's head, he'd kill him with his bare hands if he had to.

"Professor?"

Simon looked at Charlie expecting to see the same haggard, worried face he'd seen for the last few hours.

"Told ya," Charlie said, grinning from ear to ear. He mopped his brow with the bar rag and nodded toward the door. "She's back."

Simon turned and Elizabeth was standing in the doorway. She looked tired and pale, and more beautiful than ever. He strode across the bar, one step behind his heart, and gathered her into his arms in a crushing embrace. "Oh, love," he rasped. God, to feel her in his arms again.

"I'm all right," she said.

He pulled back to look into her eyes. He needed to see her face to be sure.

"Really," she said with a small smile.

His hands cupped her cheeks as he searched her eyes. Her skin was warm, alive, but even that reassurance didn't stop himself from sliding them down her neck.

She pulled away and looked at him accusingly. "What are you doing?"

"I had to be sure."

"You mean, you know?"

"Charlie told me."

She pulled back, her eyes clouded with confusion and betrayal. "Charlie knows?"

"Lizzy!" Charlie said.

"I'll tell you later," Simon whispered, before Charlie pulled her into a bear hug. Her body tensed as Charlie held her arms.

"You look all right," Charlie said, as he held her at arm's length. "Was so worried, thought I might have kittens."

"I'm all right, just tired," she said wriggling out of his embrace.

Charlie stood awkwardly for a moment still holding her arm. "Sure. Course ya are."

"We're going home," Simon said and eased her out of Charlie's grasp.

"Right. Yeah," Charlie said, and smiled at Elizabeth. "Sure glad you're okay, Lizzy."

Elizabeth nodded, her eyes glinting with mistrust, and slipped her hand into Simon's. "Let's just get out of here."

Simon hurried them along the dark streets. As much as he wanted to know what had happened, he needed to feel she was safe, and their little flat was as close as he could get.

Once they were home, Elizabeth stood in the middle of the room, her arms wrapped around her chest. Simon came up behind her, and she jumped when he put his hands on her shoulders. She stepped away and looked up at him, before turning away. "I need to take a bath."

He caught her arm. "Elizabeth—"

She squirmed out of his grasp. "Please?"

She looked so small, so vulnerable. All he wanted to do was wrap her in his arms and never let go. But right now this wasn't about what he wanted. "Of course," he said and let his hands fall to his sides.

She went into the bath and turned on the taps. Simon stood on the threshold and watched as she slowly undressed. Her hands shook as she struggled with the buttons of her dress, and Simon stepped forward and covered her trembling hands with his own. He undid the rest and then stepped back to lean against the door jam. He'd give her the distance she needed, but she was not going to be out of his sight.

Without looking back, she stepped into the hot water. The little room filled with clouds of steam. Wisps of water vapor, hotter even than the heat of the summer night, snaked up like tendrils of smoke.

Simon breathed in the cloying air and waited.

The water ran until it nearly spilled over the sides. Elizabeth didn't seem to notice. She sat huddled in the tub, barely moving.

He shut off the taps and knelt down next to her. Her skin glowed red from the scalding water. His heart ached at the sight of her—curling in on herself, trying to burn away the memory of the night.

"Come on, love," he said, and eased her out of the tub. She stepped onto the mat, and he wrapped a towel around her shoulders.

She sniffled and looked up at him, tears filling her eyes. "I'm sorry."

"Shhh," he whispered, and pushed a wet lock of hair from her face. He took her nightshirt from the hook on the back of the door and eased it over her head.

"Let's get you in bed," he said and led her back into the bedroom.

She crawled to the middle of the bed and leaned back against the headboard, clutching a pillow to her chest. Simon sat on the edge of the bed and once again resisted the urge to take her into his arms.

"I don't think I can do this anymore," she said softly, looking as helpless as he felt.

"Tell me what happened."

Her brow wrinkled and fresh tears threatened to spill out of her eyes.

"Please," he said hoarsely. "I know this is difficult, but I...I have to know. Did he... Did he touch you?"

"No," she answered and Simon felt one of the fists that clenched his heart ease its grip.

"He was a perfect gentleman," she said with a bitter laugh, "when he wasn't threatening you or Charlie." She squeezed the pillow tighter, and he saw the sense of betrayal in her eyes. "Charlie knew? All along he knew what King was and he didn't say anything?"

"I think I understand his reasons, but don't worry about that right now," he said and took hold of her hand. He'd made a complete cockup of the situation until now. And it was time for things to change. "I know it's difficult, but I need you to tell me what happened tonight. Everything that happened."

Slowly, she eased out of her despondency and recalled every facet of the evening, regaining strength in the telling. She didn't know where she'd been taken. The limousine had curtains in the back, and they'd remained closed for the trip. Judging from the distance she'd traveled, she guessed it was somewhere uptown, but couldn't be more specific than that. She described the lavish apartment and recounted the details of King's change with chilling precision. The academic part of Simon's brain catalogued each detail of the creature's appearance, while all his heart wanted to do was to tell her to stop, to blot out the last twenty-hours and spirit her away.

She told him all she could remember of their conversations, including the chilling revelation that King had been not only following them, but actively investigating them. Who knows what, besides his grandfather's ring, King had gotten from Smitty at the pawnshop. Simon tried to remember the scene to see if they'd inadvertently let any telling details slip.

"I guess there's nothing to do but wait," she said finally. "It's only a week until the eclipse."

"Too much can happen in a week," Simon said, as he pushed off the bed and started to pace.

"What else can we do?" she asked, and then quickly read his expression. "We can't leave. He'll follow us."

He gritted his teeth and shook his head. "Have I mentioned how much I hate this?"

"I know," she said. "And I'm so sorry about your grandfather's ring."

Simon dismissed it, but there was something very troubling about it, something he couldn't quite put his finger on. Perhaps King had taken it as tangible proof of his knowledge about them. "It's not important," he said. "We'll find some protection tomorrow. Go to St. Patrick's and get supplies: holy water, crosses."

He didn't actually put much stock in the idea of religious icons affording them protection, but if there was even the slightest chance they might help, he'd get them.

"I don't remember reading about any accounts of vampires that match your description," Simon said, his need to categorize and analyze giving him a respite from the helplessness he felt. "The veins are somewhat similar to the Danag of the Philippines, but the eyes are all wrong."

"Maybe having a soul mutated him somehow?"

"Perhaps. You don't remember any particular odors?"

"No. Why?"

"Some species give off a slight metallic scent. Some attribute it to the blood they'd consumed. Others, ancient alchemists, believed that if you could find the proper ore, you could forge a weapon to kill them."

"You don't see a lot of forges on the lower east side."

"No," he said with a small grin. "But I'm sure there are factories not far away. It's something to consider. Silver shouldn't be that hard to find, although I doubt we could afford very much."

"And we're not even sure it would do any good."

She pulled the pillow tighter to her chest, and he sat on the bed next to her. Her beautiful blue eyes filled with tears again, but she fought against them, trying to be strong. Simon moved closer to her, and she settled into his arms. He rested his chin atop her head. He would do what had to be done. Whatever that meant, whatever it took, he'd find a way to protect her.

"It will be all right," he said and kissed the top of her head. "I promise."

Chapter Twenty-Three

"**D**OESN'T STEALING IT DE-HOLY it or something?" Elizabeth whispered, as they dipped another vial into the shallow holy water font. She wasn't religious, but stealing from a church couldn't be good.

"Shhh," Simon urged with a nervous look around.

Old St. Patrick's was a heavily frequented church. They'd almost been caught twice by people passing by on their way to pray.

"Can I help you?" said a familiar voice with an unmistakable Irish lilt.

Oh boy. "Father," Elizabeth said as she turned around.

"And what exactly would you be needin' with, well, the entire day's holy water?"

"It's a funny story really."

"Oh, is it now?"

"Not exactly funny-funny, but... Tell him Simon," she said with a nudge to his ribs.

Simon rolled his eyes and recapped the small vial. "I don't expect you to understand or even believe me, but we need this to fight a vampire."

Elizabeth dropped her vial. "Sorry," she said and scrambled to pick it up.

Father Cavanaugh sighed and nodded. "I see. Perhaps we should continue this in the back?" he said, and gestured to a door in the rear of the church.

Elizabeth started down the main aisle, then self-consciously doglegged through a set of pews to the far aisle. There was always something about churches that made her vaguely uneasy. It wasn't the quiet. After all, she loved libraries. She'd never put her finger on it. She always thought it was the formality of it all, being told where to sit, what to believe.

Softly murmured prayers filled the silence. As she watched Father Cavanaugh and Simon whisper something to each other, she realized what it was. It was secrets. Everyone there always seemed to know something she didn't. For all her conviction, for all her words about believing being enough, a part of her always questioned, always doubted. She wasn't raised in any particular religion and for the first time she envied those who were. She looked up at the brilliant sunlight streaming through the stained glass. How comforting it would be right now to give herself over to an all-knowing something.

"Elizabeth?" Simon said, pulling her from her tangled thoughts.

"Coming."

They followed Father Cavanaugh into a small back room. Cherry wood cabinets and a shining metal drum, like a water dispenser, lined the far wall. The Father gestured to a beaten leather couch.

"You've some experience with vampires?" Simon said in a very businesslike way, as if he asked the question every day. The Father nodded. "I thought as much."

Father Cavanaugh pulled up a rickety wooden chair and sat down. "And it seems, so do you."

"What can you tell me?" Simon asked.

"A man of few words, I see. I respect that, but may I beg a little indulgence? I'm an old man and prone to ramble on a bit, I'm afraid," he said with a wink at Elizabeth.

She could feel Simon tense, even as he leaned back against the cushions. "Of course."

The Father inclined his head and then turned his attention to Elizabeth. "What have ya seen, lass?"

"How'd you know it was me?"

"A demon is always drawn to the innocent."

She laughed nervously. "I'm not exactly what you'd call innocent, but thank you."

The priest leaned forward in his chair. "It's a purity of the heart they seek. To sully the unsullied."

Simon grunted and shifted in his seat.

"And if they have a soul?" Elizabeth asked.

The father rocked back in his chair. "I see."

"Well, I bloody well don't," Simon bit out. "Soul or not. What difference does it make?"

"Every soul is worth saving."

"Not this one," Simon said.

The Father settled back in his chair and clasped his hands. "And why would that be?"

"He's after my wife."

Elizabeth felt a thrill at the words. Sure, it was a fib, but she felt like his wife, or what she imagined it would feel like.

The priest smiled genially. "Coveting your neighbor's wife is a sin, but hardly reason enough to be kept from Heaven."

"Murder, extortion. You can take your pick of sins. And honestly I don't care," Simon said. Ever since the Father had side-stepped Simon's questions about the murder, he didn't seem to have much faith in the man.

"I didn't come here to find a way to save a man I'd just as soon see dead," Simon continued.

"Simon!"

If Father Cavanaugh was insulted he didn't show it. His placid face betrayed nothing. "Why did you come here? Aside from liberating some of my holy water?"

Elizabeth chimed in before Simon could. "That's all we came for, but now that we're here, maybe you can help us?"

She felt Simon shift in his seat and quickly continued before he said something insulting. "We know a little bit, but our practical experience is, well, different."

"And what experience is that, child?"

"King. I guess you've probably heard about him."

"I'm acquainted with Mr. Kashian. We've spoken on occasion."

Simon snorted and Elizabeth stilled his tongue with a gentle hand on his forearm. There was something odd about the way the Father looked when he mentioned King, but she put it out of her head. "I had dinner with him last night. Not that I wanted to, but he... persuaded me. And then, I'm not really sure why, but he told me about what happened to him."

"Did he now?" the father said, both surprised and troubled. "Isn't that interesting."

"That isn't the word I'd use," Simon said tartly.

The Father smiled sympathetically. "No, I suppose not. Forgive me, you were sayin'? He revealed himself to you? But he didn't attack?"

"No," Elizabeth said, "he didn't."

"It's some pathetic game to him," Simon said.

"Oh, no. This is no game," the Father said. "Another creature wouldn't have hesitated."

Elizabeth shivered. That's exactly what King had said to her. Simon clutched her hand in his and gave it a comforting squeeze, but she could feel the tension in his grip.

"It's a terrible truth, I'm afraid," Father Cavanaugh continued. "Used to be quite a problem here. Although, I fear Tammany Hall may be spawning something new." He smiled ruefully. "Politics."

Good grief. She knew the government was corrupt, but demons too? It was too much to think about, and she tried to push the implications out of her mind. One problem at a time.

"Used to be?" Elizabeth asked. "Is that because King... killed them?"

The Father clasped his hands in his lap. "It's a wicked debt to owe, is it not? Better a lone wolf than a pack?"

"Unless that wolf is after your wife," Simon said. "You'll forgive me, Father. Under different circumstances I'd love to discuss the past, but it's the present that concerns me. Soul or not, Kashian has made his motives perfectly clear. I intend to protect my wife by whatever means necessary. If you have something that might help me, I'm in your debt. If not, we'll try elsewhere."

"Simon—"

"No, no. He's quite right, my dear. And of course, I'll do what I can to help you."

Elizabeth let out a shaky breath. "Thank you."

"You came for holy water and crosses, I imagine?"

"If you can spare them."

The priest smiled kindly. "I think I can manage that, but I'm afraid they won't help you. In the spirit yes, but not the flesh."

Simon leaned back and narrowed his eyes. "So it is a myth."

Elizabeth had been hoping Simon was wrong about that. He'd always doubted the claims of religious icons affecting vampires, but it sure would have been nice if he'd been wrong. "All the books I've read, all the research?"

"Propaganda," Simon said. "Another way the church exerts its control. Another in a long series of misinformation campaigns to keep people depending on the church for things it can't provide."

"Or perhaps to give them faith," Father Cavanaugh said. "Where's the harm in helping quell people's fear? To give them a feeling they have power over the Evil that surrounds us. Faith is the best protection."

"That's wonderful in the abstract, and I'm sure it comforts children before they go to bed at night," Simon said and leaned forward. "I wish we were dealing with fanciful notions and things that only haunt people's dreams, but this is real. This isn't some amorphous darkness lurking around the next corner. This is a creature, flesh and blood standing in front of me and threatening to take everything I hold dear. You'll forgive me for being blunt, but I didn't come here for God's help. I came for something much more practical."

"I find God very practical."

Elizabeth rushed to diffuse the situation. "He didn't mean that the way it came out."

"Don't apologize for me, Elizabeth. I meant what I said. We came here for weapons, nothing more."

"I understand," the priest said. "But not all weapons are forged in steel. The most powerful weapon against Evil is inside you. Your faith."

Simon snorted, but Elizabeth tried to ignore him. "What if... I'm not very religious, Father. I don't really know what I believe about God."

"Ah, but you have faith."

"I don't know," she said. She thought she did, but the last twenty-four hours had made her question lots of things. She'd believed they could face anything together, but there didn't seem any way out of the mess they'd gotten themselves into.

Father Cavanaugh looked from Simon back to Elizabeth. "You two love each other?"

"Yes," she said without hesitation.

"And you believe in that. You believe in your love for each other?"

Elizabeth nodded.

"That's God," he said. "He goes by many names, many faces, but God is simply that—love. I find God in this church, in the faces of my parishioners. One man may find it in nature, in the majesty of a tree or a river," he said and then looked directly at Simon. "Or another man may find it in a woman's smile. Wherever it's to be found, it's to be cherished. When you find it, you hold onto it and nothing, no force, no evil can take it from you. It's yours forever. And that, my dear, is something very powerful."

Elizabeth had never thought about faith in such simple terms. It had always been something vague and just beyond her reach. If love was the answer, she thought as she looked at Simon, she had that in abundance.

"That's a poetic notion, Father," Simon said. "But I fail to see how that will save our lives."

"Not your lives perhaps, but your souls."

"You'll forgive me if my concerns are slightly more immediate," Simon said.

Father Cavanaugh seemed troubled by Simon's curt dismissal, but with patience born of years of practice, he nodded calmly.

"If we can't use holy water or crosses," Simon said. "What can we use? What can you tell us of his weaknesses?"

The Father sighed and his hands clenched before he spread his palms on his knees. "I'm afraid, I can be of very little help there."

He obviously knew things he wouldn't, or couldn't share.

"I see," Simon said, clearly angry at the priest's withholding, and rose from the couch. "Thank you for your time. Elizabeth?"

She smiled apologetically at the priest and stood. "Thank you, Father. You've been a great help."

"It was my pleasure, child. You're welcome here anytime."

Simon barely waited for her to catch up as he started for the door. After the cool sanctuary of the church, the midday sun beat down on them with a vengeance.

"Sophistry," Simon mumbled to himself and pushed out a frustrated breath. "I should have known that would be a waste of time."

"I don't think it was."

He looked like he was about to give her a scathing rebuttal, but his expression softened as he gently touched her cheek. "Perhaps not," he said. "Regardless, we should find stakes. There's likely a hardware store not too far. There must be other weapons we can find." He loosened his tie and rolled his neck. "Damn heat."

"Simon, I don't think going all Rambo is going to help." He stared at her blankly, clearly not following the reference. "I mean, I'd feel better with some sort of protection, but—"

"But what? Against my better judgment, I've agreed to abide by your wishes and stay in this...city. But I will not let another day go by unprepared."

Arguing was futile and the heat sapped her strength. It was impossible to remain angry with him. She knew how difficult it was for him to stay in town. How difficult all of this was for him. "All right," she said. "But aside from getting stakes, what can we really do?"

"Over there," he said. "The telephone office."

"We're gonna kill him with long distance charges?"

"That was beneath even you," he said, but couldn't hide the smile tugging at the corners of his mouth.

She stepped closer and fiddled with his tie. "You're testy when it gets hot, aren't you?"

"Elizabeth, please," he said and pulled the tie from her hands. "This will take subterfuge. Do you think you're up to it?"

"I can fuge with the best of them."

"I'll take that as a yes," he said and stepped back and looked at her appraisingly. "Do you have any lipstick?"

Now that was an odd question. "Umm, no."

"Nothing to be done for it, I suppose."

"Gee, thanks."

Simon ignored her sarcasm and narrowed his eyes. "Lick your lips."

Maybe the heat really was getting to him. There was a nice shady spot over by the newsstand. "I think you need to sit down."

"I need you to cause a diversion. Use your feminine wiles."

"Oh. Oh!" she said, realizing what he'd been talking about. She pulled the collar of her dress down and arched her back, pushing out her breasts. Shifting her hips to the side, she looked at him coyly. "Little ol' me?"

His frown deepened. "Maybe this isn't such a good idea."

She pouted, and he shook his head. "Come along, Matahari."

"Be careful with that," Elizabeth said, as she closed the door to the apartment behind them.

Simon carefully eased a mason-sized, glass jar out from under his jacket. "Would you stop nagging?"

"When you put the acid down, I'll stop."

It was insane, she thought. Brilliant, but insane. Religious icons aside, there were only four ways to kill a vampire—a wooden stake through the heart, beheading, burning, and exposure to sunlight. Too bad tanning beds hadn't been invented yet. King was just vain enough to try one.

The wooden stakes were easy enough to come by. A visit to the local hardware store and a few tent stakes later, they were set. Beheading, aside from being absolutely disgusting, was more difficult. That left fire. Burning the host body would also destroy, or release, the demon. Or so the books said. Carrying around torches was a bit too Mary Shelley and rather impractical. She doubted King would agree to a picnic in Central Park.

That's when Simon hatched his crazy scheme to acquire other means. While she'd caused her diversion in the telephone and telegraph office, Simon had slipped into the battery room and somehow managed to pilfer a jar of sulfuric acid. It wasn't difficult really. She'd gone in first, face flushed from the heat. Of course, she'd run in place outside first to get a good sheen of sweat and that slightly out of breath helplessness look down. The two men on the desk were more than solicitous. A demure smile laced with batting eyelashes and an appreciation of their gallantry was all she needed. The heaving bosom was a bonus.

"We'll keep it out of the way in the corner," he said, as he gently placed the jar on the floor.

Elizabeth sat down on the bed and picked up one of the tent stakes and tried unsuccessfully to twirl it in her hand. "I still don't get it. Acid's a good weapon, I suppose. The flesh it burns and all that, but it isn't exactly practical to carry around."

"We need to be prepared for all situations."

It was no use trying to talk sense into him. If he could have walked down the street with a broadsword, he would have.

"We should think about acquiring a gun," Simon said, giving one last glance at the jar in the corner. "But I'm afraid we're a little short of funds."

"I'm not very fond of guns. And besides, we already know from practical experience that it won't stop him."

Simon frowned. "Yes, but he has men who work for him. We need to prepare for every contingency. Perhaps we can acquire some silver bullets."

"No guns. They make me nervous."

"Well, for now we'll have to make do with what we have," he said and sat down next to her. He picked up one of the wooden stakes and slipped it into his inside breast pocket. "You'll have to start carrying a purse. I'm afraid your dress doesn't leave much room for concealed weapons."

"I thought that's what you liked about it," she said coyly. Before he could sigh and remind her, yet again, that this was serious, as if she needed reminding, she stood and smiled triumphantly. "I've already worked that out."

She put her leg up on the bed next to him, lifted the hem of her dress, and slipped a stake neatly under her garter belt. "What do you think?"

He blinked a few times and then narrowed his eyes. "That is…disturbingly sexy."

"Is it?" she said and knelt on the bed, moving to straddle his lap.

His arms snaked around her waist and pulled her closer. "Very," he said, and leaned in for a kiss, but stopped just short of her lips. "You will be careful, won't you?"

"One more week and hopefully, it'll all be over."

His forehead creased with worry, and Elizabeth reached up to smooth away the lines. "I'll be careful. And you, try not to rile King."

He gathered her hand in his and brought her fingers to his lips. "I won't start anything," he promised, leaving unsaid the vow that, if need be, he would finish it.

Chapter Twenty-Four

THE AIR WAS THICK with sweat and smoke in the club that night. The sweltering heat from the day hadn't dissipated, and seemingly every denizen of the city was out looking for a place to slake their thirst. Charlie's club was more crowded than ever before. It didn't seem to matter that the room was stifling, or that the booze just made people thirstier; they came in droves. They crammed extra chairs up to tables meant for two, and pulled up crates when the chairs ran out. Shoulder to shoulder, hot and sticky patrons crushed against the bar, until it was nearly impossible for Elizabeth to maneuver from table to table.

Around ten o'clock, King arrived. His customary table emptied quickly as the people scurried out of his way. With as much calm as she could muster, she walked to his table. "What can I get for you?"

His dark eyes danced over her body in smooth appraisal.

"We're kinda busy tonight," she said and nervously shifted her tray from one hand to the other. Courage, Camille, she told herself. One more week. Play it cool.

"I can see that," he said without taking his eyes from her.

"So, you want something or not?"

"I hope you're feeling better today."

"I'm fine."

"Mmmm. And I imagine you feel more secure with your... protection." There was a hint of anger mixed with the amusement in his tone.

Did he know everything they did? "Yes. I do."

He took a dramatic breath and leaned back in his chair. "I can see where your husband has his. The bulge in his coat is quite telling. But, where, I wonder," he said and ran his gaze up and down her body, "have you hidden yours?"

"You forget yourself," she said tightly.

He leaned forward and eyes sparked. "I think it's you who've forgotten who I am."

"No, I haven't," she said, taking a long breath that calmed her jangled nerves. How was she supposed to play it cool when it was hotter than blue blazes in here?

"No, I don't imagine you have," he said, easing back in his chair. "You'd be wise not to."

Could he even have a conversation that didn't include a threat? "You've already made that much clear."

"I'm glad we understand each other. It wouldn't do to have a misunderstanding at this point, would it?" he said, as his gaze fell on Simon. "They can be so...unpleasant." Despite the heat, she felt a cold shiver, which was quickly followed by a wave of anger. His eyes flicked back to her and he smiled, seeming to enjoy her discomfiture. "Thing's needn't be that way, of course. They can be rather...pleasant, if you let them."

Her stomach heaved at the way he shaded the phrase with innuendo and dark promises, but she'd be damned if she'd let it show. "I really should get back to work. Did you want something to drink?"

"No, nothing. I simply came to check on my...interests."

"The club's doing well," she said, ignoring the implication of his not so oblique reference.

He grinned indulgently. "Yes, things are going well. Very well."

"Have a good night then."

"I already have."

She marshaled a weak smile and made her escape. King lingered for a few minutes, quietly surveying his domain. She could feel the weight of his eyes on her back as she moved around the club. But, thankfully, he left and the night progressed without another incident.

Over the next few nights, the stress of waiting for King's next move was starting to wear on them. Simon, true to his word, kept himself in check, but the tension at work spilled over into the day. They sniped at each other, pushing buttons better left alone. And it seemed the whole city shared their frustration.

The unbearable heat wave that gripped New York shortened everyone's fuse. Hot, muggy air enveloped the city day and night. Dark clouds loomed perpetually on the horizon, but the storm refused to break. Anxious energy crackled in the air like electricity.

Even the normally congenial patrons at Charlie's were beginning to show the strain. Bickering replaced conversation, and Lester had to break up two arguments before they broke out into full scale brawls.

That Friday night, an older, well-dressed gentleman entered the club and walked over to a recently emptied table against the wall. His tailored, herringbone suit and shock of white hair would normally have brought a few stares, but the heat had sapped everyone's curiosity along with their good natures. He folded his lanky frame into the rickety, wooden chair, crossed his long legs and melted into the dark wall behind him.

Dix didn't even notice him at first. She was busy counting the hours till closing, dreaming of a cool bath to wash away the day's grime. Eventually, she sidled over to his table to get his order.

"Whiskey," he said in a gentle, rich baritone as he pulled a small notebook from his breast pocket.

"We got all kinds," she said between snaps of her well-chewed gum. "Whatcha want? Scat? Panther?"

He smiled politely, his grey eyes were cool and soothing. "Whatever you suggest."

"You're English, huh?" she said, the thought taking the last of her energy.

"Guilty as charged."

"The Professor is too," she said, nodding her head toward Simon. "Don't suppose you know him?"

The gentleman cast a cursory glance at the piano and shook his head. "No, I'm afraid not."

Dix shrugged and dragged a finger under her eye to rub away the dripping mascara. "Ya never know. It ain't..."

The rest of her reply was drowned out by a commotion at the door. Three young men in their twenties tripped into the bar making enough noise to wake the dead.

Dix tugged at the top of her bustier. "Now, we got trouble."

"Charlie Blue, you old stinkaroo!" the shortest of the three bellowed. His pug nose glowed red from the heat and the four sheets he rode in on.

Charlie hurried around the bar and caught the man before he fell face first into the bar. "Come on, Jimmy. Why don't you and the boys go on home. Looks like you've already had enough for one night."

"I'm all right, old man," he sneered and pushed away from Charlie. "We just saw Crash Murdock get the tar thumped outta him and I plan on celebratin'!"

One of the other boys squished up his pudgy face—he looked like a cherub that was kicked out of heaven—and pushed out his thick lips in a pout. "I'm tellin' ya, the fix was in."

Jimmy cackled and slapped him hard on the back. "You're just sore cause you lost that fin, Eugene," Jimmy said, drawing out the last syllable. Judging from Eugene's reaction, his name was a sore point. "Come on Roy, drinks are on fat boy."

Eugene grumbled under his breath, and the trio pushed their way through the crowd. Charlie put up a hand to signal Lester to let things be. For now. Maybe, just maybe, they wouldn't cause too much trouble.

They commandeered a table not far from the piano and plopped down into the chairs. Elizabeth walked over to take their orders. "What can I get you boys?"

Jimmy smirked and cocked his head to the side. "I can think of a few things."

"Why don't you sit down, sweetheart?" Roy said, inching his chair back and patting his broad thigh.

Elizabeth shook her head. After a month of waiting tables, this sort of thing was old hat. "You boys want drinks or don't ya?"

"Ooo, she's got moxie, this one," Jimmy said with a wink to his pals.

Roy grinned and waggled his eyebrows. "That ain't all she's got."

"Call me when you make up your minds," Elizabeth said and turned to leave, but Jimmy grabbed her arm.

"Now, why are you runnin' off so fast?" he said. "Not that I mind the view. You're just as good goin' as comin'. But I think I'd like you comin' best."

Elizabeth tried to wrest her arm from his grip, but his dirty fingernails dug into her arm. Jimmy yanked harder and pulled her onto his lap. Grabbing her roughly about the waist, he tried to kiss her. His stale breath was hot and fetid.

"Come on, baby," he purred, as he squeezed her backside.

"Let go," she said, and managed to get to her feet. Reacting with pure instinct and adrenaline, she slapped his face.

He smiled, even as the red mark blossomed on his cheek. "Like it rough, huh? You're gonna have to do better than that if you—"

The rest of his sentence never made it past his snarling lips. The words and a good portion of nose cartilage were smashed back by the force of a hard fist connecting flush with his face. The power of the punch sent his chair toppling. He landed on the floor with a clattering thud.

Everyone in the club fell silent, waiting like a derelict old fireworks factory hoping for that errant spark. Jimmy pushed himself upright and gingerly covered his nose. He looked up to see Simon flexing his hand, towering over him.

Jimmy coughed through the blood that dripped over his chin and gushed down the back of his throat. "You broke my nose," he gurgled.

"Next time I'll break your bloody neck," Simon growled.

God, it felt good to hit someone, Simon thought, as he clenched his fist. He glared down at the man, still sitting stunned on the floor, willing him to stand up so he could hit him again. Jimmy was too shocked at the sight of his own blood to move. Tacitly satisfied, Simon turned his attention to Elizabeth. "Are you all right?"

"I'm fine. That was—Look out!" she cried, and tugged on Simon's sleeve. He ducked, barely missing being hit in the back of the neck by Roy's rabbit punch.

Simon stepped aside, and Roy's momentum caused him to careen off balance. He staggered and Elizabeth stepped forward, lifted her tray and clobbered him on the back of the head. The metal dented with a resounding bang. Stunned, Roy lurched forward and fell onto a small table that gave way under his weight.

Simon blinked in surprise. "Elizabeth?"

"What?" she said innocently.

Eugene grunted and wedged himself out of his chair. "So you wanna play, huh?" he said, and charged at Simon. There wasn't time to react, and the two of them crashed into another table. The stake in Simon's pocket dug into his ribs. Teacups flew in every direction, hitting the floor and shattering into jagged shards. Freshly ordered whiskey dripped from the remnants.

"We just got that," a man lamented, more concerned about the wasted booze than the pile of humanity at his feet.

"Told you we should have gone to Lenny's," his friend griped, oblivious as Simon pushed Eugene off his chest.

Like cinders from a wildfire caught in the wind, smaller skirmishes flared up all around the room. Lester and Charlie did their best to put them out before they grew too hot. The blistering around the edges festered enough to keep them away from the main attraction.

Simon laid into Eugene with vicious blows. All sense of purpose was gone, only blind rage remained. All his pent up frustration was unleashed in each strike. He pinned Eugene to the floor and pummeled into him. His hard fist mashed into the man's soft face. Eugene cried out for mercy, but Simon didn't care. He gripped the man's shirt front and hit and hit and hit.

All thoughts of pity had evaporated in the heat and the unquenchable anger. It wasn't Eugene he was hitting, but King. In his mind, all he could see was that swarthy bastard's face, smirking at his helplessness. Eugene couldn't fight back, all he could do was try to fend off the blows.

Roy recovered from the blow to his head and pushed the broken table to the side. He jumped up, grabbing Simon by the collar of his coat, and pulled him to his feet.

Elizabeth tried to intervene, but Roy swatted her aside like an annoying housefly. A kid in a man's body—twice as strong as he was smart—he spun Simon around and cracked him hard on the chin. Simon tried to find where Elizabeth had gone, but the world dimmed. Like in an old fashioned movie, his vision tunneled, a circle of light fighting against the fade to black. Desperate to find her, he tried to push away the encroaching darkness.

He stumbled and grabbed onto to whatever he could, then opened his eyes to see Jimmy's grinning face. The prospect of a good fight (a good fight being one where they outnumbered the other guy three to one) pushed all worries of his flattened nose aside, and he punched Simon in the gut. Bile rose in Simon's throat as his diaphragm did its level best to fly out of his mouth. He gasped for air, but his chest burned like he'd been skewered with a fiery poker.

Elizabeth scrambled to her feet and grabbed Jimmy by the shoulder. Cocking her arm, she lunged into the punch. Her father's advice rang in her ears. Keep your wrist tight! Don't tuck your thumb in! Turn your hand over right before your arm extends!

Her tiny fist smashed into Jimmy's head right under the temple. Her knuckles popped as the tendons stretched and snapped back like rubber bands. It hurt like hell, but she set her feet and was about to throw another punch when, out of nowhere, Lester stepped in.

A blow to the temple was an E ticket ride to what boxers called queer street. Lester took him the rest of the way.

Without missing a beat, Lester grabbed Elizabeth by the arms, picked her up and set her aside. She was about to step back into the melee when another set of strong hands clamped around her arms.

"Let him do his job," Charlie said.

Elizabeth struggled in his grip and watched as the bouncer did what he did best—bounced.

Roy had picked up a chair and raised it over his head to finish Simon off, but Lester was too fast. He lunged forward and slugged Roy with a swift, straight right. Roy stumbled and dropped the chair. Lester delivered a quick one-two combination and Roy crumpled to the floor.

As quickly as it had started, the fight was over.

Jimmy lay unconscious, his broken nose oozing blood, Eugene, long since having given up, sat huddled on the floor, and Roy had enough sense left in his head to know when to call it quits. He was no match for Lester and he knew it. Everyone knew it. "Just havin' a little fun."

"Get your boys and get out," Lester said. "Or would ya like me to show ya the door? Up close and personal like?"

Roy flushed and finally shook his head.

Simon staggered to his feet as Roy brushed past. He started forward, but Lester put a strong hand on his shoulder. "S'all over, Professor," he said. "Sorry it took me so long. A few others tried to join in."

Simon shrugged out of his grip, the searing pain in his back slowly subsiding.

"Come on, Jimmy," Roy said, as he slapped him back to consciousness.

As Eugene crawled across the floor to his side, Jimmy came back around. He looked up again, only to see Simon glaring down at him. Cutting his losses, he blearily got to his feet. Lester stepped forward and escorted the trio to the door.

Charlie let go of Elizabeth and turned to the rest of the bar. "All right. Show's over. Club's closed."

The patrons buzzed with the excitement of the fight and reluctantly made their way to the door. A few even stopped at the bar to even up tabs with Dix, who'd been hiding behind it.

Elizabeth came to Simon's side. "Are you all right?"

He nodded, although it was clear from the pinched look on his face, he wasn't. "And you?"

Elizabeth knew better than to push him. "My butt's seen better days," she said, rubbing the spot where she'd landed.

Simon started to laugh, but the movement was too painful. He sufficed with a weak smile and a touch of her cheek.

She wrinkled her nose. "You reek."

His tuxedo, what was left of it, was soaked with alcohol. He tried vainly to straighten the hem of his jacket, running his hands over the sopping material. When they hit the bulge in his pocket, he cursed under his breath.

Elizabeth's brow furrowed with worry. "What is it?"

"The watch," he said and pulled the gold chain from his pocket. If the watch was damaged, there would be no way for them to return home.

He opened the clasp and they both sighed in relief. It was undamaged.

Neither of them saw the older gentleman with the thatch of white hair watching them, his eyes growing round with shocked recognition at the sight of the watch. Stuffing his small notebook into his breast pocket, he quickly joined the throng headed for the door.

CHAPTER TWENTY-FIVE

THE STORM THAT REFUSED to break held true to form and hovered northeast of the island. The heavy cloud cover kept in the heat like the lid on a boiling pot. Finally, the next day, the clouds broke and the sun triumphantly poked through. Simon had insisted they stay in as much as possible to lessen their exposure to King and his men, but Elizabeth was going stir crazy inside their little apartment. Eventually, she managed to cajole Simon into taking a walk to break the monotony.

They took the subway up to Fifth Avenue and the Vanderbilt gate entrance to Central Park. The plush green setting was an oasis in the cement jungle of the city. One step across the threshold and the dull grays and browns, the sooty air, and screaming of car horns faded away.

Brilliant sun glittered off the glass panes of the Conservatory as they walked deeper into the park. The shores of the great reservoir stretched out in front of them. They walked along in peaceful silence under the shade of a grove of trees circling the perimeter. The paths diverged and meandered, but Elizabeth's step didn't falter; she knew exactly where she was going and Simon was content to follow.

They crested the top of a small hill and Elizabeth stopped. "This is what I wanted to show you," she said, pointing across the velvety grass.

Standing on a slight knoll in the distance was a castle. The design was simple, but the effect was magical.

"Belvedere Castle," she said. "Is that cool or what?"

"How did you know this was here?"

"When things were...well, you know. After Coney Island when I went for walks to think, I found it. Thought I was seeing things at first. Not exactly what you expect to find in the middle of New York City, but there it was. It seemed like a peaceful place."

Simon took her hand in his. "I'm sorry."

She smiled and shook her head, then looked back at the castle. "It's hollow inside, you know? No guts, just an empty façade. At the time I thought it was pretty darn ironic, but... I kept coming here anyway, to think."

"I don't suppose I was exactly your knight in shining armor at that point."

"More like the village idiot."

He chuckled softly. "Well deserved."

"If the big, pointy shoe fits," she said with a grin and turned to look at him. His chin was bruised and his green eyes were bloodshot from lack of sleep. "You were pretty knightly last night, being all chivalrous and coming to my rescue."

"I'm glad you think so," he said and started them down the path. "Although, if I remember correctly, you held your own rather well. Where did you learn to fight like that, or am I better off in ignorance?"

"Daddy. Thought it was a good idea for me to learn a little self defense. What about you?"

"Boarding school. My first year I learned how to take a punch. My second, how to give one."

"And your third?"

"That it's better to avoid them altogether."

"Very sage for a teenager."

"Well, I am British."

Elizabeth smiled and pulled them toward the shade of a small grove of trees. The grass was thick and lush and she started to ease off her shoes. "Do you miss it?"

"Boarding school? Hardly."

"No, England."

"I...what are you doing?" he asked, as she steadied herself and tossed her shoes aside.

She let go and lifted up the hem of her dress and undid her garters. "Taking my shoes off."

"I can see that."

"Then why'd you ask?" she asked with a grin, as she rolled down her stockings.

"Elizabeth."

"What? I'm just gonna wiggle my toes in the grass. It's been weeks since I've felt real grass," she said, then sighed happily as her feet touched the cool blades. "You should do this. It feels great." He arched an eyebrow as if to say—are you insane? She shrugged and wiggled her toes some more. "You don't know what you're missing."

He shook his head and sat down to watch her revel. She padded around in a small circle, stopping in front of him. "So, do you miss it?"

"England? No, not very much."

She gave up her circling and sat down beside him. "Really? Not homesick at all?"

"There are some things, but no. I haven't thought of it as home in a very long time."

Elizabeth reached out and squeezed his hand.

He looked down at her hand, bruised knuckles and all. "It doesn't matter."

She smiled and nodded, even though she felt a pang of sadness at the way he just accepted things. She leaned back in the grass, silently urging him to follow. A little awkwardly, he lay down next to her, propping himself up on an elbow.

She inhaled the fresh scent of the newly mowed grass. "This is nice, isn't it? Away from everything." When he didn't answer her, she tilted her head to the side and was surprised to see him looking over her shoulder and frowning. "What?" she asked, craning her neck to see what had caught his attention.

"Nothing," he said with a forced smile, as he tugged gently on her hand.

She rolled onto her side and cradled her head in her hand. "That nothing was definitely a something."

"Do you miss Texas?"

She knew he was changing the subject and considered calling him on it, but thought better of it. "No, not since Daddy died. Anyway, the idea of Texas is much more appealing than the reality."

"And Southern California?"

"Sort of. I miss my TV."

Simon snorted. "Americans."

"Oh, please. What do you miss, your tea set?"

"As a matter of fact, I do," he said with a scowl, but she could see the ghost of a smile fighting against it.

"I miss my car."

"That dilapidated, old piece of scrap?"

"Snob."

He chuckled and crossed his long legs at the ankles. "It's odd, but I miss grading papers."

"You never graded papers. I graded papers."

"Then I miss you grading papers."

She laughed and shook her head. "What else do you miss?"

"My books. And an electric shaver."

Her hand stayed to caress his cheek. He closed his eyes for a moment, and the smile he'd been fighting curled his lips.

"You're doing pretty well without it," she said, gently running her fingers along his jaw line. "But you won't have to fight with the safety razor much longer," she said, hoping the hint of sadness she felt didn't show through. "Only four more days, and if the watch works we'll be right back where we started, like none of this ever happened."

Left unspoken was the question—what if the watch didn't work? A momentary flush of anxiety coursed through her, but it soon passed. The watch would work. It would.

It was hard to believe that it was almost time to go home. The idea should have been comforting. They could get away from King, get back to their lives. But what exactly did that mean? His life before didn't include her, not in the way it did now. Maybe things really would go back to the way they were.

As if sensing her thoughts, he leaned closer and held her hand tightly. "As improbable as it is," he said, his eyes crinkling at the edges with wonder, "it has happened."

The way he looked at her, awed and loving, made her heart race. He wasn't talking about going back in time, or working in a speakeasy. He was talking about her, about how he felt about her. She took a deep breath and let it out slowly.

He reached out and cupped her cheek. "And I wouldn't change it for the world."

Slowly, never taking his eyes from hers, he leaned in and kissed her. Just feeling his lips on hers, made her feel like he was touching all of her, lifting her up, pulling her into him. After a breathless moment she pulled away. He continued to stroke her cheek, but she shook her head and got to her feet.

"Come on," she said, holding out her hand to help him up. "Let's go home."

They made love slowly, stretching out each moment, each touch, then drifting into the next. Hazy afternoon sunlight filtered through the sheer curtains. Dust motes caught on a warm breeze danced in the air.

Simon trailed his fingers along Elizabeth's back. Her lithe muscles tensed as she arched into him and buried her head in the crook of his neck. Her skin was like silk, smooth and sensual to his touch. No matter how long he held her, it could never be enough. Everything about her made him want her all the more. The soft, breathy sighs urging him closer. The feel of her hand in his. The way her eyes grew impossibly dark as she whispered his name. Everything conspired to wipe away the fears he'd held close for so long, until all he could see, all he could feel, was her.

She sighed, her warm breath a feather's touch along his neck. He wrapped his arms around her, pulling her body into a secure embrace that could barely echo the need he felt for her.

Simon closed his eyes and remembered the way her face had looked moments before, flushed with passion. The tendrils of hair cascading across her cheek, her lips swollen from his kisses, and he could see her pulse beating beneath the skin. Every detail, from the pale freckles on her shoulders to the supple curve of her calves seared into his memory. If he were an artist, he was sure he could recreate her in the dark. His hands knew every facet of her body. The remarkable softness of the skin below her belly. The sound of her breathing. The seductive way she always seemed to smell like a forest after the rain, clean and new.

He maneuvered his head around and kissed her brow. "All right, love?"

"Mmmm," she purred and nuzzled into his neck, kissing the edge of his jaw. "More than."

He held her a bit more firmly and wondered if he should have told her what he saw at the park. There was no reason to worry her, and doubtless she'd caught on and was trying to spare him the worry.

He hadn't gotten a good look at the man, or men. There seemed to be more than one, although he couldn't be sure. Ever since her revelation that King had been having them followed, he'd had the sense they were never alone. Today at the park was the first time he'd actually seen their shadow. Always keeping a discrete distance, but ever-present, the thick man in the black fedora had trailed them through the park. He should have noticed him sooner. Not that there was a bloody thing he could do about it. Four more days, he told himself. Four more days.

Elizabeth pushed herself up and re-settled on top of him, folding her arms over his chest and resting her chin atop her laced hands. "What's wrong? And don't nothing me. You were grinding your teeth."

He thought about putting her off, but she had that look in her eyes. It would be more trouble than it was worth. "We were followed today."

"I know. Black hat. Built like a fire hydrant."

Damn her. "Why didn't you say anything?"

"Why didn't you?"

Her Socratic method of arguing was frustrating to say the least. Especially when she had a point. He sighed and pushed his head further into the pillows. "I don't know."

"I've been thinking..." she said. He narrowed his eyes suspiciously and she smirked. "Very funny. I think we should tell Charlie we're leaving soon. We can't just disappear one day without so much as a by your leave."

"By your leave?" he asked with a chuckle.

"I was daydreaming about Belvedere castle. Forsooth, pray tell and all that."

"Someday I'll show you a real castle. Leeds perhaps." His smile faded. "But I don't think it's wise to tell Charlie our plans."

"Might not be wise, but it's right. He's been a good friend, Simon. We need to warn him. Who knows what King might do."

"It's still a risk."

Smiling, she scooted down his body and kissed his chest. "Just a tiny one," she murmured between kisses. "An itty bitty one."

She slowly eased her way down his chest to his stomach. "Let's live dangerously," she whispered against his waist, before brushing her soft lips against the sensitive skin.

"Elizabeth," he started softly, but the rest of his sentence was lost in the feeling of her silky hair brushing against his hip. He tried to remember what he was going to say, but all coherent thought was gone. Charlie was suddenly the last thing on his mind.

Closing time was Elizabeth's favorite, and not only because it meant the long work day was over. But there in the quiet of the club, the chores almost finished, when it was just the four of them, she felt a sense of belonging. The stillness of a place usually so bursting with life was all the more remarkable and cherished. A few nights a week, she, Simon, Charlie and Dix would linger at the club, share a drink and the consolation of shared experience. For the most part, she and Simon were no more than a willing audience for Charlie. He'd regale them with stories of the night when he was a boy and saw the last of the great bare knuckle fights. Gentleman Jim Corbett had beaten his idol, John L. Sullivan, in the brawl to end all brawls. He told them where he was when he heard President McKinley had been assassinated. And blushed when he recounted his ill-fated, one-time only, theatrical debut in Jilly Stein's Traveling Burlesque Show.

Of all the things she was leaving behind, she was going to miss Charlie the most. When she finally told him they were leaving, he hadn't protested, hadn't asked them where they were going. They warned him that King might try something and to be careful, but Charlie just heaved a big sigh, nodded and asked if they needed any traveling money.

Elizabeth felt a lump form in her throat. Last night she and Simon had nearly wrecked the place. Their salaries over the next two weeks wouldn't pay for the damage they'd caused, and here Charlie was offering them more.

"No, please," she said, and reached out to stop him from digging into his pockets.

"If you're worried about payin' me back, you can send it when ya get settled," he offered.

"No, you've given us too much already," she said and looked over to Dix, who was busying herself with the last of the night's chores. "Both of you."

Dixie looked up from the pile of dishes and forced a weak smile to her face.

The big barkeep pulled a ragged handkerchief from his pocket and wiped his face. "Wasn't nothin'," he said, trying to hide his sniffles. "You just drop Ol' Charlie a line now and then, all right?"

Elizabeth's heart dropped. In four days, if everything went as planned, she'd be home in the future and Charlie Blue would be long since passed. "Sure," she said, hesitating, before stepping forward and pulling him into a hug.

He returned it fiercely before pulling away and nodding firmly. "You take care, ya hear?" he said and then stuck out his meaty hand to Simon. "You watch over her."

Simon solemnly shook it. "I will, and thank you."

Charlie snuffled again and cleared his throat. "Aw, nuts," he grumbled and turned to rearrange some perfectly well arranged bottles. "I'll see ya tomorrow."

"Charlie," Elizabeth said, casting a quick glance at Simon. "You don't have any money in the stock market by any chance, do ya?"

Simon hissed her name in warning under his breath, but she couldn't let Charlie loose everything after all he'd done for them.

"Naw," he said. "S'all tied up in the club. Why?"

Thank God. "Just curious."

"We should be going," Simon said pointedly.

"See you tomorrow," Elizabeth said, as Simon hurried her to the door.

Once they were outside Simon glared down at her. "Really, Elizabeth. What would you have done if he'd said yes?"

"I know, but I couldn't leave thinking I could have helped him. This is Charlie we're talking about. It's not like I took an ad out in the Times."

Simon didn't seem moved. "It was wrong," she continued. "Very wrong. I'm a bad Elizabeth. Forgive me?"

He sighed and shook his head. "You are incorrigible." It had been a big risk. There was no telling the ripple effect of one simple change in the timeline. She'd been rash in trying to help Charlie, but she didn't regret it.

Simon put his arm around her. "I wouldn't have you any other way."

The understanding look in his eyes said more than words could. They walked down the street in thoughtful silence, neither noticing the two-toned sedan as it pulled into the alley behind Charlie Blue's.

Chapter Twenty-Six

FATHER CAVANAUGH STARED UP at the placid, marble face of the statue of Saint Patrick. He'd always found the countenance soothing and had taken solace from it many times over the years. He would sit in the closest pew and gently run the heavy wood under his palm. It reminded him of the smooth beads of his rosary. He'd rubbed the same spot so often that even the wood oil used to polish the benches couldn't help. He liked to think of them as a testament to the struggle. Worn, but still strong.

In his thirty years in the priesthood, he'd striven to find the same sort of peace he'd seen in the face of the saint. Not that he counted himself worthy of such things, but even priests had dreams. And nightmares.

"Are you all right, Father?"

Father Cavanaugh startled at the voice of his assistant pastor, Father Peter Fitzpatrick. The lad tried so hard, too hard sometimes, to be all that he thought a priest was. He was earnest enough, and his heart was truly given to God, but he was so young. It was hard to see past the pale, freckled face of the choir boy he'd known those years ago and see the man who stood before him now. Especially today, he thought, as he absently massaged his arthritic fingers. Normally, the signs of age served to remind him how far he'd come, but today they seemed to harken how little time there might be left.

He had heard many late night confessions, but Dixie's knock on his door in the early hours this morning and the conversation that followed had left him with a difficult decision. Knowledge can be a burden.

He smiled at the young father. The boy would have to be a man to face the things this parish would show him. He wondered if he'd done the right thing sheltering the boy from the darker side of things. He wanted Peter to find his footing before he revealed the truth of what it meant to be pastor in these times. Perhaps he had waited too long.

The younger man's pale brow wrinkled in concern. "Father?"

"I'm sorry, Peter," he said, never having broken the habit of using his given name. "Just looking for wisdom."

That seemed to unnerve the younger man, and he tugged on his ear. It was a nervous habit that always made the older man smile. Father Cavanaugh stifled a chuckle. The poor boy couldn't conceal his feelings if his life depended on it.

"Is there anything I can do, Father?"

Father Cavanaugh smiled kindly. "No, no. It's nothing for you to concern yourself with. But I will be rather busy this morning. Several meetings," he said, waving casually toward the office door. "Would you be a good lad and make sure I'm not disturbed?"

"Of course, Father."

Father Cavanaugh patted Peter's shoulder as he passed by. Opening the door to his office, he hoped for a few minutes to plan his opening remarks, but saw there wasn't time for that.

King Kashian flattened his gloved palms on the desk. "You're late."

"You're late," the waitress said with a grin.

Simon looked up from his menu. The diner was busier than normal and the din was at a new high. "Pardon?"

She shrugged. "You two always come in at the same time s'all. Breakfast at one in the afternoon," she said shaking her head and snapping her gum. "You want the usuals? Oh, I asked Fred about getting that Chinese tea stuff you're always askin' for. He said, 'They want chink, they can go across town.'" She looked over her shoulder at the squat, little man behind the counter and gave him a quick wink, before turning back to the table and snapping her gum. "Course, Fred's an ass."

Simon chuckled and put down the menu. "The usual will be fine. Thank you, Helen."

The woman smiled dreamily, as she always did when he used her name. He'd learned quickly how far a British accent could take him with most women.

Elizabeth waited until Helen left before rolling her eyes. "You really are shameless."

He merely arched his eyebrows in mock innocence. Elizabeth shook her head and went back to reading her section of the paper. Simon watched her for a moment. How had he been so lucky to find her? Such a marvelous woman. And wearing, he noted with an appreciative smile, his favorite dress. The green set off her hair, and set his mind wandering to rather pleasant places.

"Oh, the Marx Brothers are still playing at the Roxy," Elizabeth said. "Wouldn't that be great? To see an early talkie in the theater."

Simon grunted noncommittally and scanned the front page.

"Come on, it'll be fun. We only have two days left."

He shook his head and put down the paper. "It's too dangerous." Her face fell and he sighed. "Besides, 'The Cocoanuts' is really one of their lesser films. You're not missing much."

His comment had the desired effect, and her lovely face went from frowning to astonished. "You like the Marx Brothers? What else haven't you told me?"

He grinned and went back to his paper. "Many things. Many, many things."

Elizabeth laughed. "No doubt. I'm gonna use the restroom. Try not to flirt too much with Helen while I'm gone."

"I would never do any such thing," he said, pleased she couldn't see his amusement behind the paper.

The headlines were much the same as they were back home—murder, corruption in the government and an unhealthy obsession with sports. The more things change, the more they stay the same.

"Here ya go," Helen said, as she returned and poured their first cups of coffee. "Order's comin' right up."

Simon put down the paper and thanked her with a smile. She winked and moved on to her next table. The coffee was dark and thick. Definitely one thing he wouldn't miss. He leafed through the paper, searching for the crossword puzzle. Doing it together had become something of a daily ritual, but he could never remember what section it was hidden in. Finally, he found it buried in the back with the obituaries.

He quickly scanned the puzzle, looking for cornerstone clues, when Helen returned with their breakfast plates.

"You need anything else?" she asked.

"No, thank you."

"Just give a whistle."

He nodded, but his thoughts had strayed. Elizabeth was certainly taking her time. Shrugging it off, he took another sip of the bitter coffee.

When half the cup was gone and Elizabeth still wasn't back, he began to worry. He tried to concentrate on the puzzle, but with every passing second he grew more anxious. The words on the page blurred under his scrutiny.

Giving in to the apprehension, he slipped out of the booth and walked toward the counter. Helen was there picking up an order. "Have you seen my wife?"

The waitress shrugged. "She went in the ladies' last I saw."

He was probably over-reacting, but the seed of doubt had been sown. Simon wouldn't be able to relax until he was sure. He walked through the storeroom toward the back. The passage was dimly lit by a single exposed bulb hanging too low from the ceiling. It swung back and forth in a slow arc, casting an alternating wave of shadow and light on the door.

Simon knocked and waited for an answer. When none came, he tested the lock. It was open, and he pulled it slightly ajar. "Elizabeth?"

Again, there was no answer, and he opened the door the rest of the way. The tiny room was empty, the faucet left running. His heart tripped and stuttered, before he reined it in. She'd gone out for some air. That's all, he told himself. "Is there a back door?" he called out to Helen who'd been lingering in the hall.

"Yeah, right back there," she said, gesturing behind him.

Simon hurried down the short, dark hall and threw open the door. It clanged against the building, shivering on impact. Bright sunlight streamed into the alley, burning his eyes, as he stepped out. His pulse galloped, refusing to be contained.

"Elizabeth!"

He looked quickly up and down the filthy alleyway, determined to find her standing there among the empty packing crates and battered trash bins. She simply had to be there. His mind couldn't grasp any other thought. He ran to the mouth of the alley and stumbled into the crowd of pedestrians coursing down the busy street. Blaring horns and idle chatter receded like the tide. Blood roared in his ears, deafening everything but the pounding of his heart.

Turning back to the doorway, a single discarded shoe caught his eye. No. Dear God. No. He knew, even before he held it, that is was hers. Frustrating hours spent buying it and precious minutes taking it off flashed in his mind. The leather strap at the back was torn. He clamped his eyes shut, but the images of her struggling, fighting for her life battered away at him. While he'd sat doing the damn crossword puzzle! His fist tightened over the shoe.

Elizabeth was gone.

The wooden steps creaked under his weight as he took them two at a time, running up the stairs to their small apartment. He pulled open the door and called out her name. Cold silence answered him.

He knew it would. Knew she wouldn't go off without telling him, but in his panic he'd gone to the one place that still held hope she'd left of her of her own volition. It was far better to think she'd lost her senses than accept the truth staring him in the face. He'd pictured this moment in his mind so many times. Jagged shards of his nightmares cut into his thoughts. Each memory chipped away at his denial, a piece of flesh shorn away from his heart.

He'd let his guard down, just for a moment, and it had cost him everything. His chest burned, the realization striking him like a blow to the solar plexus. Forcing air into his lungs, he swallowed his dread and tried to clear his mind.

She was alive. He could almost feel her. Whether it was madness that told him so or a bond beyond the mortal world he didn't know, and didn't care. She was alive. Those three words would be his mantra until he found her, until he held her in his arms again.

His hand clenched around the shoe he'd carried back. The sharp edge of the heel digging into his palm brought him back to the present. He would find her, or die trying. Muttering a string of curses for having wasted so much time already, he set her shoe down next to the armoire and went where he should have gone in the first place.

"Where is he?" Simon demanded.

Charlie's eyes widened behind the peek hole slot. "What's wrong?"

Simon pounded his fist against the heavy metal. He didn't have time for this. "Open the bloody door!"

Charlie quickly complied, and Simon grabbed him by the shirt collar. "Where's King?"

"Professor—"

"Where?"

Charlie's big hand clamped around Simon's wrist and tried to pull him off. "Take it easy. What's happened?"

"He's taken Elizabeth, that's what's bloody happened. Now tell me where he is."

"You can't—"

Simon's fist lashed out like a striking snake and hit Charlie flush on the jaw. The big man's head jerked back, but his jaw must have been made of iron. The blow didn't even stagger him. He grabbed Simon's free hand and twisted him around, easily putting him in an armlock.

"Let go of me," Simon growled.

"Not 'till you talk sense."

"Didn't you hear what I said? King has Elizabeth."

Charlie spun Simon around again and shoved him backwards. "I heard you. And you think you're any match for him? He's got ten men twice as strong as I am. You go in there half-cocked, and you'll get yourself ten kinds of killed. That ain't gonna help Lizzy."

A part of Simon's mind knew Charlie was right, but the rest was drowning in desperation. He shook out his hand. The knuckles throbbed, and he perversely welcomed the pain. "If you won't help me, I'll find someone who will," he said and started for the door.

Charlie blocked his path and held up a hand. "I didn't say I wouldn't help."

"Then tell me where he is."

"Everything all right, Charlie?" Dix asked, appearing in the doorway to the storeroom.

Charlie never took his eyes off Simon. "No," he said. "Things ain't."

Dix rubbed a chill from her arms. "What happened?"

Simon grunted and rolled his shoulders. All this talk wasn't getting him any closer to Elizabeth. Didn't they understand?

"Professor says King's kidnapped Lizzy."

Simon barely heard her gasp. Charlie's words rang in his ears. The truth of it spoken aloud made his gut wrench.

Charlie frowned, his thick brow wrinkled in thought. "You didn't tell anybody you were leavin', did you?"

Simon shook his head. "Just you." As soon as the words left his lips, the thought took root. "Just you," he repeated his voice sharp with accusation.

Charlie shoved out his barrel chest and met Simon's glare. "I'd cut my own throat before I'd put Lizzy in danger. We didn't say nothin' to nobody. Right Dix?"

When she didn't answer, both men turned to look at her.

A patina of sweat had broken out on her forehead. She shuffled her feet nervously, her painted fingernails digging into the soft flesh of her arm.

"Dix?"

She swallowed and finally lifted her chin. Tears puddled in her eyes. "I'm sorry."

Chapter Twenty-Seven

CHARLIE SHOOK HIS HEAD. "What are you sayin', Dix? You didn't tell nobody, did you?"

Her eyes closed and black, mascara tears streaked down her face. "I'm sorry," she said, choking back a sob. "I—"

Simon snapped out of his shock and lunged toward her. He grabbed her arms in a fierce grip. "What did you do? Who did you tell? Talk or so help me God—"

She blubbered insensibly, and Simon shook her violently. It was all he could do not to put his hands around her neck and strangle the truth out of her. He'd never wanted to strike a woman before, but he could feel the rage burning inside to a fever pitch. With one final shake, he shoved her away before the final tether on his control broke.

Dix staggered back, loose strands of hair, matted down by tears, clung over her face. She trembled and wiped a shaky hand under her nose. "I'm sorry. I didn't have any choice."

Charlie took a few steps closer, but stopped when she cowered back. "It's all right," he said with a quick glance at Simon. "Tell us what happened."

She sniffled and took a few, hiccupping breaths. "I didn't want to tell him. You gotta believe me," she said. Her eyes darted to Simon before looking back pleadingly at Charlie. "I didn't have any choice. King made me do it."

Charlie inched forward and laid a gentle hand on her shoulder. "Did he hurt ya?"

"No," she said and wriggled out of his touch. She looked over at Simon. "I didn't do it to save my own hide, if that's what you're thinkin'. I know you don't think much of me, but I'm better than that."

Simon forced himself to look at her, but didn't trust himself to speak.

"Then why, Dix?" Charlie asked. "Why'd you do it?"

"For you," she whispered.

Charlie blinked in surprise. "Me?"

"After work, he'd come by. Sometimes here, sometimes on my way home, and he'd ask me things. About them. I didn't say nothin' at first, but then he said there'd be a price to pay if I didn't. I couldn't let nothin' happen to you, Charlie."

"You should've told me," Charlie growled. "Wasn't your choice to make. Don't ya see what you've done?"

"I did it cause I love you, Charlie."

Charlie looked thunderstruck, and took a step backward.

"And so Elizabeth pays with her life?" Simon spat.

Dix patched together what little pride she had left and set her jaw. "You woulda done the same thing. You can't tell me you wouldn't."

Even the truth in what she said couldn't salve the sting of betrayal. He'd been a fool to trust them, to trust anyone.

Charlie leaned against the bar, stunned. Whether it was from what she'd done or why she'd done it, Simon didn't care. They were wasting time. "Where's he taken her?"

"I don't know," Dix said. "Really. I don't know."

"Charlie?" Simon said. "Tell me where he lives, or I'll walk out that door and question everyone I see until I get an answer."

The barkeep heaved his big chest and seemed to come to a decision. He walked around to the back of the bar and reached under the counter. "You ever shoot before?"

Simon looked at the pistols in Charlie's hands. "Only rifles."

Charlie nodded grimly and shoved the revolver across the bar. "Good enough. I got these after the break in. Figured they might come in handy," he said and tucked a Colt into the waistband of his pants.

Dix jumped forward and gripped his arm as he tried to walk past. "You'll get yourself killed."

Charlie took her by the shoulders. "You go to your sister's in Hoboken. I'll call ya when the coast is clear."

"Charlie," she pleaded, but he shook his head and walked around to Simon.

Simon picked up the revolver and wrapped his fingers around the heavy metal. "This won't stop King."

"We're gonna have to get through a lot before we even get close to Kashian."

Charlie stood at the ready and Simon shook his head. "I can't ask you to—"

"You ain't askin', but I'm goin'," Charlie said. "Come on, I got a car round back. You're gonna need all the help you can get, Professor."

Simon felt a quick rush of denial, but Charlie was right. He did need help, and for once he had to be man enough to admit it. He nodded sharply and started for the door. The sooner they got to King's, the better. Out of the corner of his eye, he saw Charlie turn once more back to Dix. "You get to your sister's," he said, then gently touched her cheek. "You shoulda told me."

With one last look, he joined Simon in the doorway, and the two men headed off to face King Kashian.

Charlie's Studebaker swerved through the late, afternoon traffic, snaking its way uptown. The oppressive heat wave was back, and Simon felt a trickle of sweat run down his cheek. Through the dirty car window, he could see a storm brewing in the distance as it crawled its way down the coast from the north. Both men sat forward in the car, shoulders hunched, muscles corded, minds racing.

The cars around them belched thick, black exhaust that coated Simon's throat. He swallowed down the oily taste that clung to his tongue and burned his lungs. Gray buildings and black trucks passed by in a blur as

Charlie maneuvered them through the jammed street. The once frenzied city now seemed to be moving at a snail's pace, and Simon leaned forward, silently urging them to move faster.

"We'll park it around back," Charlie said, as he ducked the car into an alley off Park Avenue. "I know the desk clerk. He runs a book out of the back room, so you let me do the talkin'."

Simon nodded and checked the gun in his jacket pocket. He tested the heavy weight of it, resting the grip in his palm. He flipped open the cylinder and ran his fingers over the back of the shells. Six bullets. There wasn't time to wonder if that would be enough. Flicking his wrist, the cylinder snapped back into place, and he slipped the gun back into his pocket.

They entered the upscale residence hotel through the back door. Charlie waved a hand, signaling for Simon to wait, and then peered around the corner and into the lobby. The gray marble floor was studded with elaborate columns, an echo of a Roman coliseum. Oddly appropriate, Simon thought, as they prepared to step onto the floor. A well-dressed couple left their key with the clerk on their way out through the revolving door. The room was empty. It was time. Charlie nodded once, and with frightening ease shed the urgency that had surrounded him and casually walked to the desk.

The clerk was a hard looking man with thinning hair, slicked back with too much brilliantine. There was an upturned scar at the corner of his mouth that made him look like he was perpetually smirking.

"How's it, Mack?" Charlie said.

The man's scarred lip twitched. "What you doin' here, Blue?"

Charlie wasn't phased by the cold welcome and grinned. "Got a hot tip on the seventh at Pimlico. We do a little business?"

Mack's eyes landed on Simon and narrowed.

"Don't worry 'bout him," Charlie said. "He's all right."

Mack didn't seem convinced but nodded and shoved away from the desk. Simon and Charlie followed him into a little room.

The dim light from a large radio dial glowed in the corner, as the always incongruous "Yes, We Have No Bananas" crackled through the static.

Making sure the door was closed behind them, Mack took a small pad from the breast pocket of his uniform jacket. "How much?"

Charlie casually walked past him. "It's a good one. You might wanna lay down a little something. Dexter here," he said, nodding his head toward Simon, "He knows the track doctor."

Mack's face lit up and he took a step toward Simon. "You do? That's—"

Once Mack's attention was turned, Charlie took out his gun and hit him hard on the back of the head. Mack slumped to the floor, unconscious before he hit the ground. The radio played on softly in the background.

Simon stared down at the crumpled form and felt a sick sort of satisfaction. One less obstacle in his way.

"He's got a head like a brick. He'll wake up soon enough," Charlie said and eased open the door. "We gotta move, Professor."

Simon clenched his jaw and nodded. He was ready to do whatever it took to get Elizabeth back. His hand strayed to the gun in his pocket, as they hurried down the short hall to the elevators.

The doors were already open as the car sat on the ground floor waiting. The operator nearly fell off his stool when Charlie and Simon stepped inside.

"Penthouse," Charlie said.

The man righted his red felt bellboy cap and stood up looking like a defiant organ grinder's monkey. "Who're you?"

Simon pushed him against the paneled wall. "Never mind that. Get this thing moving."

The little man shook his head and was about to protest, when he felt the cold barrel of Charlie's gun press against his neck.

Simon let go of his lapel. "Now."

The man nodded quickly and worked the levers to close the door and start the car. The lift dropped abruptly with a grinding sound and then began its ascent. Simon stepped back from the operator, never taking his eyes off him. When they reached the top floor, he dug down into his pocket and pulled out his gun. As the doors opened, they moved forward in tandem, guns at the ready.

The opulent foyer was dark and empty. The light from the elevator spilled onto the marble floor.

Charlie turned back to the operator. "Don't do nothin' stupid." The little man nodded and took shelter in the corner of the lift. Simon moved stealthily across the floor into the foyer. He and Charlie exchanged quick glances. Simon slowly turned the handle and threw open the heavy double doors.

Ready for anything, it was a shock to find absolutely nothing. The long entry hall was deserted, lit only by a single wall sconce. Slowly, shoulder to shoulder, they inched their way down the dark, empty passageway.

The apartment was exactly as Elizabeth had described. Simon could almost hear her voice and he paused, nearly causing Charlie to run over the back of him. He shook off Charlie's questioning look and kept moving. He couldn't afford to think about how much he missed the sound of her voice, the feel of her. Taking a deep breath, he steeled himself again and edged past where Elizabeth had said the Rubens drawing should have been. Nothing but a scratch and a bent hook remained. Outlines of picture frames stood out in pristine white, ghostly images surrounded by the stains of age. Slowly, they made their way down the hall, checking each room as they went. Each one was empty. Finally, they reached the end of the hall and Simon saw the door he knew must lead to the room with the Egyptian artifacts.

Fully expecting it to be locked, Simon was surprised when he tried the handle and found no resistance. This room was empty too. No people, no artifacts. Nothing. It had been stripped bare, and judging from the scraps of brown paper on the floor and the hooks hanging askance on the walls, they'd left in a hurry.

"Damn it," Simon growled. If they weren't here, where the hell were they?

Charlie laid a comforting hand on Simon's shoulder. "We'll find her."

Simon kicked a leftover box and watched it skitter across the floor.

"Come on," Charlie said, and stepped back into the hall.

A shot rang out like the crack of a bullwhip. Charlie was thrown back by the impact and landed with a thunderous bang against the door jamb. He clutched his shoulder and staggered to the floor, falling into the middle of the hallway.

Simon sprang forward and tried to grab Charlie. Another shot rang out and ricocheted off the marble floor just inches away. Simon jerked his hand back inside. That damned elevator operator must have gone for help. They should have tied him up.

"Jesus," Charlie moaned, holding his shoulder.

Simon took a deep breath and stepped out into the hall, firing before his feet were set. The recoil from the gun was stronger than he'd expected, so his shot strayed into the ceiling. He recovered quickly and fired again, aiming blindly. The report of the gun was thunderous and echoed down the long hall.

Simon saw a hulking figure at the end of the corridor. He was no more than a shadow backlit by the light of the elevator. The thug tried to lunge out of the way, and Simon fired again. This time, he hit his mark. The bullet tore into the man's thigh. He lurched, but didn't fall.

Just as Simon was about to fire again, another shot boomed from behind him. Simon spun back around and saw smoke drifting from the muzzle of Charlie's gun, before it clattered out of his hand. Simon turned back toward the gunman, ready to fire again, but the shadowy figure jerked back and fell to the floor. His gun slipped from his lifeless fingers and skittered across the marble.

Simon stood frozen for a moment. The man didn't move. He was dead. Finally, Simon broke from his fugue and turned to Charlie. "Are you all right?" he asked, as he knelt at his side.

Charlie grimaced and put his revolver in his pocket. "I was shot. What do you think?"

In spite of it all, Simon laughed.

"Sure, laugh at the bleeding man."

"Can you stand?"

"Yeah," Charlie said, but he couldn't make it without help.

Simon steadied him and then saw the elevator doors closing down the hall. "Hold on to something," he said and ran forward. He sprinted down the corridor and through the foyer, managing to wedge his arm between the doors just before they closed. He shoved them open again and pointed his gun at the cowering elevator man. "I should shoot you right now. Don't give me another reason."

The little man tried to press himself into the wood paneling.

"Go and help my friend," Simon barked and pulled the stop lever. "Now!"

The man scurried out of the elevator and down the hall. He tried to support Charlie's bulk, and they shuffled back with excruciating slowness. They stepped over the dead thug sprawled at the mouth of the foyer. The man's chest was bright crimson, a blossoming stain spreading out onto the cold floor beside him. Finally, they made it to the lift, and Simon waved his gun toward the controls. "Hurry it up. Is Mack awake?"

The man trembled as he shook his head.

"Is there anyone else down there?" Simon asked.

"No. Just Vic," he said, nodding his head toward the dead man.

"Good. Now, get this thing moving."

The trip down to the lobby seemed to take twice as long as the trip up. Charlie was bleeding badly, but gathered himself well enough to walk unassisted as they slipped out the back door.

Simon helped Charlie to the car. "We need to get you to hospital."

The barkeep shook his head. "Not in the city. King's men'll be all over it."

Simon put his gun back into his pocket, vaguely aware that he had four bullets left.

Charlie opened the driver's side door and managed to heave himself up into the seat. He dug into his pocket and pulled out his gun. "You might need this."

Simon nodded and took the gun. He slipped it into his waistband.

"Better make sure it's not cocked," Charlie said with a smirk.

Simon quickly pulled the gun out. It was uncocked. With a relived sigh he put the gun back in his jacket pocket. "Very amusing."

"Can't be too careful." The brief moment of levity faded and with it Charlie's smile.

"I'll be all right. I got some friends in Yonkers owe me a favor."

Simon was torn. Charlie was in no shape to drive, but night had fallen and he was no closer to Elizabeth. If anything, he was further away.

Sensing his dilemma, Charlie shook his head. "You do what ya gotta do."

Simon heaved a sigh. How could he ever possibly thank this man? No matter what he said, it would pale in comparison to the debt he owed. A debt he could never repay.

"Give Lizzy a hug for me," Charlie said, and stuck out his hand, fingers drenched in his own blood.

"I will," Simon vowed and gripped his hand tightly, moved as much by Charlie's faith as his courage.

A wealth of understanding passed between the two men in the silence of the deserted alley. Charlie pulled his hand away and started the car with a grimace of pain. Simon stepped back and eased the door closed. Charlie put the car in gear, and with one last look, drove off into the night. The car turned the corner and disappeared from sight. Knowing he couldn't linger there any longer, Simon headed back to Fifth Avenue.

The city moved on, oblivious to the drama that played at its very heart. In a little over forty-eight hours the eclipse would come. Simon patted his pants pocket. The watch was secure. The gun was loaded. But his last chance to find King and Elizabeth had evaporated with the empty room upstairs. Or had it? With a new purpose, he fell in with the foot traffic, shoved his bloody hand into his pocket and started for St. Patrick's.

CHAPTER TWENTY-EIGHT

ELIZABETH OPENED HER EYES. White hot pain pierced her head like railway spikes. She tried to think, but her mind was still wrapped in gauze. She blinked against an ungodly bright light that sliced through the louvered blinds. All she knew was she had to shut those damn things. But when she pushed herself up, the raging headache was joined by a wave of gagging nausea. She fought to keep from retching and the effort drove the ten penny nails deeper into her brain.

She took a deep breath to try and stem the upsurge of bile, but the stale odor of rotting fish and thick, salty air had other ideas. She coughed and cradled her head. Her tongue felt tacky with a thick paste, and she could barely manage to swallow.

Dying on the spot seemed like a good idea, but she settled for not moving. She stilled in mid-movement, caught in an awkward position, half upright, and one hand curled over the top of her head, pressing cool fingers against her throbbing temple.

Slowly the fog in her head began to lift, and she dared to sit up the rest of the way. Either this was the worst hangover in the history of man, or she.... Slowly, it came back to her. Memories swimming upstream. She had been washing her hands when the door opened behind her. Just when she was about to politely remind the woman that the room was occupied, two huge men filled the doorway. A sweaty hand clamped over her mouth before she could scream. The other thug grabbed her legs, and they carried her down the hall. She'd fought as best she could, finally managing to get a leg free and kick the thug at her feet in the groin.

She'd flailed for a moment, getting in a few more shots, but he was too strong and had grabbed her ankle in a vice grip. She thought he'd torn her Achilles tendon. Looking down at her legs, she saw the red marks from his fingers just above her shoeless foot. Leaning down to massage her ankle, another wave of nausea made her reconsider the move.

They'd dragged her into a car. She vaguely remembered one of them muttering something about "getting the stuff and shutting her the hell up." Then the world faded into darkness. Until she'd woken up here. Wherever here was.

The room was small but plush. A silk duvet covered the single bed. A small, mahogany vanity with an ornate, brass-framed mirror stood to the side. Two wingback chairs upholstered in midnight blue velvet sat on either side of a small table. A crystal carafe of water and a single glass sat waiting for her.

She pushed herself up from the bed and teetered on wobbly legs before the world settled uneasily into place. She limped over to the table, poured a glass of water and gratefully drank it down.

If only the ground would stop swaying like that. Leaning heavily on the table, she closed her eyes. The distant clang of metal and a soft scraping sound were strangely familiar, but her brain couldn't find the answer.

Bleary eyed, but feeling closer to human again, she lifted one of the louvers and peered out the window. It was dark outside, save for that damnable light that hung outside her room. Squinting into the glare, her eyes slowly adjusted. A white railing stood a few feet away, beyond that, darkness. A fluttering streak of creamy white appeared then disappeared on the horizon. And then another.

The ocean.

She was on a boat. It had to be King's boat. Could she swim for shore? How far out were they? She tried to stem the tide of questions that flooded her brain and concentrate on facts. She was on a boat. Judging from the gentle, nauseating, rocking, they were still moored to the dock. Score one for the good guys.

She padded awkwardly across the carpet to the door and tried the handle. Locked. So much for one for the good guys.

She leaned against it, and the reality of her situation slowly sank in. She was King's prisoner. Maybe she always had been. Only now, the cage had just gotten a whole lot smaller.

Elizabeth hobbled back over to the bed and sat down heavily. What was she supposed to do now? Wait to be rescued? Simon would...

Simon. Her heart clenched at the thought of him. Had King taken him too? No. He wouldn't do that. But he would kill him.

"Oh God," she gasped. What if Simon was dead? She flushed with panic. No, don't think like that. Simon was alive, she told herself. He had to be.

Thunder rolled in the distance as Simon pulled open the doors to the church. He moved quickly down the center aisle, searching fervently for a glimpse of the old priest. All he saw was a dour looking woman kneeling in a pew, mumbling a prayer and caressing the beads of her rosary. Then, in the shadows at the far end of the room, he saw a stirring of black robes.

"Father!" he called out, oblivious to propriety and the glare from the old woman. He dashed down the aisle, but stopped short when he saw it wasn't Father Cavanaugh, but a young priest.

"Please, sir. A little restraint—"

"Where's Father Cavanaugh?" Simon demanded.

The young priest clasped his hands in front of him. "I'm Father Fitzpatrick. Is there something I can do for you?"

"Is he in his office?" Simon asked and started toward the side door.

"Please, sir. He's resting," the priest said trailing along behind. "Perhaps I can help you."

Simon ignored him and yanked open the office door.

"Sir, I have to insist..."

Father Cavanaugh was lying on the small couch.

"You see," Father Fitzpatrick whispered. "Come, let's..."

Again, Simon ignored him and made his way into the room. Even before he reached Father Cavanaugh's side, he knew something was wrong. A palpable presence of something malevolent lingered in the air. The way the priest was laid out was familiar. Hands clasped over his chest, a crucifix resting underneath. Then it struck him. He wasn't sleeping, he was lying-in-state.

Dead.

Simon stood over him for a moment, waiting, hoping to see the rise and fall of his chest, but knowing it would never come. Father Cavanaugh's lips were already tinged with blue. His head wasn't settled properly on his shoulders; it was shifted, unnaturally, just off-center. Simon knelt down and saw the tell-tale garish, purple bruise bulging beneath the stark white of his collar. His neck had been broken. It had to be King. He'd killed him and then posed him in this mockery of respect.

"Father?" Father Fitzpatrick said, fear and uncertainty making his voice quiver.

"He's dead." Uttering the words cut the final thread Simon had clung to. Without Father Cavanaugh, he had nothing to go on. No leads. No way to find Elizabeth.

The young priest cried out and fell to his knees. Crossing himself, he mumbled a litany that faded with Simon's hopes.

Was it just this morning life seemed to be open before him? Elizabeth at his side, the future waiting to take them. And now, he'd seen death. Twice in the last hour, like a ghoulish specter nipping at his heels, lurking behind every corner, suffocating him.

Hearing the Father Fitzpatrick's cry, parishioners crowded the doorway. Simon couldn't breathe. He had to get out of that room. Desperate to escape the sobs and cries of dismay slowly filling the cathedral, he shouldered past the onlookers and stumbled down the aisle.

He threw his weight against the heavy doors and staggered into the night. A bolt of lightning burst overhead, illuminating the street like a photographer's flash, capturing a moment, stopping time.

A single rain drop spattered the sidewalk. Then another and another. Soon, a sheet of despairing rain cascaded down. Umbrellas blossomed like black flowers in a potter's field.

Simon made his way down the street, needing to get as far away as he could from the church and the shadow of death. Carried on a tide of anger and desperation, he pushed ruthlessly through the crowd.

And the heavens above raged.

Elizabeth paced the short length of her quarters, feeling absurdly like a peg-legged pirate. She didn't want to take off her one remaining shoe. It was silly. Even if she did manage to escape, there was no way she could run away wearing only one shoe. But there was something too vulnerable about being completely barefoot, so she limped back and forth across the Berber carpet. If nothing else, maybe she could wear a hole in the deck.

She'd already canvassed the room for anything she might use as a weapon. Simon had taught her well, and the diversion kept her mind off things. They'd taken her hidden stake, but there were a few things that might come in handy. She wrapped the silver, handheld mirror in a pillowcase and broke the glass. The jagged pieces would be as good as a knife, if she didn't manage to slice her own hand in the bargain. She tore the hem off the sheet and bound one of the ends. The remaining blade was painfully small. Better than nothing, she thought, as she slipped it under the pillow.

The water carafe was heavy enough to be a decent bludgeon, but she doubted she'd get the chance to use it. That left the hurricane lamp, a ready-made Molotov cocktail. The wick cast a deceptively warm glow around the room.

Quite the cozy little prison.

She heard men's voices outside her window and peered through the slats. The two men she recognized as the ones who'd taken her from the diner maneuvered a dolly across the deck. A large barrel with Spanish lettering nearly skidded off its perch. Rain had started to fall, and the wooden planks were slippery.

"Boss'll kill us if we lose this rum," one of them said.

"Shut up and help me." They struggled to right the huge cask and trollied it down the deck out of view.

She pressed her face close to the glass and was startled by a knock at the door. She heard a key slip into the lock and quickly hobbled over to the bed. Sitting and bracing herself near the pillow, she took a deep breath.

The door opened and King stepped in. He grinned broadly, his handsome face contradicting the truth that lay behind the mask. "Ah, you're awake. How are you feeling?" he asked, helping himself to one of the chairs by the table. "No worse for the wear, I hope."

She balled her hand into a fist to keep from slipping it under the pillow and grabbing her makeshift knife. "I've been better."

He took off his rain soaked fedora and shook the water from the brim. "Sorry about that, but you weren't exactly cooperative. Or so I hear."

"My first time being kidnapped. Didn't know there was a protocol."

King chuckled. He was almost giddy. "I assume you've found your quarters adequate. If there's anything you desire, you need only ask."

"Got an extra key?"

"Now, now. No reason to be difficult. We're about to embark on a glorious journey together."

"And where are we going?"

"I was speaking metaphorically, but business before pleasure. Just a quick trip up the coast tomorrow, if the weather clears. Then we'll have all the time in the world to get to know each other."

"Are you speaking metaphorically again?"

King leaned back and rested his palms on the arms of the chair. A monarch on his throne. "You needn't be afraid of eternity, Elizabeth. Imagine the things we'll see. Civilizations rise and fall in the blink of an eye. All of it ours to behold. For eternity. Together."

Her heart was pounding now. She was sure he could smell the blood coursing through her veins. "And if I refuse?"

"You won't."

"You seem pretty sure of that."

"I'm a man who gets what he wants. I wanted you. And here you are," he said, gesturing expansively about the room.

"It's fate," he said and reached into his breast pocket. He pulled out Sebastian's ring and set it on the table.

He tugged off one of his gloves and rested his hand on the table, an exact duplicate on his finger. "What else can explain this? A one of a kind, suddenly two. A rather blatant sign, don't you think?"

Elizabeth shuddered at the implications. "Quite a coincidence," she said, casually slipping her hand further under the pillow.

King smirked. "Fate. So, you see," he said as he tucked Sebastian's ring back into his breast pocket. "It's destiny. You can't fight it."

"And the fact that I'm in love with another man?"

"A mistake. You are, after all, only human."

"Love isn't—"

The sudden crack of King's hand slapping the table made her jump. The sharp edge of the mirror fragment cut into her fingers.

"Don't lecture me on love!" he shouted, and stood up so quickly his chair fell back against the wall. His face began to change, arteries bulged from his neck. She could see him struggling to rein in the demon. He paused and with a great force of will, returned to humanity.

"The priest tried that this morning," he said in a thinly controlled voice. "He shouldn't have interfered."

"You didn't...." Dear God. Not Father Cavanaugh.

"He was a fool. Even until the very end, he spouted his endless drivel about love and redemption. Telling me what I can and cannot have. Nothing in this world is given freely. You have to take what you want, before the world takes it from you," King said and then seemed to realize he'd said too much. He squared his shoulders and pulled his glove back on. "He was an obstacle between us. I simply removed him."

She felt sick again, but would be damned if she'd show him weakness now. "So you killed him."

"Regretfully."

"Regretfully? Is that the demon or your soul talking? Or can you even tell the difference anymore?"

"Do not speak of things you don't understand."

"You're right, I don't understand. I don't understand how someone with a soul could do the things you've done."

"I did what was necessary," he said, anxiously moving around the room, teetering on the edge of madness.

"Necessary for what?"

"For us to be together."

Elizabeth steeled herself. It was a gamble, but, after all, she was a gambler's daughter. When you're dealt aces and eights, the only thing you can do is go down fighting. She played her last card. "We'll never be together."

"We are. We will be," he said like a plaintive child. "Forever."

"No, we won't. You can take my body. You can kill me. You can turn me into a creature like you. But you will never get what you want."

In one quick movement he crossed the room. His fingers dug into her shoulders, and he jerked her to her feet. His dark eyes flared. "I will!"

Elizabeth wanted to scream, to turn away in revulsion, but she'd made her final stand and wasn't going to back down now. "You can't make someone love you," she said and saw the uncertainty flicker across his face. "And if you really loved me, you'd let me go."

His fingers dug painfully into her arms, as if he could control his demon by controlling her. "Let me go," she repeated, her voice barely a whisper.

The strong line of his jaw clenched and unclenched. Finally, he lowered his gaze and released her arms. Hope flared in her chest. She held her breath, only aware of the pounding of her own heart and the incessant tapping of raindrops on the windows.

He stared down at the small bit of carpet between them. "You will love me," he said quietly, then raised his eyes. "It's fate."

The rain was as unrelenting as the man. Simon prowled the streets of Manhattan hour after hour. Sometimes swept along in the crowd and at others shouldering against them, but always searching. He'd even gone back to Mulberry Street and pounded on Rosella's door. He should have tried the psychic earlier. Now, it was too late and there was no answer. Everywhere he went there was no answer. Every straw he grasped slipped between his fingers until he was raw with the effort. Every minute that passed hollowed him out that much more, until the hope he'd clung to was frayed to a single, gossamer strand.

Saturday night bled into Sunday morning. Hours slipped by as Simon scoured the city. Torrential rains pounded down from above. People scurried past, dashing from cover to cover, as Simon walked on. Block after block. Dead end after dead end. Exhausted, but unable to stop moving, Simon kept searching.

Sunday afternoon disappeared into night.

Oblivious to everything but finding Elizabeth, Simon ignored the chill that soaked through his clothes and the muscles in his legs that threatened to give way. His vision blurred and he leaned against a brick wall, pausing for a moment. Where in God's name was she?

"Here," came a woman's voice in the distance.

His head snapped up, and he saw her through the driving rain. A slim figure in a green dress barely discernable through the striated landscape. She waved happily in his direction before turning to knock on a door. The wall opened and she stepped inside.

"Elizabeth."

He ran down the almost desolate street and skidded to a halt, nearly falling on the slick pavement. It was only a wall. Brick and mortar.

He fought the urge to laugh. Was he going mad already?

Footfalls echoed to his right and a man rapped smartly on an indistinct door. The peephole slid open and the man muttered, "Bee's knees." The mysterious door slid open and the man stepped inside.

He must have misjudged the distance. Elizabeth was inside that door. Simon pounded his fist against it until the slot opened and a pair of hooded eyes gazed back.

"Let me in," Simon rasped.

"Password?"

He'd just heard it and already it was fading from his mind. He heard Elizabeth's voice in his head, "Oh, Simon. Find something and grip it."

"Bee's knees," he said and bounded into the dark, smoky room as soon as the door opened.

He wiped the rain from his face and scanned the room. She was at the bar, but even before she turned around, he knew it wasn't her. Maybe he'd known all along. She didn't look anything like Elizabeth. It was a frightening testament to his desperation, and he felt his grip on that single thread slip. He leaned against the bar and rested his head in his hands.

"You want somethin'?"

"What?"

The stocky bartender slammed a bottle of bourbon onto the bar and scowled. "I said, you want somethin'?"

"No."

"This ain't a flophouse. You drink or you get the hell out."

The rich amber of the alcohol sloshed against the side of the bottle, inviting him into oblivion. He took out a dollar and laid it on the bar. The bartender grinned. He must have known he had a live one. He poured the first drink and shoved it to the edge.

The bourbon burned all the way down, but Simon scarcely felt it. He wondered if he'd ever feel anything again. He knew following the woman into the club was delusional at best. Glancing around the bar, the people were no more than shadows, vague images of life blurring around him.

He drank two more shots in quick succession, throwing them back without thought. Tired, hungry and soaked to the skin, the alcohol blindsided him. His elbow slid off the bar and he barely caught his head before it smashed into the hard wood.

"Watch it buddy," a man groused to his left.

Simon lifted his wobbly head and glared as best he could with double vision. "Piss off."

The man shook his head and turned away.

"Hate this bloody city," Simon growled. "Give you something then take it away. Poxy, fucking, sodding city. King Kashian... Bloody bastard!" Simon nearly knocked over his glass. "Thinks he can take her away. Thinks I won't find him. Oh, but I'll find him. King! King Kashian!" he called out, spinning away from the bar.

The crowd fell silent as he staggered forward, an instant pariah. People pulled away as he shouted, "King!"

Simon felt a hand clamp on his shoulder and tried to pull away. "Let go of me!"

"Vinny, show this palooka the door."

Another hand gripped him. Before he could even begin to struggle, the pavement flew up to meet his face.

His head hit the concrete with a sharp crack, and the pain shot straight through to his neck. He touched his forehead and felt the lump already beginning to grow. He managed to push himself up and looked down the oddly tilting street. A few shuffling footsteps later he clung to the cold, wet side of a building.

He pushed himself along and heard the echo of footsteps trailing behind. They stopped when he stopped. Was he still being followed? Whirling around, he nearly lost his balance and a strong hand reached out to steady him.

"Careful there, son."

Simon narrowed his eyes, blinking through the rain. The black night slowly encroached, shunting out what little light there was. Through the shrinking tunnel of consciousness he stared into the kindly face and choked back a sob. It couldn't be.

"Grandfather?"

CHAPTER TWENTY-NINE

TEA—CHINESE GUNPOWDER. THE SMELL was unmistakable. Strong, slightly bitter and somehow the essence of peace. This must be a dream, Simon thought. A counterpoint to the nightmare images still dancing across his mind. A magic lantern show of the macabre.

He took a deep breath, and the insistent odor forced him back the last few paces to consciousness. Blinking against the bright pinpricks of light that stabbed his eyes, he rolled onto his side, and a new fragrance filled his senses. Elizabeth. Soft and fading, but one he'd know among thousands. Hope flared in his chest and then died a premature death. An empty bed and no Elizabeth. The last twenty-four hours fell back upon his shoulders with a crushing weight. He buried his head in the pillow and breathed in the sweet smell she'd left behind.

"Drink this," came a voice from behind him.

Simon spun around on the bed with such force he thought his throbbing head would fly off his shoulders.

He was sure it had all been a dream, a delusion. But there, not more than five feet away, in their little apartment, stood his grandfather smiling and holding out a cup of tea. He blinked a few more times and rubbed his eyes. Maybe he was still dreaming?

"Come on, lad. Drink your tea."

His wits slogged through the mud of hazy memories. His hand took the offered cup, but his mind could barely manage to cobble a thought. "How did you...?" he asked before trailing off, unable to cipher out just one question.

Sebastian Cross smiled patiently, his grey eyes crinkling at the edges. "Ah. How indeed?"

He retrieved his own cup and sat down at the small table. "As to the tea, Mrs. Larsen graciously offered her hotplate and tea service. Delightful woman. Lives in 304, I think. Second cousin to Amundsen. Good man, Amundsen. Brilliant explorer," he said and took a sip from his cup. "And as to the tea itself. First rule of time travel, my boy. Always bring your own tea."

Simon stared at him blankly. "But you're—" He couldn't finish the sentence and shook his head.

His grandfather looked just as he remembered him. The herringbone suit, the knot in his tie off-center as it always was. White hair unruly as ever. Exactly as he was that last night thirty years ago. How many times had Simon wished to see him again? So many things left unsaid and not one of them would come to mind.

"Are you real?" Simon asked, sounding every inch the little boy he felt.

"Quite."

Simon placed his cup on the end table and stood, but his legs weren't up to the task and he faltered. As he had been so many times before, Sebastian was there to steady him.

"Take your time, son."

Simon looked into the weathered face smiling back kindly and swallowed the lump in his throat. He held on to the older man's arm, afraid to let go.

They stood together for a moment, the decades falling away. Years of longing settled in the dust. Simon gently squeezed his grandfather's arm and when he found his voice, it was roughened with profound emotion. "It's good to see you."

Sebastian patted his cheek. "And you too, my boy," he said softly before clearing his throat. "Now grab your cuppa and come have it at the table like a civilized person."

Obediently, Simon did as he was told, although he never took his eyes off the older man, sure he'd disappear if he did. "There are so many questions. How did you find me? What are you doing here? I—Elizabeth!" Simon said, the fog finally beginning to clear. Nearly spilling all of the tea, he thrust the cup onto the table. His head pounded even louder from the quick movement, and he gripped his forehead.

"Easy there, lad. You're in no shape to go running off after her now."

That caught him off guard. "You mean you know? About Elizabeth?"

Sebastian nodded gravely. "I do."

"But how?"

"All in good time. Drink your tea before it goes cold."

"I don't want any bloody tea."

"Simon," he said in stern voice. "Sit down," he added more gently. "Please?"

Grudgingly, Simon did as he was asked. "How do you know about Elizabeth? Do you know where she is? How did you even find me?"

Sebastian put up his hand to halt the stream of questions. "As to the latter, I've been following you on and off for some days now. Or rather, following the man that was following you. queer business, that. Very troubling. As to how I arrived here," he said and took out a gold pocket watch. "The watch. And if I'm not mistaken, yours will have the same scratch, here below the engraving."

Simon took out his watch and, sure enough, the same mark marred his watch. It was, after all, the same watch. But how could it be in two places at once? Simon's already spinning head couldn't begin to fathom the complexities of time travel. He cleared his mind as best he could. "But why are you here now? Are you here to help me?"

"An assignment from the Council. I had assumed you were here for the same reason. I'm ashamed to admit I didn't recognize you straight away. I saw you at that club, Charlie Blue's. You're quite the scrapper," Sebastian said proudly.

"You were there? The fight was days ago. Why didn't you say anything? Come to me?"

"I didn't know who you were. I saw you with the watch and assumed you were sent by the Council. But why they would send another member was puzzling. I sniffed around a bit, asked a few questions. When a man told me your name, I was absolutely gobstruck. I shouldn't have been. I always suspected you might join the Council, follow in my footsteps. You never did care that others thought I wasn't batting on a full wicket," Sebastian said with a laugh.

"But the more questions I asked, the murkier it all became. And your direct involvement in the culture was a clear violation of the prescripts of the Council."

"What council?" Simon asked, and rubbed his temple. "I don't understand. What does this have to do with Elizabeth?"

"The Council for Temporal Studies. I'm in the anthropological department with emphasis on occult studies. It's a fine organization, if a bit overzealous on occasion."

"There are others like you?"

"I'd like to think I'm unique," Sebastian said with a wink. "But, yes. There are several other field operatives. Temporal explorers. What I can't understand is how you came by the watch if it wasn't given to you by the Council."

"Elizabeth and I..." Simon started, "It was an accident."

"Ah. The waitress. Your wife?"

"Yes. No. Not exactly. It's a long story."

"Why don't you tell me about it?" Sebastian said in a voice that was nearly impossible to refuse.

"There isn't enough time. I have to find her," Simon said, as he looked out the window. It was still raining. The skies darkening. "What time is it?"

"Nearly four o'clock."

"The eclipse is in five hours," Simon said, pushing back his chair. "I have to go."

"You don't know where to look. Why not sit down and regain your strength? My back's killing me. You must weigh fifteen stone now. You should probably have that head looked at. You've got quite a lump."

"There isn't time for that."

"Rest for a few minutes. Sit down and tell me what's happened. Together we'll find a solution."

Sebastian's calm resolve battled its way through Simon's fear, just as it had when he was boy. Slowly, he let himself be led back to his seat. "Since I arrived here, I've been counting down the hours till the eclipse and now that it's almost here... What I wouldn't give for more time."

"Time's odd that way, isn't it? Drags on interminably when you want it to pass, and it's gone in the blink of an eye when you want it to linger."

"I should have been more aware. More careful. I knew he'd probably try something like this," Simon said more to himself than to Sebastian.

"Who?"

"King. He's kidnapped Elizabeth. Taken her God knows where."

Sebastian's tea cup clattered on the table. He cleared his throat and arched a bushy eyebrow in forced nonchalance. "King Kashian?"

"You know about him?"

"He's the reason I'm here. My assignment was to study him and what happened at..." Sebastian's forehead wrinkled. "That's why I went to the pub. Our records showed he frequented the establishment. Was part owner, I think. I had no idea he was involved in Elizabeth's disappearance."

"He is."

"You're well acquainted with him, I take it?"

Simon clenched his fists. "You could say that."

"Is it true then? Does he have a soul?"

"He thinks so."

"Fascinating. Did he tell you how it happened? It's most unusual."

"I don't care about King," Simon bit out. "All I want is Elizabeth back. And to go home."

"Of course," Sebastian said too quickly. "But perhaps some things are better left to their proper end."

"What do you mean?"

"We mustn't interfere with the period we visit. I understand the lure of involving yourself in the lives of those we study. All too well. But you shouldn't muck about in such things."

"I'm not here to study anyone. I told you it was an accident. Elizabeth and I were examining the watch when it activated." Every mention of her name made his heart break into another piece.

"That must have come as quite a shock," Sebastian said in sympathy. "I wish I could see the faces of the Council when they find out not one, but two people have managed to break their security. They're really quite strict about it. What I don't understand is why they didn't confiscate the watch. I assume, in your time I'm dead."

Simon frowned. How could he be so casual about it?

Sebastian took a sip of tea and smiled philosophically. "I don't expect to live forever."

"The family hid the watch," Simon said, not saying that they'd hidden everything that reminded them of him, including Simon himself. "I only recently inherited it."

"Ah. Ashamed of me even in death. They're nothing if not consistent. Well, I'm glad you have it."

"I'm not. I wish I'd never seen the cursed thing," Simon growled and pushed away from his chair. He walked restlessly toward the window. The storm outside raged on. Sheets of gray obscured the fading light. He gripped the window sill. "First the nightmares and now, this...nightmare."

"Did you have dreams? Prescient dreams?"

Simon turned back to Sebastian. "How did you know?"

"An uncommon side-effect of the watch. There's a temporal wash given off, a sort of blurred fissure in time around it. Most people aren't sensitive enough for it to register. It's a rather remarkable gift really."

"It's bloody awful, is what it is. You have no idea the things I've..." His voice trailed off. He couldn't bring himself to tell Sebastian about the dreams. He turned back to the window. "I have to find Elizabeth. She's... she's everything to me."

"She must be a remarkable woman."

Simon closed his eyes for a brief second and then stared out into the darkening street below. "She's stubborn beyond measure, thoroughly reckless and idiotically optimistic. All and all completely maddening."

Sebastian chuckled.

Simon turned to face him. "And I love her more than I thought possible."

"I know the feeling, lad. A day doesn't go by that I don't think of dear Nora. God rest her soul. Your grandmother was an angel that walked the earth. For too short a time."

Simon had barely known his grandmother. She died in an accident when he was very small, but he remembered her voice and, of course, the stories Grandfather told over games of chess.

Suddenly, a thought occurred to him. It was so obvious he couldn't imagine why he hadn't thought of it sooner. He pulled his watch from his pocket. "The eclipse. When it comes, I can set the watch to the day before yesterday and save Elizabeth. It's so simple."

"Also impossible, I'm afraid."

"Why?"

"A failsafe built into the watch. Once you travel through a time, you can never return to it. I'm sorry."

"Maybe you're wrong."

"Don't you think I tried when Nora was killed in the accident? No man can resist that temptation. The Council knows that. The failsafe is designed to protect the timeline. Certain things are meant to be."

"Not this."

"You have to consider the possibility. The Council—"

"Sod the Council and sod their bloody timelines!" Simon yelled as he slammed his fist down on the table. He took a breath and straightened. "This is Elizabeth. And I will do whatever I must to get her back."

"Now, Simon—"

"Don't coddle me! I'm not a child anymore."

"No, you're not. You're man enough to know that what you want isn't always what's best. There are rules, Simon. I'm breaking the rules I've lived by for forty years just talking to you."

"Why?" Simon demanded.

Sebastian cleared his throat and set down his teacup. "Because I couldn't stand to see you lying in the gutter."

"Why?"

"Because I love you, of course."

"And I love Elizabeth."

Sebastian took a deep breath. "You should have been a barrister," he said and then gestured to the chair.

Simon huffed out an impatient breath and then sat.

Sebastian ran his hand through his shock of white hair and sighed. "There'll be hell to pay for this when I get back. The reports I have on King are detailed, but there are gaps. No one wrote a living history of events, so my information is bodged together from various sources. Not all of them necessarily reliable." He paused and looked around the small room, clearly stalling for time.

"Go on."

"It was reported that King died today. Some time this evening."

"That's the first good news I've had in a long time," Simon said.

"Yes, well. It seems he was killed in some sort of explosion or fire. The details are rather sketchy. He was last seen this evening on a yacht, the Osiris, at a small marina in New Jersey."

Unbidden, images from Simon's nightmare of Elizabeth in her small rowboat flashed before him. "A yacht?"

"Yes, his destination wasn't clear. But," Sebastian said, his grey eyes growing troubled, "everyone on board perished."

For the first time since Elizabeth had vanished, Simon felt a faint glimmer of hope. If only he could get there in time. "What marina? Do you know the specifics?"

"It isn't necessarily reliable information, Simon," Sebastian said as he plucked at the cuffs of his jacket.

"What aren't you telling me?"

"Things will play out as they should. I'm only trying to spare you."

"Tell me."

Sebastian took a sip of tea and made a face. "Gone cold."

"Grandfather, please? I have to know."

"There was a report of a woman on board. It could have been someone else, there's no guarantee it was your Elizabeth. Perhaps it was another body."

Simon's mind reeled. It was just as it had been in his dream.

Sebastian leaned forward and rested a hand on Simon's knee. "There are certain things we have to accept, lad."

"Not this," Simon said and stood. "What marina?"

Sebastian sighed. "Brown's Point Marina in Keysport," he said as he got to his feet. "We'll go together."

"No. You have to promise you'll stay here," Simon said. "In this room until the eclipse."

"Balderdash. I'm not letting you run off to face King alone. Don't be ridiculous."

"You don't understand. You have to stay here. Promise me you will?"

Sebastian squared his shoulders and jutted out his chin defiantly. "Out of the question."

The unstoppable force glared at the immovable object. The future and the past pulled him in opposite directions, until Simon thought he would be split in two. "Don't make me force you to stay. By God, I will if I have to. I can't have your death..."

"My death?"

"Please? I couldn't bear it if...Stay here."

Sebastian released Simon, his eyes impenetrable. He stared at him for a long moment and then nodded. "You'd better hurry, son."

"Thank you," Simon said softly and then it dawned on him: this would be the last time he would see his grandfather. "There are so many things I wanted to say."

"Consider them said," Sebastian said and took Simon's hand, covering it with both his own. "Now hurry, and for God's sake, be careful."

Simon studied the older man's face for the last time. "I will," he promised and squeezed Sebastian's hand firmly before letting go. He nodded once and then turned on his heel and left the room without looking back.

CHAPTER THIRTY

THE ONLY THING WORSE than a raging storm was a raging storm on the ocean. Even as Simon struggled to keep his footing on the muddy, treacherous slope, he could see the whitecaps whipped up into a frenzy by the fierce wind. The sea churned wave after merciless wave onto the shore, dragging out the sand into the murky, bone chilling depths beyond.

He'd paid a fortune to the cabbie to take him through the Holland Tunnel to New Jersey, but far more precious was the time it had taken. More than two hours eaten away, leaving one golden hour until the lunar eclipse. He looked up into the black sky and wondered if he'd even know when it came. The moon was blanketed behind an endless cloud that seemed to cover the whole of the earth. Not that it mattered. Nothing mattered if he didn't find Elizabeth.

He would find her; he was sure of that. His nightmares had led him to this place, to this moment in time, where the images that had tortured him would come to their inevitable end.

His foot slipped on some loose pebbles, and he grabbed the thorny edge of a bramble bush to keep from falling. The thorns dug into his palm. Fresh rivulets of blood mixed with the rain and puddled in his hand. His fingers curled into a fist. He wasn't beaten yet. There was no power on this earth that could keep him from trying. Elizabeth was alive, and he'd pay whatever price that was asked to keep her that way.

The hillside he stood on gave him a good view of the marina below. It was a private dock, no more than five slips, surrounded on the shore by a chain link fence. Two men carried large casks out of a small warehouse at the base of the dock to a yacht sitting at the end of the pier. A third stood at the gangplank barking orders.

Simon crouched down into the undergrowth. If he was going to have a chance in hell of confronting King, it would have to be on the shore. There were too many men around the boat. But if they made any move to leave, he'd take his chances there.

Fate decided to throw him a crumb. Another man emerged on the gangplank and stopped to talk to the supervisor. A flash of lightning lit the night sky. King.

Simon hurried down the rest of the hill, skidding to a halt at the base of the fence. It would leave him exposed to climb over it, but there was nothing to be done for it. The gate was well secured with a heavy chain. Patting his jacket pockets, he felt the outline of the guns. They might not kill the bastard, but from what Elizabeth had said about that night in the storeroom, they would slow him down. He could feel the stake in his inner breast pocket, pressing against his chest, and he was warmed by the thought of shoving it into King's heart.

The metal fence shook and rattled under his weight. He clambered up the side, but his jacket got snagged on one of the twisted ends of wire. He yanked at it, but he was still caught. He gave it another tug and the jacket came free, but one of the guns fell from his pocket and landed on the wrong side of the fence. Damn it. He was vulnerable enough without trying this stunt again. One would have to do. Easing over the fence, he landed in a crouch and crept to the back of the storehouse.

Pressing himself against the back door, he waited and listened. Muffled voices came from the other side. He strained to hear King's among them. Then he heard the unmistakable voice that sounded like oil dripping on silk. Bastard.

The voices faded away as the men trundled another barrel back to the boat. The thin sliver of light shining under the door died. With the cover of darkness on his side, Simon gripped the rusty knob and eased it open. King stood silhouetted on the opposite side of the room and watched his men wheel the last barrel down the pier.

Simon eased the gun from his pocket and stepped into the room. He was sure the pounding of his heart would give him away, but King didn't seem to take any notice of him. Simon took another tentative step forward and raised his gun.

"I was beginning to wonder," King said calmly, his back still to Simon. "If you were ever going to arrive."

He turned around slowly, his white teeth gleaming in a wickedly perfect smile. "Not that you would have been missed."

Simon's fingers tightened around the handle of the gun and he cocked the trigger. "Where is she?"

King laughed softly. "Waiting for me."

"Waiting to tell you to go to hell, I'd imagine. In fact, it would be my pleasure to give you a hand with that," Simon said and pulled the trigger.

The first bullet was high, and the door jam next to King's shoulder exploded in a shower of splintered wood. King didn't flinch and started forward. Simon strode forward meeting King step for step, the distance between them swiftly closed.

The second bullet hit King in the shoulder and knocked him off stride, but only for a moment. Simon fired again and again; both bullets hit King square in the chest. The impact stopped King in his tracks, and his shoulders rolled forward as he struggled to keep his legs under him.

The metallic click of trigger against empty chamber told Simon he'd run out of bullets. He tossed the gun aside and reached for his stake. King staggered, and Simon lunged forward, prepared to drive the wood into the bastard's cold heart. But King's reflexes were too fast, and his hand shot out and held Simon's forearm in a crushing grip.

King's face twisted into a mockery of a smile. "Pathetic," he sneered and squeezed Simon's wrist. The bones almost snapped under the pressure, the stake fell uselessly to the floor. An icy pain shot up his arm. King tossed him aside.

Simon crashed into the wall. Ignoring the screaming pain in his wrist, he pushed himself up.

King watched, clearly amused and pleased to have a chance to play with his prey before the kill. "I wasn't going to kill you," he said calmly, nearly recovered from the onslaught of bullets. "I thought it might curry favor with Elizabeth to keep you alive, but I think I'm going to enjoy listening to you beg for mercy. Not that you'll get it," he added with a grin.

He stepped forward and hit Simon with a brutal backhand that sent him rolling along the wall.

Spikes of pain lanced through Simon's temples, but he regained his feet. He stood tall and as firmly as he could. "You do know you'll never get what you want."

King stalked closer. "I always get what I want."

"You'll never have Elizabeth."

"I already have her," King said, punctuating the statement with another cruel blow.

Simon could barely stand. It took all his energy to keep from giving in to the welcoming darkness that slowly pressed down on him. He lifted his chin and met King's eyes. "You don't. You might kill me—"

"I think I will."

"But I'll take the one thing you want with me to my grave," Simon said, finding an untapped well of strength in the force of his words. All of his weapons had been useless against King, except for one. It was an astonishing epiphany—simple and pure. Father Cavanaugh had tried to tell him, and he'd been too stubborn to see it. Elizabeth had given it to him, and he'd denied its power. Until now. "Her love will always be mine."

King's mouth twitched with anger, and his fists clenched. Eyes once black now glowed an unearthly yellow. Bulging veins popped out on his neck and sharp white fangs curved over his lip. Face to face with one of the creatures he'd searched for all his life, Simon wanted nothing more than to destroy him, to obliterate the grotesque perversion of life.

"She will love me!" King snarled. "As I love her." He grabbed Simon by the arms and held him in a vise-like grip.

Simon shook his head. "I feel sorry for you."

"For me? You're the one that's about to die."

Simon managed a weak smile. "But I'll die for love." King's eyes flashed brighter, but Simon kept on. If this were his final piece, he would say it. "You're not even capable of it. You may exist forever, but you'll never live. Not even for a moment. You'll never know how love feels."

A deep, demonic growl rumbled in King's chest and he bared his fangs, prepared for the kill, but drew up short as a voice rang out in the darkness.

"King!"

The vampire turned. Sebastian Cross stood only a few feet away. King threw Simon against the wall and then advanced on the old man. He'd barely taken a step when Sebastian tossed the contents of a glass jar at King. A wave of clear liquid splashed onto King's face. Instantly, his skin began to burn from the powerful acid. Acrid smoke billowed off the burning flesh.

King roared in fury. With reflexes far too fast for the old man, he grabbed him and sank his teeth into the soft flesh of the man's neck. Soft, gurgling sounds and the fetid smell of burned skin filled the small warehouse. Sebastian clutched the front of King's jacket in a futile effort to push him away. Ever increasing splashes of blood fell at their feet.

The acid had burned away the side of King's neck and the bulging vein ruptured. All the blood he drained from Sebastian poured out of the gaping hole.

With a furious snarl, King tossed Sebastian aside. Still gripped in the dying man's hand, King's front pocket tore away.

King stumbled toward the door. Smoke danced off his face as the acid continued to eat away at him. He pushed himself out the door and staggered into the driving rain.

Fueled by rage and unyielding pain, King made his way down the uneven planks of the dock.

"Jesus, Boss!" one of the henchman cried when he saw King through the rain.

"Get this thing moving!" King bellowed.

"What happened to you?"

"I said," King raged, grabbing the man by his shirt, "get this thing moving."

The man paled but quickly nodded and called out to the others. "Get the bow line! Cast off."

King shoved him away and boarded the boat as the men set into action, untying the mooring lines and pulling in the gangplank. In a maniacal fury, he threw open the door to Elizabeth's room. She whirled around and gasped at the sight of him.

"You will love me," King growled as he stalked closer.

Disgust and fear flashed across her face, spurring his wrath. Her hand moved quickly to her throat. He saw the gleam of a jagged shard press against her neck.

She pushed the makeshift blade to her skin. A trickle of blood slid down her pale neck. "I'll die first."

King froze. The demon strained inside him, barely reined in. It could smell the blood. Wanted to taste it. But his soul still held on.

He lunged forward and gripped her wrist, wrenching her hand away from her neck. She struggled against him, and his mind clouded over as his own inner battle raged on. He shoved her away, and she fell back onto the bed. How easy it would be to take her now. To feel her pulse ebbing into his. To take what she wouldn't give.

He looked away from her for a moment and caught sight of himself in the mirror. His soul gave him that gift. But now, it was more than a curse. There was no hint of the man he once was in his reflection. Grotesque burns left his skin slagging off the side of his face. The white of his cheek bone, scoured by the acid, shone through the blistered mass. The skeleton of the beast.

Elizabeth took advantage of his distraction and bolted for the door, but King grabbed her before she could make it past him. He spun her back into the room, but she wouldn't stop fighting. She tried to get past him, hands clawing, grabbing for anything she could in a frantic attempt to escape. Her fingers curled around the base of the hurricane lamp, and she swung it at him. King pushed her back and leapt out of the way.

The lantern crashed to the floor. Oil spilled out onto the carpet and caught fire between them. The flames spread quickly, slithering along the floor like a mass of snakes. The wall of flame licked higher and higher between them. Thick smoke filled the tiny room.

Between the flashes of orange and red fire, King saw Elizabeth. She was trapped inside the room, imprisoned by a wall of flame.

She coughed and covered her mouth, but the smoke was too thick. Frantically, she tried to ward off the searing heat and find a way past the flames, but it was no use. The flames were too high, the fire too strong. There was no escape. She was going to die. She stopped struggling and lifted her head, and her eyes met his.

Beautiful, defiant and alive. Something stirred deep inside him. A cold, dead heart struggling to beat.

In that moment, her life meant more to him than his own. The battle was won.

King stepped into the flames.

"Grandfather," Simon gasped as he pulled himself up and stumbled to Sebastian's side.

The older man was alive, barely. He coughed as blood bubbled from his mouth and dribbled down his chin.

"Why did you come here?" Simon asked desperately and tried in vain to stop the blood that oozed from the wound in his neck. "Don't move. I'll get help."

Sebastian's eyes focused on Simon, and he managed to lift his hand to touch Simon's. "Too late for that, my boy." "No!" He couldn't watch him die. Not again.

Sebastian gasped for breath and another coughing jag wracked his body.

"Grandfather."

Sebastian squeezed Simon's hand. "My watch," he said. "Put my watch in my hand."

"No, you—"

"I can't die here. I have to return to my own time."

"You're not going to die," Simon said fiercely.

Sebastian managed a weak smile. "I wish I could have seen you grow into such a fine man."

"Don't say that."

Sebastian's eyes drifted over Simon's shoulder, seeing something far off and undefined. "We're running out of time. The watch."

Simon's hand trembled as he pulled the gold watch from Sebastian's pocket. He placed the watch in one hand and saw the other held a scrap of black cloth torn from King's suit and resting in his palm was the scarab ring. In that instant, he was that ten year old boy at the foot of the stairs again.

"Do you have your watch?" Sebastian asked. "You need to be ready. The eclipse is nearly here."

Automatically, Simon pulled out his watch and showed his grandfather. Sebastian nodded in approval. "Good lad."

Simon dropped it back into his jacket pocket and covered Sebastian's hand with his own. "I told you to stay in the room."

Sebastian shook his head. "I've had a good life. Yours is just beginning."

"No."

"Running out of time," Sebastian said, his eyes glassing over for a moment. "Simon..."

"Yes?" Simon said, leaning closer.

"You made a fine man. I'm so very proud of you."

A sob escaped Simon's throat.

"Now go," Sebastian said his voice barely a rasping whisper.

Simon hesitated, his heart severed in two.

"Go."

King stepped through the flames. Struggling to breathe, Elizabeth stepped back until she pressed herself against the wall and could go no further. Flames covered King's arms. He quickly shed his burning coat and grabbed the comforter off the bed. Wrapping it around her, he lifted her into his arms. Elizabeth pushed weakly at his chest, but the smoke was too much for her and she started to lose consciousness.

Simon's words echoed in his ears: *"You may exist forever, but you'll never live. Not even for a moment. You'll never know how love feels."*

His existence hadn't amounted to anything, until this one moment. The thing he'd been searching for wasn't something to be taken at all, but something to be given.

King cradled her to his chest and plunged back through the wall of flame. Kicking the door open, he stepped out into the driving rain. The water slowly doused the small fires that burned away at his clothes.

His men shouted and tried in vain to put out the fire in the cabin, but it was too late. The flames had grown too strong. Soon they'd eat their way though the floor and ignite the barrels of rum in the ship's hull.

King crossed the deck to the railing, his precious burden still in his arms. He pulled back the blanket from her face, and the cool rain began to bring her around. Elizabeth looked up at him, her eyes bleary and unfocused.

For the first time in his life, as man or demon, he understood what it was to be alive—to love someone. "Tell him," he said. "I do know how it feels."

Without another word, he lifted her over the railing and tossed her into the sea.

Simon ran out of the warehouse. The boat was already a hundred yards from the dock and moving further into the night. Simon paused, his heart pounding against his ribs. How could he have waited so long?

A bright, orange flame shot up from the boat's deck. And another. The boat was nearly engulfed in fire. Simon ran toward the water, tossing his jacket aside. Heavy waves broke against the sand, crashing down with a deafening roar. Icy cold spray stung his cheeks as he fought against the power of the sea. His legs felt like lead weights in the thick salt water. Just as in his dream, the boat drifted further away. This was the moment his nightmares became reality.

"Elizabeth!"

He was in up to his waist when a blinding light burst on the horizon, quickly followed by a thunderous boom. Simon's heart stopped as the explosion shattered the night. Fire blossomed on the sea. Burning embers rained down, snuffed out as they hit the cold water. Waves crashed into his chest, and he stood too stunned to move. Flames engulfed the ship. Burnished scarlet flickered on the dark ocean—a bonfire slowly consumed by the watery depths beneath it.

His nightmare played out before his eyes in red and black. There was no past, no future, nothing by this endless abyss. He stared out blankly as the sea swallowed the fire and the remains of the ship sank below the waves.

He didn't know how long he stayed there. It didn't really matter anymore. Time ceased to have meaning. With nothing to look forward to and only regrets to look back on, Simon slowly turned back toward the shore.

Debris washed around him. Broken pieces of a life he might have had tumbled at his feet. His legs as numb as his heart, he stumbled on the sand. Was this what a living death was like? He'd been willing to die for her love, but he couldn't face living without it. Gentle waves lapped at his feet, silently mocking his wish for a tidal wave to come and swallow him whole.

He looked out at the vast nothingness of a black sea at night. Random pieces of flotsam and jetsam bobbed the surface, only to disappear again. Brown, grey and green. Green. His head snapped around as the flash of color caught his eye. Not more than twenty yards away, a pale green shape floated in the water.

Elizabeth.

He ran toward her, his heart sinking with each step. She lay face down in the water, a broken plank of wood caught under her chest. Her hair streamed out like an angel's halo in the dark water.

His hands shook as he reached out and took her by the shoulders. He knew what he'd find. He'd seen it a thousand times in his nightmares. Carefully, he turned her over. A gash sliced across her forehead, spilling blood down the side of her face.

"No," he rasped, as he pulled her body to his.

He stood in the water holding her. The rain had stopped, but his tears fell.

Her head lolled back and he lifted it up, cradling her limp body so very carefully. His fingers trembled as he stroked her cheek.

"No."

The waves buffeted against him as he carried her through the shallow water to the shore. Laying her down on the sand, he tilted her head back and leaned down until his cheek hovered over her mouth.

No breath.

His heart pounded in his chest as he blew two quick breaths into her lifeless body. He would bring her back. He'd shove his very soul into her if he could.

Still nothing. Her neck was ice cold, and he couldn't feel a pulse. He laced his fingers over her chest and thrust down.

"Come back," he said. "Damn it, you come back to me!"

More compressions and still her chest didn't rise. He could feel her slipping away from him, but he be damned if he'd let her go.

He wasn't sure, but he thought her eyes fluttered. His heart skipped a beat. He cupped her cheek, willing life into her. "Elizabeth!"

She coughed and water spilled out of her mouth. She gasped for breath, and Simon eased her head to the side. Finally, her eyes opened.

"I knew you'd find me."

"Oh, love," Simon gasped and gathered her into his arms.

He looked to the heavens in thanks. The clouds had parted, and the moonlight shone brightly now. A dark sliver grew larger across the face of the moon. The eclipse had begun. They didn't have much time. Simon slipped his arms under her and stood. He carried her down the beach back to where he'd cast off his jacket. Kneeling down, he gently set Elizabeth on the sand. Simon's hands trembled as he fumbled through his pockets. Where was it? Finally, his fingers brushed over the cold metal and he pulled out the watch. The black disc already partially covered the moon dial. Simon grasped her hand tightly.

"Don't let go," she said, and gripped his hand with both of her own.

Simon tightened his grip. "Never."

The blue light sparked off the watch and snaked up his arm. Nothing would separate them now. Electric blue energy engulfed them. The world around them vibrated with frenetic energy. And they fell again into blackness.

Simon woke to the gentle sound of a crackling fire. He opened his eyes, and his living room coalesced around him. Two wine glasses sat on the coffee table on either side of a small mahogany box. His entire body ached, and he lifted a hand to massage the pain in his temple. Disorientation faded and the memories came back.

"Elizabeth." Dear God, what if she hadn't made it back?

He pushed himself up from the chair and saw her on the floor. She lay in heap, her legs and arms akimbo. His heart leapt into his throat. She moaned and opened her eyes. "Thank you God," he said as he knelt down by her side.

"It's all right," he said as he stroked her cheek. "I thought I'd lost you."

"Gonna have to try harder than that." Her voice was soft and rasping, and the most beautiful thing he'd ever heard.

He gave a short laugh that made his ribs scream in protest. She closed her eyes and let out a breath.

"Did we make it? Or is this a dream?"

"No," he said, brushing his fingers below the cut on her forehead. "Not a dream. Are you hurt badly?"

She shook her head and tried to sit up.

"You shouldn't move," he said, pushing back gently on her shoulders.

She wrinkled her forehead, grimacing in pain and bringing a shaky hand to touch the cut. He gripped her hand in his, reminded of a time a few weeks, or was it decades ago when he'd done the same thing.

"You look like hell," she said, touching the bruise on his head.

Her clothes were soaked and sand covered her side. Blood trickled down her cheek and stained the collar of her dress. "You're one to talk," he said. "You should go to hospital."

She shook her head. "I hate hospitals."

"Elizabeth—"

"I'm too pooped to be prodded."

"You'll have a scar."

"Give me character," she mumbled.

"Elizabeth."

She closed her eyes. "Can't you kiss it and make it better?"

"You're impossible."

"And inclined to stay that way," she said. "But if you don't help me up, I'm gonna fall asleep on your floor."

"No sleeping. Not yet. Take it slowly," he said as he helped her sit up. "Good. We'll move to the sofa now, all right?"

"I'm not an invalid," she said, but swayed on her feet and gripped his arm. "Except for now."

He maneuvered them to the sofa, and she sank down into the cushions with a groan. She nodded her head toward the coffee table. "I'd feel better if that thing were locked up."

Following her gaze, he saw the watch resting on the floor under the table. "Agreed."

Painfully, he leaned over and picked it up and quickly put it inside the box. He slammed the lid closed. If he never saw the damned thing again, it would be too soon.

"Much better," she said and leaned her head back against the cushions.

"Right," he said, turning his full attention back to her. Gently, he pulled her matted hair away from the cut.

"Is it really over?" she asked, wincing as he checked the depth of her wound.

"It seems so," he said. "You really should have that tended to."

"I know."

It felt surreal to be back in the quiet of his house. The stormy beach and the fight for their lives seemed like a dream fading from reality into memory. The abrupt shift back to normalcy left him oddly ill at ease. The once familiar surroundings felt more foreign than comforting.

They sat in silence for a few moments. Elizabeth's small fingers played over his, slowly tracing the tarnished band of gold on his ring finger. "What happens now?"

"We take you to hospital."

"No, I meant, with us," she said, her expression so endearingly unsure. "Everything's different here."

He covered her hand with his. "Not everything," he said, gently cupping her cheek. "As far as I'm concerned, there's only one thing that matters. Elizabeth, if I have you, the rest of the world can hang. It doesn't matter what place, what time. 1929, 2029, nothing can change the way I feel."

She smiled and wiped the tears from her eyes. "Simon."

"Welcome home, love."

"It's good to be home," she said and leaned in to kiss him. He put his arms around her and gladly obliged.

THE END

ABOUT THE AUTHOR

MONIQUE MARTIN was born in Houston, Texas, but grew up on both coasts, living in Connecticut and California. She currently resides in Southern California with her naughty Siamese cat, Monkey.

Monique attended the University of Southern California's Film School where she earned a BFA in Filmic Writing. She worked in television for several years before joining the family business. She now works full-time as a freelance writer and novelist. *Out of Time* is her first novel.

She's currently working on an adaptation of one of her screenplays, her father's memoirs about his time in the Air Force's Air Rescue Service and the sequel to *Out of Time—When the Walls Fell*, due to be released in the fall of 2011.

Email Monique at **writtenbymonique@gmail.com** or visit her page on the web at **moniquemartin.weebly.com**.

An excerpt from

WHEN THE WALLS FELL
coming soon from
Monique Martin

ELIZABETH STRUGGLED against the disconnected feeling until she felt her head definitely connect with something. Something... leafy? Managing to right herself, she stared at the offending bush before remembering to check for any witnesses. Thankfully, she was alone. Very, very alone. Damn you, Simon.

She'd spent the last day and a half trying to soak up the reams of information Travers had given her and trying not to think about what she was leaving behind. Besides, if everything went well, it would be like she'd never left. Except for the arguing and gargantuan emotional chasm they'd have to cross. But she'd leap the Great Divide when she came to it. Right now she had a job to do, and twigs to get out of her hair. So much for the two hours she'd spent wrangling it into her best Gibson Girl imitation.

Travers had meticulously given her a crash course in Victorian society. Just the word society had been enough to make her pulse race. Living with Simon had given her a glimpse at how the better half lived, but they weren't exactly on the social circuit. The closest she'd ever gotten to consorting with the horsey set was getting tips from the touts at the track. She was part of the great unwashed and had the dirt on her cheek to prove it. Thank God, Travers had insisted she stuff that kerchief into her sleeve. She glanced quickly around and spit into before wiping her cheek.

A smooth start. Taking a header into a hedge and spitting. Her head pounded, but it was heck of a lot better than the headbanger's ball she'd suffered through last time. Taking a deep breath she felt her ribs squish her innards. The corset she could have done without. Torquemada had nothing on whatever sadist invented it. Compressing her breasts into some sort of one-eyed, monobosom monster, squeezing the life out of her stomach and thrusting her hips backward, it successfully contorted her body into what society of the early twentieth century deemed an acceptable shape. It was all she could do not to rip the dang laces and start the bra-burning age a few decades early.

Not being able to breathe was the least of her worries. She'd managed to arrive without passing out. Point one for her. But she hadn't managed to move from that spot. Quickly, she took stock of her surroundings. Large oak trees canopied expansive, outlandishly colorful flowerbeds. Flaming oranges and deep reds swirled in complicated pattern amongst a vibrant purple like some tapestry gone mad. Enclosing the entire thing was a large, boxwood hedge, with whom she was already well acquainted.

This looked like the right place. Travers had said that if everything went well she'd arrive in Mrs. Eldridge's garden. It was secluded from the street, thanks to her friend the hedge, and she could arrive without scaring the living bejesus out of anyone. Herself notwithstanding.

Satisfied she was in one piece, and having stalled longer than was necessary, Elizabeth took a well-measured breath and headed for the front path. All she had to do was utter the simple code phrase Travers had given her and Mrs. Eldridge would give her whatever else she needed.

As she edged up the path, the mansion loomed even larger. Gothic and imposing. Steeply pitched gables and sharp arched windows made it look more like a cathedral than a home. The fleeting image of being held prisoner inside one of the pinnacle towers flashed in her mind. But she was no Rapunzel and her knight currently had his head up his ass. Just as she was having serious second thoughts, the front door opened and a young man and an elderly woman stepped out onto the porch.

"I'll be sure to give Mother your regards," the young man said as he bounded the down the stairs nearly crashing into Elizabeth. "I beg your pardon," he said quickly taking off his goggles and cap. "Are you all right?"

"I'm... I'm fine," Elizabeth managed. "Thank you."

He smiled disarmingly. "The thanks is all mine," he said and then turned back to the elderly woman. "Where have you been keeping her?"

The woman, who simply had to be Mrs. Eldridge, lifted her pince-nez and arched an eyebrow. "In the garden, it appears."

The young man turned back to her and laughed. "You have," he said and waved a hand in the general direction of her hair, "an intruder."

Elizabeth patted at her hair.

"If you'd allow me?" he asked, and before she could protest, plucked a leaf from her hair.

"That was embarrassing," Elizabeth mumbled.

He turned on that smile of his again. "I think it was rather becoming. And I'll cherish it always," he said as he stuffed the leaf into his breast pocket. "Maxwell Alexander Harrington the Third, your humble servant," he added with a bow.

The older woman sighed and lowered her glasses. "You are incorrigible."

"You'll have to forgive me," he said, not taking his eyes off Elizabeth. "Love does strange things to a man."

"Ignore him," the woman said. "Riding in that new motorcar of his has scrambled his brain."

For a long moment, he didn't react, just simply stared at Elizabeth. It should have been discomfiting, but he exuded an earnestness no amount of brashness could cover. Handsome by any standards, he was the very definition of the All-American Boy--tall, easily over six feet, sun-streaked hair and dimple in his chin you could crawl inside.

"And your manners," the older woman prompted. "How you could possibly be a relation of mine is beyond me."

"She's my distant aunt," he said by way of explanation.

"And growing more distant with every passing moment."

Elizabeth liked her immediately. She was Helen Hayes with attitude. "I didn't mean to interrupt."

She waved her hand dismissively. "No, no. Maxwell was just leaving. What can I do for you, dear?"

Elizabeth's throat went dry. This was the moment of truth. "Mr. Holland sent me."

A brief flicker of surprise and then recognition crossed the woman's face before she smiled as though Elizabeth had just complimented her prized petunias. "Oh, isn't that lovely," she said coming down a few steps and holding out her hand. "I haven't heard from him in ages. Won't you come inside dear and you can tell me how everyone's doing?"

Just like that Elizabeth was being shuttled into the house.

"Another of your secret liaisons, Aunt Lillian?" Max said trailing behind.

Mrs. Eldridge never stopped escorting Elizabeth inside and merely said over her shoulder, "Goodbye, Maxwell," and promptly shut the door behind them. Once they were a few feet into the entry hall she squeezed Elizabeth's arm gently. "Welcome to 1906, dear."

Visit
moniquemartin.weebly.com
for the latest news on this and other forthcoming books!

Made in the USA
Lexington, KY
02 January 2014